The Maori King

SALZWASSER
VERLAG

J. E. Gorst

The Maori King

Reprint of the original, first published in 1864.

1st Edition 2022 | ISBN: 978-3-75259-310-5

Verlag (Publisher): Salzwasser Verlag GmbH, Zeilweg 44, 60439 Frankfurt, Deutschland
Vertretungsberechtigt (Authorized to represent): E. Roepke, Zeilweg 44, 60439 Frankfurt, Deutschland
Druck (Print): Books on Demand GmbH, In de Tarpen 42, 22848 Norderstedt, Deutschland

THE MAORI KING.

THE

MAORI KING;

OR, THE

STORY OF OUR QUARREL

WITH

THE NATIVES OF NEW ZEALAND.

BY

J. E. GORST, M.A

London and Cambridge

1864.

Vincent Brooks, Sculpt.

Na Wi Tamihana

CONTENTS.

CHAPTER I.

INTRODUCTORY.

CHAPTER II.

WAIKATO.

CHAPTER III.

THE QUEEN'S SOVEREIGNTY.

CHAPTER IV.

THE REVOLT.

CHAPTER V.

POTATAU, THE KING.

CHAPTER VI.

THE JUSTICE ON CIRCUIT.

CHAPTER VII.

THE TARANAKI WAR.

CHAPTER VIII.

WIREMU TAMIHANA TE WAHAROA.

CHAPTER IX.

THE INTERREGNUM.

CHAPTER X.

SIR GEORGE GREY.

CHAPTER XI.

FACE TO FACE.

CHAPTER XII.

THE "NEW INSTITUTIONS."

CHAPTER XIII.

THE MAORI KINGDOM.

CHAPTER XIV.

RUMOURS OF WAR.

CHAPTER XV.

THE AWAMUTU.

CHAPTER XVI.

TATARAIMAKA.

CHAPTER XVII.

REWI MANIAPOTO.

CHAPTER XVIII.

THE OUTBREAK OF WAR.

CHAPTER XIX.

THE INVASION OF WAIKATO.

CHAPTER XV.

CONCLUSION.

THE

MAORI KING.

CHAPTER I.

INTRODUCTORY.

I FIRST landed in New Zealand in May, 1860, just after the outbreak of the Taranaki war. The entire colony was at that time absorbed in watching the struggle that was going on between a handful of ill-armed savages and the Queen's well-disciplined soldiers, and in speculating on the probability of the whole Maori population rising to join in the conflict.

People in Auckland were especially anxious about the course that would be taken by the tribes living on the Waikato River, upon whose forbearance the very existence of Auckland appeared at that time to depend. A range of forest hills was pointed out from the town of Auckland, extending from east to south, and not more than twenty miles distant. Beyond these hills, the stranger was told, lay the Waikato country, inhabited by fierce warlike Maories, whose armed bands could at any moment swarm through the hill-side forests into the plain below, to burn the houses, drive off the cattle, and tomahawk the settlers.

It was said that these dreaded tribes had some years before declined all further connexion with their British rulers, and set up a king of their own. Their choice had fallen on a very aged warrior, named Potatau, one of that nearly extinct race of Maori heroes who had been not only conquerors but cannibals. Very little was known by the colonists about this monarch's foreign or domestic policy, except that it was said he would allow no more native territory to be sold to the British Crown; and as the Taranaki war had arisen from the resistance of a turbulent chief, Wiremu Kingi, to the sale of land, it seemed not improbable that the sympathies of the Waikatos would lead to their supporting his cause in arms, and in what better way could they aid him than by making a raid upon the rich and defenceless settlement of Auckland?

The result of our government of the Maories, thus seen in New Zealand, was marvellously inconsistent with the story usually told in England. It had always been said that the Maories possessed remarkable capacities for civilization, that they had been treated with singular kindness and perfect justice, and were happy and prosperous under British rule. It was natural to inquire the cause of such unfortunate results.

The story turned out to be strange and interesting.

Our rule, when first established in the country, was hailed by the Maories with delight. Both parties commenced relations with cordial good-will. The British Government, charmed at the prospect of beginning a new system in the treatment of native races, and of illustrating the Christian philanthropy of Britain by civilizing instead of exterminating, resolved to do its duty to its Maori neighbours, to be true and just in all its dealings, and, above all, not to covet or desire Maori lands. The natives, on the other hand, were ready to accept with gratitude the promised benefits, and looked forward with joy to the time when in all respects they should become the equals of their civilized Pakeha friends. The Colonial, as distinct from the Imperial Government, had not long existed, but it had already contrived to exhibit, by votes of money and by the manufacture of several excellent laws, solicitude for the welfare of the Maories. The leading settlers, especially those who had been long in the country and had lived in native districts, spoke of Maories in terms of esteem and friendship. Only the lowest newspapers and the most ignorant class of colonists allowed themselves to indulge in abuse of their fellow-subjects; but it would be unfair to infer from the conduct of one class in time of war that there was any general or permanent enmity between the races. The Maories had enjoyed the further advantage of having all the acts of Government scrutinized in their behalf by the

Bishop of New Zealand and his missionary clergy—men of sound education and independent opinions, whose bias, if any, was rather towards the natives than the colonists. Except in the case of the purchase at Taranaki, upon which the opinions of the most intelligent persons in the colony were nearly equally divided, no act of injustice towards the Maories was alleged. Indeed, the disposition of their rulers towards them and the vigilance of their disinterested protectors forbad the idea of any wilful wrong. If a mistake had been made by us, it lay not in what we had done, but in what we had left undone. We had been so afraid of the cost of trenching on native independence, that we had forborne even to attempt to govern. No effort had been made to teach obedience to rulers—indeed, it had never been quite settled on our side who the rulers of the Maories were to be. The policy of the Government, even after the natives had gone so far as to set up a king of their own, had been one of strict non-interference. So that it was the very caution and timidity of our policy that had brought us upon the horns of a dilemma, in which we must either give up the right to govern, which we had been too weak to exercise, or plunge the colony into a war of races.

Not long after my arrival in New Zealand, the kindness of the Rev. B. Y. Ashwell, a missionary long resident in Waikato, gave me an opportunity of visiting that country. It was just at a time when the discovery, in the forest south of Auckland, of the corpse of a Maori, apparently murdered, had filled the settlers with alarm. The Waikatos, it was feared, would make this a pretext for declaring war and attacking Auckland. But the missionary did not seem to think that even the chance of actual war would expose a stranger travelling in the district to the least risk. We accordingly set out.

What most struck me, in this my first visit to Waikato, was the strange contrast between the material poverty and the mental attainments of the people. In all outward signs of civilization the Maories proved to be extremely backward; their houses, clothing, food, and way of eating were of the most barbarous description; but in reasoning, especially on political topics, in making provision for their own government, and for the education of their children, they exhibited unexpected cleverness and good sense. There were at that time numerous village schools (which, unhappily, war and excitement have since swept away), founded and managed entirely by the natives themselves. The school-houses were large and neatly built, and the scholars cleaner, better lodged, and better mannered, than the neighbouring natives. The sexes were carefully separated. The girls wore clean print frocks; the boys blue cotton shirts and duck trowsers. The pupils could invariably answer simple questions on religion, read their own language well, and in some schools showed a knowledge of arithmetic that filled me with surprise. I also passed court-houses, originally built under the guidance of a European magistrate—Mr. Fenton—whence writs were still issued and where cases were still tried. At every village the alleged murder was temperately but eagerly discussed, and clever arguments advanced in support of their unanimous demand that the murderer should be given up to them for trial.

Soon after we reached the mission-station of Taupiri, it was rumoured that a large war party was coming down the river. The few traders and settlers in the neighbourhood took alarm and began to talk of going into Auckland. Just at this crisis a case occurred which much impressed me with the forbearance and good sense of the leading Waikato chiefs. A party of natives had claimed a debt of 5*l.* from an English trader, and were threatening to strip his house if he did not pay. The trader denied the debt, and begged Mr. Ashwell to interfere in his behalf. A letter was immediately sent off to Ngaruawahia, the Maori capital, which brought over the next morning a gentlemanly, well-dressed chief, who was said to be one of the king's councillors. He inquired into the trader's case, and decided that the 5*l.* should be deposited by him with a Maori clergyman until the matter could be further examined. He then talked in a deliberate quiet way about the murder. News had come, he said, that the murderer was discovered, and that he was a European. The natives were all determined to demand his surrender for trial. The governor had called their king "child's play," and they were resolved to show that they were in earnest. When Maories committed offences against Europeans, they were given up to the governor for justice—so now, as one of their men had been killed, we must in our turn hand over the murderer.

A few days later a war-party of about 300 men passed Taupiri in three large canoes, headed by Wiremu Tamihana, or, as Europeans call him, William Thompson, who, since the recent death of Potatau, the king, was considered the greatest man in Waikato. Potatau's son, Matutaera, who had succeeded to the vacant throne, was a weak man, entirely under Tamihana's influence. The war-party stopped at Taupiri, and the chief came on shore to beg Mr. Ashwell not to be alarmed. He said that, whatever happened, Mr. Ashwell's house and family were "tapu" (sacred), and no one would dare to meddle with them. He also invited me to continue my journey up the country, and especially pressed me to visit his schools at Peria, in the Thames Valley, offering to send with me a young chief, a cousin of his own, to guard against the least risk of danger.

The acquaintance thus commenced with William Thompson became afterwards more intimate. I visited him just before he went down to Taranaki, and was present at the gathering of his tribe and the discussion that took place as to whether he should go, and what he should do on his arrival. The pacific intentions which he declared at that assembly were considered by the New Zealand Government, to whom they were reported, as a mere pretext to disguise an intended assault on Auckland. Even the missionaries doubted Tamihana's sincerity. Yet everything which I had heard him promise in the Waikato, he punctually fulfilled at Taranaki. After his return, he sent for me to come and listen to a full account of all that he had said and done on his expedition. From his manner, he appeared vexed and mortified at the way in which his good intentions had been met by Government, and he assured me that there would very shortly be war in Waikato, as the governor was going to attack their king, whom they were determined never to surrender. He gave me at the same time some account of the origin and purpose of their Maori monarchy, which he declared had been established only when they found the British authorities would do nothing to repress crime amongst them; the Maories, said he, had now lost all confidence in our Government, and would never give up their own king.

It appeared to me, even at that time, that the history of this effort of a barbarous people to create a system of internal administration for themselves must be in itself curious and worthy of record. Under a rude form of government of their own invention they had done more for themselves than we had ever done for them. Person and property were as safe on the Waikato as in the town of Auckland. Even during the excitement and irregularity consequent on the Taranaki war, neither traders nor missionaries suffered from violence. Strangers like myself traversed the country without risk. I was informed that tribal wars, which had formerly been frequent and bloody, had been entirely stopped, and that the king's magistrates had successfully put down the traffic in spirits.

When the arrival of Sir George Grey in 1861 gave some hope of a peaceful solution of the difficulty, I was appointed Commissioner and Magistrate of the Waikato country above Taupiri, to which the rest of the district from Taupiri to the sea was afterwards added. My friend William Thompson never quite forgave my defection to the Government side. He said he was sorry to find how little the Pakehas thought of me, for Paul said—"Set them to judge who are least esteemed in the Church." We always remained very good friends, and he several times interfered in my behalf against men of other tribes; but the very last time we met, he lamented over the sad downfall of his once-beloved Pakeha in becoming a thing so mean as an officer of Government.

A residence of eighteen months in the neighbourhood

of Rangiaowhia and Kihikihi, among the most violent of the king's partizans, and the frequent journeys on horseback which I made through the neighbouring districts during that period in discharge of my duties, gave me abundant opportunity of observing the practical working of the Maori king's government. A nearer view revealed its defects as well as its excellences. Constant intercourse with native chiefs of every shade of temper and opinion acquainted me with their own story about the causes of their revolt against our rule, their disposition towards our race, and the reason of their persistently holding aloof from Sir George Grey. It is but common justice to state here, that although the presence of an officer of Government in the midst of them was extremely distasteful, I was not only never treated with rudeness, but was everywhere received with the utmost kindness and hospitality. I was never plundered of a single article of property, nor subjected to the least injustice; and finally, when they broke into open insurrection, not only were all Europeans living amongst them spared, but not a cow, nor a horse, nor any kind of property, was taken from us. Our houses, our furniture, and all goods which could not be removed, were, four months after the war had begun, still remaining as we left them—untouched and unharmed.

It appears to me that the story of how a deadly quarrel arose between such a race and rulers so well intentioned cannot be unimportant or uninteresting.

But there is, moreover, another reason why this episode in our colonial history ought to be examined. New Zealand has been recently quoted as a proof of the impossibility of civilizing barbarous races. It is urged that, wherever the brown and white skins come in contact, the former must disappear, and that the old fashion once pursued by our forefathers in the back woods of America was a more merciful, because a more speedy, way of doing the inevitable work than the lingering modern method which has superseded it. Against a theory which thus despairs of justice and humanity, this book is meant as a protest. It may be our own Christianity and civilization are so imperfect, that our efforts to Christianize and civilize others are not likely to be very successful; and of this, no doubt, New Zealand is a case in point. But I hope to be able to convince the reader that the unhappy quarrel with the Maories has been the result of errors which might have been avoided by wiser people than ourselves, and that therefore the task we undertook and failed to accomplish was not an absolute impossibility, but only an impossibility to us.

CHAPTER II.

WAIKATO.

"WAIKATO" is used indifferently as the name of a river, a confederation of Maori tribes, and the country inhabited by them. The basin which is drained by the great river and its tributaries is occupied by a very large number of tribes, distinct though intimately related. They are divided geographically and politically into three sections—Ngatimaniapoto, Ngatihaua, and a group of small tribes called Waikato, over which Ngatimahuta, the king's tribe, is dominant. The name Waikato is, however, often applied to the whole confederation which the three sections have formed, not only by the colonists, who do not trouble themselves about nice tribal distinctions, but even by the Maories themselves.

The Maories of the Waikato confederation have been for many years regarded as the most important in New Zealand. Their pre-eminence over other tribes is due not to any intrinsic merit of their own, but solely to their geographical position. Their greatness has grown up with the settlement of Auckland—the richest in the

North Island—which lies at their feet, and has been for many years at their mercy. The land on which they live is fertile and difficult to be invaded; while at their backs they have a rugged inaccessible country, a retreat where they can set our civilized armies at defiance. When New Zealand was first colonized, no one supposed that in the end we should have to fight the Maories for the possession of the soil. The early settlers confidently pushed their way into the heart of native districts: homesteads of a few hundred acres, isolated in the midst of Maori villages, were bought without apprehension by European farmers, and inhabited in security by their wives and children. The Government did not hesitate to purchase blocks of land cut off by intervening native territory from the main settlements, which were retailed in small farms to settlers without a suspicion that the latter were being thereby doomed to ruin. And now that a quarrel has at last arisen between the races, the consolidation of our own territory and the formation of a defensible frontier between European and Maori land imperatively demand conquests which must entail bloodshed and suffering upon both sides.

The outsettlers of Auckland are mostly small farmers who live in rough wooden houses, scattered about the country, and surrounded by a few fields. The adjoining land is commonly an unenclosed tract of fern and forest owned by Maories or European speculators. The loneliness of a colonial life forces nearly every man into matrimony, and a family of stout hearty children is the usual result. Compared with Australian or Middle Island squatters, the Auckland outsettlers are poor; in the eyes of their native neighbours they are rich. The cattle, horses and sheep, which form their wealth run at large in the open country outside their fences. If the land is Maori, rent varying between 1*l.* and 20*l.* is demanded for this privilege; and when the title to the land is disputed by different owners it is necessary, in order to enjoy quiet possession, to pay them all. At times the wandering cattle, in their search for food, come upon native cultivations of wheat, potatoes, or green juicy maize, wholly exposed, or defended only by a rickety fence of small sticks tied up with flax. As these cultivations are often remote from human dwellings, the cattle of the settlers may and often do commit a great deal of mischief before they are found out. On the other hand, gaunt long-legged Maori pigs, roaming at large, feed in the settler's potato-fields and root up his grass paddocks, setting hedges, ditches, and dogs at defiance. A fence that is secure against a Maori pig is a thing still to be invented. So long as Europeans and Maories continue to farm on antagonistic principles—the one fencing their crops and letting their cattle run at large; the other, tying up their cattle or driving them to other regions, and leaving their crops exposed—there must be disputes whenever the two races come in contact. If the white man is intimate with native ways and can command his temper, he will generally, but by no means always, get justice. I have known cases in which even missionaries of twenty years' standing have only avoided a quarrel by submitting to grossly unfair demands. But when the white man is unskilful or passionate, there is invariably an affray, in which the Maori is sure to get the best of it. The European either has no weapons, or, having them, dares not use them; the Maori is well armed with guns and ammunition, has a dozen uncles and cousins to back him if he wants help, thinks nothing of flourishing his tomahawk a few inches off his adversaries' heads, and generally closes the argument by helping himself to a cow or a horse as "payment," which the Englishman may get back again as he can. In New Zealand it has been hitherto so notorious that a European has no chance but submission in a native quarrel, that it has become the common opinion of settlers that they are safer when unarmed. Even when the present war broke out, settlers showed very strong reluctance to take weapons into their hands. Raglan, a small settlement on the west coast, sixty miles south of Auckland, was in danger of attack from the Waikato. A shipload of arms for the defence of the settlers was sent down from Auckland. But they held a meeting, resolved that to arm was dangerous, that it was safer to trust to the friendliness of the Raglan, and the forbearance of the Waikato, natives, and so the ship was sent back to

Auckland without being allowed to unload her cargo. When it is considered how entirely the rich white men have been at the mercy of their poor Maori neighbours, how the latter are without, and yet long for, almost all the articles of wealth which the former have, the only wonder is that there has been so little robbery and violence, and that redress could ever be obtained at all. The position was hurtful to the morals of both races; Europeans were continually smarting under a sense of wrong, and Maories grew insolent and contemptuous, filled with an overweening confidence in their own powers and the unresisting patience of the oppressed race. But though every Maori in New Zealand, and especially every Waikato, despised the single European as an enemy, it did not follow that the British Government, which had always an army at command, should be as little regarded. The reason why the Waikatos never have feared and do not fear us now, even though we have invaded their country with 20,000 men, to whom they have little more than 2,000 to oppose, is the extraordinary resources their country offers for resisting invasion. It is impossible to understand the attitude taken up by the Waikatos towards the British Government without such a description of their country as will show what those natural defences are in which they place so strong and apparently so just a confidence.

The point of the Waikato River nearest to Auckland is between thirty and forty miles to the south. The river, which from its source in the snows of Tongariro has followed a northerly course for about 200 miles, here makes an elbow and turns to the west and south-west, falling into the sea through a narrow opening in the coast line, about twenty miles south of the entrance to the Manukau harbour. At the elbow a swampy creek, called Mangatawhiri, entering the Waikato from the east, forms the boundary between the Government and native land, or, as the Maories have long thought, the frontier of their king's dominions. Mangatawhiri is separated from the open country round Auckland by the Hunua forest, which consists of a range of broken hills clothed with luxuriant wood, stretching from the Hauraki gulf on the east coast to Mangatawhiri, and thence in a westerly direction between the Waikato and the Manukau harbour. The forest is about thirty miles long and ten broad; the soil is a soft clay, intersected by many swampy streams, which in the absence of bridges are almost impassable. There are many English farms and native villages in the forest and on its fringes, and the country is traversed by several tracks, passing through wood so deep that armies might lie in ambush amongst the leafy undergrowth within a few yards of the path. The summer after Sir G. Grey's return to New Zealand, a broad metalled road was made by General Cameron and the British army through this forest, terminating abruptly at the bank of Mangatawhiri, and a large redoubt was built near the road end.

A pretty wooded bluff overhanging the Waikato, at a place called Te Ia, just below the junction of the Mangatawhiri, was at the same time stripped of its trees, and an ugly-looking stockade perched upon the top.

A traveller coming down to the river, from the Hunua forest, sees before him, to the south, beyond the picturesque foreground of woods and islands, a barren plain, covered with lakes and swamps, amongst which the distant river threads its way. The horizon is bounded by hills, between twenty and thirty miles distant. This is the Taupiri range, beyond which Ngaruawahia, the Maori capital, and the great fertile plains of Upper Waikato lie.

There are two ways of going up the country—by water or by land. The former is very tedious. The Waikato is a broad rapid stream, and canoes must crawl along under the bank, brushing past the luxuriant vegetation, and creeping under dark overhanging trees, to avoid the worst of the current. The river-bed is full of snags and shifting banks of soft pumice sand. About twenty miles above Mangatawhiri, the stream expands to a width of more than half a mile, and becomes so shallow, that, except in time of floods, even the lightest canoes have to plough their way along the sandy bottom, which in places rises so close to the surface that the crews have to jump overboard, and lift and shove their craft across the bar. There is one channel three or four feet deep, even in summer-time; but this is stopped by numerous stumps of trees, formerly growing in what is now the bed of the river. Occasionally it is possible to relieve the monotony of the journey, by getting out of the canoe and walking along narrow tracks leading from one Maori village to another; but the banks generally abound in forest swamps, high fern, and "toetoe" grass, eight or ten feet high, and are intersected by deep muddy tributaries, so that the unwary stranger often finds himself entangled in a maze of vegetation, with an impassable swamp between him and his canoe, and no sign but the shouts of his Maori rowers to tell him that the river is so near at hand. It takes two long days to ascend by water from Mangatawhiri to Ngaruawahia, a distance of forty-five miles; whereas the return down-stream requires only about seven or eight hours of easy paddling. The Waikato natives, therefore, before the recent innovation of bullet-proof steamers, were secure from attack by river; while a descent from Ngaruawahia on the settlers in the Hunua ranges and neighbourhood has been always quite possible and easy.

The land route formerly lay along the left, or western bank of the river, but this has now been abandoned for an easier road on the opposite shore, and the old track is choked up with fern. Five miles of low swampy country, with deep creeks to cross, and thickets of dense jungle and flax, interrupted by an abrupt hill on the river-bank, called Koheroa, separate Mangatawhiri from the village of Meremere. At this place the track leaves the river, and crosses twelve miles of barren undulating fern country, sometimes skirting clumps of forest, and sometimes passing between vast swamps, to the village of Rangiriri, where it again meets the Waikato river. At Rangiriri a rampart and ditch have been made, to stop an invading army; but nature has there placed an obstacle much more formidable.

The Waikato river and the Waikari lake, between which the road must pass, are here separated by an island of flax, the ground of which is sometimes only swampy, and sometimes entirely under water. The strong stiff leaves form so impenetrable a covert, that the natives are often days in finding cattle and horses that have strayed into it. I remember an occasion when an English girl, who was riding through this flax thicket, preceded and followed by horsemen, missed her way and was lost for an hour, although it does not take ten minutes to cross from side to side. In this island an army might lie hid, invisible and invulnerable, for the flax-leaves will turn a rifle-bullet, and unless completely surrounded by troops on the river-bank, above and below the island, and by boats on the Waikato and Waikari, would have a safe retreat in case of need.[1] Beyond the Rangiriri flax swamp, the road runs

[1] In the battle at Rangiriri, the news of which has arrived while these sheets are passing through the press, the Maories trusted too long to the earth-work. A large body had their retreat to the swamp cut off, and were taken prisoners.

by the river bank through the village of Paetai, and over flat gravelly soil, presenting no difficulties beyond a few swamps and streams, deep and dangerous after heavy rains. Five or six hours will take a good rider from Meremere to the Taupiri range. The country passed over is poor and thinly inhabited: good land lies in strips along either bank of the river, and in the islands made by the branches of the stream; but the rest of the country, except a few fertile patches on the lakes, consists of barren fern, and large swamps in a state of transition from water to dry land.

The Taupiri range crosses the course of the river obliquely from the north-east to the south-west. It is composed of steep clay hills, clothed with the usual New Zealand bush. The river penetrates the range by a short and narrow gorge. The hills on either side approach in some places to the very brink of the deep rapid river, forming a steep bank of slippery clay; in other places a flat margin is left, choked up with tall fern, "toetoe" grass, or "tutu" bushes; while the dense forest, with which the whole range is continuously clothed, affords both a place of concealment and a secure retreat to a party of defenders. At the upper end of the gorge, and on the east bank of the river, stands the pretty conical hill of Taupiri; the narrow passage between its base and the river is a strict "tapu" (the only inconvenient one in the district), so that neither man nor beast may proceed on that side of the river. A piece of paper pinned to the base of a flagstaff, and sheltered from the rain by a little thatched roof, informs the traveller that there is a King's ferry at the place, and that by hoisting the flag which hangs up under the thatch, he can obtain a canoe from the village opposite. A man and horse are ferried over at a charge of 1*s.* 6*d.*, and sheep, cattle, &c. at regular tariff prices.

From this point the great Waikato plain opens out, bounded on all sides by distant mountains. At the southern and most fertile end are the chief villages and cultivations of the powerful Waikato tribes. The distant hills are their strongholds—refuges in which they could set an invading, or even an occupying, army at defiance.

Ascending the river, which here runs in a strong current at the base of the pretty wooded hills, through which it afterwards passes, Ngaruawahia, the capital of Waikato, distant five miles from the entrance of the plain at Taupiri, is at last reached. Here the river is divided into two branches, of nearly equal size: the Waikato, a deep rapid blue river, comes rushing down from the distant mountains of the south; and the Waipa, a dark sluggish stream, crawls slowly in from the west.

Of all royal towns in the world, I should think Ngaruawahia the meanest, and the least likely to repay the trouble of conquest. The most conspicuous object is a huge flagstaff, the palladium of Maori nationality, by the side of which is the King's house, a common "raupo" building, like a low barn, with one door, and a small window in the gable end. The interior was, when I last saw it, more than two years ago, very prettily decorated with coloured reeds, arranged in patterns, and tied with stained flax, after the common native fashion. Palace and flagstaff are guarded by a few sentry-boxes, and scattered round are a dozen or so of the ordinary native houses. A hundred yards behind the village stands a curious wooden erection, something like a small summer-house, painted white, and surrounded by a ditch and bank, as a protection against pigs. This is Potatau's tomb. The reader will think this a meagre description of a metropolis, but I have named every object of interest. The Maories are very much ashamed of their chief town, and would not allow a photograph of it to be taken, when the attempt was made.

Beyond Ngaruawahia, the Taupiri range of hills curves gradually to the southward, and joins a chain of rugged limestone mountains, which runs parallel to the west coast, and rises to its greatest height in the peaks of Pirongia. At the base of these hills the Waipa flows in a singularly tortuous course, following on the whole their direction. It is a very deep river, full of snags; the banks are steep, and covered with rank vegetation. The soil along the course of the river, and especially on some of the alluvial flats between the reaches, is of the richest description. Small villages, with their cultivations, are nearly continuous for a distance of forty or fifty miles up the river. Whatawhata, the largest of these, about twelve miles from Ngaruawahia, though the distance by river is at least twenty miles, is only a few hours' journey from Raglan, an English settlement on the west coast. However, the limestone ranges between the two places are of so rugged a character, that, although there are several horse and cattle tracks from Raglan to the Waipa, they are considered quite impracticable for all military purposes.

The Upper Waipa is inhabited by the Ngatimaniapoto tribe. This, the largest and most powerful in New Zealand, is also the most inveterate in hostility to the white race. They were the first of the Waikatos who took part in the Taranaki war, where they lost few men, and obtained a great deal of plunder. Since hostilities were suspended at Taranaki, in 1861, Rewi Maniapoto, the leading chief of this tribe, has been ceaseless in his efforts to renew the war, and has been, in fact, the chief instigator of the present outbreak.

The numerous streams which unite to form the Waipa river rise in a rugged but fertile country, beyond the south-west corner of the great plain. This picturesque region of deep brooks and wooded hills is inhabited by wild and reckless men, of the same Ngatimaniapoto tribe; and here, deep embosomed in hills and forests, stands the village of Hangatiki, one of their chief strongholds, which has often been proposed as the capital of the Maori kingdom, instead of Ngaruawahia. The Ngatimaniapotos, in their inaccessible homes, are, and feel themselves to be, perfectly secure from attack; and being accustomed, in their visits to Waikato and Auckland, to outrage Europeans as they please, have come to regard us with the most sovereign contempt. I give one illustration of their audacity. A half-caste girl, whose mother was a Ngatimaniapoto of Hangatiki, was in domestic service in Auckland, where she had been educated. The tribe having, according to native custom, a voice in the disposal of all the daughters of their women, wished her to come up the country and marry a native. She refused. Upon this, a party of a dozen went down, carried her off in broad daylight from her mistress's house in the neighbourhood of Auckland, and took her in triumph past our police, our soldiers, and our redoubts, to Hangatiki. It is fair to add that, as she still persevered in her refusal, she was not forced into the match.

The Waikato branch of the river south of Ngaruawahia is a clear rapid stream, flowing at a considerable depth below the general surface of the country. The banks consist of pumice sand, and are high, steep, and quite bare of vegetation. For fifteen miles above Ngaruawahia the land is barren; only one small village,

Pukete, is passed. Above this lies the district of Horotiu (a name sometimes given erroneously to the river itself), the dearly-prized possession of the Ngatihaua tribe. Wiremu Tamihana, the chief of this tribe, though an uncompromising supporter of Maori nationality, has always laboured to keep peace between his race and ours; and since he succeeded in stopping the Taranaki war there has been a constant feud between himself and Rewi, the chief of Ngatimaniapoto—the former striving to prevent, the latter to promote, a fresh struggle. The Ngatihaua suffered very severely in the Taranaki war, which they persisted in joining, in spite of Tamihana's protests. This decadence of the tribe of course much weakened the influence of their chief in the Maori assemblies.

Horotiu is a perfectly level plain of light rich soil, with a gravelly subsoil, extending inland from both banks of the river. Detached clumps of trees dotted all over the plain give it a beautiful park-like appearance, while the land between is covered with cultivations and villages, the chief of which is Tamahere, where Wiremu Tamihana was born and where he has large estates. This is the general gathering-place of the tribe. Large crops of wheat were grown in this district in the season preceding the outbreak of the present war, and the English grass and clover, whic has spread over the plain, has turned it into an excellent grazing ground for cattle, horses, and even sheep, which several Ngatihaua chiefs were beginning to keep.

The eastern boundary of Horotiu is the Maunga Kaua, a rich wooded range of hills, in which are several villages. It takes three hours to cross Maunga Kaua into the upper valley of the Thames, which is another fertile district belonging to the Ngatihaua tribe. Upon the slopes of Maunga Kaua, looking down upon the Thames valley, is Peria, a large native village, the usual home of Tamihana. Two rivers, the Waiho and the Piako, run down this valley to the Hauraki gulf. The landing-place for large canoes is a day's journey below Peria, with which it is connected by a good cart-road, made by the natives themselves. The produce of the upper Thames valley is carried by this road to the landing-place, thence in canoes to the Hauraki gulf, and there shipped in Maori schooners, or, during summer, in large canoes, for the voyage across the sea to Auckland.

At the south of Horotiu stands Maunga-tautari, a mountain with many lofty peaks, clothed from base to summit with impenetrable forest. The Waikato river sweeps round its base to enter the Great Plain. On the slope of the mountain, high above the river, stands the village of Maunga-tautari, the residence of a powerful section of the Ngatihaua tribe, of which Ti Oriori is chief. The Maories have a proverb that Maunga-tautari is invincible. I have heard Ngatihaua chiefs, when warned that a war would end in their extermination, laugh, and, pointing to the forest-clad summits of Maungatautari, ask how long it would take to exterminate them in there. Above this point the country through which the Waikato flows is wild, mountainous, and almost uninhabited. There are, however, patches of good land amongst the mountains large enough to grow food for the whole Maori race, and grass plains wide enough to support all their cattle and horses.

The Taupo lake is reached from the Waikato plain, after a three days' journey through a most savage and broken country; from a narrow opening at the foot of the lake the Waikato rushes in a deep torrent. At the head of Taupo stands a group of snow-clad mountains, called Tongariro, amongst which the river takes its rise. The same name, Waikato, is preserved from Tongariro to the sea: the natives assert that the stream flows through Taupo without mingling its sacred waters with the lake; though, as it enters a muddy glacier torrent, and issues bright and blue like the Rhone at Geneva, one would think they had ocular demonstration to the contrary.

Having thus followed the Waikato and Waipa to their sources, it remains to describe the triangle lying between them, at the southern part of which the best land and densest population in Waikato are to be found. The country is quite level and open, with pretty alternations of wood and lakes, and is intersected by numerous streams flowing into the Waikato or Waipa.

The tributaries of the former run at the bottom of deep ravines, scored out in the pumice gravel which lies below the surface, and form the only obstacle to the advance of a hostile army over the plain itself.

Thirty miles to the south of Ngaruawahia are Rangiaowhia and Kihikihi, the largest villages in the Waikato district. Part of Kihikihi belongs to the Ngatimaniapoto tribe, and Rewi, their principal chief, lives there. Indeed, Ngatimaniapoto claims a great extent of land about Kihikihi, concerning which there is a chronic feud between them and the Waikatos of that place and Rangiaowhia. The two villages are separated by the river Mangahoe and a belt of swampy wood not a mile wide, but passable only in the summer season. At other times it is necessary to make a circuit of about six miles along a cart-road, which crosses Mangahoe by an old and rotten bridge.

On the bank of Mangahoe, close by this bridge, stands a mission station, called by natives Te Awamutu, and by Europeans Otawhao, after an old pa once renowned in the Waikato wars. Here Sir George Grey stationed the commissioner of the district, and established an industrial school for teaching trades to the Maories. The land upon which it stands forms part of the debated territory—Waikato gave it to the Church Missionary Society, and Ngatimaniapoto disputes the validity of the gift. A white church and spire, surrounded by English trees, green fields, and neighbouring settlers' houses, make the place look like home. The pretty contrast to the brown scenery around reminds the exile of the villages in Cambridgeshire. Maori houses and cultivations are scattered about the neighbourhood. Many Europeans had lived permanently in these parts, years before the war, as small farmers and stock-keepers; others as traders; others as artizans; while some took charge of flour-mills driven by water power, of which there are as many as three at Rangiaowhia and two at Kihikihi. Indeed, any one recently visiting this district would have been struck with the signs of bygone wealth and prosperity: the natives own carts, horses, and working bullocks, and in peaceful times used to grow quantities of wheat, which supplied a great part of the consumption of Auckland. In those days the roads from Rangiaowhia and Kihikihi were frequented by drays carrying wheat, maize, and potatoes to a landing-place of the Puniu, a navigable branch of the Waipa, whence canoes used to go down to a creek near the mouth of the Waikato, two miles from the English village of Waiuku on the Manukau, and return laden with shirts, sugar, tobacco, and, too often, rum. But recently all this prosperity has vanished. The natives grow little more than is necessary for their own consumption; the mills are out of repair, the milldams breaking down, the traders gone, the bridges rotten; the roads deserted, except by armed men, and women carrying their baggage, or drays with food to be wasted at some great meeting for establishing that Maori nationality which is their one absorbing object.

In truth, the extreme poverty of the Waikato natives is one of the chief obstacles to their subjugation. There s very little in their villages which they would mind losing. Their cultivations, if fenced at all, are only fenced in the rudest and slightest manner; they do not grow live hedges, as the land is occupied but for few years, and they look forward to exhausting it and going elsewhere. They do not enclose grass paddocks, because the wide, open country, in which English grass and clover spread like weeds, affords abundant pasture for their horses and cattle. Their houses are of the very meanest description, being a mere frame of poles covered with bundles of dried flag (called "raupo"), with a sliding board for a door and a hole for a window, erected in a few hours, and requiring constant repair to keep the fabric from falling to pieces. The only crops which they house for winter use are potatoes, wheat, and maize. The first are kept in pits dug in the ground, and lined with dry fern; the two latter are packed in baskets of flax, and stored in what they call "patakas," little wooden houses, standing on posts high above the ground, which are the most valuable erections in the village. The maize is prepared for eating by being steeped in pools of stagnant water till it rots, when it is taken out and boiled. The nauseous mess is then poured into a huge bowl, round which the company sit, dipping in their hands and sucking up the stuff with the greatest relish. In summer, large crops of melons and pumpkins are raised, and eaten as fast as they ripen; and for fruit, there is abundance of peaches, which grow wild about the country. It will be evident from this, that, if there be time to remove the women, children, pigs, cattle, and horses, which constitute Maori wealth, the loss of a village is no great blow to the natives, who can find abundant virgin soil elsewhere. To burn their standing crops and raupo houses would, no doubt, exasperate them, but would scarcely crush them into submission.

On the other hand, the habits and customs of the natives qualify them for carrying on a long-continuous war—which was, indeed, their normal condition before the introduction of Christianity. The soil is so fertile, that, with ploughs and bullocks, very few days' labour will produce food enough for the year. The time of agricultural labour is holiday in a native village; the grown men and elders sit lazily amongst the fern, smoking their pipes and discussing the latest manœuvre of the wily European foe; while women are scraping potatoes to roast with a fat pig in the native oven, perhaps with the addition of a fragrant piece of dried shark, to give a relish to the dinner. Three or four pairs of oxen, driven by stout, clean-limbed lads, are dragging as many ploughs through the rich loamy soil;

and smaller boys are following the plough, and putting in seed potatoes; while the children of the village, stark naked, are shouting and rolling about in the fern. In summer-time, you may come upon a threshing-machine, fixed on a sunny hill-top, to which all the oxen and carts of the place are drawing loads of wheat, from which the machine is noisily producing huge piles of straw, whereon the population of the village, except the few who are at work, lie basking in the sunshine, some sleeping, some munching peaches and apples, and some, in knots of two or three, discussing the everlasting King movement, and when the great war with Sir George Grey is likely to begin.

Having gone through the labour necessary for growing their food, they are at leisure to do what they please, and mostly spend their time in travelling about the country. I have known Porokoru, an old man of eighty, set off from Kihikihi, on foot, to attend a meeting in Cook's Strait, as a deputy from the King, with no other clothes than a long calico night-shirt, and return on foot, after an absence of three months, in the same garment, certainly never washed in the interim. In the spring, isolated cultivations are often met with, where promising crops are growing, and not a human being is to be seen for miles. One old man or woman will take care of an entire village for weeks, while the inhabitants are miles away, feasting or fishing. Maories travel with very little luggage. A blanket, tied with flax to the pommel of the saddle, is usually all with which they encumber themselves on a land journey. In a canoe expedition, they take food, as well as pots and kettles, and perhaps a few spare clothes, which their bullocks or wives carry to the river. To public meetings, or to any mischief, their double-barrelled guns and cartouche-boxes go too. The travelling-dress is adapted to the country, being a blue-checked shirt. If they have trousers at all, they carry that garment tied round their necks. Thus they are quite ready for rivers, swamps, or any other obstruction in their path. In fact, trousers in New Zealand bush are a mistake; the country is too new for them, and the attempt to wear them only entails constant mortification. The natives say the roads about the country are quite good enough for them, and dash through swamps and rivers without hesitation or harm. Not that they have the least objection to good roads, as such. About Rangiaowhia there are excellent dray-roads in every direction, constructed by the natives themselves. The smaller rivers, which it is possible to ford on horseback, are crossed in several places by hand-bridges; and roads are made through swamps by logs of wood, or bundles of a shrub called "manuka," which in time create a firm bottom. There is a very bad place just above Ngaruawahia, where the horses of the King's visitors were constantly getting bogged. A malefactor, convicted by the native runanga of bigamy, was sentenced to build a bridge over this, and set to work accordingly. However, after doing half, he became tired, and ran away; and the bridge is, as far as I know, still incomplete. But the sentence will never be forgotten; and if the man survives the war, he will, no doubt, have to finish the work some day. But to projects for roads which would make their country accessible to our troops, they have always made a most determined resistance. Having heard how England was civilized by the Romans, they are resolved not to be civilized themselves in the same way. The road which Sir George Grey made through the Hunua forest to Mangatawhiri was regarded with extreme dislike, and the troops thereon engaged would have been attacked, had it not been entirely upon Queen's land. In 1862, Wiremu Nera, an old chief, living near Raglan, tried, at Sir George Grey's instigation, to make a road thence to the Waipa. The whole of Waikato rose in alarm; and had the attempt been persisted in, there would certainly have been war. Wi Tamihana wrote to Nera, that the forests and the swamps were the bulwarks of Waikato, and entreated that he would not deprive his children of their protection, and leave them open to destruction; and Te Paea, the King's sister, a relative of Nera, went and with her own hand pulled up the sticks that marked the road. No money would now induce them to take off the tapu at Taupiri, and allow a road along that bank of the river, or to allow bridges to be made over the Waikato, or any of its tributaries below Ngaruawahia; although above, at Maunga-tautari, they have, with great labour, bridged the Waikato with a single enormous tree, at a place where the river runs between two perpendicular rocks.

The feeling of the people on this subject was clearly expressed to Sir George Grey, at the first meeting he attended in Waikato. Tipene said: "The roads are not simply for fetching food from a man's farm; it is that fact which creates fear. At Taranaki, the road being there, your guns reached the pa. Our fear is, lest that strange cart, the cart of terror, should travel on it. But for this fear, roads would have been allowed long ago." Tipene, who was thus addressing Sir George Grey, was the chosen orator of the King party, and the feelings he expressed were those of nearly every native in Waikato. The fact that a whole race should, at a time when we were making the most friendly professions, believe us bent on war, proves the utter distrust with which the Maories had come to receive everything that issued from the British Government, and affords strong presumption of some radical mistake in our treatment of them. It will be my object, in the succeeding chapters, to trace the growth of this distrust in the minds of the natives, and to explain its causes.

CHAPTER III.

THE QUEEN'S SOVEREIGNTY.

THE claim of the Queen of England to exercise the rights of sovereignty over the natives of New Zealand is founded on the Treaty of Waitangi. This treaty was made at the Bay of Islands, in 1840, between Captain Hobson, the first Governor of New Zealand, and the Ngapuhi chiefs, and was afterwards hawked about the country to be signed by any chief who could be persuaded to do so: each man who signed got a blanket. According to the Maori version of this treaty—which differs from the English text, of which it purports to be a translation—the Queen of England guaranteed to the Maories the full *chiefship* over their lands and other property, and the chiefs yielded to the Queen the right of buying such plots of land as the owner might please to sell. They also gave up to the Queen the whole *governorship* over their lands, and the Queen promised them the full rights of British subjects. The word for *chiefship* is *rangatiratanga; rangatira* signifies a chief or gentleman, as opposed to a common fellow or to a slave. The word for *governorship* is *kawanatanga*, *kawana* being the Maori way of writing and pronouncing the foreign word *governor*. It would be out of place to discuss here the sense of making a treaty at all with a people destitute of any government that could secure the observance of conditions on their side. Those only who contrived the treaty can tell how they thought they were binding the Maories by the form gone through; and those only who explained the treaty to the chiefs who signed can tell what success they met with in teaching so complex an idea as that of governorship, or sovereignty, to savages so entirely ignorant of the thing as not even to have a word in their language to express it. It is quite certain, however, that the conditions of the treaty have not been much observed by either side. Maories have always thought their own right arms the best guarantee for the chiefship of their lands and other property; and I know of no instance, except the dubious Waitara case, in 1860, where the Governor has interfered to protect a man in his chiefship according to the terms of the guarantee. The Crown's right of preemption has been enforced, not by forbidding natives to sell, but white men to buy. The former have constantly sold and let land to private persons; the only checks to the practice were, the difficulty the purchaser had in getting a Crown grant of what he bought, and a colonial law, never enforced, imposing a penalty for using native land. What the Maori chiefs thought they gave up under the name "whole governorship of their lands," it is impossible to tell; but as they themselves never possessed rights of sovereignty over the people, it would be idle to discuss whether they could give such rights away. If the Queen has no more right to sovereignty than the chiefs who signed the Treaty of Waitangi, her title to the allegiance of the Maories will not bear examination. The last article of the treaty, if faithfully kept, would indeed have conferred on the British Government an indisputable claim to the gratitude and obedience of the native race. If we had educated the natives in civilization, and fitted them for the enjoyment of those full rights, as British subjects, which the Treaty of Waitangi promised, nothing would have been heard of "land-leagues" and "king-movements."

But no claim on the Waikatos can be founded on the treaty, for the simple reason that they never signed it. It was, indeed, taken to Waikato, and six old men put their names to it, and got their blankets. Potatau—at that time the principal chief of Waikato—refused to sign, though pressed to do so. Te Waharoa, a great warrior, the principal chief of Ngatihaua, never signed. Wiremu Tamihana's argument—"I am chief of Ngatihaua, which is an independent tribe: my father, Te Waharoa, was chief before me; neither he, I, nor any of my people, signed this treaty, therefore we are not bound by it"—is logical and unanswerable.

It is quite true that, since the treaty, we have always

supposed ourselves to be sovereigns over the Maories, and that, until the "king-movement," no protest was ever entered by them against the claim. This is not surprising, when it is remembered that the Queen's sovereignty was, in native districts, a thing so purely ideal, that it never clashed with the self-will of the native tribes, nor even with their right to make war on each other. So absolutely was Waikato neglected, that Mr. Ashwell stated before a Committee of the House of Representatives, that, during nineteen years before the "king-movement," he could not remember more than three or four visits to the Waikato by officials.[1] The Maories have been told that the Queen was a hedge around the island to keep off the French, Americans, and other nations, who would have treated them with less humanity than ourselves. To this kind of sovereignty they never had, and have not at the present moment, the slightest objection. But sovereignty, or government, in the sense of a power strong enough to put down robbery and murder, and increase the common happiness by enforcing obedience to laws for the common good, was a thing unknown to the natives of New Zealand when they signed the Treaty of Waitangi, and unknown to loyal and disloyal alike at the present day. It was not that the Maori race did not present scope for the efforts of a paternal sovereign. For years after the treaty, tribal wars were so common, that

[1] N. Z. Parl. Papers, 1860. F. No. 3, 864.

Tamihana describes them as "a river of blood" flowing through the land. But to really govern the Maories would have been costly; the revenues of the colony were required to pay for the government and improvement of the European race; the imperial treasury had no funds to spare; and it was therefore thought most economical and prudent not to attempt to govern at all, to abstain strictly from interference in purely native affairs, and merely to purchase, by presents and pensions, the good-will of the principal native chiefs. This has gone by the name of the "Sugar and Flour Policy," because to distribute large quantities of sugar and flour was the keystone of the system. It may be questioned whether it was good economy to undertake the sovereignty of the Maories at all; but, having once undertaken it, to introduce our property, women, and children into the midst of a savage and warlike race, which we neglected to civilize, was the most ruinous policy in the world. What the Government was so long afraid to attempt, because it was difficult, has now become impossible; and a lavish outlay of money, half of which, ten years ago, would have secured lasting peace, has now failed to avert a war, expensive to England and ruinous to the colony. Lest this should be thought an exaggerated account of the neglect of the British Government, I shall quote the opinions of the last two Governors of New Zealand. Colonel Browne, in a memorandum, dated May 25th, 1861, says: "Some of the most populous districts, such as Hokianga and Kaipara, have no magistrates resident among them; and many, such as Taupo, the Ngatiruanui, Taranaki, and the country about the East Cape, have *never been visited by an officer of the Government*. The residents in these districts have never felt that they are the subjects of the Queen of England, and have *little reason to think that the Government of the Colony cares at all about their welfare*."[1] Sir George Grey, in a dispatch to the Secretary of State, dated 6th December, 1861, writes: "Ten years since, the urgent necessity of introducing simple municipal institutions among them (the natives) was pointed out, and the first step taken to induce them to refer their disputes to our courts. But, though various proposals have been made for facilitating a further advance towards these objects, the matter has been practically left nearly where it then was."[2] That is to say, the first step towards fulfilling our undertaking to govern was taken eleven years after the treaty, and no further step was taken for ten years more. Is it to be wondered at, that during these dilatory proceedings, the Maories got tired of waiting, and set up an independent government of their own?

During the entire period of twenty-one years nothing like a native service had ever been organized. On this subject Colonel Browne, in the minute above quoted,

[1] N. Z. Parl. Papers 1861. E. No. 3 A.
[2] Ibid. 1862. E. No. 1, sec. II. 17.

writes:—"In the Hudson's Bay territory, and in other colonies where the Europeans have assumed the duties connected with the government of partially civilized tribes, it has been found necessary to have officers regularly trained and educated for those duties. . . . In New Zealand the Government *is, and always has been, unable to perform its duty,* for want of a sufficient number of agents so trained and qualified for the service required of them. I am therefore strongly of opinion that the Native Department should be entirely remodelled; that a Native Service should be established. . . . Without some such system the Government will never be able to take its proper part in establishing institutions for the native race, or obtain any real hold upon their confidence." Strange words for the Governor of New Zealand to have to use twenty years after the Treaty of Waitangi. In their lack of proper agents the Government had often to send into native districts men deficient in intelligence or character, or in both, who presented most unfavourable contrasts to the many men of unblemished reputation with whom the natives were familiar as agents of the missionary societies. Indeed the missionaries have constantly rendered service to the Government as political agents, both in ordinary and extraordinary times; though they have never been willing to perform judicial and other governmental functions, which they regarded as inconsistent with their duties as missionaries. They have constantly supplied information about the feelings of the natives, and suggestions for their improvement; and have often used their influence with success to prevent disturbances. What the missionaries did not do, was generally left undone. Thus the Government was in most native districts either unknown or known only to be despised.

The measure to which Sir George Grey refers, as the first step taken to induce the Maories to refer their disputes to our courts, was an Ordinance for appointing Resident Magistrates, to exercise jurisdiction in civil cases between Europeans and Maories, where the amount sued for did not exceed 20*l*. There were, however, no means whatever of enforcing the decision given, at least where the Maori was the losing party. To provide for cases between the natives themselves, a number of chiefs were appointed assessors, of whom each party could choose one to sit in judgment with the magistrate. But unless, after the hearing, both assessors agreed in opinion, no further proceedings could be taken. The magistrate could only demand security before hearing the case to ensure obedience to his judgment if given.

This ordinance is evidence of the good intentions of the Government towards the native race. Unhappily very few resident magistrates were appointed in pursuance of the design, and those few were almost all stationed in English settlements. It is not so much in contriving as in executing that our government of the New Zealanders has uniformly broken down. Like Shilpi the Builder, we have regarded "the tongue as a constructor rather than a commentator."

In pursuance of the Resident Magistrate Ordinance, several chiefs were appointed, with small salaries, to act as assessors. These men, being without English instruction and guidance, generally set up as independent founts of justice, and administered law with much vigour and little equity. The fines levied on their victims were often so enormous, that it was simply impossible they could ever be paid. Ti Oriori, of Maunga-tautari, whose legal acumen would do credit to Lincoln's Inn, was accustomed to assign an hour to the hearing of each case: when time was up, he promptly cut short the pleadings or the evidence, and gave his decision. In one case where his judgment was palpably wrong, the losing party expostulated after the sitting of the court, and explained the rest of his cause: Ti Oriori said he was very sorry for him, but he never allowed a case to be re-heard. This enterprising judge was very useful to European squatters in the Waikato, enforcing their claims against natives in his own court, and charging a commission on the amount. Heteraka Nera, who held an illegal but perfectly formal court at Raglan, whence writs, summonses, and subpœnas were duly issued, once condemned a Maori to pay a certain sum and costs. After waiting three years for the money,

Heteraka waylaid the defaulter at the house of the English magistrate, whither the latter was come to receive some money, and informed the magistrate that he was about to levy execution after the primitive fashion of knocking the man down and taking the money out of his pocket. The magistrate expostulated and begged him, if quite determined, at least to wait till the man was off his (the magistrate's) land, and not make a disturbance on his place. To this Heteraka consented, and accordingly this energetic judge, with two comrades, chased the recusant from the magistrate's house, overtook him, knocked him down, took his money out of his breeches pocket, helped himself to the fine, the costs of the hearing, 1*l.* as the costs of this singular execution, and then gave him back the rest of the money. The whole story was told by Heteraka himself, in a letter asking for more forms of summons to be sent him from the native office. The Waikato was almost the only native district to which an English magistrate was appointed, but as a gentleman unacquainted with the language and ways of the natives was selected for the post, in fact, the very magistrate mentioned in Heteraka's story, the appointment was not followed by any results.

But though the Government was unable to do anything to cure the state of anarchy which prevailed in all native districts, the progress of colonization did much indirectly to increase the evil.

The Government, having constituted itself by the

Treaty of Waitangi sole purchaser of native land, was bound to do its best to supply the insatiable appetite of the rising colony. The interests of the latter plainly required that the Land Purchasing Department of Government at least should be kept in working order, and the watchfulness and criticism of the colonists secured a high degree of efficiency in this part of native government. Before the settlers became sufficiently numerous to excite native jealousy, land was eagerly sold by the Maories. It was the easiest way to acquire money, and the establishment of Europeans in any neighbourhood was thought very advantageous. But the sale of land soon began to lead to quarrels and bloodshed amongst themselves. Wi Tamihana says that they never quarrelled about their lands until we appeared as purchasers. Whether this be strictly true or not, it is clear that our readiness to buy would make land feuds more frequent and bitter. To people with territories far greater than they could occupy, land was comparatively worthless; but as soon as it became possible to exchange land for money, the value in their estimation rose enormously. Old claims were revived, former gifts disputed, and blood was shed to secure the title to so rich a prize. For example: Pehitukorehu, an ancestor of the Ngatimaniapotos, conquered the Ngatiraukawa tribe in battle and drove them from their stronghold, Otawhao, and their lands in that neighbourhood, to beyond Maunga-tautari: so little did he value the land—many square miles in extent—of which he thus became the master, that he gave it away to his friends and kinsmen, the Waikatos of the Ngatimahuta tribe. They occupied the country, felled the forest, and cultivated without dispute for years. Some dozen years ago the Waikatos sold a few acres of their land to settlers. The jealousy of the Ngatimaniapoto was aroused; they asserted a claim to the land, re-occupied a part of it, and the Waikatos were obliged to promise that no more should be sold without their consent. Ever since that time a feud has been going on which has several times nearly broken out into open war, and the Ngatimaniapoto dispute the validity of the sale to the present day.

Afterwards, when from causes shortly to be explained, natives were no longer generally willing to allow land to be sold, it was no uncommon practice for one party claiming a piece of land to offer it to Government for sale without the knowledge of the rival claimants; and though every precaution was taken by the Land Purchase Department, there is no doubt that in some such cases sales were effected. There are several pieces of land in Lower Waikato which have been partly paid for, and are marked down in our maps as the property of Government, which friendly and loyal chiefs assert to be their property, and to have been fraudulently sold. These fraudulent sales, or at any rate the universal belief in them, increased the eagerness of the natives to assert claims to all land in which they thought they were entitled to share, lest while they neglected to do so sales might be effected by others without their knowledge.

In the very rare cases of grave offences committed against Europeans, Government was obliged to have recourse to negotiations for the surrender or punishment of the offender. In cases of this kind valuable assistance was frequently rendered by the missionaries. Potatau, who lived at Mangere, six miles from Auckland, was always consulted in the case of a difficulty in Waikato, and he could generally obtain redress.

Even in the streets of Auckland itself the natives have generally been able to defy the majesty of the law. No native could be imprisoned for drunkenness or rioting without the risk of war; and with our unarmed men, women, and children, hostages in native districts, it was a risk the Government dared not run. On some particular occasions the Governor did venture upon asserting his authority, but drunken and insolent young Maories, with whom the police had instructions not to meddle, were common frequenters of the streets of Auckland even down to the date of the present outbreak.

Having thus shown how little the most elementary duty of a ruler—the protection of life and property—was performed by the British Crown, it remains to describe the action of Government upon the education of the race, taking the word education in a wide sense, not as equivalent to mere schooling, but as including all the instruction and training necessary to fit the natives to enjoy liberty and govern themselves. There is no doubt that every act of every Government has more or less effect upon the character of the governed, but in the case of a country like New Zealand it is the duty and interest of her rulers to institute special and direct measures for educating the uncivilized part of the community. This would have been the more easy task, inasmuch as the Maories were not only willing but eager to accept our teaching upon all subjects, even long after they repudiated our authority as rulers.

The mode in which the New Zealand Government promoted the education of native children was by yearly grants to the Church of England, the Wesleyans, and the Roman Catholics, under whose superintendence schools were established. In Waikato there were three Church of England schools, two Wesleyan, and one Roman Catholic. The Government did not reserve to itself any right to control the spending of the sums which it bestowed. It was merely a subscriber to a large amount, and exercised just so much influence as was conferred by the power of withdrawing the subscription at the risk of affronting the ecclesiastical magnates. It is true that in 1858 a Colonial Act was passed specifying certain conditions on which the yearly grants were to continue; for instance, that the children should have industrial training, regular instruction in English, and should sleep on the school premises. These conditions, sometimes from sheer impossibility, were not always fulfilled, and no means were used to ascertain or compel their observance. According to the Act, the schools ought to have been visited each year by an inspector, but no one was appointed to the office. The duty was several times performed by amateurs, usually gentlemen of high position in the colony, but their reports, though full of valuable suggestions, never produced action on the part of Government. When mission-schools were first established, children crowded into them ; it was the object of each religious body to get as many as possible into their own schools, lest they should be outstripped by their rivals in the work of proselytizing. The result was that most of the mission-schools speedily became too large for the funds by which they were supported. The Government could neither give more money, nor did it dare to put a limit on the number to be received into the schools. The managers, therefore, hampered by their efforts to educate many children with little money, were obliged to screw down the costs to the lowest possible amount. Boys and girls were kept in the same school, with deplorable moral results ; the girls worked as domestic servants, the boys as out-door labourers ; the food given was not better in quality, and was sometimes less in quantity, than they would have got in their own villages ; their clothing was ragged and sordid; their bedrooms, bare of the furniture and decencies of civilization, crowded with children, some sleeping two and three together in narrow bedsteads, others huddled in dirty blankets on the floor; and all this because the managers could not afford the luxuries of cleanliness, privacy, and better nourishment. These remarks must not be understood to apply equally to all the mission-schools. It was possible for a very expert manager, as for example the Rev. A. Reid, of the Wesleyan Infant School at Waipa, to counteract some of the bad tendencies of the system, but in other cases they produced their full fruits. Thus for several reasons the natives grew more and more unwilling to send their children to the schools; they were afraid of their girls getting entangled in connexions with boys of other tribes; they thought the children badly fed and clothed; they were disappointed at their being employed on common uninstructive work instead of learning trades; and lastly, they grew so distrustful of Government as to dread even gifts that proceeded from that quarter. The Roman Catholic priest, in order to set up a small school at Rangiaowhia two years ago, had to tell the natives that his funds came from Bishop Pompallier and not from Government.

The political education of the adult natives was provided for by a newspaper, published in parallel columns of English and Maori, and distributed gratis. Of the stuff thus circulated amongst them as political wisdom, it is impossible to speak in terms of sufficient contempt. If Maories are conceited enough to think themselves wiser in State-craft than ourselves, the dreary columns of the *Maori Messenger* are an ample explanation of and justification for their conduct. Successive governors and colonial ministers have vainly laboured to cure the dull idiocy of this newspaper. It is not that it has been impossible to find clever men and good Maori scholars to edit it; but when it is remembered that such editor is a paid subordinate of a timid and divided Government, and that in his writings he must affront neither the King-natives nor the Queen-natives, neither the Governor nor the Native Minister, neither Churchmen nor Wesleyans, neither missionaries nor colonial shopkeepers, the incurable badness of the paper is sufficiently explained. Perhaps, after the character I have given of this journal, my readers will not think it of much consequence how it might be circulated—possibly the Native Department is of the same opinion. At any rate, most of the principal chiefs in Waikato, including the King, William Thompson, and the majority of the Ngaruawahia Council, have never been supplied with this instructive reading. On the other hand, Te Wharepu, who is also called Pukewhau, the principal chief of Lower Waikato, has a copy sent regularly to each name: though the mistake has repeatedly been pointed out to the proper authority, and to other chiefs, the native office addressed copies long after they were dead and buried, even when funeral sermons had been preached on them by the very paper itself.

To promote the social advancement of the Maories, presents were made to them of ploughs, horses, and flour-mills. It may be questioned whether it was wise to give such things, rather than let them be earned by honest labour; but the policy of keeping the natives quiet by bribes to the chiefs, required gifts of some sort, and ploughs and horses were certainly better than money, which might have been spent in rum. A far more hurtful practice was to lend money to favourite chiefs, which was rarely and unpunctually repaid. The habit of lying was thereby largely promoted, while those who received such aid soon became pauperized, as they found out how much easier it was to beg or bully the Government out of what they wanted, than to get it by labour for themselves. It had come to be commonly observed, that, in most districts, chiefly, as I believe, from this cause, the King natives were of a much better stamp than the Loyal ones, at least as regarded honesty and self respect.

The possession of ploughs, carts, and mills, has not, on the whole, improved the character of the Maories. The effect has been to enable them to grow produce for their own consumption, and for the purpose of purchasing the few European articles they need, in less time and with less trouble than before; to abridge the hours of labour, and increase their leisure. This leisure they occupy in endless "runangas," or public meetings, at which their grievances are the chief topio of discussion. A little civilization has made them idle, and idleness has made them mischievous. These bad results have, however, been slow in showing themselves, while the material prosperity and increase of wealth were immediate and apparent. Rangiaowhia, in particular, became, many years ago, the scene of extraordinary prosperity. An English labourer was established there to teach agriculture; mills were built, carts and ploughs were given; roads were made; vast tracts of land were cleared of fern, ploughed, and covered with beautiful crops of wheat. Better houses were built—even a brick oven was constructed, to bake bread for the village. The natives, delighted with the prospect of becoming wealthy, gave eight hundred acres of their best land to support an industrial school, where agriculture, tailoring, shoemaking, and various European trades, were to be taught. A hospital, with a resident doctor, was also promised; but these promises were never fulfilled. Yet all this proved to be a mere hollow semblance of peace and prosperity. The natives grew wealthy, but were savages still; customs which rendered amalgamation with Europeans difficult remained in full force; and the lesson of submission to some sort of constituted authority had yet to be learned. About this time, from causes which will be explained in the following chapter, a deep and wide-spread feeling of discontent began to prevail among the natives; the more intelligent and thoughtful revolted against the whole system of treatment that they had received from Government; land leagues, to prevent further sales to the Crown, were proposed in many places; and a native king, who should unite all the tribes of New Zealand into one people, began to be talked of. This was a difficulty that the "sugar and flour policy" could not meet. Gratitude for past, or the hope of future gifts, might keep a few chiefs loyal; but it was manifestly impossible to bribe every native with ploughs and horses, to do as Government wished him. A leader only was needed, to raise a standard of separation from British dominion, and to unite all the tribes into a national party.

The Government were warned, by one of their own officers, of the danger. Mr. C. O. Davis, an interpreter, who possessed the most extensive information about native doings, said, in an official memorandum:—[1]

"The natives generally consider themselves an independent nation, and not amenable to British law. They discuss this subject with great seriousness, and many of the tribes are warmly advocating the election of a Maori king, who will, it is supposed, be able to settle all their grievances, and quiet the troubles of the land.

[1] Parl. Papers, 1860, F. No. 338.

"It may be asked, What is being done to lessen the discontent which prevails everywhere among the native people? The influence of the missionary bodies, in regard to the Maori population, has ceased; at present it is a mere shadow. The influence of Government is daily becoming less, owing, in a great measure, to our want of system. It is altogether a mistaken notion to suppose that we are attaching the natives to us, and securing their allegiance to the Crown, by the bestowment of presents and granting loans. In most instances this is positively injurious, fostering idleness and covetousness, and causing the chiefs to lay aside that self-respect which raised them so far above the generality of barbarians."

CHAPTER IV.

THE REVOLT.

WHEN the English first began to settle in New Zealand, they had little reason to fear that the natives, who were continually quarrelling and fighting among themselves, would ever become united, and therefore formidable. Before our arrival, the Maories lived in a state of continual warfare; and the first use made of the new comers by the Ngapuhi tribe, among whom the earliest settlers planted themselves, was to obtain from them a supply of guns and ammunition, with the help of which they invaded Waikato, and drove their ancient enemies with great slaughter to the upper districts and hills. Lower Waikato remained for long afterwards an uninhabited wilderness, the former inhabitants not daring to return to their ravaged homes. After a time, the Waikatos also obtained guns and powder; they could then encounter their enemies on equal terms, and, after several bloody battles, the Ngapuhi invasions of Waikato were discontinued. Disunion was exhibited not only in battles between distant tribes; even in the same village, and amongst near relations, there was rarely unanimity on any one subject. Maories are, in their opinions and sentiments, the most independent people in the world, and exhibit an individuality which would delight Mr. John Stuart Mill. I have known laws passed at Kihikihi or Rangiaowhia, at an evening runanga, prohibiting the sales of pigs and potatoes to Europeans, followed next morning by a rush of old women to Otawhao to dispose of the forbidden articles; and instances are numerous in which one thoroughly resolute and obstinate man, or even woman, has defeated the intention of a whole war-party. From people of this sort Europeans, united and civilized, had nothing to fear, unless some extraordinary accident should combine the discordant factions.

There was great variety in the modes in which the progress of colonization affected tribes and individuals, and also in the light in which they regarded the conduct of Government; but the ultimate effect produced was uniformly a strong discontent, and a desire, amounting to a passion, for separate and independent nationality. The cause of what is called "the king-movement" has been much disputed among New Zealand politicians. The fact is, that there has been no single cause. Different sentiments attracted adherents, who joined in the scheme with different views; and as one set of motives after another was in the ascendant, the character of the movement itself was continually changing.

Wiremu Tamihana and the Ngatihaua tribe, who were the first to set up Potatau as king, declared that they did so to supply that want of government which has been described in the last chapter, which they severely felt. In a letter written to Colonel Browne, in 1861, to defend his personal conduct in regard to the king-movement, after mentioning various tribal wars which he had stopped, Tamihana writes: "I thought that a great house should be built as a house of assembly for the tribes that were living at feud in New Zealand, and would not cleave one to the other. The house was built—it was Babel. Then I applied my thoughts to seek for some plan by which the Maori tribes should cleave together and assemble together, so that the people might become one, like the Pakehas. The Ngatipaoa were invited, and they came to me, and joined the talk for good. Afterwards the Ngatimatera were invited, and they came; afterwards the Ngatiwhakaue were invited, and they came; afterwards the Ngatiwhanaunga were invited, and they came. However, they were mere meetings; evil still went on—the river of blood was not yet stopped. The missionaries behaved bravely, and so did I; but the flow of blood did not cease. When you (Colonel Browne) came, the river of blood was still open, and I therefore sought for some plan to make it cease; I considered how this blood could be made to diminish in the island. I looked at your books, where Israel cried to have a king to themselves, to be a judge over them; and I looked at the word of Moses, in Deuteronomy xvii. 15,[1] and at Proverbs xxix. 4,[2] and I kept these words in my memory through all the years; the land feuds continuing all the time, blood still being spilt, and I still meditating upon the matter. In the year 1857, Te Heu Heu called a meeting at Taupo, at which sixteen hundred men were present. When the news of this meeting reached me I said, 'I will consent to this, to assist my work.' I began at those words of the Book of Samuel viii. 5, 'Give us a king, to judge us.' That was why I set up Potatau, in 1857. On his being set up, the blood at once ceased, and has so remained up to the present year. The reason why I set up Potatau as a king for me, was because he was a man of extended influence, and a man who was revered by the people of this island. That, my friend, was why I set him up. To put down my troubles, to hold the lands of the slaves, and to judge the offences of the chiefs, the King was set up. The runangas were set up; the magistrates were set up; and the Faith was set up. The works of my ancestors have ceased; they are diminishing at the present time. What I say is, the blood of the Maories has ceased."[3]

[1] "Thou shalt in anywise set him king over thee, whom the Lord thy God shall choose: one from among thy brethren shalt thou set king over thee: thou mayest not set a stranger over thee which is not thy brother."

[2] "The king by judgment establisheth the land."

[3] N. Z. Parl. Papers, 1861. E. No. 1 B. 20.

It was not, however, the bloodshed in war only that made the urgent necessity for some kind of law. The teaching of Christianity had destroyed the old barbarous customs of tapu, and all the superstitious reverence for priests and chiefs, which had supplied the place of law and government; but neither the missionaries nor the Government had been able to substitute a better system in the place of that which had been pulled down: thus the natives were left in a state of absolute anarchy, where every man did that which was right in his own eyes. Europeans of the lowest class settled among them, enjoyed equal licence, and—far out of the reach of magistrates and police—sinned with impunity, propagating all sorts of evil among their native neighbours.

I give as an example, a detailed account of one matter which natives like Tamihana considered a grievance. One of the most lucrative articles in which the Pakeha-Maories trade is rum, of which large quantities are consumed in native districts. Maories are not slow to see the mischief which this traffic is doing; they have been taught by the missionaries that it is certain destruction to their race—and the example of the Red Indians has been held up to them as a warning. Many of the Waikato chiefs have made strenuous efforts to keep spirits out of the district altogether. Tamihana saved his tribe from demoralization by the ingenious plan of making each European settled in his territory sign a bond to pay 1*l.* for every native found drunk on his premises. The sale of spirits to natives is forbidden by a colonial law, under a penalty of 10*l.*; but the law is evaded by general conspiracy. A native wishing to buy spirits arms himself with a written order from a European to a dealer to supply the bearer with so many gallons; he pays his money, gets the rum, and makes himself and comrades drunk. In a few cases in which informations have been laid either by some officious philanthropist, or by the natives themselves, when the rum has been bad (for the provincial police dare not offend their employers, the publicans, by enforcing an unpopular law), the resident magistrates have ruled that the fictitious order from a European exonerates the seller. In this way hogsheads of spirits have been sold, not only in remote country districts but in the very streets of Auckland, under the blind eyes of the law. I have known loyal natives in the employment of Government enter intoxicated into the native office and leave it unrebuked and undischarged. Soon after Sir George Grey's return to New Zealand, in consequence of fresh complaints by William Thompson of the persistence with which the traffic in rum was still carried on, an officer was sent to explain the existing law and to declare the Governor's readiness to make (as under an Act of the Colonial Legislature he has power to do) a special and more stringent regulation for the Waikato district if petitioned so to do. The message was attentively listened to by the king's runanga at Ngaruawahia, and the messenger was told that if he went back to Auckland and searched the records of the native office, he would find that years ago the Government had been petitioned by the whole of Waikato on this very subject, and petitioned in vain. A few soft-hearted chiefs proposed to write a fresh letter to Sir George Grey, but the majority said—"No; let the papers of the native office be searched." The office was searched, memorials were found from nearly every tribe in Waikato, sent when the King movement was yet in its infancy, setting forth the evils of rum-selling, and crying to Government for help to put down the trade. Minutes were found suggesting an excellent regulation to meet the case, with written approvals by the Governor and Colonial Ministry. There the matter had stopped just short of action, and the papers had gone into a pigeon-hole. But the natives, unacquainted with our admirable administrative system, in which the gravest mistakes may be made by the most subordinate officials, thought that their interests were wilfully overlooked; and that the consumption of rum, on which the Government depends for a large part of its revenue, and many influential colonists for their incomes, was more cared for than their welfare.

It is not likely that amongst the New Zealanders, or any other people, many would be wise enough sincerely to desire order and laws, and though we cannot doubt that this was the real design of some who promoted the King movement, it was certainly not that of all. Many of those who joined in Waikato, and most of those who joined from tribes out of Waikato, did so because the King was to hold the lands of his adherents upon trust not to permit sales to the Crown. Unwillingness to sell land has gradually grown up amongst the natives. With some it is unwillingness to sell at all; with others it is unwillingness to sell on the terms prescribed by law. No feeling of the kind existed at the outset. Immense tracts of country were readily parted with to the earliest settlers for very trifling considerations. The land was little valued by them as soil; they cared only for the enjoyment of what we should call territorial dominion, and it was for this, and not for mere soil, which could not at that time be exchanged for money, that they fought in early days. By sale to Europeans, while Europeans were few and weak, no power or territorial dominion was parted with. The purchaser became one of the most valuable possessions of the tribe: the chief called him "*my* Pakeha," and the tribe called him "*our* Pakeha." He traded with them, procured them guns, helped them in their wars, promoted their importance, and was at the same time dependent on them for protection, and completely at their mercy. If the Englishman was a gentleman and a capitalist, he was a consumer of surplus produce, an employer of any young men who took a fancy to do a day's work, an example of civilized life and agricultural enterprise to the ambitious, and all his greatness and grandeur were their possession and redounded to their credit. But as the number of Europeans increased, these relations were altered; a sale involved parting with the dominion of the soil; towns sprang up, inhabited by strange and powerful white men, who neither knew nor cared for the original proprietors. If the native visited the spot where he was once lord and master, he found himself insignificant and despised in the midst of a civilization in which he did not share. The hopes of social advancement which the natives had formed when they first consented to share their country with the stranger, were disappointed. They did not fail to contrast the rapid alienation of their land with the slow improvement of their condition, and they feared that at this rate their lands would be gone before they had attained the desired equality with their white neighbours. Every function of Government seemed paralysed in comparison with the Land Purchasing Department. They were willing to sell their land for civilization and equality, but at no other price. Despairing of obtaining these boons from Government, the desire to withhold land altogether became nearly universal, in order to check the aggrandizement of that power which might hurt them as an enemy, but did not much benefit them as a friend.

Besides this deep-rooted feeling, which made almost all natives dislike selling for any price, or in any manner, there were particular objections felt to the mode in which land-buying was conducted. In most cases the Maories thought themselves cheated in the price. The average Government price was sixpence per acre;[1] the upset price at which it was sold to colonists, ten shillings. The difference between these sums, after deducting the expense of surveying, formed a considerable source of colonial revenue. No doubt both races benefited by the various objects on which this revenue was expended, but the benefits received were not appreciated by the untutored native mind. They only looked at it as a commercial bargain. Government monopolized the right of buying land, bought at sixpence and sold at ten shillings an acre. If they might sell direct to settlers, they might get ten shillings instead of sixpence: therefore, it seemed to them, that they were cheated by the Government monopoly. No man likes to be taken in. It is well known to settlers that Maories will let their corn and potatoes rot, rather than take a less price than they consider just. "In passing up the river," reports a Government official,[2] "I observed several large mounds, which the natives said were potatoes, belonging to Ngatinaho, which they had been taking to Waiuku for sale, but, on hearing of

[1] From 1850 to 1861, 6,000,000 acres of land were bought from the Maories in the North Island for 160,000*l.*, which is at the rate of 6⅜*d.* per acre. N. Z. Parl. Papers, 1861. E. No. 1, K.

[2] Parl. Papers, 1860. E. No. 1, C. 3.

the low prices, had buried." They act in much the same manner with their land.

The immense number of conflicting claims to almost every piece of native land has already been noticed. One of the earliest settlers in New Zealand thus describes the disputes incident to a purchase in former times:[1]—"I really cannot tell to the present day, who I purchased the land from; for there were about fifty different claimants, every one of whom assured me that the other forty-nine were 'humbugs,' and had no right whatever. The nature of the different titles of the different claimants were various. One man said his ancestors had killed off the first owners; another declared his ancestors had driven off the second party; another man, who seemed to be listened to with more respect than ordinary, declared that his ancestor had been the first possessor of all, and had never been ousted, and that this ancestor was a huge lizard, that lived in a cave on the land many years ago—and, sure enough, there was the cave to prove it. Besides the principal claims, there were an immense number of secondary ones—a sort of latent equities—which had lain dormant till it was known the Pakeha had his eye on the land. Some of them seemed to me, at the time, odd enough. One man required payment, because his ancestors, as he affirmed, had exercised the right of catching rats on it, but which he (the claimant) had

[1] Old New Zealand. Page 76.

never done, for the best of reasons, *i.e.* there were no rats to catch, except, indeed, pakeha rats, which were plentiful enough; but this variety of rodent was not counted as game. Another claimed because his grandfather had been murdered on the land, and—as I am a veracious Pakeha—another claimed payment because *his* grandfather had committed the murder! Then half the country claimed payments of various value, from one fig of tobacco to a musket, on account of a certain *wahi tapu* or ancient burying-ground, which was on the land, and in which almost every one had had relations, or rather ancestors, buried, as they could clearly make out, in old times, though no one had been deposited in it for about two hundred years; and the bones of the others had been (as they said) removed to a *torere* in the mountains. There was one old man who obstinately persisted in declaring that he, and he alone, was the sole and rightful owner of the land: he seemed also to have 'a fixed idea' about certain barrels of gunpowder; but as he did not prove his claim to my satisfaction, and as he had no one to back him, I, of course, gave him nothing; he, nevertheless, demanded the gunpowder about once a month, for five and twenty years, till at last he died of old age. It took about three months' negotiation before the purchase of the land could be made; and, indeed, I at one time gave up the idea, as I found it quite impossible to decide who to pay. If I paid one party, the others vowed I should never have possession, and to pay all seemed impossible; so at last I let all parties know I had made up my mind not to have the land. This, however, turned out to be the first step I had made in the right direction; for thereupon all the different claimants agreed amongst themselves to demand a certain quantity of goods, and divide them amongst themselves afterwards." This account is a caricature of the state of native titles, but a caricature of that sort which gives a more truthful notion to a stranger than an exact picture.

As time went on, the task of buying native lands grew more and more difficult. Claims were made, not for the purpose of getting a share in the price, but to stop the sale altogether. Such claimants were not to be bought off by money. Natives are hard enough at driving a bargain, but are not so mercenary as the settlers generally suppose. The few who wished to sell came to be regarded as traitors to their race, to be put down at all hazards. On the other hand, it was impossible for Government to conceal its anxiety to buy, or its favour for those who were willing to sell. When the Chief Land-Purchase Commissioner became head of the Native Department, all presents made by Government came to be regarded as bribes to sell land. To offer land for sale was the readiest mode of revenge open to the losing side in a quarrel. It was in this way that the celebrated block of land at Waitara came to be offered by Teira to Governor Browne. Secret and dishonest sales were sometimes effected, and from this cause jealousies and quarrels became more frequent and bitter, until the absolute necessity of escaping from these destructive quarrels made all anxious to place the land under a King.

Takerei, the greatest landed proprietor in Waikato, when asked by a Committee of the New Zealand Assembly to give an account of the origin of the "King movement," replied as follows:[1]—

"The people sought a protector for themselves similar to yours. You have a Protector. They proposed to elect a King for themselves to protect them, to be a 'mana'[2] over them and their land. The idea was this—the Queen should be a 'mana' over the Pakeha and over the land which you have acquired. The same with respect to the Maori King. There should be no interference with the portions of land that had been acquired by the Queen, but only with the land which was under the Maories. A single individual should not presume to sell land, whether in the West or in the East, in the North or in the South. It should not be yielded to the control of one man. If the great Runanga of the tribes consented, then only would it be right; but for one man to sell would not be right; although the land was his

[1] Parl. Papers, 1860. F. No. 3. 1721.

[2] The English word most nearly corresponding to "mana" is "power."

own, it should lie with the great Runanga to agree or to object to the disposal of it. The reason for this was lest trouble should arise in the midst of us Maories and the Pakehas. This is the law that has been laid down for the land held by the Maories of New Zealand. This, that I now make known to you, is the thought of the people, that of all the chiefs of Waikato, Ngatihaua, Ngatihinetu, Ngatiapakura, Ngatimaniapoto, Ngatituwharetoa, Ngatirahungaru, and Tauranga. This was the cause of the Maori King being set up; it was for a 'mana' over the people and the land."

It must not, however, be supposed that all natives desirous of stopping the further sale of land became adherents of the King. The desire was almost universal. Land-leagues existed out of Waikato, and before the "King movement." Wi Kingi of Taranaki was head of an independent land-league, and only joined the King, in 1860, to get the help of Waikato in the Taranaki war. Waata Kukutai, of the Lower Waikato, who has always professed loyalty to the Queen, and is now our ally in the Waikato war, is as strongly opposed to selling land as Rewi Maniapoto or Wi Tamihana; but the Maori King-league having always proclaimed the prevention of land sales as one of its chief objects, and possessing a strong physical force to support the principle, is naturally looked up to by those who wish to hold back land, and has therefore a strong tendency to absorb them into its ranks.

The chief cause of the younger and less thoughtful Maories joining the "King movement" was the consciousness that they were regarded by a large majority of their white neighbours as an inferior and degraded race. Even men like Tamihana, who had other and more sober grounds for their disaffection, were powerfully influenced in their conduct by this mortifying reflection. Their political inferiority had been shortly before made clear to them. A Constitution had been conferred on the colony of New Zealand, framed, as Mr. Chichester Fortescue tells us (speech in House of Commons, April 11th, 1861), "in forgetfulness of the large native tribes within the dominions to which it was intended to apply." Under this Constitution local and general assemblies were frequent, in which speeches were made, and hot discussions took place, as to how the colonists should exercise the right of governing the country. The natives were soon made aware that these assemblies were to frame laws touching matters in which they were interested, and which they would be expected to obey; for instance, in 1856, a bill was introduced to enable the Governor, in cases where Maori offenders were not given up to justice, to lay under an interdict the whole district to which they might belong.

At the same time, the opinion of the law officers of the Crown, to whom the question of the right of Maories to exercise the elective franchise was referred by the Duke of Newcastle, was:—"That natives cannot have such possession of any land, used or occupied by them in common as tribes or communities, and not held under title derived from the Crown, as would qualify them to become voters under the provisions of the New Zealand Constitution Act."[1] Thus the Maories were shut out from all share in the assemblies to which, as they well knew, many of their friends, including the Bishop of New Zealand, declared they had a right to be admitted. The native race has never been unwilling to accept guidance and instruction from white men, whose superior knowledge in mechanical arts and in the science of law-making they admit and admire; but to become a subject race, and accept the whites as dominant over them, was felt to be a degradation to which their savage independence could not stoop. They will never submit to the Colonial Government of New Zealand until the colonists alone, without help from England or Australia, shall prove themselves masters in the field. In imitation and rivalry of the colonial assemblies, meetings were held in various parts of the country, at which their own interests and their relations to the white race, were discussed. They wished to remind the framers of the New Zealand Constitution of their existence, and they did so by setting up an independent King.

They were still more painfully conscious of their social than of their political inferiority. To view men

[1] N. Z. Parl. Papers, 1860. E. No. 7.

whose skin differs in colour from our own as "damned niggers," is a weakness of our Anglo-Saxon character, which proves our civilization and Christianity far from perfect. It destroys all chance of our gaining the affections of our native subjects in any part of the world; for uncivilized men will forgive any amount or kind of wrong sooner than a single personal insult. The Maories are exceedingly sensitive of any appearance of personal slight. I once heard a company of them discussing the character of a most estimable missionary, the only drawback to whose usefulness is, that he has a stomach so delicate that he cannot eat food prepared by natives. This was the very point in his conduct with which those whom I overheard seemed most impressed. Nothing can exceed the kindness and respect with which men like Sir George Grey and the Bishop of New Zealand behave to natives; they treat them as "gentlemen." The same remark applies to the superior officers of the Government, the clergy, the more highly-educated colonists, and the older settlers. But the ignorant mass of townspeople judge of the natives from their not very prepossessing exteriors, and never having had experience of the good qualities which, as all who have lived amongst them acknowledge, lie concealed beneath, give free vent to their arrogance and contempt, and speak of the Maories, both publicly and privately, with disgust and dislike. Men habitually told that they emit a disagreeable smell, are not likely to feel a very strong affection towards the race that smells them. I know that the petty rudeness of Europeans is so disagreeable to many chiefs in Waikato, that they dislike going into Auckland, or any of the English villages, and are very shy of visiting at English houses. Their own behaviour to strangers affords a striking contrast, not very creditable to ourselves; a chief of the highest rank will unsaddle the horse of his guest with his own hands, and either pitch his tent or give him the best house in the village to sleep in, covering the floor with freshly gathered fern and new flax mats. The women set to work to cook, or, if their own meal is nearly ready, a portion is set apart for the stranger before the others partake. Any one who in return invited one of the principal men in Waikato to accompany him to Auckland, could not fail to be shamed on the road. A shakedown of straw in an inn stable, bread and meat bought at a shop, or a meal in the inn kitchen, given as a great favour at the Englishman's solicitation, would be all the hospitality he could procure. I have heard the Bishop of New Zealand say he is quite ashamed to travel with his native deacons, men who dine at his own table and behave there like gentlemen, because he cannot take them into public rooms where a tipsy carter would be considered perfectly good society. No ordinance of Government can alter this state of things, any more than it can alter the treatment of negroes in New York, but the insult is not the less exasperating to those who suffer. The colonial newspapers are full of affronts, grave and petty, to the natives, not intended of course to annoy them, but to please the European readers. These all come round to native ears. The *Southern Cross*, an Auckland newspaper which usually advocates a "physical force" policy, used to be regularly taken in at Ngaruawahia and read aloud by a native girl who understood English perfectly. No doubt its opinions were considered to be those of the Government and the whole English race.

Books on New Zealand have never revealed the shameful extent to which half-caste children, both legitimate and illegitimate, have been abandoned by their European fathers. Desertion of wives and children is only too common throughout the Australian colonies, where the ease with which a man can shift himself out of one jurisdiction into another, makes that the easiest way of getting rid of an unpleasant burden. In a native district, where there is no chance of knowing when the father means to abscond, and no magistrate at hand to appeal to for even a maintenance order, desertion is especially easy, and has been largely practised. In every village in Waikato these abandoned little half-castes are to be seen running about wild, like dogs or pigs, growing up in filth and barbarism, inheriting the vices of both races and enjoying the care of neither. What is done for them is not generally the work of the civilized and Christian European, but of the savage half-heathen Maori. The mother's relations give food and an occasional ragged shirt, and treat the children on the whole with kindness; but they feel the wrong and dishonour done them by the white man, and it does not increase their love and respect for the white man's race. I well remember one pitiable object—a poor, pale, stunted lad of fourteen, with wasted limbs and a hacking cough, dressed in winter time in a ragged cotton shirt—who was at work at bullock-driving and potato-planting in a village not far from Rangiaowhia, whose father I afterwards learned was a wealthy Auckland citizen and a member of the Provincial Assembly. Whether such an evil was curable by legislation or not, at any rate the cure was not attempted. In 1857, Mr. Fenton, then magistrate of the Waikato district, addressed to the Government a memorandum as follows:—"The law providing means of enforcing legal maintenance of illegitimate children by the father should be published and put in the Book of Laws. Moreover, some additional provision should be made to prevent the father leaving the country, until sufficient security is given for the regular payment of the maintenance-money. *The frequency of examples of desertion, most shameless and heartless in themselves, has tended to lower the character of the Europeans generally in the eyes of the natives,* whose clannish ideas are too apt to convert the sin of the few into the act of the multitude."[1]

At the close of this catalogue of Maori grievances, I must, to avoid misconstruction, state that I am quite aware there were wrongs on both sides, and that the European race has had just grounds of offence against the Maori. My reason for not enlarging upon these here is, that the cause of the King movement, with which we have now to do, was the sense of wrong felt by the natives for what their side had suffered; of the wrongs they had done, they were, like mankind in general, unconscious. At the time the King was set up, the hostile feeling was not nearly strong enough to create a desire for war, but there was quite enough to make the mass eager for separation and independence, and to this the easy and rapid success of the King party is to be attributed.

The above were, so far as I have been able to ascertain, the feelings and sentiments floating in the minds of the natives at the time when the proposal to set up a King of their own began to be agitated. Some may have been influenced by one cause, others by another, but all tended to produce a common sense of discontent. Once possessed of a common grievance, it became the obvious interest of all to sink minor differences, and combine to assert their separate nationality. The necessity of union was industriously

[1] N. Z. Parl. Papers, 1860. E. No. 1, C. 3.

preached by Wiremu Tamihana and others, at all the large public meetings, which are frequent amongst the natives. The fable of the bundle of sticks, which, with others, has been translated and circulated, took their fancy, and was related over and over again.

CHAPTER V.

POTATAU, THE KING.

At the beginning of 1857, while affairs were in this crisis in Waikato, Wiremu Tamihana paid his last (I believe his only) visit to Auckland. He has said that his chief object in going was to see the Governor, and lay before him the lawless condition of the country, in order that some plan might be arranged to cure the existing evils. He was also anxious to have a European magistrate stationed at his own village. He was, however, received coldly, and his requests were slighted, although nobody can now recollect how or why. He complains of some subordinate officer having treated him with great rudeness when he tried to obtain access to the Governor. It is quite certain that somebody took upon himself to refuse the Chief admission to the Governor's presence. He saw Mr. McLean, the Native Secretary and Chief Commissioner of the Land Purchasing Department, and asked him for a loan to erect a mill. He was refused. A notorious opponent of land-selling, he was not one to be looked on with any favour by a land-buying Government. Before leaving town he visited a friend, and complained to him of the treatment he had received: his friend replied—"You see that your application has been thrown under the table; therefore, if you wish to erect a mill, or raise your own social condition, you must set about it yourself in earnest."[1] Mortified and disappointed, he returned home to meditate on the advice he had received. It readily commended itself to a proud, self-reliant man. He determined to ask no more favours from the English Government, but to work out what his countrymen wanted without that help which he had just been denied.

The fruit of this resolution was the following circular, which was sent about the Waikato district:—

"February 12th, 1857.

"To all Waikato,

"This is the agreement of Ngatihaua, for Potatau to be king of New Zealand:—

"Friends—Our desire is great that Potatau should be set up in this very year. Do not delay. Hasten the assembling of the 'runangas!' Hasten the establishment of the scheme, and when it is done the documents will be collected, and the day will be fixed for instituting

[1] N. Z. Parl. Papers, 1860. F. No. 3. 332.

him. Be speedy. You will write to the remote tribes that they may hear.

From Wiremu (Tamihana) Tarapipipi, and all Ngatihaua, to Waikato, to Kereihi, Pukewau, Harapata, Toma, Ruihana, Waata Tengatete.
"Be speedy."[1]

This was not the first proposal for the election of a king, nor the first nomination of Potatau to the office. The desire for a king had existed for six or seven years previously: the only difficulty was to find some chief to place on the throne who would be accepted by all. A meeting attended by 1600 natives had just been held by Te Heu Heu at Taupo. Much mystery had attended this national gathering. A platform had been erected, on which was the inscription—"Look to the land; look to the sea." At this meeting it was distinctly proposed that Potatau Te Wherowhero, the great chief of Waikato, should be king. When Tamihana heard of the proposal he resolved to do his best to carry it into effect. He therefore at once published the formal assent of Ngatihaua in the letter above quoted.

Potatau Te Wherowhero was almost the only man in New Zealand whom the natives would have agreed to make king over them. He was revered not in Waikato only, but generally throughout the tribes of New Zealand as one of the most renowned warriors of a former gene-

[1] N. Z. Parl. Papers, 1860. E. No. 1, C. 1.

ration. He had led the Waikatos in their bloody and desperate battles with the Ngapuhi invaders, in which they had to struggle for existence, as well as in wars with southern tribes, in which the Waikatos became in their turn aggressors. The name Te Wherowhero, by which he was first known to Europeans, means "The Red Man:" he got the title from being the first of his people to obtain and wear a scarlet blanket, which in the early days of our settlement in New Zealand was regarded by natives as a great treasure. The name Potatau, which signifies "He that counteth by night," was given him at the death of his wife, for whom his love was so great that he sat sleepless night after night while she lay dying—"counting," as the natives said, "her last hours." The only man in Waikato, who could vie with Potatau, was Wiremu Nera Te Awaitaia of Whaingaroa. He had been Te Wherowhero's fighting general in all the old wars, and when Wi Nera was converted to Christianity, Te Wherowhero said, "I have lost my right hand." He had been the faithful ally and companion in arms of Te Waharoa, Tamihana's father, in the savage wars which that ferocious old warrior had waged, and the son always treated and spoke of his father's old friend, even when they had become political opponents, with filial reverence. Out of personal regard, Tamihana would, no doubt, have preferred Wiremu Nera as king; but Potatau was a man of more extended influence, to whom a greater number would agree to yield allegiance, and therefore sinking his private wishes, Tamihana gave in his adhesion to Potatau, and thereby secured his election. Tamihana ever after regarded himself as the king-maker. "It was through me," he said at a public meeting, "that we did this deed." And his friends always pointed to him as the "root" of the Maori Kingdom.

When the assent of Ngatihaua, the natural supporters of Wi Nera, had thus assured Potatau's election, an unexpected difficulty arose from the old man's reluctance to accept the office. "I am nothing but a snail," he said. "What can a snail do?" He declared he would be an arbitrator between the tribes, in their land quarrels, but nothing more.

At length, he was persuaded to be present at a meeting of all the Waikato tribes, summoned to Rangiriri, in April, 1857; the avowed object of which was to install him King of New Zealand.

The Government was at last aroused from its lethargy to a consciousness of the dangerous excitement which prevailed. Colonel Browne determined to attend the Rangiriri meeting in person.[1] He left Auckland, accompanied by Mr. McLean and Mr. Richmond (one of the Colonial Ministry), arrived at Rangiriri, and, finding the meeting postponed, proceeded up the Waikato country, as far as Otawhao. He there fell in with Te Heu Heu, the great chief of Taupo, on his way to attend the

[1] N. Z. Parl. Papers. F. No. 3, A. 1.

meeting. Te Heu Heu, according to his usual custom, began to talk quietly, but soon worked himself into a towering passion. He told the Governor, that if the lowest Englishman chose to visit the Maories, he was welcome, and received all the hospitality in their power to afford, sharing their own food and shelter; but that if a chief of the highest rank visited Auckland, he was refused admittance, and neglected by all, except the Governor and one or two of the officers of Government. He said, and with truth, that Englishmen living among natives were often men of desperate character, who got drunk, and ill-treated both men and women; whose cattle trespassed on native lands, and who, instead of making compensation, abused the injured in language which, by Maori custom, ought to be punished with death. For all this they could get no redress; the English were, by degrees, obtaining the best of their lands, and the Maories would soon "be eaten up, and cease to be." For these reasons they were determined to have a King of their own, and Assemblies of their own. They would not interfere with the English in the settlements; but the laws they intended to make should be binding on all who chose to reside among the natives. Finally, he said that, in all this, they had been advised by one of our own people.

After this, the Governor rode to Rangiaowhia. At the entrance of the village he was saluted by a discharge of fire-arms, and welcomed in a loyal address.

Thence he was conducted to a native house, where an abundant repast had been prepared for him and his followers, who by that time were numerous. In the evening, three of the most important chiefs dined with the Governor at the house of Father Garavel, the Roman Catholic priest. After dinner, one of the chiefs inquired what view the Governor took of the intended election of a King; and the subject, thus introduced, was discussed at length in the most courteous terms. It was evident to the Governor that this matter was uppermost in the thoughts of all with whom he conversed during his journey; and he learned that all the tribes, from Otaki, near Wellington, to Mangere, near Auckland, were united in their views. It was clear that they did not understand the term "king," in the sense in which we use it; but, though they constantly professed loyalty to the Queen, attachment to the Governor, and a desire for the amalgamation of the races, they did mean to maintain their separate nationality, and have a Chief of their own selection, who should protect them from any possible encroachment on their rights, and uphold such customs as they were disinclined to relinquish. Only on one occasion, at Waipa, did any one presume to speak of their intended King as a Sovereign, with rank and power equal to the Queen's; and this speaker the Governor cut short, leaving him in the midst of his oration.

On his return to Rangiriri, the Governor arrived at

the same time as Potatau. The natives who had already assembled, including the principal chiefs of the Lower Waikato, made speeches to the Governor, in Potatau's presence. They asked for runangas, a European magistrate, and laws. To these demands the Governor assented; he promised to send a magistrate to reside on the Waikato, who should visit the native settlements, and, with the assessors, administer justice periodically. He also promised to have a code of laws framed, applicable to the circumstances of the natives. All the men then took off their hats, and cried "Hurrah!"[1] Potatau declared that he would be guided by the Governor's advice. He was a dying man, and should bequeath his people to the Governor's care.

After this meeting, Colonel Browne returned to Auckland, fully persuaded that the determination to elect a king would be given up. On the recommendation of Mr. Richmond, Mr. Fenton, an able solicitor, was appointed Resident Magistrate of Waikato and Waipá. He was instructed to visit periodically the native villages on the two rivers, or as many of them as he could, for the purpose of holding courts, assisting the people to devise bye-laws, and guiding their deliberations on public matters. No village was to be visited without the general consent of the people. Mr. Fenton was to report the names of persons fit to act as assessors, taking care to secure the assent of both chiefs and

[1] N. Z. Parl. Papers, 1860. F. No. 3, 816.

people; but such recommendations were to be subject to the Governor's approval. It was, also, to be explained to the natives that their bye-laws could not be made binding on both races, until the assent of the General Assembly was obtained to a measure to be proposed for that purpose. All fees and fines received by the Court at any village were to be appropriated, first to payment of the assessor's salaries, and afterwards to the direct benefit of the village, in a way to be agreed upon between the Government and the inhabitants.

Meanwhile, the great meeting at Rangiriri was going on. The following account of it is abridged from *The Southern Cross*, of June 5th, 1857:—The guests were mustering for several days at Kahumatuku. The last to arrive were the Ngatimaniapoto. On Friday, May 10th, the whole body started down the river, at a tremendous pace, to Rangiriri, twelve miles distant. About fifty canoes conveyed the guests. The entertainers were about equal in numbers: several Europeans were with them. After the usual reception, Ngatihaua formed four deep, and, proceeding to a large open space, planted in the centre the flag of the new dynasty. This was white with a red border and two red crosses (symbols of Christianity); upon it the words "Potatau, King of New Zealand."

Saturday was devoted to eating and drinking. The bill of fare included bullocks, sharks, baskets of fresh and dried eels, baskets of patika and mataitai, bags of sugar, kits of potatoes and kumeras, 1500 pounds of tobacco, besides flour, &c. &c.

On Monday, the 11th, business commenced. The number present was about 2200. Their tents and houses extended for about three-fourths of a mile. About ten o'clock the open space began to fill. Almost all the Maories wore native garments, or blankets. This day was devoted to the reconciliation of old hostilities. Songs were sung by the chiefs of different tribes; and, by common consent, all ancient hatreds were to be buried in oblivion. A solemn compact was made that there should never again be war between any of the tribes present.

On Tuesday, at ten o'clock, a long procession appeared from the southern end of the town, headed by Ngatihaua, bearing the King's flag. The Maories composing it were dressed in black cloth suits. They planted the flag as before, and arranged themselves in long rows on one side of the open space. The leaders and chief speakers were in the centre, each man provided with paper and pencil for the purpose of taking notes. There they sat for half an hour. At last, the Union-Jack was displayed on a little hill, about a quarter of a mile off. Another soon appeared, further inland. Presently a procession started from the hill, headed by Waata Kukutai, bearing the flag, and occupied part of the opposite side of the square.

Immediately after, another body advanced, bearing flag No. 2, joined the other party, and both flags were planted opposite to that of the King. The third side of the square was filled by natives who had not joined either party. At the fourth side appeared the native teachers, headed by Hoera and Heta.

Proceedings now commenced by Heta reading prayers, including that for the Queen, and Hoera gave a short discourse on temper and moderation. The following were the most remarkable speeches :—

PAORA.—God is good. Israel was His people. They had a king. I see no reason why any nation should not have a king, if they wish for one. The Gospel does not say we are not to have a king: it says, "Honour the king; love the brotherhood." Why should the Queen be angry? We shall be in alliance with her, and friendship will be preserved. The Governor does not stop murders and fights amongst us. A king will be able to do that. Let us have order, so that we may grow as the Pakehas grow. Why should we disappear from the country? New Zealand is ours: I love it.

TAKIRAU.—That is the road—that word "friendship." But it applies to both sides. Our King will be friendly with the Queen. Their flags will be tied together. (Hoists the King's flag, and ties it to the Queen's.) I say, let us be like all other lands that have kings, and glory and honour. Let the blessing of God, which rests on other lands and their kings, rest upon us. If I asked the Queen to leave her throne, I should be wrong; all I ask is, that the dignity which now rests on her should rest on our King; so that this land may be in peace, and may be honoured. Let the Queen and the Pakehas occupy the coast, and be a fence round us.

WIREMU NERA.—I am a small man and a fool. Ngatihaua, be not dark, Waikato listen, Taupo attend. My name has been heard of in the old day, and sometimes it is still mentioned. I am going to speak mildly, like a father. My word is this, I promised the first Governor, when he came to see me, and I promised all the rest, that I would stick to him, and be a subject of the Queen. I intend to keep my promise, for they have kept theirs; they have taken no land. Mine was the desire to sell, and they gave me the money. Why do you bring that new flag here? There is trouble in it. I am content with the old one. It is seen all over the world, and it belongs to me. I get some of its honour! What honour can I get from your flag? It is like a fountain without water. You say we are slaves. If acknowledging that flag make me a slave, I am a slave. Let me alone.

This speech made a deep impression, for Wiremu was the most renowned warrior present; it was followed by half an hour's silence.

WIREMU TAMIHANA.—I am sorry my father has spoken so strongly. He has killed me. I love New

Zealand. I want order and laws. The King can give us these better than the Governor; the Governor has never done anything except when a Pakeha is killed. He lets us kill each other and fight. A King would stop these evils. However, if you don't like the King pull down the flag. Let Rewi pull it down if you wish it.

REWI stepped forward without speaking, and in anger took the King's flag, threw it at the foot of the Union-Jack, and sat down again.

TARAHAWAIKI (considerably excited, rehoisted the flag).—I love New Zealand. It shall not lie down in this way. Let it look at the sun and we will support it.

WAATA KUKUTAI.—Let the flag stand, but wash out the writing on it. Let us not talk like children, but find out some real good for ourselves. We cannot do it by ourselves. The white men have the money, the knowledge—everything. I shall remain a subject of the Queen and look up to her flag as my flag for ever and ever. If you follow your road you will be benighted, get into a swamp, and either stick there or come out covered with mud.

TARAHAWAIKI got up again, rather angry, and the meeting was becoming excited, when Hoera called out, "Let us pray." All were silent, and he read prayers, and the proceedings terminated.

On Wednesday, stations were taken as before.

POTATAU TE WHEROWHERO appeared on this day, surrounded by his friends, and occupied the fourth side of the square. After prayers he spoke as follows:—Wash me, my friends, I am covered with mud. Love gospel and friendship. Ngatihaua work, continue to work. The Kotuku sits upon a stump and eats the small fish; when he sees one he stoops down and catches it, lifts up his head, and swallows it. That is his constant work. Wiremu, you understand your work. When the sun shines we see him. (Here he sang a song).

HOANI PAPITA.—Fresh water is lost when it mingles with the salt. This chief then sang a song for the land, that it should be retained, and the whole 2,000 joined in chorus.

TE HEU HEU of Taupo then spoke with violence, enumerating the causes of quarrel which the Maories had against the Europeans; the indignities shown to chiefs by the lower orders in the towns, their women debauched, men made drunk, chiefs called "bloody Maories," &c. He advocated total separation of races and expulsion of Europeans by force. He was at last stopped by some of the chiefs, and compelled to sit down.

HEMI PUTINI then, addressing Potatau, said, Declare yourself about the flags, you have heard our views.

PAORA placed the King's flag about a yard from the Queen's, and tied them together, then marked a ring in the ground round each. REWI deepened the ring. KUKENA, uncle of Potatau, then came forward, and amidst a dead silence, lowered the flag half-mast, and tied it to the Union-Jack.

TIPENE.—Don't you be sad (to the Kingites), and don't you be joyful (to the loyal party), for though the flag is down the writing remains.

After a few more speeches and songs, the meeting separated.

On the following day the King's flag was despatched to the tribes in the south, to summon them to a larger meeting, which should either induce Potatau to accept office, or appoint some one else in his stead.

The whole party then adjourned to Ihumatao, a native village on the Manukau, about eight miles from Auckland, where a second meeting was held, at which the same men were present and made the same speeches.

This meeting was not attended by any agent of the Government, but the Bishop of New Zealand, Mr. Buddle, the head of the Wesleyan body, and several other missionaries and gentlemen were present. The Maories were warned by their European friends of the mischief that must ensue from the establishment of a separate sovereignty,—"Give up your King," said Mr. C. O. Davis; "you will be torn to pieces by the Pakeha." Such warnings were not likely to deter the natives from their purpose. Maories are not easily frightened by mere threats.

After the Ihumatao meeting, Wiremu Nera and most of the loyal natives, as well as Te Heu Heu, visited the Governor in Auckland. But even the former in all their conversations insisted on the maintenance of a distinct nationality. All evinced jealousy of the Assembly, and a strong desire for one of their own. The friendly party wished for their own Assembly and the Governor, the others desired their own Assembly and a King, but all were agreed on the maintenance of a distinct nationality. A letter was also received from Hoani Papita, and the other chiefs who had so cordially welcomed the Governor to Rangiaowhia, announcing their determination to persist in electing a king.

The Governor was at last thoroughly roused to a sense of danger. He felt that the establishment of a distinct nationality in any form, would end sooner or later in collision; and that, if the agitation for a king were persisted in, it would bring about a conflict of races, and become the greatest political difficulty we had yet had to contend with in New Zealand. For these reasons he considered it highly important that the European population should in future be as little scattered as possible. Instructions were given to the Land Purchase Commissioners to endeavour to connect and consolidate crown lands, and to make no new purchases of isolated lands without special authority. But this course was adopted too late. The actual intermixture of crown and native territories throughout the North Island, and especially on the Waikato frontier, and the general unwillingness of the natives to sell more land, made such consolidation impossible. A clear line of demarcation between the territories of the rival nations could not be obtained without war and conquest.

At the same time it was confidently hoped by the Governor himself and the Colonial Ministry, that Mr. Fenton's mission would allay the excitement, and avert the dangers to be apprehended from the election of a king. This mission and its results will form the subject of the following chapter.

CHAPTER VI.

THE JUSTICE ON CIRCUIT.

THE duty which Mr. Fenton was sent into the Waikato district to discharge was of such importance, and his own narrative of his proceedings reveal so much of the actual state of native feeling at that time, that I shall try to give the reader an abridgement of Mr. Fenton's voluminous journals, even at the risk of producing a disjointed story.[1]

On the 13th of July, 1857, the new magistrate of Waikato left Auckland, with a Maori companion, carrying "200lbs. weight of books, paper, and ink." On the way they met a Waikato chief, named Huirama, who told them that a meeting was to be called to induce Potatau, their chosen King, to leave Auckland, and settle at Ngaruawahia; and repeated the common opinion that fights and disorders could be stopped by nothing but a King, to whom all would give support. The Government had tried long enough, and had failed. Huirama further informed them that he was

[1] These journals are printed in the New Zealand Parliamentary Papers of 1860. E. No. 1, C. 3.

going to Auckland, to ask for 100*l*. to buy iron-work and stones for a mill, but intended his friend Hone Kingi to ask for it, because, being a loyal man and a Queen's magistrate, he was more likely to get attention from the Government.

Passing on, without further incidents worth mention, the new magistrate and his companion arrived at the village of Taupari,[1] near the mouth of Waikato. The inhabitants were eager to establish and make trial of the new court. Books and printed forms were distributed, and three writs issued, for which 1*s*. a-piece was paid.

Waata Kukutai and a friend were to be assistant-magistrates; an old gentleman named Po, a retired cannibal, President of the Village Council; and Arama Karaka said he should be a lawyer, and charge 5*s*. to any one who employed him. But in the midst of all this, there occurred an illustration of the proverb—"Paper and ink, and little justice." A native arrived to ask assistance against a European neighbour, who would not pay rent for a cattle-run. It appeared that there were several owners, and the settler judiciously denied all their titles. Mr. Fenton told the complainant that as the dispute concerned a Maori title, the magistrate could not interfere; and that the law could afford him no protection until he held by legal tenure.

The court at Taupari was held in an unfinished

[1] N.B.—Taupari must not be confounded with Taupiri.

house, roofed with tarpaulins. One end was fitted up with seats, desks, and docks for the magistrates, witnesses, and suitors, separated by a wooden rail from the general public. From the slowness of witnesses and the vast amount of impertinent matter introduced, the three cases occupied an entire day. One witness was a boisterous old Maori chief, a great orator. He began a speech in the witness-box exhorting the magistrates to be just and give judgment for his friend the plaintiff. After going on about two minutes, he was asked if he knew anything of the facts of the case. He said—"No; but he wanted to speak up for his friend." He was told that his assistance was not wanted, that he must at once leave the box, and, if he wanted to make a speech, must go out of doors. Every one expected a scene, but he quietly walked away, and after the Court rose he made an apology, saying he would misbehave no more.

A village council, which was to have followed the court, was stopped by rain. From the same cause Mr. Fenton could not get his Maori friends to turn out and paddle up the river in time for the next court at Tuakau. The magistrate was four hours behind time, and the defendant in the only case, a European, tired of waiting, had left the place; whereupon the Maori plaintiff hinted that if his remedy was gone the defaulting magistrate ought to pay. There being no other case to be tried, the natives, who were supporters of the King, invited Mr. Fenton to a meeting in a large wheat-chamber at the old pa, which, as agent of the Government, he thought it his duty to attend. The usual complaints were made of Government neglect: they had written to the authorities about establishing a ferry at Waikato Heads, but got no answer at all, so they had begun the practice of either charging 20s. or leaving the traveller all night on the beach at the wrong side of the river. They also complained that Government did not prevent their women from running away to the low houses in Auckland; and urged that as they gave up criminals, so the Government ought to give up their women.

On reaching Paetai, Mr. Fenton found a capital Court-house finished. The timber for the posts and rafters had been all adzed smooth, and the roof was lined with reeds; but the desks and internal fittings were very inconvenient, and there were no doors or windows, such articles being beyond the power of Maori workmanship. The place where the great King meeting had been held was then covered with springing wheat. After issuing his writs, the magistrate had to turn carpenter and work for two hours at the fittings of his court-house. In the interval between his arrival and the opening of the court, one of the native defendants ran away to the hills to avoid service of a summons. The only other case was one in which Pukewhau, the principal chief of Lower Waikato, was plaintiff. This was so intricate that Mr. Fenton could not see his way through, and was obliged to order it to stand over till his return.

Still continuing to ascend the river, Mr. Fenton, at Mr. Ashwell's Mission Station, met with Takerei, upon whose co-operation the chance of influencing Upper Waikato mainly depended. There appeared to have been a schism at Takerei's village of Whakapaku, between himself and his relatives, who were ardent supporters of the Maori King. Takerei had threatened to leave the place and establish a new settlement a few miles off, at Karakariki. He also complained that a donation of 40*l.* had been made to Porokoru, an old warrior living at Otawhao. This gift excited Takerei's jealousy, for he did not understand why the Government should give money to a man who stood on the Maori King's side at the great Paetai meeting. Mr. Fenton could give no explanation himself, supposing that it was a mistake arising from the native office being ignorant of Porokoru's sayings and doings. The Auckland officials, however, had acted with a full knowledge of all the facts. The virtue that had outweighed the vice of treason was that Porokoru had recently sold land.

From Taupiri Mr. Fenton went up with Takerei to Karakariki, where he was kept talking till midnight. The next day being Sunday, service was held in a native house, small, full, and stifling with heat and smell. In the evening there was a meeting about establishing a new settlement, where law and order could be carried out without interruption. Mr. Fenton thought it better not to attend, but heard them talking far into the morning. Takerei however came to call him at an early hour, saying that all expected him to speak upon the subject. He therefore went to them and said that if their relatives persisted in forbidding the entrance of law into Whakapaku, they could do nothing but leave the place and establish a new settlement. The law could only be carried out where all consented to obey. In the early days of New Zealand Christianity, it had often happened that the Christian party was obliged to set up a separate settlement, but gradually the Maori party joined them, until the old pa was abandoned. So it would have to be in extreme cases now. Finally, he advised them to be careful to select a good site and lay out their village in a regular way. After this advice they requested him to take the entire management of the migration. Mr. Fenton said he did not approve of Karakariki, as the land was not very good, and there was no firewood handy. So they all got into canoes and paddled about the river, landing at several places, none of which however seemed to combine all the advantages they required. At last they came to the Maka, a splendid flat of several hundred acres, covered with fern and koromiko, surrounded by forest containing many kinds of trees. Mr. Fenton approved of that place, marked out a line for the houses, with space between each, and directed the court-house and church to be placed in the centre, and patakas and stores in the rear: all the houses were to face the river. Having thus provided for Takerei and his brother malcontents, he proceeded on his circuit.

The next place visited was Whatawhata, where the people were in a state of alarm and vexation at a summons they had received from the King party, either to join, and surrender their lands to the King, or else leave their village and settle upon the territory of the Queen. The Whatawhata people urged upon Mr. Fenton the necessity of the British Government openly recognising their friends, and discountenancing the agitators, who were their enemies. They insisted that applications for assistance from hostile tribes should be refused, and the white men managing their mills should be recalled, and that Maories should thus be taught how utterly they were dependent upon the Governor for everything. At present, said they, it was the general opinion that the Governor did not give more encouragement to the loyal than to the disloyal.

No cases were tried at Whatawhata, and Mr. Fenton paddled down again to Karakariki. There he found Tarahawaiki and all the Whakapaku people discussing with Takerei and his followers about the separation of settlements, and about a project of Mr. Fenton's for advancing grass-seed to them on credit, for sowing their waste lands. The King party said, that they had heard that sheep also were to be given by the Governor, and that such a gift was very bad, and was only meant to make the Maories tame; moreover, that if the wool was sold to repay the money, the bodies of the sheep would not be discharged from the debt. As to the grass-seed, they said that the name of the Queen would stick to all the land covered with grass, and that they would not have the name of the Queen in Waikato; and that Taupiri would go, with a great deal more nonsense of that sort. Takerei replied: "We are near relations, and I shall speak plainly. Mind your own business. We do not ask you to join us. The land is mine, as you know, and I shall do what I like with my own land. If you wish to remain poor, you may do so. I intend to grow rich." Another speaker said that he saw the Maori kingdom meant eating fern-root and wearing mats: he would not interfere with the digging of fern-root, and they must not interfere with the growing of wool. One cause of the opposition of Tarahawaiki and his friends was vexation at Mr. Fenton's not having called to see them on his way up the river; and a second cause was jealousy of the position and influence which Takerei's loyalty had already gained.

Mr. Fenton had heard from Takerei that the great Ngatimaniapoto tribe, which has since become our most formidable enemy, was anxious to receive a visit from him, and had returned 1*l.* 17*s.* which had previously been collected for the King, to the subscribers. Indeed, the chief, Rewi Maniapoto himself, had met Mr. Fenton at one of the landing-places on the Waikato, and invited him to Kihikihi. Takerei, however, wanted to put off the visit till the next circuit, as he proposed to go with the magistrate, but had not yet got his wheat in, and seed-time was already past. To this delay, Mr. Fenton—who found the duties of the whole district more than he could satisfactorily perform—agreed. It was a golden opportunity lost.

Before returning to Auckland, Mr. Fenton visited the Ngatihaua tribe, who were energetically working, under Wiremu Tamihana, for the Maori King. They had appointed six men to mark out the boundaries of their land which was to be handed over to the King's custody. Ti Oriori of Maunga-tautari, one of their chiefs, had written a letter to Mr. Fenton, reporting a case of murder, and requesting him to come to Maunga-tautari to hold an inquiry, as Tamihana was trying to get the murderer tried by Maori law, and wanted him, if guilty, to be put to death.

Mr. Fenton wrote in reply, that he would not go unless the people collectively would agree to accept and abide by the law, and wrote to invite him, as otherwise he might find his orders disobeyed. Subsequently, although no invitation came, Mr. Fenton, after thinking deeply over the question, resolved to go, as if on a private visit to Ti Oriori; since it was most important to see the disposition of so powerful and intelligent a tribe. He found the current of Waikato above Ngaruawahia very rapid, and it was hard work to paddle a canoe against it. It was dark before he had reached Te Rapa, where he sent a messenger to Arikirua to fetch Ti Oriori. The people at Te Rapa told him that the boy said to have been murdered was still alive, and the magistrate went to bed, uncertain what to believe. Next morning, however, three men, riding from Arikirua to Whatawhata, called at the village. They said that Ti Oriori was too ill to come to see Mr. Fenton, and that a large meeting was to take place that day to discuss the alleged murder. The victim was said to have been killed by three priests, who, while going through certain incantations over the boy, got into a passion, broke his arm, and then despatched him, though at the commencement of the ceremony they had no intention of doing so. The travellers said that some proposed to crucify the worst of the men, and let the others off; but nothing would be done till Ti Oriori had judged and sentenced the accused.

Mr. Fenton stayed all day at Te Rapa, but no message came to him and no one asked him to remain longer. There was evidently a bad feeling amongst the Ngatihauas. Speaking of their mill which had been broken and become useless, "Yes," said one, "the Pakehas are a humbugging people." Two or three men came to Mr. Fenton privately and said they were tired of agitation but dared not say so, as the multitude had resolved that all the Queen's friends should leave the territories of the King and live on the Queen's land. So Mr. Fenton returned from his attempt to visit Ngatihaua without any result good or bad.

On the way back to Auckland Mr. Fenton again visited Paetai. He found the natives alarmed and excited by a visit from Huirama, who had just returned from his visit to Auckland, where he had succeeded in getting blacksmiths and carpenters to build his mill, though Government had not given him the expected help. He told the Paetai people that they would be driven from their lands if they did not recognise and subscribe for the King. This had made them very uneasy. They asked Mr. Fenton—"What are we to do if the King party commence to carry out their threats by force? are we to resist? If we protect the Governor's dignity, will he protect us? Which side affords us the best chance of quiet? If we join the King, we know the Governor will make no difference in his behaviour to us, but if we join the Queen we are not certain that the other party will be as indifferent."

A few cases were heard at Paetai, and that difficult case of Pukewhau's was again adjourned for further evidence.

The hardships of the journey, constant wet, indifferent food, and talking instead of sleep at night, subjected Mr. Fenton to a violent attack of influenza, which compelled him to return speedily to Auckland, and confined him to his room for many days after arriving there. The entire journey had occupied rather more than six weeks, and did not produce the expected effect of inducing the natives to abandon their design of electing a king.

As the result of experience acquired in this journey, Mr. Fenton made three practical proposals to the Government:

(1) Maories never cultivate the same piece of land for more than a few years successively; they then abandon the half-exhausted soil to weeds. At every village visited, Mr. Fenton found acres of land covered in this way with dock: he proposed, therefore, that the Government should advance a quantity of grass-seed, and get the Maories to sow it upon the cultivations immediately before they were deserted, so that they might thereby be converted from mere noxious wildernesses into pastures. The magistrate's attention had been particularly directed to a great piece of land stretching for three-quarters of a mile, from Mr. Ashwell's Mission Station down the west bank of the Waikato, about 300 or 400 yards in depth, and hemmed in and sheltered towards the south-west by the mountains which form one side of the gorge through which the river flows. The place was free from fern and native growth, having been under cultivation during that same year. Mr. Fenton had taken the pains to ascertain the names of the owners, and to obtain their

consent to the place being sown with grass-seed supplied by Government, the cost of which was to be repaid by instalments. The matter was looked upon by the proprietors as a settled arrangement, and they accordingly prepared to execute their part of the engagement. This scheme was, as appears from Mr. Fenton's own narrative, regarded with jealousy and dislike by many natives, and the fear of provoking a quarrel was the reason assigned by Government for not performing what Mr. Fenton had promised. It is true that land-buying which provoked many quarrels was not suspended from the same humane motive, but there is a clear difference between the two cases. In the latter we were pursuing our own interest; in the former, only that of our native friends.

(2) Mr. Fenton's efforts to introduce law and civilization among the Maories soon led him to the conclusion that some power was necessary to *enforce* obedience to the decisions of magistrates. He thought it would be very unwise and a dangerous imperilling of such prestige as we had, to attempt to enforce civil procedure in the European manner; but proposed that either the Governor or the Magistrates of the district should call a meeting of native assessors, at which even such men as Ti Oriori would attend, and by a resolution of such meeting bind them to undertake the duty of enforcing obedience to law. He desired that it should be made clear to them, that since law was offered and taught to

them as a boon, and by no means forced upon them, it was their business to see the law respected and obeyed. Summoning such meetings as these appeared of the very highest importance to Mr. Fenton. But no such council was ever called.

(3) Experience showed that the practice of the native office in conducting correspondence and other business directly with the natives, without referring to or informing the local officer, was a source of many evils. In the first place, there was often an actual conflict of authorities. Pukewhau was sent for to Auckland on the very day when he ought to have appeared as a litigant before the local officer under pain of having his case dismissed. Moreover, when the natives discovered that the district authority had little or no influence with the Governor, his power as an officer was materially diminished, and respect for his decisions decreased proportionally. At the time when Mr. Fenton was magistrate of Waikato, it was most important to throw as much power as possible into his hands, because the political department of Native Government in Auckland had become entirely absorbed in the Land Purchasing Department, so that every political event was estimated by its tendency to aid or hinder the acquisition of land. Moreover, the local agent of necessity always knew more of facts and people in his own district than persons resident in Auckland. Even the Governor himself cannot obtain

reliable information by direct intercourse with the natives. When a Maori is in the Governor's presence, it is difficult to get him to tell out plainly his thoughts, fears, and wishes. He generally sticks to safe generalities. Polynesian politeness forbids the introduction of any topic known to be disagreeable to the person visited. In Mr. Fenton's days, the Maories visiting Auckland were possessed of two fears—first, of offending the Governor; secondly, of offending the Native Department. Mr. Fenton therefore proposed that all ordinary business transacted with the natives of a district should pass through the local officer's hands. It is hardly credible that so simple and obvious an administrative reform, though often talked of, has never down to the present day been practically made.

After the establishment of the new Circuit Court, the next phase in the history of the Government of the Maories was a departmental battle between the New Zealand Ministry and the Native Office. The Colonial Ministry had at that time much less share in the management of native affairs than they now possess. They had a mere right to be informed by the Governor of what he proposed to do, and to give their opinion thereupon. The Governor was not bound to follow their advice, but could act on his own judgment even when opposed to theirs; and the Native Department, which executed his decrees, was responsible neither to the ministers nor to the Colonial Assembly. But the exceptional measures taken to counteract the King movement in Waikato had been a joint plan of the Governor and Mr. Richmond, the Colonial Treasurer, who was devoting his whole mind and most of his time to the solution of the Maori problem. Mr. Fenton was a *protégé* of Mr. Richmond, from whom he received all his instructions, and at whose suggestion he had been appointed in preference to another person, recommended by the Native Office. The whole plan of the Circuit Court and the new magistrate appointed had from the first been very unpalatable to Mr. McLean, the Native Secretary and his subordinates, who, as might be expected from the connexion of their department with the English Home Government, were always more or less jealous of the colonial ministers. The Waikato became a bone of contention between the colonial and imperial departments of New Zealand Government. The latter regarded Mr. Fenton as a colonial interloper, who should be put down on all possible occasions, and he on his side was nothing loth to take up the quarrel, in which he was backed by his patrons the colonial ministers.

Mr. McLean thought he had good grounds for objecting to much that was being done in the Waikato district.

The loyalty of Mr. Fenton's adherents was far more a love of prospective gifts and salaries than of law and order. The Queen party were abandoning their cultivations, and all other useful industry, and were talking of nothing but being made magistrates, wardens, or jurymen, under which designations they all looked forward to some lucrative employment under Government. Mr. Fenton's chief supporter in Lower Waikato, Waata Kukutai, a very conceited young man, and the head of a small party of his own, was intensely disliked by his countrymen. He was a spendthrift, who had squandered away large sums of Government money—borrowed, but never repaid—and who possessed an insatiable capacity for more. He was pleased with the title of magistrate so long as he could carry out the laws in his own way without restraint; but that a magistrate himself should be under the law, was an idea that found no room in the thoughts of a man who had never learnt to obey. Upon one occasion, having received a check from Government for exceeding his jurisdiction, he was very much offended, and indicated, if he did not explicitly state, that he should throw up his office in disgust. Takerei, the only one of Mr. Fenton's friends that possessed any influence among the dominant tribes of Upper Waikato, was a man of a singularly covetous and greedy disposition. He owed the Government 210*l.*; and, at the rate of his requirements in land, grass-seed, and sheep, his loyalty was becoming very expensive. He was, moreover, animated by an ambition to supplant his relative, Potatau, in the consideration of the Government. At an interview with the Governor, he proposed himself as the sole medium of communication with the Queen party, and President over all native magistrates in the Waikato district. Mr. Fenton's circuit had caused great excitement, and the natives were becoming divided into two parties, "Queenites" and "Kingites," between whom a bitter spirit of opposition had sprung up. The magistrate was regarded as the counsellor and prompter of the former. Instead of taking pains to conciliate the old chiefs, and win them over to his schemes, he threw himself into the hands of the younger men, and tried to construct a party of his own amongst them. The older chiefs said that the combination of young chiefs, in favour of Mr. Fenton, was like a rope of sand, and would disappear if Potatau held up his finger. Potatau was highly affronted. He told Mr. McLean; who went to visit him at Mangere, that he was going up the Waikato to live. He had often been invited to do so, but had always declined, as he preferred living quietly among the Europeans. He was not consulted now, he said, as he had formerly been, with reference to the affairs of his district. The Government were acting with the younger members of the tribes, and carrying out changes without his concurrence.[1] Mr. Fenton had never been to Mangere to see him. He had heard a great deal about the subdivision of territory and the distribution of grass-seed and sheep. He

[1] N. Z. Parl. Papers, 1860. F. No. 3.

intimated that it was an interference with his rights and prerogative to sow the great flat at Taupiri, a property of his own to which he was much attached, without first consulting him, and finally declared that he should yield to the solicitations of his people, leave Mangere, and go to live in the Waikato country. This was at the end of the year 1857.

From these various causes, Mr. McLean gave in the following official opinion to the Governor:—"The most distant recognition of any adverse party to Potatau in his own district, would be attended with results more injurious to the real interests of the Europeans than any other step that could be taken; not only from its giving an undue prominence and appearance of stability to the position he proposes to assume, but from the paucity of the numbers, and subordinate character and position of those tribes which would alone follow such a course —in which, moreover, they could be retained only by influences of a mercenary nature."[1]

In consequence of this representation, Mr. Fenton was removed from the control of the colonial ministers, and placed under the orders of the Native Department, of which he had hitherto been the rival and the critic.

At the beginning of 1858, Mr. Fenton was permitted to make another circuit in the Waikato district, where he was instructed to confine himself entirely to his judicial duties as a magistrate. On this visit he had

[1] N. Z. Parl. Papers, 1860. F. No. 3, A. 3.

the further task of taking a census of the native population.

The first place visited was Tuakau; but as the court-house was not finished, and the excuses of the people for their delay were unsatisfactory, no justice was there administered. At Taupari there was no business to do; Waata Kukutai had disposed of all the cases before the English magistrate's arrival. The court-house was completed except the windows. Waata inquired whether windows would be supplied by the Government, as his court-house was useless for want of them in windy weather, and it was not possible at any time to keep papers there. Mr. Fenton could give him no information on the subject. On the way up the river, many questions were asked about the grass-seed project, but Mr. Fenton was not able to give any information how far the plan would be assisted or encouraged by the Government.

The task of taking the census caused the magistrate some uneasiness. A stupid woman told the people that he was writing down the names of King's people, and Queen's people. He was afraid this would do harm in the unquiet districts; but he pacified them by saying that he merely wanted to know the numbers and distribution of the people, so as to arrange the court-houses conveniently.

At Kahumatuku, a court was held and two cases tried. In one, an action for slander, the defendant was

Whakapaukai (*Anglicè*, Gorging Jackie), the most impudent and bare-faced robber in the Waikato district, who has since set the Governor and the Maori king alike at defiance. He was difficult to manage. When rebuked for his improper language he said that it was not his fault, that he did not understand the new system, and that he was an old fool; that he did not come willingly to the court, but came because he was compelled, and therefore they should not be angry with him. However, notwithstanding his contumacious language, he paid the damages given to the plaintiff.

Several of Mr. Fenton's native friends told him that the census was sure to cause misunderstanding among the tribes of the interior. Waata Kukutai had been engaged to accompany the magistrate, but it was now thought better to send the loyal chief back, lest his presence should excite suspicion.

Passing on to Ngaruawahia, Mr. Fenton found the King's house already built, and an opposition house a few rods in front. Another tribe was building a third house, and there was some talk of not allowing the King's flagstaff to be erected. The opposition was headed by Wiremu Nera, who had an old grudge against Potatau about land on the West Coast, which was the real reason of his opposition to the King party. Nera's tribe claimed Ngaruawahia as their ancient domain, and refused to allow Potatau and his adherents to settle there. A great meeting was to take place in

April, which would be attended by tribes from the South, at which Potatau was to be installed King.

At Whatawhata there were many cases awaiting trial. When the business was disposed of, some very young men made a complaint against the native magistrates. After a patient hearing, Mr. Fenton found that (apart from some slight mistakes, resulting from ignorance or inexperience,) the conduct of the magistrates had been good and firm, and that the complaints arose from the dislike the young people felt to the restraint under which they were held. They said they were quite willing to submit to the decision of the court when the European magistrate presided, but the native magistrates were not so good. Mr. Fenton found at Whatawhata that the census would not be of much value, as far as the proportion of children was concerned, from the vague ideas of Maories as to the age at which a person becomes adult. Only the infants were put down as children; boys and girls were classed amongst the adults.

On this occasion, Mr. Fenton, in company with Takerei, ascended further up the Waipa than he had done on his former circuit. They were much annoyed at being constantly stopped by parties of natives, who insisted on presenting them with cooked food. The houses and people were very miserable.

At Kopua, where there is a Wesleyan Mission-station, the people expressed their desire for law and their willingness to build a court-house, and a promise was given that they should be visited in future circuits. Thence Mr. Fenton and Takerei "poled" up the shallow river to Awatoetoe. The people of this place pressed the magistrate to consent to the erection of a court-house and the establishment of law. But they were told that the place was too remote to be included in the regular circuit of the European magistrate. They replied that they were the Queen's subjects, and had a right to have law administered among them; that this necessity was so strongly felt, that great numbers of the Maories were trying to find out a way of governing themselves, for every one felt that murders and wrongs must be stopped among them as well as among the Europeans, but they did not wish to join this party, which was ignorant and principally led by old Maori chiefs. This place was amongst the hills, three days' journey from Taranaki, and the chief subject of conversation among the people was the native war at that time raging there.

Mr. Fenton overheard some people saying that the King party were organizing policemen and soldiers to repress disorder, but the conversation dropped when they saw he was listening. He thought the objects of the agitators were too little understood in Auckland. The agitation seemed to him to be simply the effort of a people wishing to be governed, to govern themselves in default of anything better.

When the subject of the census was introduced, the people of Awatoetoe told Mr. Fenton that he would get no information higher up in the central district of Ngatimaniapoto, and that his presence on such an errand would cause great uneasiness.

Next day there was a meeting and a feast. The banquet consisted of eels and pork. More mention than usual was made of the King. After the feast, Mr. Fenton formally consented to their building a court-house, but would not promise that any magistrates would visit them regularly. In the evening there was a meeting about a disputed eel-weir; the magistrates declined to act, when called upon, on the ground that the dispute concerned land. It was as well they did, for Ngatimaniapoto had taken possession with an armed party.

Next day the ground was marked out for the court-house, and Mr. Fenton went away, collecting his census papers as he pulled down to Kopua. One tribe would not make any return, as they thought the Governor wanted to know how many men there were, that the Pakeha and Ngapuhi might come down to fight them. The Maories in this Upper Waipa country were in the lowest stage of poverty; their houses, clothes, and everything belonging to them, were most wretched. They had nothing inside their houses and little outside, and expected to have to eat fern-root during the winter. The mill had not turned its wheel for five months.

Mr. Fenton doubted whether he should thence visit the large villages of Rangiaowhia and Kihikihi, but as the people there knew he was in the neighbourhood, and had not asked him to go, he took it as a broad hint to stay away, and staid away accordingly.

At Mr. Ashwell's Mission-station, he had a long interview with Ti Oriori, who assured him that all the Ngatihaua tribe wanted was law and order; they thought the only way of getting it was by establishing a government among themselves. He was glad to see that the Europeans, whom they knew to be far wiser than themselves, were at last beginning to govern in earnest. He and most of his people were quite ready to join Mr. Fenton now that they saw the affair was not a mere pretence. Ti Oriori said that the old chiefs of Ngatimahuta must not be taken as representing the opinions of the kingmakers; they were the advocates of a return to old Maori customs. Ngatihaua, on the contrary, wanted nothing but government and progress, showing, as an instance, that they had supported the sowing of grass, and he himself had procured and sown some of the seed first sent up.

At Paetai a meeting had been held in Mr. Fenton's absence, at which it was resolved that he should discontinue circuits and live there permanently, or else that some other European magistrate should be appointed to live at Paetai. The people offered any quantity of land,—the idea being that the magistrate could occupy his spare time in farming. This offer he was, of course, forced to decline. At Rangiriri there was a land-feud going on, in which he refused to adjudicate. The native magistrates here were beginning to complain of the weight of their labours, saying they would soon be the poorest of their tribes.

Only once during his term of office did Mr. Fenton venture to send a Maori to gaol. A native stole linen from a dwelling-house in Auckland, escaped up the Waikato, and took refuge in the hilly country about Pirongia. Two of Mr. Fenton's probationary magistrates went after him, caught him, and brought him down to Kahumatuku, where he was tried, sentenced, and sent in charge of native police to Auckland gaol. His friends, who had vainly offered money to atone for the crime, were very angry, and complained of the magistrate's conduct. Wiremu Nera, to whose tribe the culprit belonged, told the Government that it was very rash to take such steps in the district, and that it was fortunate the man belonged to his tribe, as, had he belonged to any other, a collision would have been inevitable. He himself felt aggrieved that he had not been first consulted. As the hunt had been so successful, Mr. Fenton wished to reward his two probationers as an example, and therefore recommended their appointment to salaried offices. This appointment had been previously promised to them by the Governor, whenever Mr. Fenton should recommend it.

On arriving in Auckland with their prisoner, they, in pursuance of the recommendation, went and called upon officers of the Native Department. These officers told them that all such recommendations must come from the Native Office—that the officers of that Department were the only heads of the Maories; and with this gratifying information the men were sent back, without being either appointed or allowed to see the Governor.

I have told this story to show how completely the Native Department had reduced the Waikato magistrate to a state of subjection, and how the official mind, even at the antipodes, cannot restrain itself from those petty jealousies, which, however harmless in a highly civilized society, are fatal folly in the government of a half-savage race. Shortly after this occurrence, Mr. Fenton was altogether relieved of his functions, and the field was left clear for the Maori King.

Thus ended the first practical attempt to govern the Maories. To extinguish Mr. Fenton was no doubt a great triumph for the Native Department, but has since turned out rather a costly one for the British Empire. The abortive measures of the Government made the revolt of the Waikatos much more complete than if nothing had been done at all. The Maories know as little of our domestic intrigues as we of theirs. It appeared to them that the Governor had made promises at the Paetai meeting which had not been fulfilled. The King party were encouraged in their turbulence and claims of independence by seeing how evidently the Government was afraid of them, and those who desired to see law and order established amongst them at last lost all faith in their British rulers, and characterized their conduct as "maminga," or, in plain English, "humbug."

For example, in 1858, a chief of Paetai, named Honi Kingi, was deputed by several tribes to see the Governor as to the delay in carrying out what had been promised. He could not obtain an interview. He thought himself insulted. The tribes by whom he had been deputed were of the same opinion, and they soon after joined the King party, of which they had previously been determined opponents.[1]

It is useless now to conjecture what might have been, if the attempt to solve the New Zealand difficulty by active efforts to govern and civilize the natives had been at that time persevered in.

A committee was appointed by the New Zealand parliament in 1860, to inquire into the abortive attempt to introduce Civil Institutions of government into Waikato. This Committee, after examining all the papers and a large number of witnesses, European and Maori, reported as follows:[2]—"The Committee, with

[1] N. Z. Parl. Papers, 1860. F. No. 3, 75.
[2] Ibid. F. No. 3.

the light of two years' subsequent experience before them, do not perceive sufficient reasons for suspending the work in which Mr. Fenton was engaged. Without in any degree mitigating the real causes of agitation in the native mind, his withdrawal disheartened a large and influential body of natives, including many influential chiefs who had associated themselves with him, and were actively engaged on the side of Government. They were disappointed and humiliated at the sudden abandonment of their undertaking. Many of them joined the King party, and this, amongst other causes, has tended to irritate and give a more malign aspect to the King movement itself." Wiremu Tamihana was invited to attend to give evidence, but he wrote to the chairman: "Friend, what is the good of our talking after the evil has taken place? Had you written to me when the evil was small, it would have been well, and I should have come to see you; but now, that the evil has attained full growth, what is the good? Behold the kindling of fire, when little it can be put out, but after it has spread it cannot be extinguished."

It is quite clear that Mr. Fenton's plans would have required much modification to insure success. To encourage a population in litigation, to teach them to play at courts, and amuse them with the formalities of an attorney's office, could never have led them to civilization. But it was quite possible to gain an influence among them by humouring their enthusiasm in this pursuit, and then to use the influence so acquired to direct them to better things. This, Mr. Fenton had already begun to do. He was trying to get an agricultural instructor appointed by Government; he persuaded many to sow grass and take to sheep-farming, and he showed every disposition to promote their social advancement. There were difficulties, no doubt, but no reason for supposing them insurmountable. The worst part of Mr. Fenton's theory was his dependence on the "runanga" as an instrument for enforcing obedience to the law. The name "runanga" was used by the Maories to denote assemblies of a particular kind, which were in use before ever Europeans came into the country. The Runanga was a sort of council of war, held in war time to discuss war questions. It was formed of the highest chiefs, but inferior men were not excluded, though the reverence then paid to the chiefs forbad the rest to take any prominent part in the discussions. As time went on the Runanga began to take notice of other matters, and to grow more and more democratic, until it degenerated into a promiscuous gathering of men, women, and children, which usurped the whole legislative and judicial function of government. Such an institution was obviously unfit to teach a barbarous people to obey constituted authority. The worst part of Mr. Fenton's practice was his failure to humour and conciliate the old Maori chiefs, whose power for mischief was great enough to ruin the best devised scheme. But both these were corrigible errors. At any rate nothing can excuse the entire abandonment of the attempt: if Mr. Fenton was rash, some more prudent officer should have been put in his place. Our own divisions and jealousies were the real causes of failure. No man could succeed in bringing a race of haughty independent savages under civilized rule, whose official superiors gave him criticism instead of advice, and thwarted, instead of supporting, his authority.

As the European magistrate left the Waikato, Potatau went into it and was duly installed King at Ngaruawahia in April, 1858. The Governor trusted that "time and absolute indifference and neglect on the part of the Government (which still continued to pay Potatau a salary of *50l.* per annum afterwards increased to *100l.*) would teach the natives the folly of proceedings undertaken only at the promptings of vanity."[1]

Treating this great national agitation as nothing, was a policy in great favour with New Zealand statesmen. Mr. Fenton fell into a like error. "Although I find this King business," he says, "a nuisance and an obstruction, I always tell the Maories it is nothing, and advise them to take no notice of it."[2] There is no doubt that such statements did much mischief. They were false and the natives knew it. The Maories contrasted the declaration of Government, that their King

[1] N. Z. Parl. Papers. F. No. 3, A. 6.

[2] No. 3. Parl. Papers, 1860. E. No. 1, C. 3.

was unworthy of notice with the warnings of their Pakeha friends, that they would be "torn to pieces" for establishing him. And when they were afterwards informed that the King was not such a mere trifle, and had always been regarded by Government as a serious danger, the discovery did not increase their esteem for either the resoluteness or the truthfulness of their rulers.

Every one acquainted with the native affairs of New Zealand knew from the first that there was real danger, and that any act which the natives should regard as a common grievance would turn the harmless and ridiculous King into the head of a formidable hostile confederacy.

We shall learn in the next Chapter how such a common grievance was supplied to the Maories, without loss of time, at Taranaki.

CHAPTER VII.

THE TARANAKI WAR.

THE country of Taranaki had originally been occupied by the Ngatiawa tribe, but in 1834 it was invaded and conquered by the Waikatos and Ngatimaniapotos under their chief Potatau, who at that time went by the name of Te Wherowhero, or the Red Man. The whole land was laid utterly waste; and of the original inhabitants, some fled away into other districts, others were carried captive into Waikato, and only a small remnant, who took refuge in the mountains of Cape Egmont, were left behind.

In 1839, Colonel Wakefield, the agent of the New Zealand Company, determined to buy the rich but deserted territory, and made every effort to buy it fairly. It was first purchased from the exiled Ngatiawa chiefs, who were living on both sides of Cook's Straits; in the year 1840, thé interest of the remnant of Ngatiawa, still resident at Taranaki, was also bought; and finally, in 1842, the rights which the Waikato tribes alleged as conquerors, were purchased from Te Wherowhero at the price of 150*l.* in money, and about as much more in merchandise.

After the arrival of the New Zealand Company's colonists, and the formation of the settlement of New Plymouth, several of the fugitive Ngatiawa, considering that the presence of the English would secure them against another attack from their enemies the Waikatos, returned to Taranaki and began to cultivate land within the limits of the 60,000 acres which had previously been sold to the Company. Several of those who had been carried as slaves to Waikato, and whose rights Colonel Wakefield had therefore not thought it necessary to purchase, were about the same time set at liberty by their now Christian masters, and began to return to their former homes.

Such of the natives as thus repossessed themselves of their old lands at Taranaki, denied the validity or completeness of the New Zealand Company's purchase; but when the title of the buyers was investigated, in 1844, by Commissioner Spain—a judicial officer specially appointed to investigate the fairness of the purchases of the Company from the aborigines—he pronounced this sale both valid and complete, and awarded the whole 60,000 acres, with the exception of certain burial grounds, cultivations, and reserves, to the New Zealand Company.

The Commissioner's award was received by the natives with such disappointment and anger, that the authorities became alarmed, and sent off an express to Governor Fitzroy, at Auckland, asking, in the most pressing terms, for military assistance, as the only security for life itself. The Governor immediately went down to Taranaki, assembled the Europeans and Maories, and informed them that he did not agree with Commissioner Spain's opinion, and should not confirm his award. After various impediments and delays, the block on which the settlement had been made, consisting of about 3,500 acres, was bought over again for 350*l*., and the rest of the land was virtually abandoned to the native claimants.

When the news of this transaction arrived in England, Mr. Gladstone, then Secretary of State for the Colonies, wrote to Governor Grey, who had meanwhile superseded Captain Fitzroy—"I indulge the hope that you may have found yourself in a condition to give effect to the award of Mr. Spain in the case of the Company's claims at New Plymouth; and, in any case, I rely on your endeavours to gain that end, so far as you may have found it practicable, unless, indeed, which I can hardly think probable, you may have seen reason to believe that the reversal of the Commissioner's judgment was a wise and just measure."

Governor Grey, however, never did find himself in a condition to give effect to Commissioner Spain's award.[1] Some of the natives, who were parties to the original sale, and had been amply paid for the land they disposed of, said that they should stand by the

[1] N. Z. Parl. Papers, 1860. E. No. 2, 16.

previous Governor's arrangement, and repudiate the first transaction, nor would they even for any further payment permit Europeans to occupy the land. The arrangement by which Governor Grey proposed to end the dispute was, that ample reserves should be marked out for the resident natives and those likely to return, but that the rest of the territory should be reserved for the Crown; whilst, in fulfilment of Captain Fitzroy's promises, the value of the land so reserved should be assessed, and those natives who established valid claims to any part of it, should receive corresponding sums of money in payment.

To this arrangement, however, the Maories would not assent. There was a good deal of talk on our side about an "intention to enforce it," and hopes were from time to time held out of the natives giving way, and of the European settlers being put in possession of their lands. But, relying on their numbers and strength, and on the declaration of Captain Fitzroy, the Maories persisted in their original determination to restrict the settlers to the 3,500 acres so ignominiously bought by the former Governor. Exiled chiefs from Cook's Straits, and slaves from Waikato, persisted in returning and taking possession of what they chose to call their own property. Among others, Wiremu Kingi, one of the principal chiefs of Ngatiawa, and a body of followers, made up their minds to migrate from Waikanae in Cook's Straits to their original possessions on the

Waitara, a small river about twelve miles north of the town of New Plymouth. Governor Grey, who heard of this intention, sent word to them that a ship of war should stop their migration. Wiremu Kingi repudiated the idea of acting by stealth, and said he would let the Governor know when they were coming. The whole party finally went up to Waitara by sea, but Governor Grey did not send the threatened man-of-war.

The Ngatiawa did not, however, prosper on the lands so unjustly seized by them, and so weakly yielded by the British Government. The country became the scene of the most bloody and atrocious land feuds between those who desired to sell and their opponents. Murders and counter-murders were perpetrated on the public high-roads and amongst the farms of the settlers with circumstances of the most sickening barbarity. The most horrible of these atrocities was the murder of Wi Kingi's relative Katatore, which was planned by a chief named Ihaia, to revenge the death of his relative, whom Katatore had shot for persisting in cutting the boundary of a block of land sold to the Government. The deed was thus described by an eye-witness:[1] —"One of them presented a gun at Rawiri's heart (Rawiri was a comrade of Katatore), and fired. He was badly wounded, rolled from his horse, struggled with his enemy for a short time, and was seized by his hair and tomahawked in an awful manner. It was a

[1] *Taranaki Herald*, Jan. 16, 1858.

sickening sight to see the poor fellow imploring mercy, the blood streaming down his face in torrents, and the ruthless savage protracting his agony by a pause between the blows. Katatore dismounted, and fled up the road; he was shot down about 800 yards off, and his head fearfully beaten with a gun; he was also tomahawked." The man who hacked Rawiri to pieces,[1] lived in a well-furnished house in New Plymouth, and was remarkable for his intelligence and extensive mercantile transactions with the settlers. The scene of the massacre was the Queen's high-road.[2] The Government feared that if the natives were permitted to fight with each other on the settlers' farms, the latter would sooner or later become entangled in the quarrel. A proclamation was therefore issued, declaring that the Queen would levy war upon all persons who unlawfully assembled in arms upon Crown land. But this had not the effect of stopping the bloodshed. One Maori faction was, in cruelty, just as bad as the other, but the land-selling side met with a much greater share of sympathy from the settlers and Government. Ihaia in particular, who planned Katatore's murder, received an amnesty from the Government, [was lauded as a "friendly, honest character,"[3] by the Provincial Council of Taranaki, and is at this moment the cherished friend and ally of the British Government.

[1] N. Z. Parl. Papers, 1860. E. No. 2, 23.
[2] Ibid. E. No. 2, 24. [3] Ibid. E. No. 2, 26.

At length, after many years of bloodshed, Wiremu Kingi succeeded in establishing a close land-league (not connected with the Maori King), and in the beginning of 1859, gave notice to Governor Browne that no more land was to be sold in a district extending from the settlement of Taranaki to Mokau, and advised him to pay no attention to any offer of land within that district.

Soon after receiving this notice, Governor Browne visited Taranaki, and made a speech to the assembled Europeans and natives, in the course of which he stated, that he never would consent to buy land without an undisputed title, but that he would not permit any one to interfere in the sale of land, unless he owned part of it.[1] Upon this Teira got up, and offered his land at Waitara for sale, which the Governor agreed to buy, provided a good title could be made out. Wiremu Kingi then rose and said: "Listen, Governor! Notwithstanding Teira's offer, I will not permit the sale of Waitara to the Pakeha. Waitara is in my hands, I will not give it up!—Never!—never!—never! I have spoken!"—and he and his followers rudely and abruptly left the meeting.

Of the subsequent investigation into Teira's title, which was spread over nearly a whole year, no record has been preserved.

[1] N. Z. Parl. Papers, 1860. E. No. 3, 23. Encl. 1.

The subordinate official who conducted the inquiry, came to the conclusion that Teira and his friends were the sole proprietors of Waitara, and had a perfect right to sell. Accordingly, in the spring of 1860, Governor Browne tried to take possession. Wiremu Kingi resisted. Military force was called in, and the Taranaki war was the immediate result.

As to the policy of this war, there can be now no question; events have proved that it has entailed on the Colony of New Zealand, calamities of which it is still impossible to see the end. But, while condemning the policy by the light of that wisdom which experience has so dearly taught us, it must not be forgotten that in the immediate quarrel between Governor Browne and Wiremu Kingi, the latter was most clearly in the wrong. The case which was afterwards made out for him by the Bishop of New Zealand and Sir William Martin, which enlisted the sympathies of all the Maories in his cause, and which disturbed the confidence of the British Government in the justice of their own officer, was not the ground on which Wiremu Kingi made war. He is no hero, but simply a grey-headed savage, of a coarse and bloodthirsty disposition. The breach in the land-league, of which he was the head, and the prospect of losing Waitara, to which he was strongly attached, aroused his rage. He had before resisted land-selling by force, and was ready to do so again. Whether his claim to a right to prevent the sale was good or bad, he did not choose to submit it to the British Government for investigation. "Waitara is in my hands; I will not give it up!" was his ultimatum.

The real circumstances of the case were such as would inevitably irritate a passionate man to madness. At the time of the original migràtion of Wiremu Kingi's party from Cook's Straits, there was still considerable fear of an invasion from their old enemies, the Ngatimaniapoto. It was, therefore, agreed by the whole tribe, that instead of Wiremu Kingi settling on the north bank of the Waitara, where his own possessions were, the whole tribe should live together upon Teira's land, on the south bank, for mutual protection against the common foe.

It was in consequence of this arrangement that Wiremu Kingi originally established himself on Teira's land, where he laid out cultivations, and built substantial houses. There they all lived happily together, until disturbed by the accursed land-feuds, which caused perpetual dissension amongst them. At length Teira, out of spite to Wiremu Kingi, sold Waitara to the Government, the effect of this sale being to turn the latter suddenly, and without compensation, off land which he had considerably improved by building and cultivation, and which, under the original agreement, he had certainly an equitable right to hold.

It seems quite incredible that circumstances so material to the case should have escaped the notice of the officials concerned in the purchase, and have remained undiscovered for three years, until they were accidentally found out, by Sir George Grey's interpreter, in private conversation with the Waitara natives. The facts were certainly unknown, not only to Governor Browne, but even to Wiremu Kingi's advocates. It will be readily believed, that had the Governor been informed of a circumstance so material, the Waitara block would never have been purchased.

Giving any further history of the Waitara controversy, or expressing any opinion thereupon, is a task which I gladly avoid, as not relevant to my subject. Volumes have been written on the subject, which are certainly calculated to produce a strong conviction on most people's minds that the "undisputed title" which Governor Browne required is not possessed by the Waitara block, and, probably, not by any native land in New Zealand. I pass on to the point with which we are more immediately concerned, namely, upon what grounds, and in what manner, the Waikatos mixed themselves up in the quarrel.

During the year 1859, the Waikato King-party had been putting out feelers in every direction.[1] In December, Whaitere of Hangatiki called at Waitara, on his way to the south, and secretly left one of the King flags there. The acceptance of this flag would have been considered as a sign of accession to the King, and,

[1] N. Z. Papers, 1860. E. No. 3, A. 1.

especially, as a pledge not to sell land without the King's consent. When Wiremu Kingi found out that the flag had been left, he accused those who sanctioned it of treachery. A division ensued. Wiremu Kingi left the Pa, and went to live elsewhere, while the other party kept the flag, and began to erect a flag-staff. At the beginning of the year 1860, a deputation from the Ngatiawa and Ngatiruanui was sent to the Waikato[1] (apparently without Wiremu Kingi's consent) to give in the allegiance of those tribes to the King. The deputation consisted of sixty young men. They arrived at Ngaruawahia on the 10th of April, accompanied by a large number of Ngatimaniapoto, marched up to the royal flag-staff three abreast, wearing favours to distinguish the tribes, and went through a certain mummery of kneeling down and making speeches, which was supposed to constitute them true subjects of the Maori King.

While these men were still at Ngaruawahia, the news of the outbreak of war at Waitara arrived there. The principles of the King party now required that they should interfere actively to prevent the alienation of land, which had come under the King's "mana." A southern chief, named Wi Tako, was commissioned to visit Taranaki on his return home from the Waikato, and report upon the case. He gave as his opinion that the quarrel, of which he had carefully ascertained the

[1] N. Z. Parl. Papers, 1861. E. No. 1, 1.

grounds, concerned Wiremu Kingi alone, and that the rights of the Maori King were not involved therein. But Wiremu Kingi, who had hitherto kept aloof from the Maori national party, was now glad enough to get the help of such powerful allies as the Waikatos in his contest with the British Government. He accordingly wrote a letter consenting to join the league, and praying for help against his enemies.

A general meeting was held at Ngaruawahia in May, 1860, to consider the Taranaki question, and determine whether the Waikatos should join in the war or not.[1]

Wiremu Tamihana, who was one of the first speakers, said:—

"I am disturbed by the letter received from Wiremu Kingi Te Rangitake. I wish to understand the case, but do not see it. . . . I hesitate and say, Let us see our way. Te Rangitake says, the land is his: Teira says, it is his. I say, Let us find out the owner. Do not be hasty lest we make a mistake. I do not condemn the Governor, for I am not informed. . . . I do not say, let us find out that the Governor is right that we may join him, nor am I idle or unwilling to go to war if necessary, but let me have a just cause. . . . If the Governor says that this (the Maori King) is the cause of the war, I see through it. If he says that it is the land, I see through that also. But I do not speak it; that is a matter not to be spoken here, it is a hidden

[1] N. Z. Parl. Papers, 1861. F. No. 1, App. D.

word that is to be kept in the heart. We intend to keep our land, and if the Governor comes to take another piece after this, then we shall have war. . . . Let the subject be taken up and settled by the chiefs. Shall we go to the Governor or shall we join Rangitake? Let us search out the merits of the case, that if we die we may die in a righteous cause."

The whole discussion finally turned upon the question whether the Governor bought the land before or after it came under the Maori King's "mana." "The question is," said one of the latest speakers, "was the flag first or the money first? If the land was paid for before the flag reached it, the Governor is right, if not, then the matter cannot rest where it is. If the mana and flag went before, we must contend for our land."

Mr. McLean, the Native secretary, who attended this meeting on behalf of Government, gave a very clear account of the Waitara purchase. He was listened to with great attention, and his speech was apparently producing a great effect when Te Heu Heu, of Taupo, rose, and with the remark—"It is night," broke up the meeting.

Many of the Waikato chiefs were heard to say that Mr. McLean's words were quite correct. Old Potatau also corroborated his statements, and was very angry with Te Heu Heu for so rudely interrupting the speech. The Ngatihaua offered to light large fires, that he might have an opportunity of completing his statement that night, for they had resolved on other grounds to leave the meeting early the next morning. Unfortunately this offer was not accepted, because Mr. McLean fancied that he would have an opportunity of continuing his statement to the whole assembly by daylight. However, when the morrow arrived and Ngatihaua had gone, he found the other natives so busy preparing to erect a new flagstaff, that they could not be induced to assemble. After waiting some time in vain, Mr. McLean struck his tent and departed.

It is not the custom at Maori meetings to pass definite resolutions; indeed, it would be useless to do so, as the majority have no means of forcing the minority to conform to their decision. The only use of these gatherings is to make public opinion heard, so that each man, in determining for himself what he will do, may know what chance there is of being supported therein by comrades.

The speeches delivered on this occasion made it clear that the whole body of Waikato were not yet prepared to back Wiremu Kingi's quarrel at all hazards. Still, much passive sympathy had been expressed, and many had shown great eagerness to pick a quarrel as soon as possible with the Pakeha, and have a trial of strength. This party had a strong though secret supporter in Rewi Maniapoto, whose intrigues were so successful, that, at length, a band of volunteers from Waikato went down to take part in the Taranaki war. Epiha, a

Waikato of Kihikihi, was the leader. Rewi persuaded him that Potatau and the chiefs of Ngaruawahia wished some of them to go. The untruth was eagerly received by Epiha, who longed to take part in a war in which he hoped to gain personal distinction. Before, however, actually setting off, he wrote a letter to Potatau, saying that if Potatau disapproved, though he should be already on the way to Taranaki, he would return. It is said that, in fact, an imperative order was despatched by the Ngaruawahia Council to recall the too zealous chief; but Epiha always denied having received any such order, and it is more than probable that Rewi intercepted the letter.

The pioneers of the Waikato war-party were received with intense delight by the Ngatiawa natives. In the first encounter with British troops, they gained a splendid success, contrary to the warnings which they had received from their missionaries and other Pakeha friends, who had prophesied that their martial pride would have a speedy downfall. They beat back an attack upon their Pa at Puketekauere, with a loss to the British side of thirty killed and thirty-four wounded.[1] The news of this victory, enormously exaggerated, fired all the adventurous young men in Waikato with enthusiasm. They were eager to share such glorious deeds, and seize the opportunity of distinguishing their names. Numbers, therefore, chiefly from Ngatimaniapoto and

[1] N. Z. Parl. Papers, 1860. E. No. 3, 52.

the neighbourhood of Rangiaowhia, flocked to Taranaki, where they plundered the abandoned homesteads of the settlers with impunity, insulted the troops, and returned to their homes laden with spoil, and full of confidence in their own valour and contempt for the cowardice or stupidity of their foes. The warriors who thus went down to the war were influenced far more by a love of excitement than by any political motive. The King's government had nothing whatever to do with the matter; Potatau and his councillors did all they could to stop the Waikatos from going, and perhaps may have restrained a few. But most Maories choose to do exactly what they please, and would equally have gone down to fight at Taranaki, whether there had been a Maori King or no. It became the fashion for all the adventurous men to spend a month or two in the year at Taranaki, "shooting Pakehas;" and in obedience to this fashion alone, they went and took part in the war. For example, Wiremu Kumete, a Ngatimahuta chief, living at Kawhia, having planted his crops, and having nothing else in particular to do, marched down to Taranaki, joined in a most reckless assault upon one of our redoubts, in which thirty-six men lost their lives, and, according to General Pratt's despatch, fell himself. His name is handed to fame in the returns of killed as "a chief of high rank."[1] Notwithstanding this, however, he arrived in safety at his home in Kawhia, in

[1] N. Z. Parl. Papers. E. No. 1, A. 3.

time to reap his crops; and having brought his produce over to Waipa, made a peaceful expedition down to the Waiuku market to sell his goods, and buy powder and shot for the further prosecution of his warlike propensities. At Ngaruawahia, he was severely called to task by his kinsmen for taking part in the war, but defended his conduct in a playful good-humoured vein, made himself very merry over some Englishmen because he had been killed in the "Governor's newspaper," went on to Waiuku, sold his produce, came home again with whatever it was that he had bought, and would, no doubt, have gone again to the war, had not hostilities been by that time suspended.

But though most of the Maori warriors were thus animated by pure love of mischief, and had no definite political object in fighting for Wiremu Kingi, it was not so with Rewi Maniapoto, who having seen the war mania fairly progressing in Waikato, threw off all disguise, and went down in person to Taranaki, to pursue his design of involving the whole Maori people in a contest for supremacy with their European rivals.

At this crisis the New Zealand Assembly met, in which a large and influential party, composed of the oldest settlers, and supported by the Bishop of New Zealand and Sir William Martin, late Chief Justice of the Colony, openly espoused Wiremu Kingi's side. Some declared that the seizure of the Waitara was the result of a conspiracy among the settlers of Taranaki, greedy for their neighbours' land; others, that Wiremu Kingi had a perfect right, as chief of the Ngatiawa tribe, to forbid the alienation of tribal land; and others, that a dispute between the Government and Wiremu Kingi, about a question of title, should have been referred to some court of justice, that it was monstrous that the same individual should be both party and judge, and that the peace of the Colony was being imperilled upon an issue that had never been tried.

No attempt was made, nor would it indeed have been possible, to keep these opinions and the discussions that ensued secret from the natives. The Governor, it is true, issued a proclamation, urging all loyal subjects to abstain from publishing opinions tending to impugn the justice of the course he was pursuing, but that was not until long after it had become known to the Maories throughout the length and breadth of New Zealand, that in the opinion of the most revered among the Pakehas, Wiremu Kingi was an injured man. The desire to interfere in his behalf grew stronger on this evidence of the justice of his cause. The Waikatos had, moreover, according to their notions, other good grounds for remaining no longer neutral. The Governor, said they, had not fought out his quarrel with his own forces; he had sent over to his friends in Australia, and their troops were continually arriving in New Zealand to his assistance. It was, therefore, right that Wiremu Kingi's friends should imitate the conduct of the

Governor's friends, by bestirring themselves to support in arms that cause which they believed to be just.

Among others, Wetini, a chief of the Ngatihaua tribe, inferior only to Wiremu Tamihana, whose relative and close friend he was, resolved to go. Tamihana by this time had ceased to doubt, and had become satisfied of the justice of Wiremu Kingi's cause, but he was not clear as to the right of Waikato to interfere in Kingi's behalf: at any rate, he strongly dissuaded Wetini from going. He used religious arguments against war; he called a meeting of the tribe, at which Wetini's proposals found only nine supporters, and for the time succeeded in holding him back. But three weeks later, a letter came from Wiremu Kingi, asking what was the use of sending him only a "disembodied flag," and why they did not personally come to help him. Wetini could bear it no longer, and in spite of his friend's arguments, denunciations, and prayers, set off with a considerable number of his tribe to the war. Tamihana's last words to him (for they parted at Tamahere almost in anger) were—"Then go, and stop there."

In the midst of these troubles old Potatau died. His last days were vexed by the anticipation of evils about to come upon his people. The abusive and threatening language of the Pakeha newspapers had reached his ears, and one of his last acts was to send a message to his old friend, Sir William Martin,—"Be kind to the niggers." His last words to his people, which afterwards became a sort of watchword with the chiefs of the King party, were—"Hold fast to love, to law, and to the faith." When Potatau was dead there was some difficulty in finding a successor acceptable to the whole of Waikato, and for a short time the Government hoped that the league would fall to pieces for lack of a recognised head. It was said that Wiremu Tamihana had always looked forward to succeeding Potatau as King, but that at the time when the latter died the former's temporary unpopularity as an advocate of peace prevented his aspiring to the vacant place. One party proposed Matutaera Potatau, the son of the late king, as successor. Another party objected to him on the ground that his abilities were too slender worthily to fulfil the office, and proposed Te Paea Potatau, his sister, instead. She was a woman about thirty-five years old, strong, intelligent, and very resolute, inheriting more of the courage and virtue of her warrior-father than his weak and effeminate son. Everybody who knows Te Paea admits that she would have made a splendid queen. The dispute was brought to an end, however, as soon as Tamihana, after some hesitation, declared himself in Matutaera's favour. The sister's claims were withdrawn, and the brother, without further opposition, was installed in his father's place.

So soon as it was known that the Waikatos in considerable numbers had joined the Taranaki war, the excitement and terror in Auckland became intense. Ngatimaniapoto had several times distinctly proposed to carry fire and sword into that province, which lay, without troops, exposed, and at their mercy. At length the danger reached its height when the corpse of a Maori, with gun-shot wounds in the head and hand, was found in the woods near Patumahoe, a small native village lying between the Manukau Harbour and the lower part of the Waikato.

The hasty inference, that a Maori had been murdered by a European, spread like wildfire among the already excited natives. Those on the spot were with some difficulty pacified by the officers of the Native Department, and prevailed on to abandon their original intention of making a promiscuous onslaught on the neighbouring European villages to avenge their countryman's death. But no sooner was the danger of attack from the natives of Patumahoe over than a fresh alarm was raised as to the intention of the Upper Waikatos. It was just the case in which the King party felt bound to interfere. Their union had been ridiculed by the Governor as "child's play," and here was an opportunity for showing that they had the resolution of men. The only question they would entertain was, whether there were sufficient grounds to fix the crime on a European; should that be proved, they resolved to demand the surrender of the criminal for trial by them, or in default to declare war.

It was fortunate for Auckland that Rewi and the Ngatimaniapoto had already gone to Taranaki, so that the business fell into the hands of Wiremu Tamihana and the Ngatihaua. A large gathering was made at Ngaruawahia, whence a fleet of canoes, filled with from 300 to 400 armed men, under the leadership of Matutaera Potatau, the young king, and Wiremu Tamihana, went down the river, bent on holding an inquest upon the murdered body of their countryman.

They stopped a day at Paetai, when the war dance was performed in all its grotesque horror, and the excited natives afterwards sat down to discuss further proceedings. Their leaders then proposed that the fighting men should not go further down the river until some other inquiries had been made, but they had not influence enough over their followers to carry their point. A letter from Ihaka, the chief of the dead man's tribe, arrived, stating that all was settled and they might go back; but as Ihaka was known to be in Government pay not the slightest notice was taken of the letter, and the armed band persisted in going on to Patumahoe to inquire for themselves. The King and his mother returned in disgust and displeasure from Paetai, but Tamihana still remained with the party, justifying his conduct, both at the time and afterwards, by saying, that though the young men would go on to Patumahoe and he was unable to prevent them, his presence might restrain them from mischief when there. The war canoes paddled down the river to Tuakau, a village six miles below Mangatawhiri, spreading terror among the settlers, many of whom fled in panic to the town. At Tuakau they were met by several chiefs friendly to Government, and by the Bishop of New Zealand and Archdeacon Maunsell, and finding that there was not the slightest clue to the perpetrator of the deed, and that the evidence was not quite conclusive as to its being a murder at all, the Waikatos at length consented to return. There was, however, after all, the narrowest escape from collision. While discussions were going on at Tuakau, Whakapaukai and some choice spirits like himself separated themselves in two canoes from the main body, and paddled further down the river on a private expedition of their own. The absence of these men was pointed out by Archdeacon Maunsell to Tamihana, who exhibited the liveliest concern, and in great haste sent off a letter to fetch them back. The words of the letter were—"Come back, and come back in peace." He exhibited great uneasiness until Whakapaukai had re-appeared. Had there been the least hesitation or lukewarmness on the part of Tamihana, interference would have been too late to prevent certain robbery and probable bloodshed. Finally the whole party was taken back up the river without doing any further harm than giving the Auckland citizens a severe fright. The Europeans owed their salvation on this occasion to Wiremu Tamihana, the Waikato rebel.

Immediately after the Patumahoe affair had been brought to this amicable conclusion, news arrived in Waikato of a dreadful disaster at Taranaki, in which Wetini and most of the Ngatihaua contingent had fallen. Wetini and old Porokoru, who led the party, having reached Waitara eager for battle, sent off a taunting challenge to General Pratt. It ran as follows:—

"Friend, I have heard your word—come to fight me; that is very good. Come inland, and let us meet each other. Fish fight at sea. Come inland, and let us stand on our feet. Make haste, make haste. Do not delay. That is all I have to say to you—make haste.

From Wetini Taiporutu; from Porokoru; from all the chiefs of Ngatihaua and Waikato."[1]

The challenge was accepted: the combatants met at Mahoetahi, and according to a preconcerted plan, Wetini's party were surrounded by an overpowering force and cut to pieces. Four men only escaped unwounded, a brother of Wetini's fled with a bayonet sticking in his body, which he afterwards preserved as a great trophy, and all the survivors declared their only wonder was that the soldiers had allowed a single person to escape. Wetini's body was carried to Taranaki and honourably buried in the church-yard. Equal respect was paid to some man unknown, who was taken for old

[1] N. Z. Parl. Paper, 1861. E. No. 1, A. 1.

Porokoru. "It is a curious fact," says General Pratt in his despatch, "that the two chiefs who signed the challenge were both killed." It is a still more curious fact that Porokoru must have come to life again after being thus dead and buried, for he still survives to fight us gallantly in the present war.

The greatest indignation was felt and expressed by the Ngatihaua against Rewi and his men, to whose failure to support them they attributed the disaster. Rewi, on his part, says that Wetini was a rash fool, who would not listen to advice; that he sent him down messenger after messenger urging him to retire before it was too late; that his last messenger actually followed too far and was caught in the snare with the others and killed (being one of the very few Ngatimaniapoto who fell in the war); and that he could not have done more for Wetini without injury to the common cause. All this is quite true, but the loss of Wetini while Rewi sat inactive has ever since rankled deeply in the minds of the Ngatihaua, and increased the hereditary hatred between the two tribes.

The fallen chief, who as a dashing leader was a general favourite in his tribe, and was more beloved than even Tamihana himself, was loudly lamented at his home in Waikato. Every evening, for months afterwards, the women of Tamahere met at sunset to raise the "tangi" for the dead, and moaned forth the doleful dirge until nightfall. The traveller riding about the neighbourhood constantly came upon small parties, who, meeting each other, had alighted from their horses, and were sitting in the dust to howl and wail for Wetini.

But the general grief at the terrible disaster, so far from disheartening the Waikato tribes, and putting a stop to their interference in the war, as was expected by many, had the contrary effect of stimulating their zeal; and many who had disapproved of Wetini's expedition were now burning to join in the conflict, and avenge the blood of their kinsmen. Tamihana himself was strongly pressed by his tribe to lead them to battle, but though so far persuaded as to write a letter to the Bishop of New Zealand, announcing his intention of going to Taranaki, he appears to have been still restrained by reason, and did not carry out his design.

But others began to flock to Taranaki, not only from Waikato, but from Tauranga, Rotorua, and more remote places. The Ngatihaua tribe joined in great numbers, and signalized themselves by ill-judged and reckless assaults on the English positions, in which many lives were lost.

At the moment when every one expected that the petty quarrel at Taranaki must inevitably merge in a general war between the two races, the fighting was suddenly stopped by the intervention of Wiremu Tamihana, of which an account will be given in the next chapter.

CHAPTER VIII.

WIREMU TAMIHANA TE WAHAROA.

THE warriors of the Ngatihaua tribe who took part in the Taranaki war continued to be conspicuous for their reckless valour, and the extreme rashness of their imprudent leaders. Reports of disaster came, from time to time, into the Waikato, brought by wounded men returning to their villages, who joined the kinsmen of the fallen in urgently calling upon Wiremu Tamihana to fulfil his duties as leader of their tribe. At length, in the beginning of 1861, he showed symptoms of yielding to their importunity.

Tamihana had succeeded his father, Te Waharoa, as head chief of the Ngatihaua tribe. The latter, a contemporary of Potatau and Wiremu Nera, is still notorious in Waikato for the mingled ferocity and cunning which he exhibited in the wars of the last generation, in which he raised his tribe to great renown. Among Maories, the son does not necessarily succeed to his father's position, unless, in the opinion of the elders of the tribe, his own personal qualities entitle him to do so. Tamihana, however, inherits all the vigorous traits of his father's character in a less savage form. He is just as courageous and determined, and equally diplomatic. He even follows some of his father's whims, such as generally making journeys by night, never telling others when he intends to set off, and delighting to arrive in places where he is least expected. When converted, at an early age, to Christianity, he declared he would never fight again; and since that time, though living in the midst of innumerable quarrels and bloodshed, he had never, up to the time of which we are now speaking, personally engaged in war, but had consistently and successfully performed the part of a peacemaker. Feud after feud was settled by his mediation, until at last it had become usual when any difficulty arose to send for Tamihana to settle it.

Having embraced Christianity from conviction, and not from hereditary custom, and being in the habit of constantly reading the Bible as almost his only literature, he argues on religious maxims, and intersperses his writings with Biblical quotations, in what appears to us an unusual degree. It would be a mistake to suppose this the result of cant or hypocrisy. Most of the Maories are exceedingly fond of reading the books of the Old Testament, in which they find described a state of civilization not unlike their own; and though not possessed of the same critical powers as the Zulu Kafirs, they have sufficient intelligence to deduce maxims from both Old and New Testaments, which it is inconvenient to have to reconcile with the theories of our modern civilization.

The chief consideration that constrained Tamihana to visit Taranaki, was the great loss which his tribe had suffered in war, in most instances for want of a prudent leader. It was his obvious interest to endeavour to stay that slaughter of his people, which threatened soon to destroy his own influence and importance. He determined to go, however, not as a belligerent, but as a peacemaker. He did not doubt that injustice had been done to Wi Kingi in the purchase of Teira's land; and although he readily admitted that it was Kingi's duty, if he thought himself wronged, to appeal to law and not to arms, yet he maintained that the Governor's haste and rashness had forced on and commenced a war, leaving Wi Kingi no option in the matter. He felt, however, by no means certain that the Home Government would back up the proceedings of the Governor. He was aware that the Duke of Newcastle's absence in America had postponed the examination of the Waitara question, so that, after all, the war going on at Taranaki might be a useless waste of life and property. He therefore resolved to go down and propose to Wi Kingi and the fighting chiefs, that all hostilities should be stopped, and an appeal made to the Queen and Imperial Parliament. If the Queen and Parliament were willing to have the title investigated by law, it should be so investigated; but if they upheld what he considered the lawless policy of the Governor, it would be time enough to fight then. With these designs, he mustered the remnant of his tribe at Tamahere, and putting himself and Ti Oriori at their head, set off to join Te Heu Heu of Taupo, with the object of going down in a body to the seat of war, in direct opposition to the wishes of the Maori King, who throughout steadily and consistently opposed all meddling on the part of Waikato in the Taranaki quarrel.

The Government, during the whole of this critical period, had no officer of any kind, either resident in, or travelling about, the Waikato district, and were, in consequence, a prey to all the absurd and exaggerated stories that idle gossip might set afloat. So little did they understand either Tamihana's character or his motives in visiting Taranaki, that it was confidently believed that he was forming a deep and wide-spread conspiracy to attack the Auckland settlement; that he had gathered his tribe together for this purpose, that he and Te Heu Heu were only pretending to be on their way to Taranaki to mislead, but that when they had thrown Government off their guard, they would turn round and fall upon Auckland.[1]

Wi Tamihana, meanwhile, quietly pursued his way, and arrived at the Waitara on Monday, the 11th of March. Before entering Pukerangiora, a Pa up to

[1] N. Z. Parl. Papers, 1862. E. No. 1, Sec. II. 21.

which the British troops had been for months laboriously sapping their way, he halted on the north bank of the river, opposite to the English camp, to which he sent a letter, asking for a truce on Monday, Tuesday, and Wednesday, to give him an opportunity of visiting Te Rangitake (Wi Kingi) and the fighting chiefs: he stated that he was a man of authority, and his tribe would make good his stipulations. General Pratt's reply reproved him for dissimulation, and exhorted him to candour; the truce on Tuesday and Wednesday would be granted, but the peacemaker was warned in strong terms to keep his word, "lest he should be known as a deceitful man." Upon receiving this letter, it being then late in the afternoon, Tamihana went on to Pukerangiora. On the following morning a white flag was hoisted on the pallisading of the Pa, but as there was no wind to blow it out, the firing of our troops had recommenced before it was perceived. Tamihana sat down and wrote an answer to the General's letter of the previous afternoon. "I see," he wrote, "that you accuse me of deceiving you. Now listen! I am not acting deceitfully towards you. You have been crafty towards me; your soldiers have come to-day within the trench and fired. Now I know, in the first place, you are a crafty man, and in the second, you are a man without authority among your people." The mistake was explained, and an apology offered for the harsh missive with which communications had opened the day before.

The whole of the next day was taken up in talking over those Waikato chiefs who had already taken part in the war, and who, when Tamihana's pacific designs were announced, cried and shouted against him. The precise arguments by which their views were changed have never been ascertained. Tamihana's own opinion has always been, that the cause of Maori nationality, to maintain which he has made every sacrifice, is not in any way advanced by war with the Europeans. His policy has always been to make a passive resistance to our encroachments, to assert Maori independence by just and lawful acts, and to let our side, if there must be war, be clearly the aggressors. Perhaps it was this view that he urged upon the fighting chiefs. They were, no doubt, the more disposed to listen to him, in as much as all were getting tired of the war. At first it was exciting and pleasant to roam at will over the country from which the English farmers had been driven, and to push even into the outskirts of the town of Taranaki itself, pillaging houses, driving off cattle and horses, and occasionally exchanging a shot with the enemy's outposts, or picking off some foolhardy straggler. But the plunder had been looted long ago, and the war had turned into a very dull and uninteresting resistance to General Pratt's slow but certain advance up the Waitara valley. At any rate, by the evening of Tuesday they were brought to consent to Tamihana managing matters in his own way, and a message was sent to

Wiremu Kingi to desire a talk, which at that chief's request was fixed for the following morning.

On Wednesday, a meeting took place between the Waikatos and the Ngatiawa tribe. The proceedings were commenced by Tamihana, who said that he was come to Waitara to tell them the opinions of the other Maories and of the ministers of religion; he had been desirous to visit the fighting chiefs, and particularly Te Rangitake, to inquire into the causes of the quarrel, and he was now quite satisfied that the quarrel was not Waikato's but Te Rangitake's.

"No," said Wiremu Kingi, interrupting him, "neither Waitara nor the quarrel is mine: they are yours."

"No," retorted Tamihana, "they are yours."

"No, they are yours."

"Why look at a man," continued Tamihana; "his head is head; his hands, hands; and his legs, legs: you are the head, Waikato is only the legs."

"No, you are the head."

"No, you."

"Yes!" said Wi Kingi, "I am the head, Waitara is mine, the quarrel is mine. There! I give Waitara to you!"

He further declared, in answered to Tamihana, that his gift was free and unreserved, and that he claimed no further voice whatever in the disposal of the land. Hapurona, the fighting general of Ngatiawa, and Epiha and Rewi, as leaders of the Waikato and Ngatimaniapoto contingents, were successively challenged, and publicly announced their assent to the gift, and their willingness to yield the unreserved disposal of the land to Wiremu Tamihana. Thus appointed sole arbiter on the native side, Tamihana proceeded to make his award—"Waikato! back to Waikato! Te Atiawa! away to Mataitawa! Ngatiruanui! return to your homes! Let the soldiers be taken back to the town of Taranaki; Waitara shall be left under the protection of the law."

A letter was sent the same evening to the general to propose a cessation of hostilities on both sides, and that the land-question should be reserved for the decision of the Great Assembly of the Queen. On Thursday morning, an interview took place between Tamihana and an officer of the Native Department; the former repeated his proposals, and begged that the troops might be at once taken back to the town; he was told that the Governor alone had power to order such a step, and was invited, if really desirous of peace, to proceed by ship to Auckland. "What," asked Tamihana, "was the crime of Rauparaha? (a chief who was kidnapped and carried off in a man-of-war by Sir George Grey) and what was the crime of Pomare? These men's crimes were mere trifles: I am a very bad man, far worse than either of them; I am both a King-maker, and the head of this quarrel: I dare not go on board your ship, lest I should be treated as Rauparaha and

Pomare were." He offered to go by land and meet the Governor in three days at Tuakau, the nearest point of the Waikato river to Auckland—"if the Governor is afraid to come there," he said, "let him bring his soldiers to take care of him, or if he does not like to talk in the open air, let him come to Ngaruawahia: our house is there."

As it was found impossible to persuade the chief to adventure himself into our power, it was at last agreed that his proposal should be sent by steamer to the Governor at Auckland, but the general would not consent to a suspension of hostilities until an answer should be received; Tamihana in vain urged the desirability of saving human life; the general replied that it would be a waste of time, and firing would re-commence on the following morning.

On Friday our white flag had disappeared, but that of the enemy was, by Tamihana's orders, still kept flying. The soldiers entered the sap and commenced digging: no opposition was offered. They proceeded to fire upon the Maori pa. "Now," said Tamihana to the fighting chiefs, "do what you please." The white flag was hauled down and the war flag hoisted; firing continued on both sides during that day, Saturday, and Sunday. The Maories say that they did not during those days lose a man; on our own side Lieutenant Macnaughten, R.A., was killed and several men wounded. Tamihana took no part in the fighting.

On Monday Mr. McLean, the Native Secretary, arrived, and had an interview with Tamihana. He had not brought the Governor's consent to the troops being taken away from Waitara. Tamihana was much annoyed, and asked what he had come for. He thought the Governor was very foolish; however, he would have no more to do with Waitara, he had told all the Maories to disperse; Waitara was left under the protection of the law, and he should return to Waikato forthwith. Mr. McLean said that if the various tribes would cease hostilities and disperse, the Governor would treat with them separately. He would deal with Kingi and Ngatiawa at Waitara; with Ngatiruanui at the town of Taranaki; and would meet Tamihana at Mangere, a village a few miles from Auckland, to settle the affairs of Waikato. There were four matters to be disposed of; (1) the disputed land at Waitara; (2) the murders; (3) the property of settlers that had been taken or destroyed; (4) the Maori King.

Tamihana returned from Waitara, mortified and disappointed; he went down with intentions friendly to the English, desirous of distinction no doubt, but of the distinction of a peacemaker; his advances were rejected, he was accused of promoting war and rebellion, he was forced into the position of a belligerent though he had never fired a shot, and he came back under a threat of war. The Waikatos followed him sulkily; Rewi stayed behind to hatch mischief if he could, and succeeded at last in carrying off Wiremu Kingi, who might, he feared, patch up his quarrel with the Governor, to a sort of honourable captivity at Kihikihi. At Mokau, Tamihana's followers broke out into open complaints, and bitterly upbraided him with an ill-timed and useless interference in the war. He contrived, however, in some way to satisfy them, and thence made a journey round the west coast, and through the greater part of the Waikato district, to explain his policy and ascertain the sentiments of the natives generally about upholding the Maori King. After this he settled quietly down at Tamahere, hoisted a white flag, and waited for the Governor's next move. He had declined the proposed meeting at Mangere, on the ground that he feared imprisonment. He informed Europeans by whom he was visited, that they were all determined to uphold the King; that they were no breakers of the treaty of Waitangi, for neither he nor any of the Waikatos had ever signed or agreed to it, except seven old men who had been bribed with blankets to do so. He denied, however, that there was any feeling of enmity on their part towards the Queen: they had constituted Potatau their head and called him King, as a centre round which they might rally, in order that they might do for themselves what had not been done for them, namely, make laws to take the place of their old Maori customs, which were obsolete or injurious. He thought that their King should be to them what the Governor was to the Europeans; that the two races should be united by one law, and that the Queen should be a hedge around them all. At the same time they were determined not to be our subjects; they would administer English laws themselves, that is, take our laws so far as suitable to their circumstances, and carry them out among themselves without being responsible to any higher authority.

In the month of May, a clerk of the Native Office was sent with a letter to Tamihana, reminding him that a portion of his tribe and other Waikatos had, without provocation, gone down to fight at Taranaki, and asking what compensation they intended to make for the evil they had done. Soon after the receipt of this letter, Tamihana began a reply to the Governor in vindication of the Waikato tribes, but before it was finished and despatched, a printed ultimatum from the Governor was brought by an obscure native into Waikato.

This proclamation is especially worthy of attention, because it is difficult to exaggerate its effect on the minds of the natives, and its influence on subsequent events. Its power must not be estimated by that which a similar document would have on ourselves. Maories can generally read, but are furnished with very little literature, except the Bible and a few lesson-books. This fresh and exciting paper, widely distributed and carefully read at their evening meetings, where every paragraph was discussed, had an independent value as a piece of literature; while, politically, it was a distinct revelation of the thoughts and purposes of the Pakeha, and helped to decide that anxious question which was always in their thoughts, when the great war that was to deprive them of their lands would begin.

The proclamation, which was entitled "Declaration by the Governor to the Natives assembled at Ngaruawahia," was to the following effect.[1] It began by stating that at the first establishment of the Maori King, the Governor inclined to the belief that the King's supporters desired only the establishment of order and a governing authority amongst themselves; but that he soon felt misgivings, which had been justified by the event. He had not interfered to put down the Maori King by force, hoping that the Maories themselves, seeing the danger of the course they were pursuing, and that the institution of an independent authority must prove inefficient for all purposes of good, would of their own accord abandon that course. He then enumerated the wrongs that had been committed in the name and by the adherents of the native King:—

(1). The Treaty of Waitangi had been violated.

(2). Some of them had interfered between the Governor and other native tribes in matters with which they had no concern, and levied war against the Queen.

(3). Others had abetted the men who committed these outrages.

[1] N. Z. Parl. Papers. E. No. 1, B. 16.

(4). A war-party had advanced to within forty miles of Auckland, to interfere with the due course of the administration of justice.

(5). They had stopped the Queen's mail from passing over native land, usurped jurisdiction over Europeans, and committed divers other offences against Her Majesty's Sovereignty.

(6). The adherents of the King were at that very time using the most strenuous efforts to possess themselves of arms and ammunition, to effect their objects by intimidation and violence.

"*The Governor*," says the proclamation, "*cannot permit the present state of things to continue. No option now rests with him: he has been commanded by Her Majesty the Queen to suppress unlawful combinations, and to maintain Her Majesty's Sovereignty in New Zealand.*"

The document then went on to explain what Sovereignty implied:—

(1). That every man should obey the law, which guaranteed freedom to the weak as well as to the strong. [Wiremu Tamihana must have smiled at this. Sir William Martin's pamphlet on the "Taranaki Question" had informed him that the conduct of the Governor in taking armed possession of the Waitara was unlawful. Either, therefore, the Governor did not obey the law, or the law did not guarantee protection to the weak as well as the strong.]

(2). No man in the Queen's dominions is permitted to enforce rights, or redress wrongs, by force: he must appeal to the law. [What a mockery this statement must have been in the eyes of the Taranaki natives, who remembered the murder of Rawiri, Katatore, and many others, whose friends all appealed to the law for redress, and appealed in vain; or to the Upper Waikato, Ngatiruanui, Taupo, and other tribes, rarely or never visited by an officer of Government, and having, therefore, no law to appeal to.]

(3). "That men do not enter into combinations for the purpose of preventing other men from acting or dealing with their property as they think fit. This is against the law." [To the Maories, this meant, "Land-leagues are unlawful." In themselves, land-leagues are no more unlawful than trades'-unions; but the Governor's language would include trusts, partnerships, and settlements of all kinds, in one sweeping condemnation.]

4. That every man allow roads and bridges to be made on his land, when required by lawful authority. [As the Maories had no share in the government of the colony, this implied, whenever the Pakeha might choose.]

On the other hand, the Queen had, by the Treaty of Waitangi, secured to them their lands. "*By that treaty,*" are the words of the declaration, "*the Queen's name has become a protecting shade for the Maories' land, and will remain such, so long as the Maories yield allegiance to Her Majesty, and live under her sovereignty; but no longer. Whenever the Maories forfeit this protection, by setting aside the authority of the Queen and the law, the land will remain their own so long only as they are strong enough to keep it:—might, and not right, will become their sole title to possession.*"

Lastly, the Governor, after promising to establish order and laws among them, stated specifically his demands, thus:—

"1. From all: submission, without reserve, to the Queen's sovereignty and the authority of the law.

"2. From those who are in possession of plunder; restoration of that plunder.

"3. From those who have destroyed or made away with property; compensation for the losses sustained."

It is impossible to exaggerate the effect which the statements printed in italics, coming from the Queen's officer, at so solemn a time and in so solemn a manner, had upon the minds of the natives.

Hitherto they had cherished a hope that the Queen would sanction their native Sovereign, and be his protector. "How do we know," asked Tamihana, at a public meeting "that the Governor disapproves of our work? He never said so."[1] Now, for the first time, they learnt that, unless they gave up their King, the Governor had no option, but was commanded by the

[1] N. Z. Parl. Papers, 1860. E. No. 1, C. 3.

Queen to make war upon them. The question was put in the New Zealand Parliament, on what authority the statement had been made. I print the words of the despatch sent out by the Secretary of State, and of the declaration which the Government of the colony founded thereon, in parallel columns:—[1]

DUKE OF NEWCASTLE'S INSTRUCTIONS TO THE GOVERNOR.	GOVERNOR'S DECLARATION TO THE MAORIES.
. . . . "I am clearly of opinion that the attempts of the Maori Land League to prevent persons over whom they have no legitimate authority from alienating their lands should be inflexibly resisted.". . .	"No option now rests with the Governor; he has been commanded by her Majesty the Queen to suppress unlawful combinations, and to maintain her Majesty's Sovereignty in New Zealand."

The second passage printed in italics has always been a favourite doctrine with the Colonial Government, by whom it has been successfully revived at the present time. Ignoring the great principles of natural justice, the Government informs the natives that the Treaty of Waitangi is the *sole* foundation of their right to their lands, and that, but for the obligation of this treaty, the Europeans would help themselves to land whenever strong enough to do so. This monstrous theory has always been a favourite one with English colonists; and the New Zealand settlers have now a rare opportunity, by the aid of the British army, of carrying it into practical effect. The natives had the option given

[1] N. Z. Parl. Papers, 1861. F. No. 1, A. 9.

to them of submitting to the Queen's sovereignty, or fighting for the possession of their lands. They knew well enough that the former meant submission to be governed by the colonists; but their proud spirits can as little endure the rule of foreigners as our own, especially when threatened with what they think unjust spoliation if they refuse. Is it strange that high-spirited men, like Wiremu Tamihana, chose to be free, even at the risk of having to fight for their liberty?

The first copy of the Governor's declaration reached Tamihana at Te Rapa, and was read aloud by him to Rewi, Epiha, Wiremu Kingi, and other chiefs, who were on their way to a great meeting, to be held at Ngaruawahia. His audience expressed no opinion further than a want of confidence in any document proceeding from the Government.

Maories from all parts of Waikato, and the neighbourhood, began to gather at Ngaruawahia, on Monday, June 3d. The next few days, during which they continued to assemble, were spent, as usual, in talk and eating; and it was not until Thursday that any question of real importance was discussed. On that day the following points were brought forward:—

(1) The taking down of the King's flag, and breaking up the league into which they had entered to keep their land.

(2) The restoration of plunder, and payment for what had been destroyed.

(3) What should be regarded as a re-commencement of hostilities on the part of the troops.

The first question was disposed of almost entirely by Tamihana himself, who commenced by denying that the flag had ever been intended to do away with the supremacy of the Queen, as the protector of their rights and privileges: it was the badge of an agreement, made among themselves, to part with no land, and to hold meetings which should take cognizance of and suppress evil among themselves. He detailed the good that he considered had resulted from this combination: disputes about boundaries, existing at its commencement, had been set at rest; other disputes of the same kind, that had since arisen, had been quietly arranged; drunkenness, adultery, &c. had been suppressed; and they were now working to put down other evils also, that were still existing. He contrasted the good which had resulted from their combination, with the evil which had arisen from the Governor's taking soldiers to Taranaki. He denied that the flag had ever been the cause of the Waikatos going to Taranaki, but maintained that blood relationship would have driven them to it, had there been no flag. He particularized the relationship between some of the leading Waikatos who had gone to Taranaki and Wi Kingi. He expressed his good will to Europeans generally, declaring that he had never yet fought against them, but had been the means of stopping hostilities at Waitara; but he intimated that, in the event of war being recommenced, he could remain neutral no longer. He ended by saying that when the flag was set up upon any land fairly sold to the Queen, or when it otherwise interfered with the rights of the colonists, then would be the time for the Governor to interfere.

The meeting then proceeded to discuss the second point. The argument used was, that the Queen's troops had commenced the war, had attacked and destroyed Wiremu Kingi's pa, with all that was in it, had appropriated the horses and cattle, which he and others kept at Waitara, and burnt and destroyed their property; it was, therefore, unfair to demand restitution and compensation from them, while the Governor did not say a word about compensating Kingi. Moreover, very little plunder was brought away by the Waikatos, who did not go to plunder colonists, but to defend their friends from the attacks of the soldiers.

On the third head, it was resolved that the survey of any of the lands of Wi Kingi and his tribe, or the movement of troops to Mangatawhiri, or to any point which would clearly threaten a hostile movement against them, would be, as they expressed it, "a call to them to awake out of sleep."

The result of the Ngaruáwahia meeting, was a long letter written by Tamihana to the Governor. He first addressed himself to the question of the right to set up a Maori King[1]:—"When I betake myself to this work, I am rebuked. Now, when I worship God, I am not rebuked. This great name of God which is taught to me, why is this free to me? While of this name of King it is said to me, 'It is not right to use it, it is a sacred thing.' Enough, my friends, it is the practice between master and slave, that though the word of the slave be right, the master will not allow it to be right. That is the reason. Look at Deuteronomy xvii. 15.[2] Come, now, if the kings of all the countries came from Rome only, thence also might one come here. But is not the Queen a native of England? Nicholas, of Russia? Buonaparte, of France? Pomare, of Tahiti? Each from his own people. Then why am I and this people rebuked by you, and told that we must unite with you under the Queen? How was it that the Americans were permitted to separate themselves? Why are they not brought under the shadow of the Queen? for that people are of the same race as the English. Whereas, I am a foreigner, this island is not near to you. I am only near to you in Christ. Were all the different countries under one sovereignty—that of the Queen—it would be quite right; no one would differ, all this island would also be united to the rest. Instead of which

[1] N. Z. Parl. Papers. E. No. 1, B. 18. I have altered the translation in cases where the English is too obscure to convey Tamihana's meaning.

[2] "One from among thy brethren shalt thou set king over thee; thou mayest not set a stranger over thee, which is not thy brother."

the nations are separated from each other, and I also, standing here in my independence, desire to have a King for myself. Friends, do not be offended; let me make known my thoughts with respect to this great matter, which has furnished us with a cause of dispute. Is it on account of the Treaty of Waitangi that you are angry with us? Was it then that we were taken possession of by you? You are mistaken. Look at the case of two shops. The goods in one shop are sold; those of the other are not sold. Now, do you think that because of the selling of the goods in one shop, the goods of the other all went also? I say they did not go. Just so the assent of one chief did not dispose of what belonged to another. It is a similar case to that of the two shops. What harm is there in this name that you are angry about? The great things—the sacred things of God—have been given and accepted by us, Baptism, The Lord's Supper, and Marriage. And I supposed, my friends, that God's things were for us all. God did not make night and day for you only. No; summer and winter are for all; rain and wind, food and life are for us all. Were those things of yours indeed made for you only? I had supposed they were for all. If some were dogs and others men, it would be right to rebuke the dogs, and wrong to rebuke the men. My friends, why have you grudged us a King as if it were a greater name than that of God? If it were that God did not permit it, then it would be right to object, and it would be given up. But it is not he who forbids; and while it is only our fellow-man that is angry, it will not be given up. And now, my friends, leave this King to stand on his own place, and let it rest with our Maker whether he shall fall or stand. This is the end of this part of my words, and though they may be wrong yet they are openly declared.

"I will now commence upon another subject. At the beginning of this war at Taranaki, I meditated upon the haste of the Governor's wrath. There was no delay; no time given; he did not say to the Maories—Friends, I intend to fight at Taranaki. No, there was nothing said, not a word." After observing that no investigation into the rights of Wiremu Kingi and Te Teira had been made, he went on—"Do you consider that this was a just war? Is it good in your opinion to give vent quickly to anger? Yes! but in my opinion, to make haste to be angry is wrong. Paul says—'Charity suffereth long and is kind; is not easily provoked; thinketh no evil; suffereth wrong.' Friends, wherein is our Governor right, whom you believe in? Te Rangitake, who quietly reflected, is blamed by you, and the Governor, who hasted to anger, is supported and praised by you. Hence my thoughts are perplexed in my heart, for hasty wrath has been condemned by James, who has said—'Be slow to wrath, swift to hear. As it is, the precept in Proverbs xvi. 32 [1] has not

[1] "He that is slow to anger is better than the mighty; and he that ruleth his spirit than he that taketh a city."

been carried out. Friends, it is for me—for me who am a child—to get angry hastily. The proverb says, It is a child that breaks calabashes; it is a child that cries for food. Both these proverbs are for children. But for you to be so hasty is, in my opinion, wrong. Rather is it for you to act deliberately, as you have an example to go by. The Word of God is your compass to guide you—the laws of God."

He then explained the grounds which had led Waikato to take part in the Taranaki war. He enumerated four. (1) That it was Potatau who fetched Wi Kingi back from Kapiti to Waitara. (2) That some of the Ngatiawa were blood relations of Waikato. (3) They were fetched. They were written for by Kingi and Hapurona. (4) Potatau's word that land-selling should be stopped. "These were the grounds of Waikato's interference. If the Governor had considered carefully, Waikato would also have considered carefully; but the Governor was headstrong, and that was why the Waikatos went to help Wiremu Kingi. For Wiremu Kingi was a man who had not been tried, so that his fault might be seen to justify the infliction of severe punishment. You mock us when you say that this island is one, and the men in it one. For I look at the Pakehas, who madly rushed to fight with Wi Kingi.

"About the murders—my opinion is decided that they were not murders. Look—it was murder when Ihaia killed Te Whaitere (Katatore). He caused him to drink spirits, that his senses might leave him. He was waylaid and killed by Ihaia. That was a foul murder. You looked on and made friends with Ihaia. That which we regard as a murder, you have made naught of; and these which are not murders, are called so. This, I think, is wrong: for the Governor did not say to Wiremu Kingi and the Ngatiruanui, O friends, do not kill the unarmed. Nor did he direct that the settlers, living in the town, should be removed to Auckland, where there was no fighting, and there stay. He knew he had determined to make war at Taranaki, and therefore he should have told his unarmed people to remove out of the way.

"With regard to the plunder which you say is to be restored—listen to my opinion about that. The Governor was the cause of that. War was made on Wiremu Kingi, and he fled from his Pa. The Pa was burnt with fire; the church was burnt, and a box of Testaments; all was consumed with fire; goods, clothes, blankets, shirts, trowsers, gowns, all were consumed. The cattle were eaten by the soldiers, and the horses, one hundred in number, were sold by auction by the soldiers. Had the Governor given word not to burn the church, and to leave the goods and animals alone, Wiremu Kingi would have thought also to spare the property of the Pakeha. The former first commenced that road, and the latter merely followed upon it. Friends, look you to this—one hundred horses were sold by auction; property and food wasted; houses burnt with fire; and cattle eaten by the soldiers—whose work was that? The Governor's own, for he it was that commenced the work of confusion spoken of in his declaration."

This letter was received as a calm defiance. "All doubt," said the Governor, "is now at an end, and it is evident that if the Maories will not submit, this part of the colony must be abandoned by all who will not yield obedience to Maori law, of which the aptest symbol is the tomahawk."[1] Both sides began to prepare for war. Tamihana visited the tribes from Tauranga to the East Cape, to ascertain what support in men and ammunition he could count on. The Governor did not suspend negotiations, but it was known, that unless the Maories submitted within a definite time, Waikato would be invaded. The Rev. J. Wilson was sent up to Peria, to try to persuade Tamihana to have a personal interview with the Governor. To this he at last consented, but only, he said, in order that when the time came for their being enemies, the Governor might have heard his reasons. "My words," he said, "cannot go back. All I have to say is, that my words at the commencement will be adhered to. What I have to say in your presence is what I said at the commencement."

Even this slight concession was so unpopular in

[1] N. Z. Parl. Papers, 1862. E. No. 1, 10.

Waikato, that a storm of indignation arose. Porokoru and others intercepted Tamihana and told him that he might go if he chose, but they would hang him on his return. So vehement was the popular clamour that Tamihana was obliged to yield, and could not carry out his purpose.

It appeared now as if nothing could avert an immediate war of races, when the unexpected news that Sir George Grey had been re-appointed Governor of New Zealand suspended all further operations until his arrival.

CHAPTER IX.

THE INTERREGNUM.

AMONG Maories, the prompt execution of a plan alone commands that respect which is paid to strength: hesitation or delay, whatever the cause, is taken as conclusive proof of weakness. Nothing therefore could have been contrived more likely to remove what little respect the Maories still had for us and our proceedings than the two months of inaction during which Sir George Grey's arrival was anxiously expected by the colonists.

Diplomacy had brought the Government and the Maories to a distinct issue. The Governor had announced that unless certain terms were accepted he was commanded by the Queen to make war, and the Maories, after due deliberation, had firmly and absolutely rejected those terms. But instead of the uplifted sword falling, they were suddenly told that Governor Browne was to leave New Zealand, and Governor Grey was to reign in his stead. There is no doubt that many believed we were afraid to strike, and that as they could not be frightened, we had determined to try to gain our end in some other way.

The task which Sir George Grey found awaiting him on the 26th September, 1861, when he landed in Auckland, was about as difficult as can be conceived.

At Taranaki actual war was indeed suspended, but not a single point at issue in the quarrel had been settled. When Governor Browne arrived in Taranaki after Tamihana's interference, he found the Waikatos gone and Wiremu Kingi in the lands of Rewi, who would not allow him to see the Governor, but finally carried him off to rejoin his Waikato allies. The great chiefs having thus gone off, the Governor was reduced to the necessity of concluding peace with Hapurona, the Ngatiawa general. The Treaty, or Convention, or whatever it was, bore the title—"Terms offered to the Waitara insurgents," and was signed by Hapurona and twenty-four men, by "Maria, Jane, Betty," and sundry other women, and by several children, all of whom, according to the text of the document, had been for twelve months carrying arms against Her Majesty the Queen.[1] The most important stipulation therein made was, that all land in possession of the troops belonging to those who had borne arms against the Queen was to be disposed of by the Governor as he thought fit. This land consisted of territory, between the English settlement and Waitara, defended by several block-houses garrisoned by our men. In a subsequent article of the terms offered, the Governor stated that as

[1] N. Z. Parl. Papers, 1861. E. No. 1, B. 2.

he did not use force for the acquisition of land, but for the vindication of the law and protection of Her Majesty's native subjects in the exercise of their just rights, he should divide this land amongst its former owners, but reserve the sites of the block-houses and redoubts, and a small piece of land round each, for the public use, and exercise the right of making roads through the Waitara district.

In accordance with these stipulations, Mr. Rogan, an officer of the Land Purchasing Department, was sent down by Government to make a survey of the ground, mark out the properties of the various Ngatiawa owners, and lay out certain roads, and the sites of block-houses and redoubts which were to be retained.[1]

Mr. Rogan, on arriving at Taranaki, went to see Hapurona, who referred him to the Mataitawa natives, saying—"Go and see Arapeta and the people at Mataitawa. My peace is made with the Governor, as I ceded Onukukaitara, and am now under the Queen's protection. The subdivision of the land rests with the people; the Governor's object in having the land divided is good, but they are foolish blind people, ignorant of what is for their benefit, who will cause the matter to be confused." He added, in a complaining tone, that the Governor was a child in precipitating this matter at that time, before the wounds of the people were healed, and at the same time exhibited his own. In accordance with

[1] N. Z. Parl. Papers, 1862. E. No. 1, Sec. II. 9.

his suggestion, Mr. Rogan arranged a meeting with about twenty of the principal Mataitawa natives who had signed the terms of peace. They listened very attentively to the account of what the Governor had sent Mr. Rogan to do, after which Werata, a man who had signed the terms, rose and said: "I shall reply. Listen to our views on the matter of Waitara. Hapurona has given over Onukukaitara to the Governor, which we all assented to, and beyond that place we will not allow any interference." Another of the men who signed the terms followed—"You have come to inform us of the Governor's words about the Waitara. Hearken to mine. Onukukaitara has been given to the Governor for the wrong done to the Pakeha, and beyond that place the whole of the land you have described belongs to us. All the redoubts except Puketekauere, together with the entrenchments, are ours, and we have no intention of giving them up to the Governor in the way you propose. Not at all! We are satisfied with our own title to our lands, which are inherited from our fathers, and we shall have no interference with our property by the Governor; and remember, if you should come hereafter with your claim to measure, that is a path to death." Mr. Rogan found it quite impossible to survey the lands, and had to return to Auckland without accomplishing his mission. Such was the obedience which twelve months of military operations had conquered out of the Ngatiawa tribe.

As for the Ngatiruanui, the second section with which Governor Browne had purposed to treat, they took not the slightest notice of his presence in Taranaki, or of the terms of peace which he dictated to them. They retained possession of Tataraimaka—a detached block of European land about twelve miles south of Taranaki—from which, at the beginning of the war, they had driven out the thriving settlers by whom it had been occupied. During the war, Tataraimaika, like other places, had been overrun by the enemy, the farms destroyed, and the houses gutted. The Ngatiruanui now declared that they held it by right of conquest as a security for the disputed block of land at Waitara.

The attitude of Waikato was sufficiently described in the foregoing chapter:—their independence and their King they were determined to maintain at all hazards, whosoever the Governor of the Europeans might be.

The difficulty of making peace out of this mass of confusion was immensely enhanced by the impossibility of getting the Maories to believe any professions or promises that came from the British Government. The existence of this profound distrust at the close of the Taranaki war, is a fact supported by overwhelming testimony. "I should think it hopeless at the present time," said Sir William Martin, before the Waikato Committee, in 1860, "to effect anything. You must build upon confidence: and, at this time, confidence in the native mind towards Government is very small. What I mean is not that the recent proceedings of the Government have created that want of confidence for the first time, but that there is always a latent distrust of the intentions of the Pakeha, which those proceedings rekindled, and for a time increased enormously." [1]

Every pamphlet, every speech, every report of that time, alluded to the existing distrust as the chief difficulty in any future dealings with the race. The numerous officers sent by Sir George Grey into all the native districts of New Zealand immediately after his arrival were unanimous in reporting that their statements and professions were everywhere received with incredulity; and I can personally testify that any declaration made in the name of the Government in the Waikato district was usually received with the remark—"He maminga pea" (Perhaps it is a take-in.)

The causes of this distrust of our Government, which is always steadily on the increase, are not difficult to explain. The Maories in the course of their dealings with white men have discovered that the superior information of the latter renders natives always liable to be overreached. This feeling, joined to the extreme dislike which a proud, self-confident man has to be worsted in a bargain, has made the Maories, in all transactions of every kind with Europeans, suspicious and distrustful. Nothing but the most childlike truth

[1] N. Z. Parl. Papers, 1860. F. No. 3, 1228.

and simplicity will gain their confidence; and these, unfortunately, are the last virtues of which a civilized government is usually possessed. All the assertions, written or oral, made by a government, have usually some design lurking beneath them which the savage cannot fathom. He therefore feels an instinctive repugnance to admit such statements at all, unless confirmed by independent testimony. Besides this, as governments are constantly making promises, which it is afterwards impossible or inconvenient to keep, an appearance of bad faith cannot always be avoided. The New Zealand Government has been so often unfortunate in this respect, that even its own officers and the colonial public place a very slender reliance upon its promises; and the natives, who are less able to appreciate and make allowances for the exigencies of statecraft, are very blunt in their expression of opinion as to its character. I will give one example of what the natives would consider perfidy and we should call defective administration.[1] In selling territories to the Crown, many chiefs made it a condition of sale, that Crown grants for certain reserved portions of the territory should be issued to them, which would have given them a legal tenure and a right to let such lands to settlers, thus providing themselves with an income. Legal difficulties were, however, raised by the colonial law-officers as to such grants, and year after year passed

[1] N. Z. Parl. Papers, 1862. E. No. 1, sec. II. 24.

without the promises of Government being fulfilled. Soon after Sir George Grey's return, his attention was drawn to the subject, and the Government surveyor was directed to prepare a return of all cases in which Crown grants had been promised but never issued. So little care had been taken by Government to remember its engagements to the natives, that two months of unremitted rummaging amongst maps and original deeds of Cession in the Government offices was necessary before the tale of our bad faith could be furnished. It then appeared[1] that in no less than 178 cases, some occurring as long ago as the year 1848, Crown grants had been promised and the promises had never been fulfilled; and that in thirty of these cases Crown grants had actually been stipulated for as part of the consideration in the very deeds of Cession. Is there any wonder that the natives called the Pakeha "a humbugging people?"

It was expected by the New Zealand clergy and others, who had sympathized with the Maories in the Taranaki war, that the arrival of Sir George Grey would be hailed by the natives with delight, that they would rush into his arms, tell him their grievances, and follow his advice with confidence. The same opinion was also prevalent in England, whither most of the information about Maories that ever comes, comes at second hand through the New Zealand clergy.

[1] N. Z. Parl. Papers, 1862. E. No. 10.

But this supposed feeling of personal confidence did not really exist. Sir George Grey, during his former administration, had succeeded in attaching the greatest chiefs to himself, not so much by presents and pensions, of which he was less lavish than is generally supposed, but by exercising his extraordinary power of persuasion in personal intercourse. On the mass of the people he never made much impression. But at that time, the influence of the old chiefs, though decaying, had not altogether vanished; and Potatau, Wi Tako, and others, who had become Sir George Grey's personal friends, were quite capable of keeping the country in tranquillity. But the day for a policy of this kind had gone by when Sir George Grey returned to New Zealand. Most of the old chiefs were dead, and the rest had become the followers and not the leaders of the public will. The Maories had contracted a passionate desire for nationality which overwhelmed the personal predilections of their chiefs, so that Sir George Grey found his old friends either unwilling to sacrifice their patriotism to personal friendship, or powerless to persuade their tribes to follow them.

The chiefs of Waikato, Wiremu Tamihana, Rewi Maniapoto, and others, were neither to be bribed, cajoled, nor coaxed into pursuing any other object than the advancement of their Maori nationality. It is true, that Sir George Grey was more feared than the former Governor; he had a character among the Maories for deep subtlety, and his visible acts were always thought to cover some deeper scheme which he wished to conceal. It was a common saying of the Maories, that Governor Browne was an eagle, that came swooping upon them from the clear skies, while Governor Grey was a rat [no offence is implied by the name], that burrowed under ground, and would come up in their midst when and where they least expected. Moreover, the Maories understood their own position far better than their Pakeha friends. They were conscious of a firm determination to maintain a separate nationality and an independent King. They understood Governor Browne's plain declaration, that the Queen had ordered him to put the King down; and they could not divest themselves of the idea that Sir George Grey was sent to accomplish the same purpose in some way different to that which Governor Browne had threatened.

But of all obstacles to the restoration of confidence, the greatest was the necessity of keeping the large body of troops sent out to quell the Taranaki insurrection waiting in the country, in case another insurrection should break out. The expenditure in the town of Auckland, occasioned by the presence of the soldiers, was so great, and was thought to be so advantageous to the citizens, that not a hint of the real sentiments of the natives on this subject was ever allowed to find its way into the public journals, and therefore remained altogether unsuspected by the people in England;

neither was it likely that the Government would reveal anything which might deprive it of what all Governments so highly prize—the command of a large military force. But, in fact, the Maories asked themselves the simple question, Why are the troops remaining here? and as they could conceive no purpose except another war, they felt certain that the peace was hollow, and that the Pakeha was plotting some further attempt at coercion. Nothing short of the removal of most of the troops from New Zealand would have convinced the Maories that this was not so.

But though the presence of the troops caused distrust and alarm, it did not overawe the natives into submission. The Maories have never, hitherto, been convinced of our military superiority. What change General Cameron may have effected in their sentiments, it is yet too early to estimate. We have, on the whole, failed in every native war previous to that now proceeding. At first, a ridiculous estimate was made of the forces necessary to subdue New Zealand. It was said that a hundred militiamen could march from end to end of the island, and take every Pa in it. Our estimates have gradually increased, until at the present day we find twenty thousand men necessary for the conquest of a single district. In the war against Heke, the victory was won by Tamati Waka, and our native allies, in battles unrecorded in the common histories of New Zealand. At Taranaki, the loss of life—by which natives judge of success or defeat—was nearly equal on both sides; while the value of property actually destroyed or carried off by the Maories was estimated at 150,000*l*., our set-off being of the most trifling amount. Their estimate of their own powers, when talking quietly, and not gasconading at a public meeting, is moderate and just. In the open field, they say, our discipline, our rifles, and our artillery, make us irresistible; in the swamps and forests, their skill in avoiding close encounters, and their practice of ambuscades, which they call "the Maori artillery," render them superior, or at least equal, to our men. Their custom in warfare is to kill men and male children, except infants, whereever found: non-combatants are expected to move off from the scene of conflict. The better sort of chiefs have tried to adopt a more civilized mode of warfare, but in vain. They cannot control their people even in peace, and are not likely to do so in war. Murders—as we call them—thus committed, usually swell up the total of our loss nearly to an equality with theirs; and thus they have come to think that they can carry on warfare with us on pretty equal terms.

Besides the difficulties with which Sir George Grey had to contend in conciliating or conquering the tribes which had taken part in the Taranaki war, the state of the whole native population called for prompt measures of civilization and government. Actual insurrection had been confined to a small area, lawlessness and discontent were universal. Indeed, in every other virtue, except loyalty, the Waikatos surpassed rather than fell short of the other tribes in New Zealand. There was room for reform in the very streets of Auckland, where natives of unblemished loyalty defied the law before the windows of the Native Office and under the eyes of the police.

It is quite evident from the above description of the state in which Sir George Grey found affairs in New Zealand that a Governor, though possessing sole and absolute authority and a plentiful command of men and money, would have had before him a task of no ordinary difficulty.

But a hindrance, with which the Maories had nothing to do, hampered the Governor in all his efforts, and was at last the immediate cause of the final break down. Sir George Grey had not only to persuade the reluctant natives once more to submit to British rule, and to devise a plan by which they could be efficiently governed, but also to settle finally whether the people of England or the colonists were to be responsible for administering the Government of the Maories.

When the constitution was originally conferred upon New Zealand, the native inhabitants of the country were altogether forgotten. Maories were practically excluded from the franchise and from both Chambers of the New Zealand Legislature, although no special provision was made to secure proper care for their interests. Since that time a continuous struggle had been going on between the ministers of the colony and the authorities of the Imperial Government—the former eager to possess full power to govern the native as well as European race, and at the same time resisting to the utmost the corresponding obligation of providing money and men for coercing their coveted subjects should they rebel—the latter vainly striving to escape from the ever-increasing cost of protecting the settlers against their native neighbours, and as unsuccessful in either providing a government for the Maories or preventing the settlers from carrying out any particular scheme of native policy they might choose to patronize.

On the colonial side it was urged that the colonists had a much greater interest in the good government of the Maories, upon which not only their property but their lives depended, than the authorities at home; that the funds for efficient government of the natives would have to come out of the ordinary colonial revenues, the expenditure of which they had a just right to control; and that it was impossible so clearly to separate the interests of the natives from those of the settlers, that they could be entrusted to the care of different departments.

On the other hand, the answer of the Imperial authorities was, that in the first place the honour of the British nation was pledged by the Treaty of Waitangi to a certain definite policy in native affairs, and that in the second place, so long as the British Government provided the military force, which protected the settlers, it was but reasonable that the Imperial officer should have some control over matters which might saddle the British nation with the cost of expensive and interminable wars.

The very first colonial ministry that succeeded in firmly seating itself in power, began the agitation of these questions, and it has been kept up continuously ever since. But until Sir George Grey's second Governorship, the Imperial Government nominally retained the whole responsibility in their own hands. The Governor of New Zealand acted entirely on his own opinion in all native matters. A staff of secretaries, commissioners, and clerks, neither responsible to the New Zealand Assembly, nor removable by the colonial ministers, carried out the Governor's policy, both in the purchase of native land, and the general management of the Maories. But with all this apparent authority, the Governor had very little real power, in as much as his colonial advisers, whom he was bound to inform of everything that was done, had a most effective check on him. In the Statute which established the New Zealand Constitution, the sum of *7,000l.* per annum only had been placed beyond the control of the Colonial Legislature, as a provision for carrying on the Government of the natives. This sum, quite insufficient in itself to pay the expense of an effective government, including the costs of District Courts and Circuits, and the pay of the various secretaries and other officials, had besides been, to a large extent, disposed of and forestalled in the following manner.

A correspondence took place, in May, 1853, between the then Governor and the heads of the three principal religious bodies in New Zealand—the Bishop of New Zealand, the Superintendent of Wesleyan Missions, and the Roman Catholic Bishop of Auckland. Sir George Grey stated that, it having become necessary for him to recommend, for the sanction of Her Majesty's Government, the mode in which he proposed that the funds reserved for native purposes should be applied, he was prepared to recommend that the following sums should be placed at the disposal of each religious body for the purpose of native education:—[1]

Church of England	£3,500
Wesleyan Society	2,300
Church of Rome	1,200
Total	7,000

The valuable assistance was thankfully accepted by all to whom it was offered, but "Sir George Grey only procured the approval of the Secretary of State to the following appropriations, viz. :—

[1] N. Z. Parl. Papers, 1856. A. No. 7.

Church of England	£3,500
Wesleyan Society	1,600
Church of Rome	800
Total	5,900."[1]

At the earnest request of his colonial advisers, the succeeding Governor, Colonel Browne, "consented to devote to the use of schools, the remaining portion of the 7,000*l.* (viz. 1,100*l.*) which Sir George Grey had not previously appropriated to them. The Governor made this concession only because the sum was too small to be of importance, and because it had not been expended in the best manner; the salary of the Resident Magistrate at Auckland, whose duties were almost exclusively connected with Europeans, having formed one of the items."[2]

Finally, the Governor received the following instructions from the Secretary of State:—

"So far as public faith is engaged towards particular local bodies for the maintenance of Sir George Grey's scheme or otherwise, it must be strictly preserved, and you are authorized to adhere to this principle against all opposition."[3]

Thus Governor Browne was left without any funds whatever under his own control, to carry on the government of the natives.

[1] Mr. Richmond's Minute. N. Z. Parl. Papers, 1858. E. No. 1 A.
[2] Governor's Minute. Ibid.
[3] Despatch of Right Hon. H. Labouchere, 16th December, 1857.

The colonists would not consent to vote money f native purposes generally, but only for such speci objects as they approved. Governor Browne, therefore, being destitute of funds, could not exercise his theoretical right to follow his own plan, but was always obliged to consult the Colonial Ministers, who alone could supply him with the means of acting at all. Thus, at the time of Sir George Grey's return, the colonists were getting pretty much their own way in the management of native affairs, and had at the same time the advantage of being able to cast the responsibility for anything that might be wrong upon the Imperial officer, who was nominally possessed of sole authority.

The British Government had at last become weary of this arrangement, in which the advantage was all on the Colonial side, while the risk was all borne by them; which had, moreover, totally failed to give the Home Government any real voice in the management of the Maories. Sir George Grey was to put an end to the double government.

It is worth noticing that the contest between the different departments for the government of the Maories began just at the time when the latter were making up their minds to govern themselves. Since then, the influence of the colonists in native affairs, and the determination of the Maories to be separate and independent, have both steadily increased. At the same time, all our efforts to escape from the expensive luxury of owning a colony like New Zealand have been in vain. The cost of the strife between settlers and natives, which must be either advanced or guaranteed by the Imperial Government, grows rapidly, and already forms a considerable item in the annual expenditure of the mother country.

CHAPTER X.

SIR GEORGE GREY.

In the early morning of the 26th of September, 1861, H.M.S. *Cossack* ran quietly into the Auckland harbour, with the new Governor on board.

A few days later, Colonel Browne took leave of New Zealand, amidst tokens of general good-will. Few persons, acquainted with the native affairs of the colony, attached much blame to the departing Governor for the misfortunes which marked the close of his term of office. The mistakes of his predecessors, aggravated by a vicious system of double Government, were the true cause of a disaster which it was difficult, if not impossible, for him to have averted.

No sooner had the new Governor been installed in office, than addresses of welcome poured in from loyal chiefs of the North and of the South, couched in terms complimentary to Sir George Grey, and reflecting on the wickedness of the Waikatos, who, as one writer said, were "wandering sheep that had strayed on the path of Balaam the son of Bosor." But the stray sheep remained aloof, and made no sign. They were not sulky, as most people said, but were wise enough to see that their interest was to let Sir George Grey make the first move. For them to have taken any step would have been a mistake. Welcoming the new Governor would have looked like submission; and standing purely on the defensive, they had no demands to make.

The frightful calamities and the ruinous expense that a war undertaken at that time would have inflicted on the colony, rendered the Governor unwilling to announce to the Waikatos any intention on his part of enforcing the terms which his predecessor had determined to exact. He waited on, from day to day, hoping that, if he made no demands or threats, the chiefs might, out of personal regard to himself, do all that was wanted.[1] But the strength of the Maori enthusiasm for an independent King, which overwhelmed all personal friendships and extended to natives who had never seen or known the Governor, made the realization of this hope impossible.

Tamati Ngapora, an old chief, who had taken Potatau's place at Mangere, and who, though a supporter of the Maori King, had always striven to maintain peace between the European and Maori races, at last went up the country to tell the Waikatos of the pacific intentions which the Governor had expressed to him, and to get them, if he could, to send down a deputation. The natives on the river were quietly pursuing their

[1] N. Z. Parl. Papers, 1862. E. No. 1, See II. 3.

ordinary business of planting potatoes and wheat. There was no excitement, and little talk about the King and national flag, but all expressed that same quiet determination to maintain both, from which they have never varied. Tamati went up to Ngaruawahia, where he found the Court in a ferment, because the Queen had just committed the serious offence of being tattooed, in defiance of a law which they had made forbidding the practice. They held a Runanga about this freak of the Queen, fined her 10*l*., and Honi Papita, who abetted her, 5*l*.; but both criminals refused to pay. Tamati, on his arrival, sent a "message of love" with which he had been charged by the Governor, to the principal chiefs, and begged them to meet at Ngaruawahia, to settle who should go down to Auckland. Wi Tamihana, after the excitement of making peace at Waitara, and issuing his letter of defiance to the Governor, had retired to rural life at Peria, where he had been busy, for many weeks past, in company with his eldest son, a lad of fifteen, ploughing up acre after acre of land, and sowing wheat, for the support of the children in his village-school. The school was, however, much reduced in numbers, and the people of his village were naked and barbarous, owing, as he said, "to the madness of that madman who was gone." He expressed a wish to go to Auckland, and have an interview with the new Governor, but did not think his tribe would let him do so. His visiting the Governor would be regarded by the Ngatimaniapoto, and the more violent party, as an act of weakness, and would be likely to occasion an open rupture.

Wi Kingi, the hero of Taranaki, was in Rewi's custody at Kihikihi. The people of that village were gaily attired in military caps and coats, and carried rifles and accoutrements taken at Taranaki. Rewi and all his myrmidons refused even to be present at Ngaruawahia to discuss the propriety of sending a deputation to Sir George Grey. They said, "If Governor Grey will let the King stand, then we will go down to see him; but if he asks what Governor Browne did, then we will not go down." They threw doubts on the assertion that the Governor was a man of peace. "Who fought," they asked, "Honi Heke and Rangihaeta, when he was Governor here before?"

On the whole, there was little prospect of the Waikatos submitting to Sir George Grey. Their side, at least, was quite firm. Every man was resolved to stand by the King and the national flag, at all hazards.

The result of the assembly which Tamati Ngapora convened at Ngaruawahia, was that a deputation from Waikato did go to Auckland to see Sir George Grey. But the interview was not satisfactory. The natives declared their resolution to be separate and independent, in a manner too distinct to be mistaken; and Sir George Grey could merely reply by expressing general disapproval of their sentiments. The victory of Waikato was complete. They had been threatened with war, if they did not give up their King and flag. They had refused; and the Governor was not going to carry out the threat.

As the Governor would not make war, and the Maories would not submit to the conditions of peace, Sir George Grey was obliged to postpone the performance of the first part of his task for a time, and turn his attention to the second; namely, the invention of a plan for the government of the native population. A scheme was put down on paper, and promulgated as the "new policy" to be pursued in native affairs. This was received by the Governor's friends with the most lavish praise, which it was the easier to bestow, in as much as time must necessarily elapse before it could be certainly known whether the experiment would succeed or fail.

Lawlessness was justly pronounced to be the great evil of the land; and the remedy applied was a machinery not for enforcing obedience, but for making laws. Every country has some staple manufacture, and there can be no question that laws are the staple manufacture of New Zealand.

The whole native territory was to be divided into about twenty Districts, each to be presided over by an English Commissioner.

The District was subdivided into a half-a-dozen Hundreds, each of which should select two native magistrates, a warden, and five constables. These officers were to be paid by Government—a magistrate, from 30*l.* to 50*l.* per annum; a warden, 30*l.*; and the constables, 10*l.* each, with a suit of uniform every year.

The two magistrates from each Hundred were to constitute the District Runanga, presided over by the Civil Commissioner.

An Act of the New Zealand Assembly had conferred on the Governor and his Executive Council power to make bye-laws in native districts about cattle, trespass, drunkenness, suppression of nuisances, and so forth. The Governor conferred on the District Runanga power to make bye-laws on these subjects, which, if approved by the Governor in Council, would be valid under the above Act.

It is unnecessary to give more than a brief sketch of the system proposed, because the original plan underwent considerable modification before it was attempted to be carried out at all in the Waikato district.

The boon practically conferred on the natives was the distribution of about 2,000*l.* per annum in salaries to the principal chiefs in each district, and the right to pass resolutions on certain petty subjects, which, if approved by the Governor *and by the Colonial Ministers*, would be, by their proclamation, made into laws. On all the greater concerns of life, they had no power to legislate. It is undoubtedly true, that the need of the natives was not so much new laws, as some controlling authority to enforce obedience to the old ones. There is, perhaps, only one matter on which, for the sake of the Maories themselves, fresh legislation was, and still is, urgently called for. That is adultery. The English law on this subject, which has been promulgated amongst them, has produced the most frightful demoralization. Actions for damages on account of adultery, constitute a large majority of the cases heard before native Runangas and resident magistrates in native districts. I have myself seen the whole population of Peria gathered in the open air, on a summer's evening, to hear the disgusting details of vice told out by the actors themselves, before men, women, and young boys and girls, apparently without shame. Husbands retain adulterous wives for purposes of emolument. The better sort of natives are quite alive to the mischief of such gross immorality. This is the one subject upon which they have made the most strenuous efforts to legislate for their countrymen. Wi Tamihana once read me a code of laws, drawn up for the Ngatihaua tribe, which was entirely on this subject. Though far from perfect, great improvements were made on the law we had taught them. For example, no damages could be recovered by a husband after a first offence; in subsequent cases, the fines levied on the woman, and on her paramour, were converted to public use. If the offence were committed in the "whare puni" (large public sleeping-house), no damages could be recovered by the husband: it was his own fault, said the law, for being too idle to build a private house. Tamihana had urged upon the Runanga which drew up this code, to make adultery criminal, and punish it by fine levied on the offending parties for the public use; but he could not carry his point.

I am quite at a loss to know at which of the numerous law factories in New Zealand a statute to meet the wants of the natives in this particular could have been provided. The King's Runanga at Ngaruawahia, which had the best notion of the sort of law wanted, was not powerful enough to give effect to the idea. The Colonial Assembly was quite unfit for the task. There are few colonial senators who possess any special knowledge of the social habits and wants of natives; the matter did not affect any pecuniary interest in the colony; it could be neither made a party question, nor meddled with except at the risk of giving offence to the clergy; it was, therefore, altogether neglected. In 1857, the attention of the New Zealand Government was called repeatedly to this subject by Mr. Fenton, in his official capacity. He wished to bring in a Bill[1] to give magistrates "power, in adultery cases, to award punishment by way of fine, instead of compensation to the husband." "The woman," he said, "is sometimes so worthless, that no money should be paid to her husband; but still, a fine, acting as a restraint on vice,

[1] N. Z. Parl. Papers. E. No. 1, C. page 31.

would be beneficial." The necessity of legislation was acknowledged both by the Governor and the Colonial Ministry. "For these offences (adultery and seduction)," says Colonel Browne, "at present there is practically no redress, which is, of course, incomprehensible to a savage."[1] "One of the highest judicial authorities in England," write Ministers, "has lately declared, in open court, that our own law on these matters is a disgrace to our civilization. We concur in this sentiment, and feel satisfied that the English rules cannot be recommended for native adoption."[2] Yet not only has no Bill such as that proposed by Mr. Fenton been ever introduced, but the subject has never, so far as I am aware, been once mooted in the Legislature.

While it thus appears that in Sir George Grey's scheme there were no means of supplying that sort of legislation which was most needed by the natives, no provision whatever was made for teaching the Maories the great lesson of obedience to constituted authority. The five constables (whose name, for fear of offence, was changed to "messenger") were only to be employed to carry letters and serve writs.

The first tribe to which the "new institutions" were made known was the Ngapuhi, at the Bay of Islands. The northern natives, since the rapid progress of colonization had been checked by the destruction of Korerareka and the war of 1848, have been on the most

[1] N. Z. Parl. Papers, 1860. F. No. 3, A. 1. [2] Ibid.

friendly terms with Europeans. Sir George Grey's reception was enthusiastic, and the Maories were charmed with the "policy." The welcome was, on one occasion, such as would have tried the nerves of any less cool and experienced man. A crazy old chief made a most violent and hostile oration, dancing with excitement, and declaring that he would separate from the Governor and fight him that very day. He concluded by jumping upon the verandah where the Governor was seated, and offering to stab him with a long steel-pointed rod,[1] which he had brandished during his speech. He then abruptly burst out laughing, shook hands, and said that he was only joking, and was really very glad to see his old friend Grey.

Upon one point of the "new policy" the Ngapuhi audience insisted on the Governor's being very explicit. This was the amount of salary to be distributed. On this subject many questions were everywhere asked, and the answers given were so satisfactory, that all said: "Great is the excellence of Governor Grey's scheme."

Having thus experimented on the Ngapuhi, it remained to be seen what effect the "new policy" would produce in Waikato. Most of those natives who had acted under Mr. Fenton were clamorous to have Sir George Grey's institutions established amongst them. The proposed salaries would be the realization of that hope which had hitherto proved but a dream. It was

[1] Used for digging Kauri gum.

soon arranged that Sir George Grey should visit Waata Kukutai's tribe at Taupari, in Lower Waikato, where a great feast was to be held, provided of course at Government expense, to which chiefs from all parts of the Waikato were to be invited.

Before the feast took place, an opportunity occurred of explaining the proposed plan for the better government of the Maories to Wiremu Tamihana. A letter from him was received at the Native Office, reporting the following case:—The Ngatihaua had a vessel, on board which it had been decided by the Runanga of the tribe that no spirits should be carried. A Frenchman named Louis had seen her in Auckland, put three kegs of spirits on board, and arrived with them in the Piako. On hearing of this, the Maori Runanga had taken away the kegs, and given them into the charge of the owners of the vessel, in whose hands they were still lying untouched. The object of Tamihana's letter was to inquire whether the seizure of the spirits was right or wrong. Sir George Grey thereupon sent me up the country to Peria to explain that, under the proposed system, traffic in spirits could be legally suppressed, and that the Government wished to assist the chiefs as much as possible, in promoting the good of their people in this respect. As soon as my errand was told, Tamihana replied at once, that long ago he had earnestly besought help from the Government, and had besought in vain, and that he had therefore tried to set up a

Government of his own. "If a *weka*,"[1] said he, "once escapes from the snare, you never catch that same bird again." As to the adoption, however, he continued, of Sir George Grey's plan of government, it was a matter not for him alone, but for the assembled chiefs of Waikato to decide—the young men might be persuaded to agree to it easily enough, but the old men would give a great deal of trouble. For three days Tamihana remained in a state of indecision, meditating on the Governor's proposal.

At length, after this interval, Ti Oriori arrived in Peria. Tamihana always appeared to have much respect for this man's opinion, though he more than once told me that Ti Oriori was a greedy impostor. The two consulted together, and decided to go over to hold a meeting at Arikirua, in Horotiu, where the greater part of the Ngatihaua were busy putting in crops.

The Ngatihaua tribe assembled at Arikirua very soon made up their minds upon the Governor's scheme. At first they expressed some suspicion that the real object of the plan was to get them to do away with the King. Ti Oriori said that the usual way of catching owls was for one man to shake some object before the bird to attract attention, while his mate slipt a noose over its head from behind; so Sir George Grey had sent his mate to dazzle them with laws and institutions, while he was watching his chance of entangling them in the

[1] A New Zealand bird, like a land-rail.

meshes of the Queen's sovereignty. However, in the end, after some discussion, they all agreed to obey laws made in the first place by their Runangas, confirmed by King Matutaera, and finally approved by the Governor. The ground on which they admitted the Governor to a voice in enacting their laws was, that there were many European settlers resident in the Waikato country, whose interests were bound up with their own. If the Governor, they said, would allow the King and national flag to stand, all other matters would be accommodated by the whole of Waikato without any difficulty.

After this meeting, Tamihana, observing that in the multitude of councillors there was safety, got upon his horse and rode away to Tamahere to lay the matter before another section of his tribe at that place. On arrival, he sent a message round to the farms and hamlets dotted about Horotiu, summoning the people to Tamahere. At night, an excited crowd crammed itself into the village meeting-house, there to hear the plans of Sir George Grey admirably expounded by Wi Tamihana, who brought out the leading points of the scheme quite as well as any civilized orator could have done. The other speeches were all hostile and uproarious. Paora, Wetini's younger brother, the man who had escaped from Mahoetahi with a bayonet stuck in his body, made a most effective speech, abusing all the acts of the British Government, from the Treaty of Waitangi downwards. He said they would not come back again under the Queen's rule. They had so often been "humbugged" by us, that they felt certain, if they agreed to this proposal, they should be "humbugged" again. He wanted to know, whether we should send our laws to the Maori King, to obtain his assent on behalf of the Maories, if they sent theirs to the Governor. Speaker after speaker followed in the same strain, crying out with enthusiasm that they would stand by their King and their flag. The next morning, Tamihana said: "You have now heard the opinions of the men of Arikirua and Tamahere. Meet me to-morrow at Ngaruawahia: let us hear what they say there."

At Ngaruawahia a law had recently been passed, forbidding Europeans to enter the village unless by special permission. Ignorant of this innovation, I arrived there next day and sat down to talk with a Ngatihaua chief till Wiremu Tamihana should appear. Two of the King's policemen, zealous for the new law, came down to turn me away, and a whispered controversy between them and my Ngatihaua friend ensued; they urging him, and he refusing, to order me away. Not knowing the subject of their whispering, I went down to the river-side and got into a small canoe, meaning to lean over and drink. The canoe being light, turned over and soused me in the Waikato. This decided the controversy on the bank above. Even the King's policemen would not send a half-drowned man away till his clothes were dried and some food had been cooked. Before their zeal again got the better of their hospitality, Tamihana arrived, having galloped all the way from Te Rapa, where he, for the first time, had heard of the new law, and feared that I should be sent away.

Upon his arrival, the Council of the Maori King was summoned, and the Governor's proposed plan was explained. It was discussed by the chiefs of the Council in the most able and temperate manner. There was no talk then about the salaries, but much about the way in which the institutions would work, and the security the Maories would have for the preservation of their liberty and independence. They all said that if some plan of the sort had been carried out five or six years ago, there would never have been a Maori King. Their final resolution was unanimous; that if the Governor would let their King and flag stand, they would adopt his plans and try to work with him for the common good. There was a difference of opinion about having a European officer to live amongst them. Tamihana and a few others advocated it, but the majority desired to wait until confidence in the European Government was restored. However, the great meeting at Taupari, they said, to which a deputation from the King was to be sent, would take place in a few days; there they would hear Sir George Grey's intentions from his own mouth, and would be then better able to form their opinions on his policy. Their final decision was therefore postponed.

This great meeting at Taupari, upon which the Waikatos looked as the crisis of their fate, began on the 12th December, 1861, and was continued on several subsequent days. The new gifts of Government were publicly bestowed upon Waata Kukutai's tribe, and that chief was installed as head magistrate of the Taupari Hundred, with a salary of *50l.* per annum. The explanation of the plans to him and his people, and to others who wished also to be loyal and get salaries, occupied much of their time. But the most important event at the meeting was the dialogue between the Governor on one side, and Tipene and Herewini on the other. These two chiefs were selected as the spokesmen of the King party, not because of their own rank and importance, but for their talents in oratory, which were very highly estimated by their countrymen. To appreciate the importance of the conversation, it must be remembered that all Waikato was waiting to hear the Governor deliver his opinion about the Maori King, to see whether the present Governor had that commission from the Queen, to suppress their national combination, which the former Governor had announced.

The only point brought out by Sir George Grey's catechizing Herewini on the first day, was, that the Waikatos did not intend to force their King upon tribes who would not have him.[1] The Governor then said: "I felt some anxiety to know whether you

[1] N. Z. Parl. Papers, 1862. E. No. 8.

intended to force your King on tribes who did not want him, because I should have been obliged to protect them from such a course of things; but now my mind is at ease. I don't care what you call him: King or chief, I do not mind him. What I shall now do is to set to work with all the chiefs who will help me, and do all the good I can; and those who will not aid me, I shall not care for. I shall look upon each chief as the King of his own tribe; and if two or more tribes come and say—'This is our King,' I shall say—'Well, if you like to give up your chieftainship to another man, well and good, I shall not care.' I shall have twenty kings in New Zealand before long, and those kings who work with me shall be wealthy kings, and the kings of wealthy people."

The second day Sir George Grey made a long speech to the Waikatos. He said: "Salutations to you all! I have returned to this country to see my old friends, and to be the Governor of the two races—the Europeans and the Maories. You must not think I am only come as a friend of the Europeans, to punish the Maories for anything they have done. I am come as the friend of both, and as an impartial person, to see what can be done. I have been sent, with a very large force at my disposal, to put an end to war and discord, and to establish law and order; and if the force now here is not sufficient, I can have as much more as I like. I know I shall have to answer for the way in which I may use that force; not to Europeans, not to Maories, but at the Judgment Seat where I shall have to stand hereafter: and knowing that as I do, you may depend that I shall use the means at my disposal to the best of my ability, for the good of those under me. The people of Waikato may therefore rest assured, and I give them my word, that I shall never attack them first, and that they may rest in peace and quietness.

"Having now said these things, I will talk to you with reference to the points of difference between you and the Government, and tell you my news.

"The first point is, the property stolen from the Europeans. You will remember that this has been demanded to be given up, if you do not wish to be attacked. In my position as Governor, I do not care whether this is given back or not; but I will tell you what I think. You know, if in a tribe one steals from another, that the whole tribe rises and punishes the thief. Now I say that the Maories and Europeans are one tribe; and to say that I will attack the tribe that has the plunder, is to say that it is of a different tribe to ourselves, which I will not admit; and, therefore, whenever a man is caught with any of the stolen property, he will, even if it be twenty years hence, be taken before the judge, and, if found to be a thief, he will be punished. I do not pretend to say whether he is a thief or not; the judge will do that when he is caught. Now I have told you this as Governor, I will speak to you as a friend on this point. I look upon the Maories as one 'hapu' of the great family that inhabits this island. When a 'hapu' looks upon a thief as a disgrace, it says to him, 'Give up the plunder, and don't bring disgrace upon us.' Therefore I recommend you all to try and persuade the people who have the plunder to give it up. All nations are watching you, and I am jealous for you, and cannot bear to be the Governor of the Maori, and for other nations to say, 'They (the Maories) are a nation of thieves.' Just in the same way, the father of two children, when he sees one of them take things from the other, tries to make him make restitution. So, when I see Taranaki has been plundered, I know the Europeans can never feel reconciled to the Maories unless some restitution is made; and I would persuade them to make it.

"The next thing is about the roads. You seem to think that roads through the country would do no good. I think they would improve the value of the lands through which they pass; and if you think I want to spend money in making roads through the lands of people who don't want them, thereby enriching them at the expense of others, you must think me a fool. In the country of the Europeans, they have to pay the greater part of the cost of the roads before the Government helps them. In the same way, I should be very unwilling to make roads through native land, even if the owners came and asked me to do so, unless they paid part of the money. The only case in which I would pay for them would be, when the roads led to some very distant place, which would benefit other districts, besides benefiting the lands of the natives through which they pass.

"I will give you an instance of what I mean. I hear Waata Kukutai is going to cultivate on the top of the mountain (pointing to the hill behind the village). If he does not make a cart-road up to the cultivation, I shall think him a very cruel man; for, otherwise, he will kill or injure all the women, who will have to bring down the loads of produce; and the children that will be borne by them will be decrepit, and thus the tribe will be lost. But do you think I shall be such a fool as to come with troops and war to make the road? No! I tell him what will be the result if he does not make the road, and I leave it to him.

"I should like to see all the land covered with carts and horses and cattle, and all the people well dressed and flourishing; but I shall not come and cut their throats if they don't like to be so. How should I like to be judged, with a row of dead bodies laid out before me, and one should say, 'How is this?—Who slew them?' and I should have to say, 'I did, because they were foolish, and did not know what was good for themselves'? Look there (pointing to a heavily-laden bullock-dray passing), would you rather see your women laden with those things? Those men who like their women to be killed with hard work, and who do not like oxen and sheep, why, it is their own look-out.

"Another thing—you must not think that I shall let travellers, either Europeans or Maories, be stopped and plundered. It is a very serious offence. I shall not make war upon the tribe; but if ever I catch the individual, he shall be punished.

"Now, the third thing—the King—I will talk about. You heard Waata Kukutai say, I assented to the King and the flag. I must explain what I mean. If a tribe, or two, or three, or more, call their chief a King, and stick up a flag, I think it nonsense, and don't mind it. I think it a foolish thing to do, and that it may lead to bad consequences; but I shall not quarrel with them until the bad consequences come. You must recollect that this King affair is mixed up with many things that ought not to be. For instance, I hear that at the Runangas many of those people who have plundered the Europeans are present, and I think you should not associate with such wicked people. If I was in the King's place, I would not associate with bad people. I even understand that people who have been receiving pay as Assessors from Government, have been associating with these people; and I think it wrong that people who are paid for putting down robbers should mix with them.

"In the same way, I hear that the King has been making rules to prevent travellers going about. This is wrong; and if he does wrong things, and he is caught, he will be tried like another man, and punished. I can't help it: you must not misunderstand me: any man may stop people from coming on to his land; but where an accustomed line of road runs from one place to another, no man may block it up. You must be careful not to think that in this matter I shall quarrel with you all. I, as Governor, have nothing to do with it; the cause must be tried by the judge, or by your Runangas when you have them, between the traveller and the owner of the soil. I speak to you as a friend; and as the name of 'King' has been mixed with many troubles, and is much disliked by many people, I would get rid of it, and find some other name; and then, with the other chiefs of the district, I will work to establish law and order in the country. If they don't care to have me as a friend, to help them and work with them, they must do without me. I can't help it.

"I will now speak to you on one other point—the land.

"I understand that there is a jealousy that I shall buy land from a few people, and take it by force from others; you may depend upon it I shall not do this. Until all that are concerned are consulted, no land will be taken. I will not send people about the country teasing and troubling you about the sale of your lands. I should be a bad man if I did so—particularly in the Waikato—as whenever I have asked you for land you have given it to me. Did I not ask you for the land on which the Mission (pointing to it) stands, and did you not give it? Did I not ask you for land for Mr. Ashwell's station, and did you not give it? So also with other places.

"Now, as I have said so many hard things of you, I must say that I think, in very few countries, men would have so liberally given up land for school purposes as you have done; and in all countries it is said you have in this thing well done.

"Now I will tell you what I propose to do for the future. I do not mean to say, that in as far as institutions for the maintenance of law and order have not been established in the country among you, your interests have not been overlooked. You must have seen that the Europeans have been allowed to make rules and laws for themselves, and those who made them have been paid for doing so; while the Maories have been left unprovided for, and those that did make laws were ill paid. I do not feel that I am without blame in the matter myself. When I was the Governor here formerly, I ought to have seen further ahead, and what civilization would lead to and require. I propose therefore now, that wherever people live in considerable numbers, the island should be divided into districts, and Runangas appointed to make laws for them, and to determine if roads are to be made, and what share of the expenses the people of the district will have to pay. They will also determine the ownership and boundaries of land, and if it may be sold, and by whom—and whether spirits may be sold, and under what regulations. In fact, they will have to make laws on all subjects concerning their own interests, and when these are sent to me and I have consented to them, they will be binding alike both on Maori and European.

"Native magistrates will also be appointed, and people under them, to administer the laws; and all these people that are employed will have salaries, and be paid regularly on the first of each month like Europeans. You will thus see by what I have said, that the way I intend to put down *evil* is by putting up *good*, not by employing force.

"One thing I have omitted to tell you. For each district a medical man will be stationed, and salaries will be provided for the native clergymen or schoolmasters; and for each 'hapu' that wishes to put aside land for the support of a clergyman, I will endeavour to get a minister. One of the great evils has been, that there has been no opening for the young men, chiefs and others, who have been highly educated. Now I make all these openings—clergymen, magistrates, doctors, &c.—and a young chief may become one of these, and not have to go to work on his land like a common man, but live like a gentleman.

"Now don't you say I have not come here to conquer and kill you; I have come to conquer and kill you too

—*with good.* Now I have done, and if any of you want to ask questions about what I have said, I am here to answer."

After others had spoken, Tipene rose and said:—"What I shall speak about is, the King, the flag, and the plunder. You formerly were Governor of this Island; and as for us, we were with you. After your departure, we considered that we should raise up a King for ourselves, to stop blood-shedding and repress the evils of the land, and put an end to wars. Men were selling land throughout the island. We thought, New Zealand will be gone. We saw the land which had gone, covered with cattle, horses, and sheep, and men employed fencing against cattle. We then said, let the land be withheld. We began it, and others joined. We saw brother quarrelling with brother; so one man was appointed to suppress fighting and stop the blood.

"Land was bought at Taranaki; we heard it was bought improperly, and presently disturbance arose about it. We had not heard that the Pakeha was fighting at Taranaki, until the soldiers had gone on board the ships: then we heard. Now this offence was from the Pakeha; hence we said, we are strangers to one another. We are divided; you on one side, we on the other."

THE GOVERNOR.—If any tribe refuse to have your King, will you attack them?

TIPENE.—I have not yet heard of any tribe within this island that has refused.

THE GOVERNOR.—Until you give me a fair answer to that question, I shall think you refuse my words of peace.

TIPENE.—This is my reply. I do not know that any are outside. Let me hear it, and then, indeed, I shall say—we are a divided people. But we will not attack them.

THE GOVERNOR.—If any tribe sells land to us, will you attack it?

TIPENE.—We shall not consent. We and our land are with the King. We shall therefore withhold it.

THE GOVERNOR.—If the man wishing to sell his land has not pledged it to the King, will you attack him?

TIPENE.—No, he would be a stranger to us.

THE GOVERNOR.—But if he had, and afterwards altered his mind?

TIPENE.—The land will be withheld because he will have been imposing upon us.

THE GOVERNOR.—What, by force?

TIPENE.—No, we shall not strike; but if he sees us withholding it, and attacks us, then we shall strike. He will not be allowed to sell his land, but we shall not assail and kill him; we shall not do as you Pakehas do.

THE GOVERNOR.—How about the stolen property, the cattle and horses?

TIPENE.—My name for that is "spoils lawfully taken in war."

THE GOVERNOR.—How about the land of the Europeans, on which the Maories have gone?[1]

TIPENE.—Is there no Maori land at Waitara in possession of the Pakeha?

THE GOVERNOR.—What land do you mean? Do you mean the block that was fought about?

TIPENE.—I ask you, is there no Maori land at Waitara in possession of the Pakeha?

THE GOVERNOR.—What land do you mean?

TIPENE.—Waitara.

THE GOVERNOR.—If you mean the disputed land, an investigation will take place.

TIPENE.—That is well; let also the other land, Tataraimaka, be investigated.

THE GOVERNOR.—We can have no dispute about Tataraimaka. That is ours.

TIPENE.—Let the man who takes it be tried; that is a good plan for lands which are disputed. Let a trial take place.

THE GOVERNOR.—The Ngatiruanui are in quite a different position to others. They killed women and children, burnt houses, and plundered. I have not inquired into the matter; but if I were a friend, as you are, going to speak to the Ngatiruanui, I should advise them to give up what they have got, and a piece of land

[1] Tataraimaka in possession of the Ngatiruanui.

as compensation. . . . Even in distant parts of the world I heard of the conduct of the Ngatiruanuis, and felt ashamed at such things being done by Maories.

Tipene then laid his carved Maori spear at the Governor's feet, and said: "Look here. You say there is no cause; I say there is a cause. Will the vibration (striking the head of his spear) stop at the tongue, in the head of my spear? I thought your words of peace were to reach the other end." He meant that the Ngatiruanui had been their allies in war, and ought to have the same terms of peace.

The Governor said he did not wish to pursue the subject further at that time.

TIPENE.—Very well. Are your questions ended?

THE GOVERNOR.—Yes.

TIPENE.—Then I will ask a question. Are you opposed to my King?

THE GOVERNOR.—I do not care about him; but I think it is a thing that will lead to trouble. It will be stopped by such means as I have adopted, and will die out.

TIPENE.—If the King is brought to nought by your plans, well and good. You say, "What is the King to you?" We say, "It is a thing of importance to us." And the reason why we say so is this, that we have seen the good of it. The quarrels of the Maories amongst themselves have, for the last two years, diminished; and now, by means of it, many evils that have arisen have been put down without war. And therefore I say, the King is an important thing to us. Now I ask you, Are you altogether opposed to my King? If you consent to my question, we shall then work quietly; for we are not the chief cause of the King, whereas you have the final decision about your own system. So I ask you, Are you altogether opposed to my King? that you may say whether you are so or not.

THE GOVERNOR.—If you ask me as a friend, I tell you I think it a very bad thing.

TIPENE.—It has not arisen from us, but from the whole island. My question still remains unanswered. I ask, in order that the word of condemnation or otherwise may be spoken out. Will you condemn it in anger with war?

THE GOVERNOR.—I think each chief should come under the Governor; then they could all work with me.

TIPENE.—We are not going to pluck out the various tribes that adhere to us. If a man comes to join us, we shall not tell him to stop away. Letters have come to us, and money has been subscribed, from every place in the island (naming the various places, and the sums of money that had come from each). At the present time, while both races are at peace, perhaps we shall be divided, or perhaps we shall be united. Proceed cautiously in working out your plans. The only thing that remains dark is the King. Your own plan is to unite us all.

The Waikatos had expected to get a distinct pledge from Sir George Grey, in answer to the question which Tipene had been sent down to put. It was not possible, however, to elicit from him such a plain declaration of his intentions with regard to the King as they desired. The language he had used convinced them that he was at heart opposed to the King; but they remained in perplexity as to whether he would, or would not, use that large army which he had at his disposal, and which he could increase indefinitely, to put down the obnoxious King by force.

Sir George Grey's next act, however, which he publicly announced at the close of the Taupari meeting, put an end, in their opinion, to all doubt on the subject.

Many years before, the Auckland provincial authorities had commenced cutting a road from Drury through the Hunua forest to the Waikato river. The road, so far as it was made at the time of the Taupari meeting, was not metalled, the trees had merely been felled, the stumps extracted, and the ground rudely levelled. Except in dry summer weather, the road was a quagmire, through which a horse could only crawl with the greatest difficulty, sinking in most places knee-deep at every step. During the Taranaki war, the jealousy of the Waikatos had been excited at the progress of even such a road as this, and to avoid offending them, the works had been stopped, by order of the Colonial Government, about two miles short of the river-side.

Without a road through this forest, it was an idle boast to talk of invading the Waikato country. The Maories well knew this, and accordingly laughed in perfect security at the threats of Governor Browne.

Sir George Grey now determined to employ the British troops, who, since the close of the fighting at Taranaki, had been living idly in cantonments round Auckland to the great profit of the enterprising citizens, in cutting and metalling a good military road through the Hunua forest. No persons were more keenly alive to the effect of this measure than the Waikatos themselves. It would make the invasion of their country no longer impossible. That it greatly increased their respect for Sir George Grey there can be no question; they saw that this new Governor did not threaten them with what he could not perform, but, while soothing them with smooth words, was steadily and effectually taking measures to place them at his mercy. At the same time it is equally certain that the construction of this road rendered the restoration of confidence in the British Government and the peaceful solution of the native difficulty, a sheer impossibility. The chiefs of Waikato could never be misled as to the real design of this military undertaking: from the first day that they heard of it, they never swerved from the opinion that Sir George Grey's ultimate intention was —war.

CHAPTER XI.

FACE TO FACE.

THE last part of the task which Sir George Grey had come to New Zealand to perform—namely, shifting the responsibility of managing native affairs from the Imperial to the Colonial Government—was by far the easiest. In performing it he had Englishmen, not Maories, to deal with. Circumstances had luckily helped to make the change still more easy to effect.

In the last days of Colonel Browne's Governorship, the Ministry under whose auspices the Taranaki war began, was, after holding office longer than any previous Colonial Ministry, at length turned out by a majority of one. Mr. Richmond, who had devoted great labour and attention to the problem of native government, was deposed, and Mr. Fox reigned in his stead. The latter gentleman had constituted himself champion of Wiremu Kingi in the renowned Waitara controversy, and it was supposed that this circumstance peculiarly fitted him to second Sir George Grey in his attempt to settle the various difficulties by that universal remedy—the "new institutions." Mr. Fox had, in the New Zealand Parliament, declared his belief that the "King movement" arose out of a mere desire for law and order, and that the flag would be hauled down before any second magistrate who should attack it with Mr. Fenton's weapons.

When the Duke of Newcastle tried, in the previous year, to introduce a Bill into the House of Lords, providing an independent Council for New Zealand, with power to advise the Governor in native affairs, such New Zealand colonists as then happened to be visiting England raised a clamour so noisy as to induce him to withdraw the Bill. When the news of this reached Auckland, the New Zealand Parliament was in session; and with all possible despatch a colonial Bill, intended to forestall any future Imperial measure, was prepared and passed. The essential difference between this and the abortive schéme was, that by the colonial Bill the Native Council was put under the power of the New Zealand Assembly—in the Imperial measure it had been placed beyond it. The author of this piece of colonial legislation was Mr. Fox, who had always claimed for the Colonial Assembly the right of controlling the destinies of the Maories.

The offer which Sir George Grey now made, on behalf of the Imperial Government, to hand over the administration of native affairs to a responsible Minister chosen by the colonists was, therefore, eagerly caught at. It was a concession which far exceeded their most sanguine expectations. A native Council within the power of the Assembly would have satisfied them; but a Minister, who might be changed every session, and who could be therefore made to do just what the colonial shopkeepers and publicans wanted, was far better. The arrangement was at once made, and Mr. Fox became the first responsible Minister for Native Affairs.

It must be confessed that, if in the old arrangement, as regarded the possession of power without responsibility, the advantage was all on the side of the colonists, in the new one it was all on the side of the Imperial authorities. The Governor still remained absolute master of the six thousand British soldiers who kept the natives in awe; not a man could be moved without his express commands. Just as formerly, the Governor was obliged to consult the Colonial Ministry, because they supplied the money to carry out his schemes; so now the Minister for Native Affairs was obliged to consult the Governor, because the latter would not otherwise supply the physical force necessary to give effect to the colonial policy. While the colonists were nominally responsible for the government of the Maories, the Governor—who knew a great deal more about the natives than his advisers, and who was, moreover, master of six thousand soldiers—was the real ruler. The colony had enjoyed power without responsibility before: it was the Governor's turn to enjoy it now. The continuance of the double government, in which the nominal and real authority were still vested in different persons, caused constant inconveniences in the administration of affairs, and ultimately, as we shall see, a most disastrous catastrophe, which was the immediate cause of war.

Mr. Fox, on coming into office, had proclaimed to the House of Representatives, as his native policy, that he should insist on a real "face to face" negotiation with the chiefs of Waikato, with the view of removing all points of difference. The dialogue between Sir George Grey and Tipene was not enough, in Mr. Fox's eyes, to redeem the pledge; and therefore, after the Taupari meeting, he did not return with the Governor to Auckland, but set off in a canoe up the Waikato river, to make good his words by talking face to face with the leaders of the King party. He was also the bearer of specific proposals from Sir George Grey for settling the Waitara controversy. A Commission was to be appointed, consisting of two Europeans and four Maories—a European and two Maories nominated by the Governor, and a European and two Maories nominated by Wi Kingi and his friends. The Commission, thus constituted, was to go to Waitara and other settlements of the Ngatiawa tribe, examine witnesses, collect evidence, and report to the Governor upon the ownership of the celebrated Waitara block. I accompanied Mr. Fox upon this expedition.

The first person whom Mr. Fox tried to see was

Wiremu Tamihana, who, while the Taupari meeting was going on, had been waiting, with others, at Ngaruawahia to hear the result. But as soon as the news of the intended military-road reached Ngaruawahia, the whole party there assembled considered the act conclusive. Such a road, they said, could be intended for no other purpose than to bring great guns down to the Waikato river; and it was quite plain that Governor Grey was going to fight their King after all. So Wi Tamihana and his friends had dispersed and gone away, each to his own home.

Very few chiefs were left at Ngaruawahia, and the King was on a visit to the Ngatimaniapoto tribe, who were holding a great Christmas gathering at Hangatiki, far up amongst the hills. Two of those who remained behind, Patara and Wi Karamoa, met Mr. Fox at Taupiri, and questioned him most anxiously as to the truth of the report about the road. They politely expressed their own satisfaction at his assurances of peace and good-will; but they feared some of their countrymen might be incredulous, and think the road the beginning of mischief.

Messengers were sent to Peria, to try to catch Tamihana; but they only found Victoria, his wife, who said that he had gone down to a village near the mouth of the Thames, to settle some land dispute, and she didn't know when to expect him back. So, as it was necessary that Mr. Fox should deliver himself of his errand,

and negotiate "face to face" with somebody, there was no alternative but to beard the King and the Ngatimaniapoto among the hills at Hangatiki.

The Colonial Prime-Minister was, after a rough ride to Hangatiki, received with marked honour and respect. Somebody had ridden on before to announce the visitor; so that when he came in sight on the road which winds up the hill to the village, a guard of honour turned out to receive him. Forty young Maories, dressed in white breeches and blue coats, with stiff military stocks of cardboard, lined the road on either side, and presented arms as Mr. Fox rode between. His horse was taken from him by a Maori lad, and he was ushered into the best house in the village, and asked by a handsome young woman, in good English, whether he chose roast-fowl or sucking-pig for supper. The King was lodged in a house a little detached from the village, and a double or treble line of sentries rigorously excluded all approach to his sacred person. It was Saturday night when Mr. Fox arrived, and Rewi appointed Monday morning for a formal conference.

The guard-room adjoined the house in which Mr. Fox was lodged, and the evolutions of the royal army were a never-failing source of amusement; bugle-blowing and drilling appeared to go on incessantly from morning till night. The general was a very smart young fellow, one of a party that had been taken over to Europe, a few years before, in an Austrian frigate, the

Novara, which had visited New Zealand on a scientific exploring expedition. He spoke a little English, French, German, and Italian, and took care to exhibit his proficiency in each in turn. He was certainly much ashamed of the ragged regiment at the head of which we had caught him; but he said it was only a little pastime to amuse himself for a short time. On Sunday, the army was paraded and marched to church, where they looked very stiff and unhappy in their tight coats and military stocks, as contrasted with their civilian neighbours in the freedom of a simple blanket. The general carried their Prayer-books to church in a bag, and served them round to the men. Towards the end of the sermon, when he caught sight of two talking and laughing, he walked down the rank and boxed their ears with his hymn-book. Most of them were very young lads: two came privately, when off duty, to say how much they wished there was a good school to which they could go. The old men did not seem to approve of the soldiery. One veteran, as he sat with his pipe in his mouth, watching their evolutions, grunted out: "Humph! they'll spoil them for fighting, and make them fit for nothing but keeping barracks."

During the Sunday, Mr. Fox had a "face to face" interview with Wi Kingi, who coolly denied his identity. It was a common practice about that time to try to mislead the Pakeha as to the persons of the leading chiefs. They were afraid of Sir George Grey's threat that they should be taken up and tried, remembering the fate of Rauparaha. On one occasion, a Government officer was thus tricked into delivering an important message to a sham Wi Tamihana, at a place from which the real chief was far distant.

On Monday morning, everybody began to collect in the great meeting-house to listen to a speech from Mr. Fox—Rewi, with his *protégé* Wi Kingi, Reihana, and all the heads of Ngatimaniapoto were present. It was a meeting of the extreme party—no Tamihana, no Ngatihaua, and but few of the moderate chiefs of Ngaruawahia. The King did not appear. It was the worst set of men in New Zealand to whom terms of peace could be offered. Mr. Fox made his speech containing the usual professions of friendship, an account of Sir George Grey's intended system, and finally the proposal for an adjudication of the Waitara dispute. Rewi and all the leading chiefs sat mute, but they put a common man—an orator named Aporo—to reply. He fenced about in the most ingenious manner without giving any distinct pledge on any subject. He asked Mr. Fox whether he did not think that Governor Browne had been in the wrong, and Wi Kingi in the right, in the Taranaki war. Mr. Fox observed aside in English: "Why, that's exactly what I have always said in the Assembly." The incautious remark was overheard by a man who understood English, and politely interpreted to the assembly. Aporo then asked how a trial could take place about Waitara, unless Governor Browne, the guilty party, were present. He further inquired, whether he was not right in saying that he had conquered this concession for himself with his bow and spear, and whether our side would have re-examined Teira's right to Waitara if we had not been unsuccessful in the war. He finally said, that the questions of both Sir George Grey's new system, and the Waitara investigation, were too important to be rashly decided, and that time must be given for Waikato to consider. This broke up the meeting, and the crowds assembled at Hangatiki immediately began to disperse. The King, who had not been allowed to see Mr. Fox, went off, with his army and retinue of chiefs, to pay a royal visit at Kihikihi, and Mr. Fox and I rode down, with the Rev. A. Reid, to the mission station at Waipa.

It so happened that the King spent the night at a village close by the mission station, and Mr. Reid, anxious to give the colonial minister an opportunity of seeing the illustrious rebel, invited his Majesty to tea. The answer returned by his secretary was: "Mattie is too ill to come—rather do you send us some pork and a little pepper." Next morning, as we were departing, a second royal messenger arrived to beg for tobacco.

Before returning to Auckland, Mr. Fox visited Kihikihi, where many natives were assembled, including Te Heu Heu and several Taupo chiefs, who had arrived to pay a visit to the King. Matutaera and his suite were riding out of Kihikihi as Mr. Fox rode in. A deputation had arrived from the Lower Waikato to say that soldiers were actually come out to Mangatawhiri, and were making the road, to the great consternation of the Maories of Paetai and other places down the river. The tribes were assembling at Rangiriri, and proposed to attack the troops at once. The King had sent off a messenger to tell them to be patient, and not meddle with the soldiers, but wait until he came down in person to see what was being done, and take care of his children.

Rewi and the Ngatimaniapoto did not seem to feel much interest in the matter. Roads and troops at Mangatawhiri would not hurt them. They were extremely jovial. A row of eels stuck upon sticks, looking like a hedge forty or fifty feet long, was roasting for dinner, and emitting a most savoury smell. Mr. Fox was invited into their meeting-house, and Rewi joined issue with him there, and a tremendous discussion ensued. Rewi attacked all the past acts of the British Government with clever and unsparing criticism, exposing our timidity, selfishness, and arrogant assumption of superiority. It was a regular partisan speech, making out the worst possible case against us, but delivered with perfect temper and good humour, and well worthy of careful attention. I regret extremely that, having no notes of it, I cannot give the substance to the reader. After discussing the "King movement," we were invited to dine on eels and potatoes. Wi Kingi sat opposite Mr. Fox, eating out of the same basket; they had a great discussion over their dinner, about Waitara; the former declaring that no proposals from our Government would be listened to until the troops were taken off the native lands, and the whole left, as Wiremu Tamihana had proposed, under the protection of the law. Mr. Fox was then invited into his house and introduced to his wife, and they all stayed laughing and joking together for some time. Rewi, who was my neighbour at dinner, said he regretted to hear that I was going to be sent amongst them as a magistrate, because it would become his painful duty to drive me away again—why couldn't I come amongst them as a trader or a missionary?—he would gladly drive off the present missionary to make a vacancy, as he had grown quite tired of his sermons, which he had listened to for twenty years.

After dinner, Te Heu Heu began a long speech, commencing from the creation of the world, and working slowly on towards modern times, while everybody else went to sleep. At last the orator, reaching the point in the history of mankind at which he had to speak of the relations between Pakeha and Maori, went off as usual into a towering passion, and made such a noise, that all his audience were aroused thereby. Half-a-dozen of the Taupo chiefs, who hankered after the "new institutions," retired in disgust, saying with truth that Rewi and Te Heu Heu had stopped all chance of their talking to Mr. Fox. They sent a message asking for a quiet interview by themselves next day, at which the "policy," with all its circumstances of salaries, &c. was explained and accepted.

Meanwhile the King went down to Rangiriri, where the Lower Waikatos had assembled in great numbers. A large flag was flying, soldiers were drilling, and the constant horn-blowing and bugle-playing gave a military character to the meeting. The King's more fiery partisans urged an immediate attack; it was far better, they said, to fight it out at once, than to wait till the Governor was ready, and then have to fight on less advantageous terms. But the argument of the moderate party was unanswerable. The Governor's road was made entirely upon Queen's land; the very principle for which they were contending was, that every man should be allowed to do as he pleased on his own land, and therefore, on their own theory, they were bound to let the Governor alone. Maories never go to war without a "take," or ground on which to stand. In this case there was clearly no "take," and therefore, though keenly alive to the advantage the Governor was gaining, they remained at peace. It was, however, agreed by all, that whenever the Governor crossed Mangatawhiri, and so came upon Maori soil, there would be a just "take" for war, and then the whole of Waikato should rise. That he would ultimately cross Mangatawhiri, the Maories, whether of the peace or war faction, did not for a moment doubt.

CHAPTER XII.

THE "NEW INSTITUTIONS."

IN the midst of the alarm caused by Sir George Grey's supposed preparations for war, the attempt to civilize the natives off-hand, by the introduction of the new system of government, was urged forward with the greatest rapidity.

In the Waikato district, the only existing authority, legislative or judicial, was the "Runanga." This national institution, which at first was strictly oligarchic, the head chiefs meeting to discuss plans of war, and common people listening with awe and reverence to their speeches, had become the most democratic assembly that can be conceived. Women and children were admitted, and made their voices heard—even dogs and pigs were not excluded.

Mr. Hanson Turton, who succeeded Mr. Fenton as magistrate of Waikato, in a Report on the Runanga, dated Nov. 20, 1861, gives the following faithful picture of what a Runanga had then become:—[1]

[1] N. Z. Parl. Papers, 1862. E. No. 5, A.

"The Maori Court, or Runanga, was opened. Old Riwai sat as judge. The case, one of 'korero-teka' (slander), was introduced, and argued by two young men as 'roias' (lawyers), each having received a fee of 10*s*. The judge was quickly confused by them, and sent to ask me how to proceed. I replied that I was there as a spectator only, and wished to see how such cases were conducted. Plaintiff then began on behalf of her daughter, ten years of age, whose gentle birth had been maligned, and in a screaming speech, with abundance of grimaces, demanded damages of fifty pounds, to be paid down at once. On this, loud laughter arose on every side. The child's father came forward to prove how reasonable was the demand; saying, that though the mother was a slave, he was a chief, and a great one too, and that the sum was little enough for having called his daughter a slave. He was quickly supported by aunts and uncles in abundance, who all, doubtless, thought that 50*l*. ready cash would be a good thing for the family; and so they all stood up and chattered together, making confusion worse confounded. By this time, the two lawyers were nearly fighting, pacing about and speechifying one against the other; and the Court was about to decide in favour of the plaintiff, who had gained judgment solely through strength of lungs and impudence, when up jumped the defendant—a wretched old woman, and all in tatters. Rushing into the ring, she first divided the lawyers, then assailed the plaintiff, then abused the witnesses, heaped scorn on all the party, and justified the slander; then repeated it most expressively, and dared them to their faces. The whole Court was instantly in an uproar, like Bedlam let loose, each person siding off to his party, and every speaker grinning at the rest, and all speaking and rushing about together; when my interference was again requested by the judge. Order being restored, I took the case in hand, much to the discomfiture of the lawyers; and within a quarter of an hour, the whole evidence had been extracted, and the decision given. Judgment was for the plaintiff, but only 10*s*. damages; and yet all parties were pleased with the result. Even the old dame herself was content, crying out that she had never had such a sum in her life, and never should have, and they might get the money as they could. This speech was received with great applause, and a collection at once commenced, when garments and coins of various value, amounting to about 25*s*., were handed over, and laid at the feet of the mother, as a cure for her troubled mind and daughter's damaged reputation."

The Runanga above described was one held in the lower part of the Thames valley. The village Runangas throughout Waikato—and, indeed, throughout all New Zealand—are of the same character. All are a promiscuous gathering of men, women, and children, held in the public sleeping-house of the village, at bed-time;

in which certain individuals—not always the wisest or best—possess a prescriptive right to engross all the talk. The members never come to a formal vote; they go on talking, like schoolboys in a dormitory, till every one has gone to sleep. When there is difference of opinion, one side out-talks the other.

Village Runangas were chosen by the New Zealand Ministry as the foundation on which the "new institutions" were to be built. In a Ministerial memorandum on Sir George Grey's plan of native government, Mr. Fox says:—

"The Runanga, as at present constituted, appears to be little else than a gathering of the people of a particular village, or 'hapu.' Let it continue so, with the limitation only imposed that none but adult males take part in its deliberations. . . . The jurisdiction of the Runanga should, as nearly as may be in each case, be co-extensive with the lands of the hapu or hapus of which it consists. The Runanga should be empowered to make bye-laws. . . . All officers, such as assessors, policemen, pound-keepers, &c., being Maories, should be elected by the Runangas, subject to the approval of Her Majesty. . . . Each Runanga should elect one judicial officer, the assessor. . . . This officer should act alone in all cases where the Commissioner is not present, subject to the periodical revision, at very short dates, of that officer." After speaking of a District Runanga, composed of members elected from the

Village Runangas, Mr. Fox continues: "This branch of the machinery would be new to the natives, and might not, at first, work so smoothly or intelligibly as the simple machinery of the non-representative Runanga.

"Ministers attach much importance to the gradual initiation of the system, by beginning in practice from the bottom, and not from the top, in the manner which the above suggestions will indicate. . . . Ministers would hope gradually to work up to all, or nearly all, that His Excellency proposes; but they are convinced that the development of the system must be gradual, and that great care must be exercised in securing a firm foundation. They believe that in the existing Runanga such foundation exists; and therefore it is that they seek to direct His Excellency's attention particularly to that institution, and to the expediency of making it, in practice, the *point d'appui* to which to attach whatever other machinery of government it may be considered desirable to organize."

The introduction of Sir George Grey's system into Waikato was carried out in conformity with these suggestions. All native officers were elected by the Village Runangas, and no such election was ever objected to by Government. No District Runanga of select men was ever assembled.

In the Lower Waikato, most of that small party which had formerly supported Mr. Fenton's schemes received the "new institutions" with avidity. The duty of explaining the plan and "organizing" the District was entrusted to Mr. Fenton himself; but, as his engagements in Auckland forbade his remaining permanently in the situation of Commissioner, it was arranged that Mr. Armitage, a friend of his, who had for many years lived as a settler near Paetai, should succeed, at an early date, to the office.

The first place "organized" was Taupari, where Waata Kukutai was ready enough to fall in with a scheme which promised him the two things he specially loved—money and distinction. The Hundred of Taupari was constituted, and a staff of magistrates and policemen nominated, with salaries amounting altogether to 180*l.* per annum. The Runanga of the Ngatitipa (Waata's tribe) was promptly assembled, and the manufacture of laws commenced.[1] The most amusing resolutions passed were—

No. 3. "We agree that the Government should give us eight bullocks to plough the land with. The ploughs we have ourselves."

No. 5. "We agree that the Governor should give us grass-seed for our farm; but let it be clean seed—do not let there be any noxious weed mixed with it."

At a later meeting, the native officers took the oaths of allegiance to the Queen, and a special oath of office. The Runanga then passed further resolutions, asking Government to build them a wooden Court-house,

[1] N. Z. Parl. Papers, 1862. E. No. 9, Sec. II. 3.

instead of leaving them to build a raupo one for themselves; requiring a blacksmith to be sent to live at Taupari to repair their ploughs; making another application for a gift of bullocks, which they persevered in, in spite of Mr. Fenton's expostulation; and finally asking the Governor to send a doctor, an elderly man, who did not misconduct himself with women or drink rum, to cure all their ailments, of which one speaker gave an interesting catalogue. Several orators declared that if a bad one came, they would send him back again.

After this exercise of legislative functions, the Runanga proceeded to exercise judicial power. A policeman's wife was brought before Mr. Armitage and Waata Kukutai, charged with the offence of having written a love-letter to a young man of another tribe. After a severe examination by Waata, she was cautioned, and the police were directed to return her to her husband.

At a village called Te Kohekohe, a few miles above Mangatawhiri, a second Runanga was organized, composed of a very small section of Ngatimahuta, the tribe royal. Among these few people a sum of 180*l.* a-year was spent. Wiremu Te Wheoro, the head magistrate, is a very intelligent young man, really attached by something more than pecuniary interest to our side. Wiremu Tamihana always said he was the best man we had enlisted; the rest of our officers cared for nothing more than our money. Te Wheoro was the only loyal native I was ever acquainted with, who appeared to have the slightest notion that his loyalty implied any obligation to obey. An old Maori woman, who once did me the honour to paddle me down from Meremere to Mangatawhiri for a shilling, stopped her paddle, took the pipe out of her mouth, and laughed me to scorn, when I observed to her that Wiremu Te Wheoro's tribe was loyal. "Yes," she said, "there are some on the Queen's side—the two assessors, the two wardens, and the six policemen; but all the rest to a man are faithful to our King." She cast up her eyes, resumed her pipe and paddle, and regarded me for the rest of the voyage with pitying contempt.

But while the new plans were allowed to be carried on without active opposition in Lower Waikato, in the Upper District the Government was not so fortunate. An abstract resolution had been passed by the Runanga of Ngaruawahia to forbid Queen's magistrates within the King's dominions, and Patene, a mad Ngatimaniapoto chief of Mohoaonui, determined to exalt his name by carrying the resolution into practical effect. No sooner did news reach him that I had actually arrived at Otawhao, and was a guest at the mission-station, than he set out from his village on the Upper Waipa, at the head of a Maori regiment, the counterpart of that which Mr. Fox encountered at Hangatiki, bent on expelling the intruder. Patene first marched to

Rangiaowhia to arrest some Waikato malefactor, but as the Rangiaowhia people would not surrender him, they very nearly came to blows: the dispute ended by the old men taking the soldiers' guns from them, and turning them out of doors, saying that they would have no riot there. After spending a wet day at Rangiaowhia, Patene marched his forces down to the mission-station, where Mr. Clarke, the interpreter, and I, were then lodged. There was a most ludicrous scene. A large party of Rangiaowhia men went down on horseback, joking and laughing, to see the fun. Everybody had received notice of the intended performance, so that a number of Europeans from the neighbourhood, including several ladies, were assembled, and a tribe of scampish Maori boys had perched themselves upon the fences to get a good view. On the arrival of the soldiers, who had halted out of sight to put on their breeches, everybody first shook hands with everybody else, and then Patene read to the assembled public a declaration of loyalty to the Maori King, which had, he averred, been signed by 2,079 persons. As sunshine in the open road, where Patene was standing, was found to be disagreeably hot, he proposed an adjournment to the shade in the church field, so Mr. Clarke and I sat down on the church steps; the army was re-formed, reprimanded for allowing the boys to poke fun at it, manœuvred through a gap in the hedge into the field, and drawn up with fixed bayonets a couple of yards in front of us. Patene came forth and made an oration. He dwelt on the wrong committed by the Governor in sending up a magistrate, when they had passed a resolution that none should be allowed to come; it was no use saying that I had never judged a Maori—he had seen in the newspapers that the Governor had sent me up to be as magistrate. It might be a piece of Queen's land on which I was living, but he would not let me stay unless I consented to be a trader and sold blankets or tobacco, and gave up being a magistrate. All the Runangas had agreed that English magistrates were not to be there; officers of Government were worms, baits that Sir George Grey was fishing with, and if suffered to remain, some tribes in Waikato would inevitably be caught. Patene repeatedly ordered me to go. I refused. He said that this time he had told us quietly to go, but if we persisted in remaining, he should soon come back and send us away; he should take us and our goods, but without hurting either, bundle us into a canoe, and take us down to the Queen's boundary at Mangatawhiri. A bystander observed that we should have to be carried down to the canoe, and should refuse to paddle; to which Patene replied that such conduct would be quite just. The unlooked-for magisterial obstinacy put an end to the proceedings, and Patene, with many threats of a future visitation, marched the army away.

It turned out afterwards that the chiefs of the King's

party had not authorized Patene's expedition. They admitted that his conduct was very wrong, and some of them wrote to Rewi, to keep his tribe in better order, and stop all further violence. Patene was very angry when he found that his zeal was so ill-appreciated. He said he had been trying to carry out a law which had been universally agreed to; but now that his act had been condemned, he should never allow the magistrate to be driven away, and should resist any one who might try to do so at any future time.

The chiefs who thus interfered to prevent further violence from Patene, liked Sir George Grey's attempt to establish European jurisdiction in Waikato no better than the Ngatimaniapoto did; but they determined to resist the Governor in a quieter and more effectual way. The magistrate was on Queen's land, and had a right to stay there; but they had as good a right to keep all cases out of his Court, if they could. They, therefore, enacted stringent laws in all their Runangas, forbidding, under heavy penalties, any native to sue in the European Court; and so successful was this policy, that, for six months afterwards, only one native suitor ever brought a case into Court, and he had to pay a heavy fine for doing so.

The only result that appeared to be gained by the presence of a magistrate at Otawhao, was the irritation felt by the Ngatimaniapoto at having a magistrate lodged amongst themselves, after they had threatened those tribes who should tolerate one with their displeasure.

There were, of course, scattered about the villages of Waikato, plenty of discontented people, who had been somehow affronted by the leaders of the King-party. Now that loyalty had a marketable value, these men had a strong personal interest in declaring themselves upon the Queen's side. They accordingly obtruded their loyalty upon the officers of Government, claiming to be made assessors, wardens, or policemen. No advantage was to be gained by yielding to their demands; they constituted a small minority in the midst of an overwhelming hostile majority. They might, if appointed, have drawn their official pay, but they could not have made the slightest impression upon the mass of the people. So little did the chiefs of the King party care for the influence of Government assessors, that they made very little objection to assessors being appointed in the very centre of the King's dominions. It was commonly reported that all the Queen's native magistrates within the Maori kingdom paid over regularly a part of their salaries to the King, as the condition of being allowed quietly to receive the remainder. The Maories declared openly that, having formerly tried to conquer, and having failed, we were now trying to bribe them into submission. They derided equally both our attempts.

The effect of the new institutions in the Waikato

district can be best illustrated by giving the history of the reduction under law and order of the Ngatiwhauroa tribe.

Ngatiwhauroa is a very small tribe, or rather "hapu" of the great Waikato tribe, numbering only fifty or sixty men, scattered over a wide extent of country, reaching to the north as far as Paetai, on the Lower Waikato, and south as far as Whatawhata, and everywhere closely intermixed with larger and more powerful "hapus." Their principal village is Kahumatuku, a mile above Taupiri. Hona, the head chief of the tribe, was an assessor under Mr. Fenton, working without salary, in hopes of getting one. After the scheme which Mr. Fenton had begun was abandoned by the Government, Hona had joined the King party, and built a house near Ngaruawahia, to lodge in during the national assemblies, in which he took as great a part as his abilities and station allowed. For a long time the Ngatiwhauroa had been engaged in litigation with the Ngatimahuta, concerning the right to an eel-weir at Paetai; and in the beginning of 1862 the cause came on for trial. The powerful Ngatimahuta insisted on having their blood-relations, the Ngatimaniapoto, as judges. Wiremu Tamihana, who is related to the other party, demurred, and proposed one of the Hauraki tribes, as being really neutral; but his advice was not listened to, and consequently, when the trial took place at Paetai, he refused to be present. The eel-weir, as every one expected, was adjudged to the Ngatimahuta; whereupon Hona and his tribe renounced their allegiance, handed over their King's flag to the royal army, and wrote to ask me to come and establish Sir George Grey's new policy amongst them. On my arrival at Kahumatuku, they held a meeting, and stated their requirements. They demanded two magistrates, two wardens, five policemen, and a secretary—in all, ten officers for the government of fifty persons. They were very angry at the demand being refused; they said they were treated much less favourably than other tribes had been, and they particularly instanced Te Kohekohe, where the tribe was a smaller one, they said, than their own. They further asked to have the right of carrying the inland mail, which custom had assigned to Taati and the Rangiaowhia natives, transferred to them; they wished that a Queen's flag should be given them, to flaunt in the faces of the King and his Court; and, finally, by way of taking decisive revenge for the loss of the Paetai eels, they wanted to sell an acre and a half of land to a European trader, who had been for some years living in the village.

Disappointed at the coldness with which their new-born zeal for the Queen was received, they resolved to make applications in other quarters. Hona accordingly went down to the Commissioner of the Lower Waikato, and told him that his tribe lived partly in the Upper, and partly in the Lower District; that they all objected to be included in the former, but wished to be altogether in the latter. Thence Hona went on in the Commissioner's company to Auckland, to see what effect he could produce on the Government. His conditional loyalty was accepted; the Government made the arrangement desired, and Hona and his friends became salaried officers of the Queen.

A month afterwards, to Hona's great disgust, the Lower Waikato District was placed under my charge, so that I had every opportunity of observing the mode in which his new duties were performed. Against the King party he was utterly powerless. A resolution had been lately passed at Ngaruawahia to augment the King's scanty revenue by laying a poll-tax of 1*l.* yearly upon all Europeans living on native territory. One of the first persons from whom an attempt was made to collect this tribute was Hona's trader at Kahumatuku. The native magistrate and his friends made a great fuss about the insolence of the King party, and bragged about the resistance they would make to any attempt to enforce the payment of the tax; but when a canoe full of men came down from the enemy's town, headed by a young chief, who quietly stated that his instructions were to take a pound, or a pound's worth of goods, from the trader's store, and that he should do so, Hona knocked under and told the European that the best course would be quietly to pay the money. Nor was Hona more successful in attaining his desire to carry Her Majesty's mail. Taati's Runanga had decreed that no man other than a King's soldier should be allowed to carry the Queen's mail. Even a young Rangiaowhia chief, who presumed, in defiance of the law, to be carrier, was stopped at Ngaruawahia, had his bag taken from him, and given to a soldier, to carry on to Auckland, and was himself sent back home. The natives asked—"What did it matter to the Government who carried their mail, as long as the mail was regular? Government had better be content, and not give themselves unnecessary trouble."

During the whole time that Hona was a Queen's officer, he attended native meetings, visited Ngaruawahia, appeared on terms of perfect familiarity with the disaffected natives, and never, so far as I know, did the slightest service to Government in return for the salary which he received. At the outbreak of the present war, he went down with some of his tribe, and lived at a village called Cameron-town, about eight miles below Mangatawhiri; at which place Mr. Armitage, who had again become Hona's superior officer, lost his life in an ambuscade. There was very grave suspicion that to this ambuscade the Ngatiwhauroa tribe had been privy. Waata Kukutai accused Hona of being accessory to the death of Mr. Armitage, at which the latter took such offence, that he openly renounced his allegiance to the Queen, and went over again to the King's side.

The above story shows how impossible it was to force upon the Waikato District institutions to which the whole mass of the people was opposed. The only result was to draw a small minority of greedy and mercenary men into our employment, who could render us no other service than to make us utterly contemptible in the eyes of the disaffected but more honourable chiefs.

In fact, Sir George Grey's new scheme for governing the Maories, as carried out by the Colonial Ministry, proved in every place a total failure. The whole native population of New Zealand is, and has been for years, in a state of utter lawlessness and anarchy. Actual resistance by force of arms to our authority is confined to the Waikato, but lawlessness is universal. The great mischief of all is not that the Maories choose to be governed by a King instead of the Queen, but that they are not in any real sense governed at all. So long as each individual Maori can do that which is right in his own eyes, and break the laws of God and man with impunity, so long will peace and prosperity in New Zealand be an impossibility.

The only remedy that can ever cure the evils of that distracted colony is the establishment of some Government that can make itself *obeyed.* It is not the enactment of additional laws that is wanted: the country is infested with laws and with assemblies of law-makers. But the last link between sovereign and subject—a police to make the laws obeyed—is entirely defective in New Zealand, and at the present time no effort is being made to supply the deficiency. If there existed any power that could arrest and punish Maori offenders against the law, without destroying the entire race in the process, the whole difficulty would be solved.

In England we learn the lesson of obedience to constituted authority at so early an age, that we are apt to regard it as a common instinct of mankind, and to forget that it is a lesson that must be learnt before self-government is possible. With Maories it is not so. Children, like all other possessions, are regarded as a sort of common property. If a father ventured to punish his own child, the mother's family would resent it as an affront, and probably claim some payment to atone for the offence. The parent is not absolute over the child, and therefore the child never learns to obey. I have seen little children rise up and strike their parents with the full force of their infantine rage, and the parent merely put the child quietly aside without taking any notice of the blow. At a very early age the Maori boy emancipates himself from all control, and for the rest of his life does literally that which is right in his own eyes.

The new system did nothing to teach that lesson of obedience which was so much needed. The central power was divided, the Colonial Ministry and the Governor were independent and sometimes conflicting authorities, and the Maories knew it. No man could serve two masters, and an untutored love of independence prompted the Maories to serve neither. Moreover, they had come to look on Government rather as a storehouse of good things to be enjoyed, than as a superior power to be obeyed. If they could not get what they wanted out of the local officer, they went to the Colonial Minister, and if he was also churlish, they appealed to the Governor, and often in the end got what they asked for. No attempt was made to establish or support the authority of the District Commissioners. Correspondence of the most important kind, of which, however, the commissioner of the district was kept in profound ignorance, was carried on with natives by officials in Auckland; measures were taken and arrangements made, sometimes by the Governor, sometimes by a Colonial Minister, sometimes by the officials of the central department in Auckland, without consulting, and even without informing, the officer of the district thereby affected. Every one connected with Government desired to have his finger in the native pie, until at last the number of cooks became prodigious. I can enumerate at least a dozen masters from whom Wiremu Te Wheoro received conflicting orders in the course of a twelvemonth—yet that man still remains a sane subject of the Queen. The conduct of a district officer was usually estimated by the satisfaction he gave to the natives over whom he was placed, and the latter were most pleased by a lavish distribution of salaries and offices. A man who sought to spare the public purse, and not give money away without some adequate return, ran the risk of being looked upon coldly by his official superiors, who cared less for success than for the appearance of having succeeded.

The result of this was, that the loyal natives soon became more disobedient and insolent than the disloyal. In May, 1862, Arama Karaka, the chief assessor of the Bay of Islands district, and one of the most loyal Maories in New Zealand, seeing that he need fear no restraint from his patrons at Auckland, deliberately took part in a native war at Wangarei, where he attacked a chief named Tirarau, an old friend and ally of our Government. Ihaka, an assessor, living in the Manukau, told every one in the Native Office that he would obey nobody, and that Sir George Grey was not his master; and, shortly afterwards, went with a neighbouring assessor, named Aihipene, to the Waikato, and openly recommended the people to attack and pull down a native police school, which the Government were building at the Kohekohe. One of Te Wheoro's policemen, on being summoned for adultery, renounced his allegiance, sent his uniform, his oath of allegiance, and his oath of office, to the magistrate, and went openly over to the King. Another policeman, who was told by Aihipene that his uniform implied that he was to obey orders, replied, "Oh, that's the meaning, is it?" tore off coat and breeches in the street of Waiuku, flung his cap on the ground, and marched off in his shirt and his freedom. It was announced in the Government *Gazette*, that he had "resigned his office." Waata Kukutai borrowed his salary in advance from the Government in Auckland, to keep himself from going to prison for debt. The district officer was directed to stop the salary till the loan was repaid. The latter having obeyed his orders, Waata was so angry, that he wrote a most abusive letter to the Government, complaining of the underhand fraud committed upon him by the Commissioner, and threatening to resign his office. No notice was taken. Shortly afterwards, the Governor raised his salary from 50*l.* to 150*l.* a year, as a reward for his loyalty; and Waata, thereupon, applied forthwith to the Colonial Ministry for a salary for his wife, because the weight of public duty prevented him from growing food for her. Examples of this sort could be multiplied indefinitely.

The instances in which law has ever been enforced against Maories are extremely few, and could, in all the cases that I ever heard of (for I never met with a case myself), be explained by some exceptional circumstance.

No plan of native government which has yet been tried, either by Pakeha or Maori, has succeeded in teaching the good and necessary lesson of obedience.

In this respect, the plan of self-government supported by Tamihana and his friends broke down, as they themselves admitted, as completely as the Governor's; though, as a means of demoralizing and pauperizing the natives, the latter was unrivalled. In short, every scheme which depends on Village Runangas as the means of teaching and enforcing obedience, must, in the present condition of the people and Runangas, break down.

The system established by the Waikatos themselves had a great advantage over the Governor's, in the existence of a better sort of Runanga, namely, the King's Council at Ngaruawahia, which Tamihana was trying to convert into a Parliament of the entire Maori nation. But an account of the Waikato government, and an examination into its excellencies and defects, must be deferred until the next chapter.

CHAPTER XIII.

THE MAORI KINGDOM.

SINCE the introduction of Christianity into New Zealand, the political condition of the Maories has progressively become more and more democratic. The traditional power of the chief, derived from heathen superstition, is now altogether gone. Men like Wiremu Tamihana and Rewi Maniapoto have, indeed, the title of Chief, and their abilities have gained them respect and influence, both in their own tribes and among strangers; but these men only execute the will of the people, and do not guide it. In all their plans, they have to consider what their tribes will think and say; and when their own opinion differs from that of the multitude, the former has to give way. Popular passions are too strong for them; resistance would cost them their position.

In the Maori kingdom, as in all other native districts in New Zealand, the supreme authority, legislative and judicial, resides in the Village Runangas.

In making laws, the Runangas have no idea of any limit to the province of government; their regulations extend to the minutest details of private life. They make laws about behaviour on Sunday—laws against falsehood, whether slanderous or not—laws to fix the prices of pigs, corn, and potatoes—laws to fix the payment for which people shall carry the mails. In short, the Runanga is a grievous tyranny, and would be insupportable, if it only possessed power to carry its decrees into execution. Happily, the tribal government is more feeble than forbearing; so that a Maori, by obeying no laws at all, contrives to enjoy a fair amount of personal liberty.

The Runangas throughout New Zealand exercise judicial authority. In the Maori kingdom, there are, indeed, persons styled King's magistrates, just as in the Governor's native districts there are Queen's magistrates; but neither are able to exercise the power implied by the name. Physical force resides in the members of the Runanga, who carry out their decrees, when they are carried out at all, by the strength of their own right arms. No Runanga would carry out the decision of either King's or Queen's magistrate, till they had first themselves examined its justice. Thus they constitute themselves the real judges. A Maori magistrate only acts as a sort of detective and public prosecutor, and sometimes reasons and expostulates in a friendly way with offenders who will not submit themselves to his decision. Against a Pakeha defendant, it is generally easy enough to put a Runanga in motion.

No more mercy is shown by a Maori Runanga to a Pakeha, than by an Auckland jury to a Maori. But any native who feels himself strong enough, redresses wrongs received from Pakehas, without troubling the Runangas, by helping himself to a horse or a cow; and this way of obtaining satisfaction is approved and sustained by the Native Assemblies, if the original claim to compensation is just.

The laws which guide Runangas in their judgments are those which may approve themselves to the individual conscience of each member. Some quote the Ten Commandments; some, Maori custom; some, English law; some, laws developed out of their own self-consciousness. I once heard a trial before the Runanga of Peria, at which it was given in evidence that a man called Kepa had made a law that no one should go to his house while he was from home; and "Kepa's law" was accepted throughout the trial as perfectly valid; the only question entertained being whether the defendant was aware of it. Wiremu Tamihana is a diligent student of the code of laws contained in the Pentateuch, which he appears to find better adapted to the wants of an uncivilized nation than English law, and he always quotes Levitical law upon any doubtful case. Several ambitious Maories have tried to codify their laws, but their attempts have been as abortive as our own.

The Runangas do not generally succeed in administering substantial justice. This is the natural consequence of the Runanga being a popular and tumultuous gathering, in which the young and ignorant talk down their elders and betters. Again, if a just decision is come to, it is by no means certain to be carried into effect. There are no police: the members of the Runanga have themselves to execute their own decisions. When it is known that the losing party will fight rather than yield, the task is perilous. Whakapaukai long set even the Runanga of Ngaruawahia at defiance, because he gave out that he would shoot anybody who molested him. A Maori criminal, however, cannot escape from the recollection of his sentence by changing his place of abode, and losing himself in a crowd. He must either remain on the spot, or go where he is well known. From the time he has been sentenced by the Runanga, he is a marked man until the penalty is paid. The Runanga may not have power to enforce its sentences, but it has power to banish a man from society until he voluntarily submits. Lastly, the Maori custom of perpetual travelling makes even the Runanga at times inaccessible. The fountain of justice may be absent at a feast, or may have turned into a war-party and gone to fight: the plaintiff in such case is put off with the everlasting Maori answer—"taihoa" (by-and-by), which, of course, is fatal in all cases in which justice, to be of any use, must be speedy.

It must not be supposed that the anarchy of one

tribe is exactly like that of another. In some tribes "Lynch law" is administered with greater justice; in others with greater vigour. Amongst the Ngatihaua tribe the administration of justice has always been very creditable. This is to be attributed to the character and personal influence of Wiremu Tamihana and the chiefs by whom he is, or rather was, surrounded and supported. I never heard a complaint of injustice from the Europeans resident amongst his tribe. "In the neighbourhood of Maungatautari," said Bishop Selwyn before the Waikato[1] Committee, "I asked a man whether it would be safe to leave our baggage on the side of the road while we went some little distance off to a native village? The answer was—'Oh yes: nobody steals now.' And when I asked why, he said—'Some don't steal for fear of God; some from fear of the Five Pounds;' the Five Pounds being a fine put in force by the native Kai-whakawa (magistrate)."

The Ngatimaniapoto Runanga was very powerful, but not by any means just. The members had very strong prejudices whenever they thought the King's "mana" or any appearance of yielding to the English Government was involved in the case at issue. Rewi never paid so much attention as Tamihana to the domestic affairs of his tribe, so that the young men were in his Runanga supreme. They were, moreover, demoralized by the possession of Taranaki plunder, and were

[1] N. Z. Parl. Papers, 1860. F. No. 3, 1138.

violently hostile both to the English race and to the Government. At a place called Whataroa, far up the Ngatimaniapoto country beyond Hangatiki, a chief called Reihana had organized the best system of law and order in the whole country. He kept a force of eighty strong lads, clothed and equipped by the fees and fines of his Court. The culprits whom Reihana sentenced were generally made to pay their money down before leaving the Court. When a man really had no money in hand, two days were allowed him in which to obtain some; but on the third day, if the money was not forthcoming, the fine was increased. If a man was himself too poor to pay, Reihana expected his kinsmen to subscribe for him. All the proceeds of these fines went to the equipment and support of the eighty soldiers, who thus had a very strong and obvious interest in the vigorous administration of justice. Reihana had the character of being perfectly just in his judgments.

When the several tribes united to set up the Maori King, they did not thereby surrender their distinct independence. The Maori kingdom was a sort of federation which did not much interfere with the local jurisdiction exercised by the Village Runangas in the way described.

According to the native system, Matutaera Potatau, the King, had very little to do personally with affairs of state. He used to travel about, attended by chiefs, to most of the great meetings, where he was always carefully guarded by a body of drilled soldiers, and, whether at home or on a visit, seldom appeared outside his house when Europeans were present. In political matters he was scarcely ever consulted.

All public business was transacted by a Council of State, called the Runanga of Ngaruawahia, which was composed of about a dozen members, who were the elder chiefs of the Ngatimahuta tribe, and relatives of old Potatau. But Rewi, Tamihana, Reihana, or any other great men from the provinces, on a visit to Ngaruawahia, would sit with the regular members, and join in their deliberations. Common men did not presume to take part in this Runanga.

Of the wisdom of the King's Council I feel bound to speak in the very highest terms. In all questions which I have heard discussed by them, they have argued with calmness and good temper, keeping steadily to the point at issue, and facing all the difficulties. They usually came to a just decision. Calm in discussion, the strongest opposition never provoked personal rudeness. It would have been impossible to get together a body of Maories with whom the Government could have more advantageously consulted upon the management of the native race. If the King's Council had only possessed power equal to their wisdom and moderation, the present war would never have arisen. But that wise resolutions should but seldom be carried into practical effect is a weakness that appears naturally inherent in all public bodies at the antipodes.

The Runanga of Ngaruawahia often acted as a judicial body: it appeared to be the last resort in cases which no one else could settle. During the year 1862, many wrongs had been done to Europeans living in Waikato, chiefly in the Ngatimaniapoto district, which the local chiefs and their Runangas were unable or unwilling to redress. Wiremu Tamihana, who took a very strong interest in such cases, in as much as they were standing proofs of the failure of his design to establish law and order in native districts, had the subject brought under the notice of the Runanga of Ngaruawahia; and the Runanga, by his advice, claimed jurisdiction in all cases where Europeans' interests were involved. This plan, however, was displeasing to Rewi; he did not choose to part with power, or to allow the dealings of his tribe with their own Pakehas to be revised by any other body. He protested against the intended assumption of jurisdiction, and the Runanga had to abandon the pretension. All conflicts of this kind that arose between the central and local authorities, were quietly settled by the former at once giving way. The King's Council had no real power. There was no force at command by which it could compel obedience; and that was only rendered voluntarily when the opinions of the subject happened to coincide with those of the Sovereign. Even Wiremu Tamihana himself could, when he chose, turn a deaf ear to the King. During the time I was in Waikato, I often attended the King's Runanga, and the members thereof used sometimes, after we had sat talking together till a late hour, to grow confidential, and reveal their troubles. At such times, they told of the disobedience of distant tribes, who persisted in stopping roads they had been ordered to open, who turned away ministers of religion, and let land in spite of all remonstrance. Once, in the middle of a conversation of this sort, Wi Karamoa started up, and said, "What fools we must be to talk in this way, before the Pakehas are gone to bed." They all laughed, wished us good-night, and at that time revealed no more. Latterly, the Council became cautious, and wisely reluctant to issue commands, avowing openly that they had no power to compel obedience.

Indeed, as an instrument for enforcing law, the Council was less effective than the local Runangas. Its authority was not universally acknowledged. My friend Patene once told me that he had never recognized as members of the Runanga any others than Rewi, Wetini, and another; and that the men who called themselves the Runanga of Ngaruawahia were impudent usurpers. The King's magistrates appointed in each tribe added no strength to the central authority. Their power, dignity, and emolument, all depended on local sources; there was nothing to make them uphold the government of the King, as distinguished from the tribal government: they were nothing but local officers, who used the King's name as a badge of opposition to the English Government. Tamihana and several members of the King's Runanga wished to vest the whole judicial function in chiefs appointed by, and responsible to, the Maori King; but it is manifest that the project could never have been carried into effect. The Runangas would have given no help to the King's magistrates till they had judged the case themselves. If the two powers came into collision, the King's magistrate would always have had to yield. Besides, the King could give no salary, nor hold out any other inducement, which would make his magistrate prefer a barren allegiance to the more profitable and pleasant course of falling in with the passions and prejudices of his own kinsmen and companions.

There were in Waikato and the neighbourhood several bodies of young men, drilled, armed, and dressed in uniform in imitation of our troops. Playing at soldiers was for more than a year the absorbing fashion in Waikato. The men who had fought at Taranaki introduced the practice on their return, having learnt the English words of command, the bugle calls, and the corresponding manœuvres by watching our troops. Those who had not been to the war, and especially Wi Tamihana, received the new fashion with great displeasure. It was agreed that each tribe in turn should furnish a company to occupy Ngaruawahia as a guard of honour to the King: when it came to the turn of Ngatihaua, Tamihana would have nothing to do with the plan; he said his tribe were all ploughmen, none of them were soldiers; and he ended by bringing his men and lads to Ngaruawahia with a dozen ploughs and without guns, and instead of playing at soldiers, ploughed up about seventy acres of land for potatoes. Notwithstanding all opposition, however, the fashion steadily made way. Most of the soldiers were lads of about twenty; they kept themselves very clean and neat, wearing white trousers, blue coats, and white caps with a red cross embroidered in front. Their arms were nothing better than old flint muskets, only a few possessing double-barrelled fowling-pieces or rifles. They grew their own food, and were paid at the rate of threepence a-day. When the King's resources began to fail, the pay was commuted into the promise of a grant of land as a reward for military service—an example afterwards followed by the Colonial Government, except that the King promised his own land and not that of other people.

These soldiers were not at the command of the Runanga of Ngaruawahia; whether they would have obeyed their commanding officer or not was doubtful; but it was quite certain that the commanding officers were not subject to the Council. On several occasions when the services of the soldiers were requested, the chiefs by whom the various companies had been raised and equipped refused to let them be employed. When Reihana was asked to send his men to defend the gold-fields of Coromandel against the Pakeha diggers, he replied: "My soldiers shall take care of the King that is all; let the people of Coromandel take care of their own gold."

Besides the weakness consequent upon having no one to execute their commands, the Council had always before their eyes the fear of offending the local magnates. Patene was so affronted at being censured for attempting to drive away the European magistrate, that he offered to lease land to the settlers. A Kawhia chief threatened to go over to the Queen if the King's Runanga took away his second wife; and as the wife was not taken away, a Hangatiki chief actually did renounce his allegiance, saying he would belong to no society in which bigamy was to be tolerated. Lastly, the King's Council was more addicted to wandering about the country than even the local Runangas. They were invited to every Maori feast, and frequently paid visits to places far remote from Waikato. It was, therefore, impossible to get any matter attended to except by persistent importunity; every question that it was inconvenient to answer was put off to the morrow, with polite apologies that would have done credit to the oldest bureaucracy. In shelving disagreeable subjects their cleverness surpassed even that of the Colonial Government.

The account above given shows what Tamihana and the chiefs of Ngaruawahia were obliged frequently to confess, that there was no power amongst the Maories capable of really governing. They complained bitterly, however, that we had not given them fair play, saying, that instead of being allowed to devote their sole attention to domestic affairs, they had been kept by the British authorities, since they began to construct a Government, in a continual state of excitement. First, we had made an unjust war at Taranaki; then we threatened to attack and put down the King by force; and since Governor Grey had come, he had never ceased to alarm them by his attempt to bribe the King's subjects from their allegiance, and by his preparations for war. It was hardly to be expected, said they, that children such as they were could succeed, when we kept harassing them the whole time they were making the attempt. They thought the least we could do was to let them alone, and not interfere until it was conspicuous that they had failed.

But, like some other Governments, though weak in domestic affairs, in foreign policy the Maori King was strong. As the rallying point of Maori nationality, as the head of a federation to resist the encroachment of the Pakeha, the King was enthusiastically supported by all Waikato and by men of distant tribes. It was in this aspect alone that Rewi and his tribe were adherents of the King. He and Tamihana had espoused two opposite views of the purpose for which the Maori King was to be maintained. The latter desired to create a paternal sovereign to execute just laws to which all should yield obedience; and to oppose the progress of the Pakeha by passive and peaceful resistance, giving no pretext for war. Rewi, on the contrary, rejected every attempt of the King to exert, in time of peace, the least authority over any member of the Ngatimaniapoto tribe, but as the head of a confederation of Maories against the common enemy, Rewi was his most devoted subject. The measures of Sir George Grey, and especially the military preparations going on before the eyes of the Maories in every direction, while increasing their hostility to the Pakeha, strengthened their loyalty to the King, and made the alliance between the various tribes, in spite of all jealousies, far closer than it was before the operations of Government in Waikato commenced. Rewi's view of the object for which the Maori King was established became the popular view, and Rewi the popular leader. During Sir George Grey's administration, Tamihana's influence was steadily on the decline.

Tipene's words to Sir George Grey, at Taupari, that the whole of New Zealand had accepted the Maori King, were true, if they meant that the King had been accepted as an incarnation of Maori nationality, and a leader of resistance to subjugation under the Colonial Government. In this sense, all the tribes of New Zealand either support or sympathize with the Waikatos. That all have not actually risen in arms against us is no proof to the contrary; for one Maori tribe can carry on the war better, if other tribes remain neutral, and furnish supplies. During the time that I was stationed in the Waikato, the King was visited by leading chiefs from Taranaki, from Wauganui, from Hawke's Bay, from the East Cape, from Tauranga, and even from the Ngapuhi of the North; and deputations from Waikato were invited and sent in every direction, even as far as Kapiti, in Cook's Straits.

The Waikato chiefs used often to confess their great need of money to carry out their schemes. The remark was constantly made, that we got all our power by money; and that if they had as much money as we, they would be equally able to carry out their plans.

Their power of raising revenue was very small; most of their money, in fact, came from voluntary contributions. The largest donation I ever heard of was one of 300*l.* in sovereigns, collected by the Hawke's Bay natives, and sent to Waikato, just after the Taranaki war. It was said that this sum lay untouched up to the time of the present outbreak. There were, however, a few regular sources of revenue: all the money taken at ferries in the Waikato district was paid over to the King. The charges, which were regulated by a tariff, were usually 1*s.* 6*d.* for putting a man and horse across the Waikato, and 1*s.* on the Waipa and smaller rivers. The ferry at Pukete paid in one year 5*l.* to the King. The system afforded great advantage to travellers, who were thereby exempted from the extortion customary in other districts. At the much smaller streams of Mangatawhiri and Whangamarino, where the tariff was made by Queen's natives, under the sanction of the Government, the charge was half-a-crown.

Most of the local Runangas paid over to the King some share of the fees and fines which they exacted. I have heard of as much as 10*l.* at a time coming down from Reihana, of Whataroa, for the King's treasury. One of the favourite projects for raising revenue was to levy a tax of 1*l.* per annum on all Europeans resident in the King's dominions. The promoters of the scheme declared that the tribute should be imposed on all alike, missionaries or magistrates, residents on crown or native lands—all should pay, or else be driven out of the district. Others wished to postpone the measure, on the ground that it was unfair to expect Europeans to contribute until the King's Government could afford them protection from depredation. In several instances the tribute was exacted; for, although the missionaries refused to pay, and the natives had too much respect for them to use violence, with the traders and Pakeha-Maories submission was the more prudent course. I knew, however, one old man-of-war's-man, who indignantly refused to pay, and being very abusive to the tax-collectors, got himself pitched over his fence into the fern beyond. But he would not give in.

The most lucrative source of revenue was the money that found its way out of the English into the Maori treasury. The expenditure of Government money in the Waikato district was very great. The sum spent in the Upper and Lower Waikato districts between the 1st August, 1862, and 31st July, 1863, amounted to 5,950*l.*[1] Of this, 1,263*l.* consisted of salaries and pensions to natives, of which it was always said the King received his tithe. In addition to this, there was a large Post-Office expenditure, for the carriage of overland mails to Taranaki, Ahuriri, and other places. These mails were carried exclusively by Maories, selected by Reihana of Whataroa, and Taati of Rangiaowhia, who, although both strong supporters of the King, had this duty entrusted to them, and received salaries from Government for performing it.

None of the magistrates or officers of the King, except the soldiers, received any fixed pay. One effect of this was, that no man had any sense of responsibility for what he did. Every man undertook his duties spontaneously, and considered himself at liberty to throw them up whenever it suited him to do so. No power existed to make Maori officials, any more than other Maories, do their duty: they enjoyed absolute irresponsibility. It was quite impossible to fix the

[1] N. Z. Parl. Papers, 1863. E. No. 8.

blame of misgovernment, or of any public act of injustice, upon any individual or any definite number of individuals.

The account above given, of what the system which the Maories established ultimately became, makes it sufficiently clear that the King himself was a source of little danger to the peace of the colony.

For a long time after the establishment of the Maori King, so little personal hostility was felt towards the Queen, that when, during the Taranaki war, some innovators proposed to change the name of Queen Victoria in the Church Service to King Matutaera, the heretical desire was scouted. "Pretty fellows, indeed," said the chiefs of Ngaruawahia, "to want to alter the Prayer-Book." I once attended service at Ngaruawahia, and looked over the same Prayer-Book with the King. He said a loud "Amen" at the end of the prayers for the Queen. Some murmured that it was rather hard to expect them to pray "that she might vanquish and overcome all her enemies;" but it was not until much later that the practice was given up. In short, the whole system of the native organization was kept together by a feeling of distrust and opposition to the Colonial Government; but it was the existence of this distrust, and not to its peculiar manifestation in the establishment of the Maori King, that was dangerous. Of course, when the interests of one race appeared to become antagonistic to those of the other, some sort of organization was sure to have been invented, with the object of giving unity to the Maori party. As the neglect of the British authorities to perform the duties of government had already brought a Maori King into existence, this person was seized upon for the purpose, and subsequently to, and in consequence of, the Taranaki war, grew really formidable. As long as the Maori race remains disaffected, the peace of the colony will never be secure. Though the King should be killed in the present war, or though the Maories should be forced into agreeing to abjure the King system, the danger would not be thereby removed. In order to secure peace and safety, we shall have to cure the disease, not merely remove the symptoms: we must root out Maori distrust, and then the "King movement" will wither and fall of itself.

If the present unhappy war should be brought to an end before the Maories are altogether exterminated, we shall have to begin afresh the task of governing those who may remain. The utmost that war can effect is to destroy some of the obstacles which have hitherto prevented good government. A better system has yet to be created, but that cannot be done until confidence in those who are to be their rulers is implanted in the minds of the natives.

CHAPTER XIV.

RUMOURS OF WAR.

No progress was made by Sir George Grey's plans in settling any of the matters in dispute between the Maories and the English Government. The Waitara still remained in the occupation of our troops, and Wiremu Kingi was obstinate in his determination to reject all proposals for investigation into the title. It was in vain that his European friends, who had upheld his cause against the late Governor, represented that their advocacy had been based on the assumption that no opportunity had been given him of appealing to any impartial tribunal, and that, such an opportunity being now offered, his refusal to avail himself of it was shaming all who had supported him. Wiremu was stolidly indifferent to every remonstrance. "Waitara is in my hands. I will not give it up" was his ultimatum to Colonel Browne, and it was his ultimatum still. His reply to every one who argued the question with him was, "If Governor Grey wants peace, let him give back Waitara to me."

Rewi and the Ngatimaniapoto chiefs, with whom Wiremu Kingi was living, half-guest, half-prisoner, were delighted at his firmness. Rewi never liked either the award of Wiremu Tamihana, or the stoppage of the war at Taranaki, and had striven from the very first to upset the one and re-commence the other. He now declared that Wiremu Tamihana's proposal had never been carried out; Tamihana had said, "Let all parties withdraw, and let Waitara be left under the protection of the law," whereas the Governor's soldiers still held in their possession, not only Waitara, but other native lands—lands that had been placed under the Maori King—to which the Governor had no sort of claim. As for Tataraimaka, it was held by the Maories, said Rewi, as a security for the Maori land in the Governor's possession, and would be given up whenever that was restored. Rewi denied that the absolute disposal of Waitara was in Tamihana's hands; whatever the latter proposed would be considered by himself and Wiremu Kingi, and if it did not appear good to them, they should keep Waitara in spite of it. The best way Rewi could see of settling the dispute, was by the English Government confessing their error, and restoring Waitara to the lawful owners.

Wiremu Tamihana himself was very reluctant to stir in the matter at all; he had, he said, little hope of getting his proposals adopted by the rest, and when there were so many grounds of quarrel unsettled between Pakeha and Maori, what good was there, he asked, in making himself unpopular, by advocating a trial about Waitara, in opposition to the wishes of his countrymen? Suppose the Waitara dispute was settled, the strife about the King would still remain. It was quite plain that Sir George Grey intended war; his Pakeha friends might talk to him about the commercial advantages of roads, but he knew Sir George Grey better than they. The road from Drury to Mangatawhiri was being made, to bring great guns to the Waikato river, and for no other purpose. A letter was sent to Tamihana by the tribes of Hawke's Bay, who had sympathized warmly with Wiremu Kingi during the Taranaki war, expressing their surprise at the Governor's offer of legal investigation being refused, and urging Tamihana to accept it. This letter never got beyond Kihikihi, where it was read by Rewi, who prudently determined to let it go no further. Tamihana was, however, informed of the letter and its contents, and that all his friends wondered at his inaction, and were beginning to doubt the sincerity of his proposals at Waitara. To these representations he at last yielded, and formally proposed that the Governor's offer about Waitara should be accepted; but as he had foretold, only a few would listen to him, and the majority sided with Rewi.

In the mean time, Sir George Grey's military road was rapidly progressing. The old one, designed and partially made by the Provincial Government, came direct to Te Ia, where the Mangatawhiri joins Waikato. But while completing the old design, Sir George Grey added thereto a new branch, which diverged at a distance of three miles from the Waikato, and was thence carried in a direction pointing up the country, until, on arriving at the bank of the Mangatawhiri, at some distance from Waikato, it came to an abrupt end. As soon as this new road was finished, timber was conveyed along it to the bank of the Mangatawhiri, to make a landing-stage: the Maories thought a bridge was to be built at once, and their excitement became intense; but the Governor assured them he had no intention of building a bridge until the following year, by which time he was sure their opposition would be withdrawn. A large fort, called the Queen's Redoubt, capable of containing 1000 men, was constructed in the midst of the plain, near the termination of the new branch; and a second fort, in which it was reported that cannon would be mounted, was built upon a bluff, overlooking and commanding the Waikato river at Te Ia, the end of the old road. These works proved to the Maories how correct had been their original suspicion of the purposes for which the Governor's operations had been designed.

But a project for a second road, to be made not on Crown but on Maori territory, produced still more excitement and alarm. Wiremu Nera and his tribe had been persuaded to consent to a road being made from

Raglan, through the forest ranges, to Whatawhata on the Waipa: the Government eagerly offered to supply money and employ Nera's natives at high wages in its construction. When the project became known to the Waikatos, they were greatly concerned: the peril was extreme: the intended road, if made, would place Ngaruawahia at the mercy of troops landed at Raglan. For months, meetings were held between Nera's tribe and other natives who had, or asserted, claims upon the land over which the road was to pass. Every influence was brought to bear upon the road-makers to persuade them to abandon the project, but in vain. At last, a day was fixed upon which the work of cutting down trees along the line was to be commenced on the Whatawhata side of the ranges. Rewi and his men began to arm, King's soldiers were assembled, and war-meetings were held at various places on the Waikato. Things went so far, that a party, with guns and ammunition, actually set off from Kihikihi to fire upon Nera's men; but, on arriving in Whatawhata, they met a stern message from Tamihana, saying that Wiremu Nera was his father's companion in arms, and that any one who attacked the old man would also have to fight Ngatihaua and their chief. The question about the road, said Tamihana, was between Nera's tribe and the Ngatihaua, and would be sooner settled if the Kihikihi warriors would go back and mind their own business. The crest-fallen war-party, on meeting such a rebuff, had no alternative but to sneak home again. Yet the opposition to the road, though carried on without further warlike demonstration, was as strong as ever. Tamihana wrote a most eloquent letter, begging Wiremu Nera to abandon a scheme that would place Waikato at the Governor's mercy; and Te Paea with her own hands pulled up the stakes which had been used to mark out the road. Finally, Nera, finding that he had all Waikato against him, and that he could get no pledge from the English Government of support in arms, made up his mind to begin at the Raglan end, upon Queen's land. To this all agreed. A road from Raglan to the sea-slopes of the dividing range would not much hurt Waikato, and, being on Crown land, could not with justice be opposed. Nera got his men employed at 3*s.* 6*d.* a day, which was what he and they most cared about. The Government, though spending large sums with a very inadequate return in the shape of labour, purchased a great deal of very demonstrative loyalty from Nera's tribe. Thus all parties were for a while satisfied.

During the whole time that the leaders of the King party were thus disturbed by threats from without, they had to struggle also against dangers from within. The Waikato district was in a state of lawlessness, which made collision between different tribes, as well as war with the Pakeha, daily imminent. The young men who had fought at Taranaki roamed about the country with arms in their hands, tyrannizing over Maories and

Europeans, seizing cattle and horses on the most flimsy pretexts, and paying not the slightest respect to either King or Queen. The principal chiefs, who had lost all their power, still clung to the authority which their King nominally possessed, but which his Council dared not exercise lest the whole fabric of their Government should break down, and their interference result in internal war. To cure this state of anarchy, the Colonial Government was appointing officers at random, frequently men of neither education nor good manners, who went about the country giving away large salaries to their favourites among the natives, and calling their proceedings "the establishment of law and order." To the lawlessness of the "organized" districts the Government was wilfully blind; but what they would not see, the Maories jealously scrutinized, and refused to exchange their King, weak though he was, for a system which, in their eyes, had so evidently broken down.

The Runanga of Kihikihi, in particular, constituted itself patron of all malefactors whose misdeeds exhibited contempt for Pakehas, or defiance of the English Government. Yes!" said Ngata, a tall hairy chief, with a merry face, who had fought like a lion at Taranaki, and was eager to fight again—"It is quite true! We are much worse than we ever were before. We are showing off our independence." Ngata, when he made this confession, was spending the day galloping about Otawhao, from one European's house to another, announcing, with great glee, that his Runanga had passed a law the night before, that every horse, cow, or sheep, that got out of the Pakeha's fences, if only for five minutes, was to pay a fine of sixpence; and that he and his comrades were going to spend their leisure in watching the fences, and pouncing on the stray animals. All this was said without the least passion or malevolence, as rather a good joke; and, after gossiping awhile on current events, Ngata rode down to Te Awamutu, to consult the magistrate on a point of law incident to a case coming before the Kihikihi Runanga the next evening.

Ngata had just before been "showing off his independence" by stopping Her Majesty's mail. He had quarrelled with the Rev. J. Morgan, the postmaster, about the pay he was to receive for carrying the Napier mail-bag, and thereupon declared that no man should carry the mail over his land until his demands were acceded to. After the Napier mail had several times slipped past Kihikihi, in the bags that were to be carried to Taupo, Rotorua, and elsewhere, Ngata grew so angry, that he extended his prohibition to all mail-bags whatsoever, and gave due notice thereof to the postmaster. The next mail-man tried to traverse Kihikihi by night; but Ngata, who was on the look-out, pounced upon him, and carried him, bag and all, before the Runanga. The assembly gave the mail-man some tea, set the bag on end in the midst, and, sitting around, held a solemn court thereupon. It was unanimously resolved that the postmaster should be fined *5l.* for his breach of injunction and attempt to over-reach them; and that the bag should be retained until the fine was paid. Ngata rode down, next day, to announce the sentence to Mr. Morgan, and used all his powers of persuasion to induce him to pay the *5l.*, but in vain. It was, of course, quite in Ngata's power to have seized upon property to the value of five pounds; but he never did so, and retains the leather bag, stuffed with old newspapers (the letters were safe in the mail-man's pockets), to the present day.

Ngata and his lawless rollicking comrades soon ceased to feel any animosity against me, though I had been forced in amongst them as magistrate. They found the peaceful measures recommended by Tamihana and the King's Runanga, as a substitute for violence, eminently successful in reducing me to a condition of perfect harmlessness. They ceased entirely to express any wish for my expulsion. On one occasion, I rode 150 miles, to rescue a flock of 500 sheep, belonging to an Englishman, out of the hands of some half-dozen Maori depredators among the hills, and was finally referred, by the Runanga of Ngaruawahia, to a couple of young fellows, about twenty-two years old, who, in the absence of Rewi, called themselves "the Runanga of Kihikihi." They told me to mind my own business, and leave them to settle the matter. It is fair to add, that they threatened to bring a war-party on the thieves, who were thereby frightened into restoring the greater part of the flock. Only once did a Maori venture to bring a case into court. On this, the defendant, who was a half-caste, at once appealed to the Kihikihi Runanga for aid, saying that his mother was of their race, and he was an adherent of their King. The appeal was successful: a large party came down to the trial, denied the jurisdiction of the court, and by main force carried off the defendant. No notice was taken by the Government of this act; and the half-caste who so successfully set the authority of the law at defiance did, and does still, visit the English settlements with perfect impunity.

The Government of the Maori King, however, took more notice of the affair. The rescue was discussed at a large meeting, held on the Piako, when both Wiremu Tamihana and Ti Oriori argued that the rescue had been illegal. In this opinion the whole assembly, including Rewi himself, agreed. A collection was therefore made, and the sum of five pounds was subscribed, to be offered as a recompense to the English Government for the offence. This sum was unwisely entrusted to Rewi, who, instead of carrying out the intentions of the subscribers, appropriated it to some purpose the exact nature of which I could never discover.

The meeting on the Piako, here alluded to, was so

universally attended by the King's adherents, that the villages on the Waikato were deserted during the fortnight it lasted. The meeting was an important one, and produced grave results. The cause of its assembling was as follows.

The citizens of Auckland, excited by the news of the rich gold-fields discovered at the other extremity of New Zealand, in the province of Otago, found, or thought they had found, a rival gold-field in a mountainous promontory on the eastern side of the Hauraki gulf, called Coromandel. The most extravagant accounts of its richness were published in the Auckland newspapers, and became immediately notorious to the Waikatos. Unfortunately, the richest veins were supposed to lie in Maori land, which the owners would not either sell, let, or even suffer to be examined, for any sum of money offered. The Auckland public began to put a pressure upon the Colonial Ministers, who made the most vigorous efforts to induce the native owners either to sell or let the land, but in vain. The press began to advocate force, and the diggers to talk of taking the law into their own hands, and driving both Maories and Government off the place. It was exactly a case in which the King party felt bound to interfere and protect their countrymen from injustice. They therefore endeavoured to persuade the owners of Coromandel to hand over the land to their league, by promising to protect them, if attacked. With this view a meeting was called at the mouth of the Piako, on the shores of Hauraki, which was attended by the King with a large body-guard of soldiers, and by nearly every native from Waikato. On both the European and Maori side, war was thought to be imminent; a rush of diggers from Otago was expected, to "prospect" the supposed auriferous country; and it was then thought that the owners would be forced into the Maori King-league in order to obtain protection, and that a collision between the diggers and the King's forces would ensue. The Government, in their alarm, could do nothing more than continue their efforts to acquire peaceably the territory which they feared their white subjects would otherwise seize by force.

The peril was most happily averted by the tact of the Governor. The obstinate owners were few, and the chief of them a woman: it was just a case in which personal influence could tell. Sir George Grey was hastily summoned up from the South, where he was engaged in visiting his old friend Wi Tako, and discovering how general was the native discontent, and how wide were the ramifications of the "King movement." He went down to Coromandel, and persuaded the hitherto obstinate owners to do just what he wished. A large sum of money was paid for the right to dig gold on land which, as it afterwards turned out, was not worth digging; and the Maori King and his army, finding themselves out-manœuvred, retired.

A newspaper, called *Te Hokioi,* published at Ngaruawahia, in Maori, by the King party, soon after printed a very angry letter, which the Governor had sent to the King, finding fault with his going to Hauraki. The Governor said he should not permit Matutaera to march about the country with men whom he chose to call his soldiers, to the great terror of all well-disposed persons; a time would soon come when punishment should be inflicted for these evil deeds. The letter was published by the Maories, in conjunction with a reply, to the effect that, if the Governor would point out the portion of Queen's territory which had been invaded by the King and his forces, or let them know the European settlement which had been terrified, or the individual man who had suffered any damage from the soldiers going to Hauraki, the Maories would be ready to pay compensation for their conduct; but if nobody had been harmed, it was idle to talk of punishing the King for his evil deeds.

This letter of Sir George Grey produced at least one important result. It confirmed the opinion which was entertained by all the Waikatos, that the Governor was as strongly opposed to the Maori King as his predecessor had been, and that they would very probably have ultimately to fight for their independence.

In a letter written by Matutaera Potatau to the natives of Hawke's Bay, on August 21, 1863, six weeks after the invasion of Waikato, this passage occurs :—

" Friends : The Governor has not only now made up his mind. He took his determination when I went to Hauraki. Though it was to Taranaki he went, his thoughts were all the time intent on Waikato."

CHAPTER XV.

THE AWAMUTU.

THE King and his party, on their return from Hauraki to Ngaruawahia, stopped to hold a Runanga at Te Kohekohe, where their young relative Wiremu Te Wheoro was administering "law and order" as a Queen's magistrate. Finding that a design had been made for building a wooden court-house at the village, they seriously warned Te Wheoro not to persist in such an attempt. Several of them had a joint claim with him to the land, and were resolved to interfere and stop the erection of the building. The Runanga and the resolution were reported to Sir George Grey, who determined to proceed with the building, regardless of threats, and to make not a mere court-house, but a defencible barrack for a native police force.

The design was to imitate the policy of the Maori chiefs themselves, by enlisting a body of native youths, who were to be lodged in the barrack at Te Kohekohe, disciplined, drilled, and gradually and cautiously made use of, to suppress dangerous offenders like Whakapaukai and establish a real system of law and order, at least in the more loyal region of Lower Waikato.

Sir George Grey was anxious to have a similar force enrolled in the Upper Waikato, at Otawhao, but it was represented to him that any such attempt would inevitably provoke the hostility of the Maories, who would promptly suppress the institution so soon as its object was apparent. In consequence of these representations, the plan was so far changed, that instead of a police-station, au industrial school for young men and grown-up boys was substituted, which would be at once a trap to catch the King's soldiers, and might be made into a station for an effective force at some future time. There was no doubt that the design would be, sooner or later, seen through by the King party, and that a law would be passed forbidding young men to join the school. Sir George Grey was, however, of opinion that the offer of good food and clothes would be a sufficient inducement to procure disobedience of any such injunction.

The execution of both these projects was entrusted to me, as I was at that time in charge of the Lower, as well as the Upper, Waikato District.

The first plan never proceeded further than the preparation of timber for building. In New Zealand, where sawn timber can be bought only in the large towns, and where the expense of carriage is very heavy, it is a matter of economy, before erecting a building, to saw the timber required, on or near the spot. All the sawyers in the neighbourhood of Te Kohekohe were employed for several months in preparing large quantities of timber for building barrack-rooms, &c., within the stockade at Mangatawhiri and the Queen's Redoubt; and when this task was finished, they had to drink out the wages they had earned before they were willing to work again.

But at Otawhao it was possible to begin the experiment at once. A Mission-school was already there, with an estate of about 200 acres attached, called Te Awamutu, and this was given up by the Bishop of New Zealand, and the Secretary of the Church Missionary Society, to the Government, to enable the plan to be carried out with the least possible delay.

The objects which it was hoped might be attained by a school at Te Awamutu were:—

(1) The exhibition before the eyes of the Waikato natives of the advantages to be derived from the British Government. That it might be seen, especially by the young men, the most dangerous class in the native community, that the Queen's Government was able to give physical comfort and civilization in exchange for the barbarous independence still cherished by them.

(2) The training of a class of men, upon whose fidelity the Government might rely, and out of whose ranks native officers might be afterwards selected.

(3) The organization of a body of disciplined young

men, accustomed to obey, who might be used as police, and furnish the Government with an instrument for really establishing "law and order" in Maori districts.

The chief fault to be found with this scheme was, that it ought to have been begun twenty years before. At that time the natives wished to place themselves under our authority, and would have joyfully accepted us as masters. Even so recently as ten years ago, they had proved their desire for civilization, by giving to the Crown an estate of 800 acres, upon a promise that an industrial school and a hospital should be erected. For the fulfilment of this promise they had waited in vain. Before the time had arrived at which it was convenient for us to remember and keep our promises, their zeal for improvement had cooled. Some months before the new school at Te Awamutu was proposed, they had announced that, ten years having elapsed without the erection of that school and hospital for which they had given the land, they considered the grant void, and should resume possession of their property.

As these sentiments of the Waikatos were well known, it was the opinion of many that it would have been more prudent to try the experiment of enrolling a police force, or collecting the young men into an industrial school, in some other district, where there would be less risk of being interrupted in the work by jealous fears and hostile attacks. There is no doubt that such criticism is just. Had any one desired to irritate the King party, and obtain a ground for quarrel with them, no better places than Te Awamutu and Te Kohekohe could have been chosen for establishing schools and barracks.

To the Awamutu scheme, which appeared to the natives, at first sight, an act of pure benevolence, free from any sinister motives, a large number of the Waikatos were, at the outset, highly favourable. Many youths at once made application for admission, and others said they only hesitated because they could not believe Government promises, until they saw them fulfilled with their own eyes.

But this confidence on the part of the Waikatos was very short-lived. Not only were they alarmed by the report of what was to be done at Te Kohekohe, but the rumour of a new plan of Sir George Grey caused nearly as much excitement in Waikato as the original announcement of the Mangatawhiri road. The Governor told some Waikato chiefs, who visited him in Auckland, that he was going to send for a steamer to navigate the Waikato river; and when they assured him that the entrance of the vessel would be resisted by force, and that they should certainly fire upon her, he replied that his steamer should be one that no shot could pierce—that he should sit quietly reading books in the cabin while they fired upon her, and should take the rattling of their bullets against her side as a great compliment to himself. This announcement, when made known to the other natives, was everywhere taken as a distinct proof of that intention to make war, which most Maories had attributed to the Governor, from the day when he condemned the Maori King at Taupari. These reports put an end to their hesitation about the proposed school at Te Awamutu. It was evidently part of the same scheme for reducing Waikato, and must, therefore, be inflexibly resisted.

The existing buildings of the old Mission-school furnished room for not more than twenty-two persons, and in order to provide accommodation for a hundred, the number it was intended to enlist, it was necessary to purchase trees from the natives, and have timber sawn. The King was then at Rangiaowhia, with a large gathering of the Waikato and Ngatimaniapoto tribes. The proposed school was discussed. The feature of the plan which most alarmed them was, that children and young boys were not to be admitted. "We often wished," said one speaker, "to send our young men to the Mission-school. We were told, 'No; they could not learn the Pakeha's language—their lips and tongues were too stiff.' Now there is a change; the lips and tongues of the young men have suddenly become flexible, and they are pressed to go to school." They did not doubt that some hostile design lurked under the apparent benevolence; and it was resolved that no timber-trees should be sold, so that it would, at least, be impossible to enlarge the existing building. The King and the whole assembly then adjourned to Hangatiki; but no sooner were their backs turned, than certain natives, who cared more for money than the King's commands, offered trees for sale. The offer was accepted; six trees were bought, of which four were felled, and sawing commenced.

At the Hangatiki meeting, the subjects of the Awamutu school and the Governor's intended steamer were again discussed; when Rewi and the Ngatimaniapoto strongly urged that it would be by far the safest course to expel the Government officer from the district at once, by force; and as the arrival of a steamer would render Ngaruawahia no longer safe, they tried to persuade the King to retire to the hills, and fix his capital at Hangatiki. To this hostile policy, however, the Waikatos would not consent. The fact of the land at Te Awamutu being Crown land was held to justify the Government in stationing any person they chose upon it; and the steamer might prove but an empty threat. It was therefore resolved to oppose the school by those lawful and peaceable means which had proved so successful in the case of the magistrate. Great was their indignation, on returning to Rangiaowhia, to find that a sale of timber had actually taken place. A resolution was immediately passed, to take back, at least, the two trees not yet felled; but when it was represented to them that such conduct would be stealing, they rescinded the resolution and gave up the trees, though at the same time they again made a law that no more should be sold. The law, however, could not be enforced. The Waikatos of Rangiaowhia, and even of Kihikihi, persisted in selling timber; though, at the latter place, the Ngatimaniapoto expressed strong indignation, and a stormy Runanga was held over almost each individual tree. Sawing proceeded steadily though slowly, and the plans of the Waikatos for stopping the building failed.

The scheme was regarded by the younger men in a very different light; they liked good food and clothes, and knew the benefit of learning to be blacksmiths or carpenters, and were willing enough to render the obedience which was exacted from them as the price of maintenance and instruction. A large portion of the King's soldiers at Rangiaowhia, Waipa, and elsewhere, expressed their desire to leave His Majesty's service for the establishment at Te Awamutu, and even went so far as to apply for admission. Their defection so alarmed the Runangas, that a law was passed, imposing a fine of 5*l.* upon any King's soldier who left the service; and extreme displeasure was threatened by the King-party against any persons who might venture to become members of the school.

Notwithstanding this opposition, however, the number of pupils steadily increased. Ti Oriori openly pronounced himself a supporter of the school. Several young men from his section of the Ngatihaua tribe actually entered as scholars, and, with the exception of one who went off to be married, remained until the outbreak of the war. The opposition was also much weakened by a dissension which arose amongst the King-party, and for a time appeared likely to produce an open rupture. It was a controversy about religion. A Runanga sat at Taupo to discuss the relative merits of the Roman Catholic and Protestant faiths. It was argued that the priests of the former religion avowed themselves to be of no country, professed allegiance to the Catholic Church and not to the Queen, and made no opposition to the Maori nationality and King; whereas the clergy of the Church of England and the Wesleyan ministers were friends of Governor Grey, staunch in their allegiance to the Queen, and persistent in using the form of prayer for the Queen, even to the length of supplicating that she might "vanquish and overcome all her enemies," which, of course, included the Maories themselves. The argument was held by the Runanga of Taupo to be convincing. They accordingly addressed letters to Waikato, recommending all persons to change from the Protestant to the Catholic religion. A report was circulated that King Matutaera had himself become a convert; and a pastoral letter from Bishop Pompallier, the Roman Catholic Primate, to Matutaera, offering to station a priest at Ngaruawahia, was printed and published. The indignation of the Protestant chiefs was aroused. Old Porokoru, alarmed lest he should be converted, clad himself in European garments, put on a tall black hat, and attended the church at Te Awamutu for about six consecutive Sundays, where he repeated the responses, prayers for the Queen included, in a loud and indignant voice. The Roman Catholics at Ngaruawahia were warned that, if they persisted in having a priest, the opposite party would have a magistrate; and Wi Karamoa sat down in a rage and wrote to invite me to come at once, offering a house and land.

Soon afterwards, a dinner was given by the chief of Rangiaowhia, to commemorate the King's accession, to which all Europeans in the neighbourhood were invited. At the request of the natives, I took the chair, supported by Te Paea the King's sister, Wi Karamoa, Taati, and other leading Protestant chiefs. The dinner, which was served in European fashion, was excellent—roasted turkey, preserves, tarts, and bottled ale, were in the bill of fare—and every one behaved in the most decorous manner. When dinner was over, there were races and athletic sports. A day or two afterwards, the whole party came to return the visit, and dine at Te Awamutu, and, as a pledge of friendship and goodwill, wrote a letter to the Governor, inviting him to a meeting in the Waikato district.

When the dissension thus began to grow serious, the Catholic party gave way, and agreed that the priest was to be stationed at a village a few miles away from Ngaruawahia; an article was also published in the King's newspaper, explaining that His Majesty had not changed his religion, but had merely, when asked whether he approved of the Roman Catholic faith, replied—"I approve of all religions in the world," which, the newspaper observed, was the right sort of thing for a Sovereign who had subjects of different creeds to say.

In the meanwhile, the establishment at Te Awamutu was carried on with every prospect of success. Every applicant for admission was referred to those who had been already some time at the school, to make full inquiries as to the management and discipline; and was then told that he would be received and treated exactly in the same way, upon the one condition of implicit obedience. Every man and boy in the school was clothed, lodged, and fed, in a coarse, but wholesome and civilized fashion. The clothes, and everything else entrusted to the scholars, were regularly inspected, and kept scrupulously clean. A schoolmaster was provided by Government, who taught reading, writing, and arithmetic, to all; and beside this, each person was employed for five hours daily in one of the various mechanical trades carried on within the premises. Thus each had an opportunity, not only of acquiring a rough education, but of fitting himself to gain a livelihood, by practising some handicraft acquired at the school. The trades carried on upon the Awamutu estate, were those of carpenter, blacksmith, wheelwright, shoemaker, tailor, and printer. A few scholars were also employed in agriculture, and in tending cattle and sheep upon the school estate—some as their regular occupation, and others as an occasional change from in-door employment. The English artizans, employed as teachers, were chiefly men who had been living in the neighbourhood, and were acquainted with the Maories and their language. Most had previously been exercising their trades for the benefit of the district, and the only difference to them was, that they were now more systematically at work, and were engaged in instructing native apprentices. The natives of the district had now, therefore, to resort to our Government establishment for the repair of their ploughs, and for their shoes and clothes. The demand for all these services was far greater than the supply, so that there was a prospect of being able to employ a great number of Maori apprentices in every department, with certain profit. The cost to the Government of keeping up each branch of industry diminished daily. Even Rewi and Wiremu Tamihana themselves visited the school. The latter extended his patronage so far as to be measured for a pair of trowsers, for which he paid 1*l*. in advance; but Ti Oriori intercepted them on their way to Peria, tried them on, and was so charmed with the fit, that he refused to part with them, and told Tamihana he would agree to take them as a present.

The promise of implicit obedience to orders, exacted from each person on admission, was in almost all cases faithfully kept. Very few complaints were made, either by the schoolmaster and trade-instructors, of idleness and obstinacy; or by the scholars, of tyranny and injustice. The former, who at first loudly declared the impossibility of making Maori boys work, or teaching them anything but mischief, ended by as loud praises of their docility, industry, and progress in their work. A continual and almost daily inspection of all the work that was going on, enables me to testify that this praise was well deserved. The pupils, on the other hand, finding themselves happy and well-treated, and being conscious of steady progress in acquiring valuable attainments, submitted, without the least reluctance, to the restraints and discipline of the place, and were daily practised in the habit of obedience. In the main object for which Te Awamutu was established—the collection of a body of Maories accustomed to obey—there was little doubt of complete success.

The only difficulty was that of getting enough timber to build a house that would hold fifty or sixty more. The opposition of the Kihikihi natives was persistent and troublesome. The very men who, ten years before, would have given land, timber, provisions, and even labour, to establish a school of the kind, now resisted the buying, felling, sawing, and carting of timber, by the most strange stratagems. On one occasion, they entirely surrounded a saw-pit by a ring of new cultivations, which carts were forbidden to cross; and it was only by threatening to plough up the Government road adjoining the bridge over the Mangapiko, and to sow a crop of wheat there, so as to stop all communication between Rangiaowhia and Kihikihi, that a right of road through the ring of cultivation was obtained. A daring fellow, who was a great friend of Rewi's, threatened to break the saws; and when, in spite of his threat, the work still went on, he drove his cart and horse to the pit one very stormy day, when the sawyers were kept from work by fear of falling trees, and carted all the sawn timber away. An express was at once sent off to tell Wiremu Tamihana and the King, who were holding a monster meeting at Peria, of this seizure, and to demand instant restitution. The lawless violence of Rewi's friend was universally condemned; even Rewi had nothing to say in his behalf. Ti Oriori and another Ngatihaua chief, with a dozen followers, were sent over to Kihikihi to order the timber to be given up. A stormy meeting ensued, and the Kihikihi natives refused to obey the command; after talking a whole day, Ti Oriori consented to let them keep the timber, upon paying compensation for the trees and for the sawing. To this arrangement I refused to agree; I would have nothing but the timber. Ti Oriori could do no more, and he went away. Te Paea, who happened to be on a visit at Kihikihi, heard the tumult, and asked what it was all about; she was told: she then asked to have the disputed timber given to her; it was impossible to refuse her so trifling a request. "Now," she said, "I shall give the timber to Mr. Gorst." She wrote and sent a messenger to beg that I would fetch my timber which she was holding for me. "One thing," said this lady in her postscript, "I have forgotten; please give me a little tobacco." A week afterwards, when Tamihana arrived from Peria, to insist on restitution, I had the pleasure of showing him the timber, stacked upon the Awamutu land, and of informing him that the trouble was at an end.

After this defeat, Rewi and the Ngatimaniapoto appeared to withdraw all opposition, and many of the soldiers and other lads, from Kihikihi and elsewhere, began to talk of entering the school.

The good temper of the Waikatos at this period so imposed on the Colonial Government, that they determined to spend considerable sums of money, in further enlarging and improving the Awamutu school, and in other schemes for the civilization of the natives.

It was intended to erect the long-promised native hospital, on a small plot of Crown land, consisting of about thirty acres, not yet enclosed or cultivated, situated about three-quarters of a mile from Te Awamutu. One house-surgeon was to be in constant residence at the hospital, and a superior officer, under the title of Medical Commissioner, was to travel about the whole Waikato district, to heal the sick, send serious cases to the hospital, and recommend measures to improve the sanitary condition of the Maories.

The New Zealand Assembly, which had been recently in session, had shown the utmost zeal in forwarding Sir George Grey's policy. They repudiated, indeed, the bargain which Mr. Fox had made with the Governor, that the Colony should undertake the responsibility of governing the Maories; and turned Mr. Fox's ministry out of office for having made such an arrangement. Another ministry was placed in office, upon the distinct understanding, that they were in no case to be so rash as to propose any particular policy in native affairs. They were to let Sir George Grey pursue what course he pleased, and were held responsible to the Assembly only for seconding the Governor, and giving effect to his wishes, so far as the interests of the colonists would allow. The New Zealand public wished to make the Governor, whom the Home authorities had sent out, Dictator. No sooner had this arrangement been made, than a despatch arrived from the Duke of Newcastle, accepting the offer which Mr. Fox had already made on behalf of the colonists, and which the colonists had just repudiated. This brought the Government to a dead lock. The colonists addressed an indignant remonstrance to the Queen, complaining that the Imperial Government had first mismanaged the Maories, until most people thought the Queen's sovereignty could not be established without a war, and then, when affairs were in this critical and dangerous condition, abdicated their unpleasant office, and left the difficulty for the colonists to solve. In the mean time, as hopes were entertained that the Duke of Newcastle would be persuaded to alter his decision, the Colonial ministers were sent to their tasks with the strict injunction of the Assembly not to assume the dangerous responsibility. The Governor, on his side, was equally reluctant to exercise a power which his chief in England had already relinquished. It will be seen that this double Government, of which each member refused to move first, was the proximate cause of the war.

But, while refusing to assume the lead, it was the object of the colonists to show their readiness to second the Governor's plans. The sum of money, which Sir George Grey said was necessary for native government, was voted without special appropriation, to be spent exactly in the way he might desire. An Act also was passed, empowering the Governor in Council, by proclamation, to form districts in which, under certain regulations, the Maories should be at liberty to exchange their proprietary rights to land for estates in fee simple. The friends of the Maories in the Assembly expected great results from this Act. They thought the natives would barter their independence for a Crown grant of their lands. In this, however, they were entirely mistaken. The Act was hardly heard of, and was never the subject of discussion, in the Waikato District. An estate in fee simple was only useful to a native who wished to sell or let his land. In the Waikato, where selling or letting was rigidly forbidden, native title was good enough. Thus the Native Lands Act, like most other legislation on native matters, served as a topic for debate to the New Zealand politicians, and as an illustration of colonial benevolence, but had no effect, good or bad, upon the Maories. Had the law been in any way forced upon their attention, I have little hesitation in saying that it would have excited great dissatisfaction. They would have asked what right the Colonial Parliament had to legislate about their lands at all. It must not be forgotten, that the zeal for Maori nationality was wider than that for the Maori King; and that the idea of possessing a right to their lands quite independent of our will, and of any treaty or engagements with us, was universal. I know a clever and well-educated young gentleman—a half-caste—to whom Sir George Grey offered a Crown-grant of the land which he held as a Maori chief. His reply was: "Thank you, I have no objection to receive a certificate of title, but I will not accept a Crown-grant of what is already mine." We ourselves have taught the natives that the land is their own, and they regard any meddling with it, on the part of the Colonial Assemblies, as an intrusive usurpation.

CHAPTER XVI.

TATARAIMAKA.

In October, 1862, a great national meeting, to which allusion has been already made, was held at the Ngatihaua village of Peria, to which invitations were issued several months before. Sir George Grey himself was asked to attend the meeting by several Waikato chiefs; but Wiremu Tamihana did not join in the invitation. He and the principal men of Ngatihaua did not wish the Governor to attend, because Maories from distant places would be present, the language would be very free, and things might be said in the Governor's presence that would affront him, and put their hospitality to shame.

The meeting was a very large one, attended by the tribes not only of Waikato, but of Tauranga, the East Coast, Napier, Whanganui, and Taranaki. The subject which the meeting had been specially called to discuss was the everlasting Waitara. The general opinion of the Maories on this point was, that no arbitration could take place so long as the troops remained in possession of Waitara, and of those other plots of native land which were claimed under Hapurona's treaty of peace. As long as the Government persisted in keeping possession of the land in dispute, it was right, in their opinion, to refuse every offer of arbitration, and continue to hold Tataraimaka as a material guarantee for the restoration of that which was their own. The difference between what Sir George Grey proposed, and what the Maories would accept, was small, but very important to both sides. It was the old question of nationality in a different form. If both parties withdrew from Waitara, the investigation would have the aspect of an international conference; but to allow the Governor to remain in possession, was to acknowledge the Queen's sovereignty—to submit as subjects, not to treat as an independent people.

The Bishop of New Zealand, who was present at the Peria meeting, tried in vain to combat this zeal for nationality, which overpowered all other considerations. The first encounter occurred on a Sunday. Wiremu Tamihana had preached to the assembled multitude in the morning, on the text, "Behold how good and joyful a thing it is, brethren, to dwell together in unity;" and had illustrated the doctrine by relating the benefits produced by the union of the Maori tribes, once constantly at war, into one brotherhood under the Maori King. The Bishop, learning of his discourse, which had produced great effect on the audience, preached in the afternoon a different sermon from the same text, urging the great necessity of union between the Pakeha and Maori races, and pointing out the impossibility of such union, unless they agreed to submit to one law and one sovereign.

In the course of the discussions which took place during the following days, the Bishop asked for an opportunity of addressing the Assembly, which the head chiefs readily granted him. In his speech, he urged and besought the Maories, especially Wiremu Tamihana and Matutaera Potatau, whom he called upon by name, to agree to a settlement of the Waitara dispute. He further pointed out the suffering and ruin which the hostile occupation of Tataraimaka inflicted on the innocent men, women, and children, who were so unfortunate as to be its owners; and declared, that as he had stood up before the British Government, and protested against the Maori widows and orphans being deprived by force of their rights, so he now protested against the Maories' wrong, in retaliating upon Pakeha widows and orphans in the same fashion.

The Bishop's arguments, though heard with attention and respect, and though supported by several Ngatihaua chiefs, who stood up and boldly declared themselves on his side, could not alter the general resolution of the meeting. Some effect, however, was produced on Wiremu Tamihana himself. A fortnight after the meeting, he rode over with his followers to Kihikihi, and publicly demanded from Rewi and Wiremu Kingi, that an investigation should be made into the title to Waitara in the manner which the Government had proposed. Wiremu Kingi refused. A stormy discussion ensued, in which Rewi and all the Ngatimaniapoto supported Wiremu Kingi's refusal; and ultimately their opinions gained the day. Tamihana, thus baffled in his first attempt, next demanded that Tataraimaka should be given up to the owners. This demand was, however, as obstinately opposed as the former one. The resolution of the Ngatimaniapoto was immoveable. Wiremu Tamihana could effect nothing without an open quarrel. Such a breaking up of the league would sacrifice Maori independence, which Tamihana, in his love of his country and fear of Sir George Grey, was not prepared to do.

After this failure of Tamihana, it was evident that, sooner or later, one of two things must happen: either Waitara must be exchanged for Tataraimaka, or the war at Taranaki must be renewed. There always was, and perhaps even now is, a way out of the native difficulty—I mean, the acknowledgment of the Maori King, as a Sovereign independent of the colonists, but under the Queen's protection—but to that the New Zealand Government had never been willing to listen.

At the beginning of 1863, Sir George Grey astonished the Waikatos, by suddenly appearing in the midst of them. He made a rapid journey from Auckland up the country, landed at Ngaruawahia unrecognised, and stationed himself by Potatau's tomb. The village was nearly deserted; the King was at Hangatiki with most of his Council, only Te Paea and a few chiefs remained behind. They came out of their houses to look at the Pakeha visitor, and to their amazement recognised the Governor. He was received with enthusiastic good-will. All the old women turned out to "tangi" over him, according to the Maori fashion of saluting an old friend,[1] and then began to scrape potatoes and prepare food for him and his retinue, who shortly began to arrive. Te Paea said afterwards, "Why did you not make the surprise complete, by taking an axe and cutting down the flag-staff? We should have refused you nothing." In their politeness and hospitality they would very likely have refused nothing; but Rewi would certainly have put the flag-staff up again.

After talking to the people, the Governor went down the river as far as the Mission-station of Taupiri. Maori lads were sent galloping off to fetch the King from Hangatiki, and Wiremu Tamihana from Peria. Both obeyed the call. His Majesty was obliged to come from Hangatiki on horseback, a mode of travelling to which he is not accustomed. By the time he reached Rangiaowhia, the unusual exertion had made sitting on the saddle extremely painful. The King could go no further. To his bodily sores was added

[1] The old native women always show affection by a sort of whimper, which is often prolonged for hours. This is called a "tangi."

mental anxiety lest the Governor should think the inability to ride a pretence. The monarch, therefore, sent for a neighbouring missionary, the Rev. J. Morgan, and a native catechist, whom he requested to examine into his actual condition. They did so. They certified in due form that Matutaera could not sit, and the certificate was solemnly forwarded to His Excellency the Governor. I wish I could give the reader a translation in full of this extraordinary State document.

Wiremu Tamihana, however, being a more practised rider, was speedily on the spot, as well as many other Waikato chiefs. Rewi and those who sympathized with him did not attend. It was arranged that a conference should take place in a field at Taupiri. As soon as the Governor came into the field, at the further end of which the chiefs were clustered together, the crowd suddenly parted, and Tamihana rushed forward to the Governor, seized him by the hand, and with cries of welcome led him to the seat which had been placed for him as president of the meeting. The principal speakers were Taati of Rangiaowhia and Tamihana. The latter said that he was glad to see the Governor in person, and tell him that the work of the Maories in setting up a King was no new thing. It had not begun, said Tamihana, in the days of Governor "Angry-belly," as he irreverently termed the late Governor; no! it had begun before, in Sir George Grey's own time, while he was still Governor amongst them.

The Maories had the design in their thoughts long before it was actually carried out. Sir George Grey was again asked by Tamihana, as he had been asked more than a year before at Taupari, by Tipene, whether he was still opposed to their King. He replied that he never went to bed at night without thinking what he could do to pull down the Maori King. "I shall not," he said, "fight against him with the sword, but I shall dig round him till he falls of his own accord." These words made a deep impression on the audience, and were told to those not present, and quoted as the special thing which the Governor had said at the meeting.

A case had recently occurred at Whanganui, in Cook's Straits, where an English girl, walking along the high road a little in advance of her father, was seized by a Maori who attempted to assault her; her screams brought the father to her assistance, and the miscreant made off. The police arrested the man, but he was rescued by his comrades, who declared that he was a subject of the King, and could not be tried by our laws. This story was told by Sir George Grey to Tamihana and his friends, and he charged them with being guilty of the outrage, inasmuch as the man who had done it sheltered himself from punishment under the name of that King whom they persisted in supporting. To all their arguments in favour of the King, the Governor answered by referring to this case, and at last silenced them altogether.

The next subject discussed was Tataraimaka. The Governor announced his intention of taking possession of this land. Wi Tamihana replied, that, while acknowledging such an act to be perfectly just and right, he begged for further delay, in order that the well-disposed chiefs might work upon the Maories, and persuade them to surrender the land quietly. The Governor said he had waited long enough, and should now go down to Taranaki at once. Tamihana said that also was quite just, and he offered to meet the Governor at Taranaki, and accompany him to Tataraimaka, with the object of preventing the holders from resisting by force of arms. The Governor thanked the chief for his offer, but declined his company. The party present, composed of men who supported Wi Tamihana, had nothing to say against the justice of the Governor's design; they told him they would write to the Ngatiruanui, and do their utmost to get the land surrendered in peace. Had Rewi and his friends been present, no doubt the Governor's announcement would have been very differently received.

The chiefs present also remonstrated with the Governor against the threatened steamer. They had never objected to small boats and canoes; but a steamer was, in their eyes, very different: she could bring troops and great guns into their country. The Governor said he should certainly bring in his steamer, to save them trouble in paddling their canoes against the current;

she would tow the canoes. He had no doubt that, in a very short time, they would be convinced of her usefulness, and would threaten him with war, if he proposed to take her away.

After the meeting, Sir George Grey was invited to visit Rangiaowhia and Horotiu; but he was compelled by illness to return direct to Auckland. Even after he had left Taupiri, riders galloped down the river bank after him, as far as Paetai, begging that he would return.

In fulfilment of their promises, Tamihana, Taati, and others, sent letters to Taranaki, urging the Ngatiruanui to give up Tataraimaka, and intimating that if they resisted and renewed the war, no help was to be expected from Waikato. But counter letters were sent at the same time by Rewi and other chiefs of Ngatimaniapoto, as well as by chiefs of Lower Waikato, from the Paetai neighbourhood, exhorting Ngatiruanui to hold the Tataraimaka block resolutely, and promising that any attempt on the Governor's part to possess himself of it would be regarded by Waikato as a declaration of war.

Still, however, Sir George Grey hesitated; while the Colonial Ministers, true to the charge laid on them by the Assembly, refused to give advice on the matter. At last, in the beginning of March, 1863, the Governor announced that he should delay no longer to take the decisive step. Accompanied by General Cameron, Mr.

Domett (the Colonial Premier), Mr. Dillon Bell (the Minister for Native Affairs), and a large military force, he went down to Taranaki by sea. Battalion after battalion was then sent for from Auckland, until the bulk of the troops were once more concentrated at Taranaki.

After some delay, the Governor, with a strong military force, marched to Tataraimaka, and built a redoubt. Nothing but good-will was shown by those natives whom they met, although every person in Taranaki had expected, and many had laid heavy bets, that the party would be fired upon. The leaders returned in safety to Taranaki, and the troops were left quietly working at the redoubt. It must not be forgotten, that at this time, the country round Taranaki was entirely occupied by the stockades and redoubts of our troops. Not only were our own lands, and the disputed block at Waitara so protected, but northwards, beyond the frontier of the settlement, little stockades, surmounted by the English flag, could be seen dotted about the landscape; all situated on Maori land, which was ours only by right of conquest, and so long as we could retain possession by force.

On his return from Tataraimaka to the town of Taranaki, the Governor commenced a private investigation into the Waitara purchase. His interpreter was sent to the Ngatiawa natives at Mataitawa, and found out a new and very material point in the case, overlooked by both the supporters and opposers of the original transaction. This was, that Wiremu Kingi's residence on Teira's land, at Waitara, had not been merely by permission of Teira and his father, but under a general agreement, made by the tribe at the time of their migration to Waitara, that they should live together on the south bank for mutual protection against their ancient enemies, the Ngatimaniapoto. About the same time, Teira went to see Mr. Dillon Bell, who was an old friend of the Ngatiawa tribe. They happened to talk about the occasion when Mr. Bell had fallen in with the tribe on their way from Cook's Straits. Mr. Bell asked Teira to tell him all about their first settlement at Waitara; and to his surprise, Teira's narrative disclosed the same fact. In a subsequent interview, Teira, who had obviously been tampered with in the interim, tried to explain away his former admission. But the fact was too well established to be now denied, and Sir George Grey expressed a very strong opinion that this circumstance, if known to Colonel Browne, would have prevented his ever purchasing Waitara from Teira; and, having now come to light, obliged the Governor, in common justice, to relinquish the land. He, therefore, wished the Colonial Ministers to advise him to give up Waitara. The Ministers were very reluctant to do any such thing. In the first place, giving advice at all had an appearance of assuming that responsibility which the Assembly had charged them to avoid; and, secondly, they were the very men who had supported Colonel Browne's policy by the argument, that the Taranaki war was not about land but sovereignty; and that Wiremu Kingi was fighting, not because his rights were invaded, but because he did not choose to allow them to be determined by the Governor of the colony. To men holding these opinions, the discovery of a new claim possessed by Wiremu Kingi did not seem to affect the question at issue. They considered that the Governor should still hold Waitara, and should not yield possession until the rival claims of Teira and Wiremu Kingi had been publicly heard and adjusted.

While the Governor and his advisers were thus debating the well-worn Waitara question, the natives were not so quiet and inactive as they seemed. It is not Maori custom to act hastily. The occupation of Tataraimaka had taken them by surprise: the Government had so often threatened what had not afterwards been performed, that they never believed Sir George Grey would really seize it, otherwise they would have resolved beforehand how his act should be met. To fire on the party, without previous consideration, as they marched to Tataraimaka, was a measure far too rash and decisive for Maori policy.

While the troops, therefore, were building the redoubt, the natives were holding Runangas. The result of their deliberations was, that rifle pits were dug, and preparations for fighting made on the Maori land, at the edge of Tataraimaka; but it was agreed that nothing more should be done until an answer was received to the following letter:—

"Mataitawa, in the region of Taranaki,
April 8, 1863.

"To Wi Kingi, to Rewi Maniapoto, to Te Waru,[1] to Porokoru, to Honi Papita,[2] and to all their districts.

"Friends and fathers. Salutations to you in the grace of God and in the shadow of our King.

"On the 4th day of April, the Governor marched to Tataraimaka with his soldiers. His barracks are finished and stand at Tataraimaka. The determination of the people here is to wait for the word from you and from the people of this island.

"These five tribes—Te Atiawa, Taranaki, Ngatiruanui, Ngatirauru and Whanganui, have sat down at Tataraimaka. The red earth has dried on the surface—the work of the people.[3] The guns will shortly be firing continually.

"O Wiremu, what is your determination for your people who are in trouble here? Friend, if it were

[1] A Rangiaowhia chief—Taati's father.

[2] A Rangiaowhia chief, and member of the king's council.

[3] This means,—the red subsoil has been dug up, and has dried on the surface, *i.e.* rifle pits are dug.

merely a canoe of wood we should know how to act; but for a canoe of men, where should we search?[1]

"*From the* RUNANGA *of* MATAITAWA."

Before relating the answer received, and the next act of the Maories, it is necessary to inform the reader of events which had occurred meanwhile in the Waikato District; where, as soon as it was known that the Governor had actually gone down to Taranaki, the excitement became intense. The Waikatos expected nothing less than an immediate renewal of war. In this crisis, Rewi Maniapoto took the lead, and his violent and energetic measures will form the subject of the following chapter.

[1] That is to say, if it were such a thing as a canoe that were in peril, we should judge for ourselves, but men's lives are more important.

CHAPTER XVII.

REWI MANIAPOTO.

THE timber for the projected police-barracks had been mostly sawn upon English land at Mangatawhiri, whence it was rafted by Te Wheoro and his friends to Te Kohekohe. By the month of March everything was ready; carpenters were sent out from Auckland, and the work began.

Just then Mohi and Ihaka, Manukau chiefs in Government pay, paddling down the river from a meeting at Rangiriri, observed the large quantities of timber and other preparations at Te Kohekohe. Upon this, they sent messengers back to Rangiriri with this message to Waikato—"Our fate has come upon us." The Assembly sat all night debating, and in the morning messengers were sent to warn Te Wheoro that Waikato was coming down, to raft back the timber to the Queen's land at the Ia. Behind the messengers came a large band to fulfil the threat; they landed at Te Kohekohe, and an angry debate began, which lasted two days. Neri, who was present, asserted that he had a joint claim with Te Wheoro to the land, and refused his consent to the building. The Waikatos entreated, stormed, and threatened; but Te Wheoro stood firm. At last, irritated by his obstinacy, they seized some of the planks and threw them into the river. The old women of Te Kohekohe rushed to the rescue. There was a struggle between the two parties, carried on without bloodshed and without even a blow struck in anger; one party pulling out the planks as fast as the other threw them in. A few pieces only were carried away by the current, and stranded some distance below. At last the Waikatos desisted and went away, warning Te Wheoro that they should shortly return in greater force.

After a week's delay, a still larger party came down from Ngaruawahia, headed by Wi Kumete, a reckless madcap, who, being on a visit to the King, wished to signalize his zeal. I fell in with the party, halting for the night at Rangiriri, and tried to persuade them to wait till the rival claims to the land at Te Kohekohe could be adjusted. Wi Kumete was civil, but wild. He said they all knew the object of the building at Te Kohekohe, and of those up the country at Te Awamutu. They might be called "schools," but they were in reality barracks. They believed that soldiers were continually going up the country, disguised as carpenters and other labourers, and were secreted in cellars at Te Awamutu; and that guns and ammunition were carried thither, packed in casks and cases, like sugar or other goods. A law had therefore been passed, that every canoe should be searched; and, in the excution of this law, he (Wi Kumete) had just been searching one, and he would show me what he had found. Thus speaking, he ushered me into the great meeting-house, and brought out about a hundred bottles, from one of which the cork had been drawn, and the contents proved to be rum. This, he said, was a pretty way of carrying out our laws.

The subsequent history of these rum bottles is amusing. They were put in charge of Onehi, a young *protégé* of Whakapaukai, who ought to have been a boy at school, but was a King's magistrate. He kept them for a couple of months; but during the whole time was so perpetually drunk, that Wiremu Tamihana was sent for to examine into the cause. He discovered that the rum had been abstracted from the bottles, and the water of Waikato substituted. For this peccadillo, Onehi was brought up before the King's Runanga, fined, and dismissed from his office.

Wi Kumete and his party refused to delay their visit to Te Kohekohe. They nearly frightened the carpenters out of their wits, and made them only too glad to drop their work, and carry themselves and their tools away in safety. Then they threw all the timber into the river, binding it together in rafts, and sent to the officer commanding the Queen's Redoubt to know whether they should be fired upon, if they brought the timber to Te Ia; adding that, unless they were promised safe conduct, they should cut the rafts adrift, and send them floating down the stream at hazard. The officer replied that they should be permitted to land the timber unmolested. Wi Kumete, accordingly, came down with all his party, order was kept by the King's soldiers, ropes and stakes were placed along the bank to keep back the throng of spectators, and the timber was landed in triumph. So elated was Wi Kumete with his success, that, on returning from Te Ia, he held a meeting at Te Kohekohe, and proposed that they should all go up to Te Awamutu, take the Governor's magistrate, with his houses, his men, and all that he had, and land them in the same manner, and at the same place.

A Runanga was therefore held, and the following offence laid to my charge:—

On hearing of the Governor's steamer, the natives determined to assert their claim to the ownership of the river, and to make it clear that the purchases of the Crown did not extend beyond dry land. For this purpose, Neri took upon himself to survey the boundary of Mangatawhiri, and erect a post on our side of the river, bearing the notice, "This is the Pakeha's boundary; the water belongs to the Maories." In accordance with the wishes of the Government, I had this post pulled up, and wrote to tell Neri that it would not be allowed to stand on Pakeha land. Pulling up this post, which Wiremu Kumete re-planted, was considered an ample ground for expelling me.

On reaching Ngaruawahia, however, they found that Rewi Maniapoto had anticipated them by making an attack upon Te Awamutu, under the following circumstances:—

For some time past, a newspaper had been published by the King party at Ngaruawahia. The journal was called *Te Hokioi*, after a mythical bird, never seen, but only known by her scream, which was an omen of war or pestilence. Patara, a cousin of the King, one of the best men in Waikato, was editor. His articles exhibited the same kind of wit and ability, as the speeches and letters which I have so often quoted in the course of this narrative. One of his best articles was upon the subject of the intended steamer. "Successive Governors," said the *Hokioi*, "have declared to us that the Queen, by the Treaty of Waitangi, promised us the full *chiefship* of such of our lands, rivers, fisheries, &c. as we might wish to retain. Now Waikato is one of the rivers which we wish to retain under our own *chiefship*. How is it, then, that we are told a steamer is to be sent into this river, though we have not given our consent? Is this the way in which the Treaty of Waitangi is observed by your side? Pakeha friends, why do you act thus wrongfully, or trample under your feet the words of your Queen?"

It was thought desirable by Sir George Grey, to have a newspaper published in the Waikato to answer the arguments of the *Hokioi*. For this purpose it was determined that a printing-office should be established at Te Awamutu. The newspaper published was called *Te Pihoihoi Mokemoke* (The Sparrow that sitteth alone upon the House-top), and the first number was issued under the Governor's own revision, shortly after his visit to Ngaruawahia. Among other articles, was one on "The Evil of the King's Government," which, after reciting the challenge thrown out by the *Hokioi*, to declare why the King deserved punishment, exposed the lawlessness of the Waikato district, and the utter inability of the King and his Council to prevent or punish crime, citing in particular the outrage on the young girl at Wanganui, with which the Governor had already silenced the chiefs at Taupiri. The article concluded by saying that Matutaera either had or had not power to punish such a crime—if he had power, he deserved punishment for not exercising it—if he had not, he deserved equal punishment for pretending to be a King.

This article produced an immense sensation. The tribes less intimately related to Matutaera, were greatly amused, and enjoyed the hit at the King's Council; but the chiefs of Ngaruawahia were very angry. They said the "Sparrow" was written in a bad, mocking style, nothing like the calm and reasoning tone of the *Hokioi*. Some said, "Why is this press allowed among us?" others, "Why is not the press broken, and the Government-officer driven away?"

These words of the chiefs, who had hitherto restrained the rest from violence, were told to Rewi. He promptly seized the opportunity. He wrote letters to Ngaruawahia, to say that he intended to expel the press and the Commissioner from Te Awamutu. The answer was an old Maori song, sent by Wi Karamoa:—

"Oh Kahakura,[1] at the sea!
Oh Ruamano,[1] at the sea!
Hearken! our treasures are being borne away,
By Whiro, Whatino, and Wharona,[2]
By thieves wind-swift, by thieves headlong.
Cast them down! dash them down!
Fling them upon the trees!
Let them be a prey to be cast down,
A prey to be dashed down,
A prey to become the spoil of the far-famed.
Arise! Gird on!
Cast down! Dash down!
Let there be a shock,
The shock of army meeting army;
Let there be a prayer to overturn them,
To lash them.
Oh Tangaroa![3] whet thy teeth,
Sharpen thy teeth.
If thou liftest thyself up on high, Tangaroa
Shall gather together all his, against thee."

Rewi took the hint, and sent to the wild tribes of Hangatiki, to come down and do the work. I had many vague warnings from various quarters, even from

[1] Deities of Waikato.
[2] The genii of lies and plunder, and their associates.
[3] A water demon.

Rewi himself, that something was to happen. Ti Oriori took up his quarters at Rangiaowhia, assuring me he was there for our protection, as there would be trouble and darkness not only at Taranaki, but in the Waikato as well. Threats of the kind had been so common, and had so often come to nothing, that these warnings were unheeded. I had seen a letter from Tamihana to Rewi, urging the latter on no account to use violence at Te Awamutu. The writer said, that what had already taken place at Te Kohekohe would cause trouble enough, and that any further disturbance would be added by the Governor to the former one, and the two together would be made a cause of war.

Rewi paid no attention to this remonstrance. On the 24th of March, at three o'clock in the afternoon, a party of eighty Ngatimaniapotos, armed with guns, arrived at Te Awamutu, headed by Aporo, the same orator who had addressed Mr. Fox at Hangatiki. Rewi and Wiremu Kingi came with the party as far as a native house, about three hundred yards from Te Awamutu, where they sat while the mischief was done.

Aporo led his men to the front of the printing-office, which was close to the public road, and at a distance from the other buildings. They there halted and had prayers. An Englishman and native, who were printing inside, came out and locked the door in their faces. After prayers, without asking for the key, they began to break open the door. Pineaha, a Maori employed on the station, stood up before them and said: "It is enough. You have met, now go outside again and let us talk to-morrow—Mr. Gorst is not here." Aporo said: "I shall not delay. Mr. Gorst heard of my intention, but he refused to believe, so now break open the office." They then cried out—"Seize him, seize him"—and several men took hold of Pineaha and dragged him to one side. The office was broken open, and they began to remove the contents—packing the type in cases, and dragging out the press, in the course of which performance one of its legs was snapped off. While this was going on, Patene, who, since his own failure, had always vowed he would resist any attempt to drive away the Government officer, arrived, dressed for the occasion in black pantaloons, a light summer coat and waistcoat, and a new black silk hat. He ran into the office, which was crammed with Maories, half a dozen of whom he successively ejected. Pineaha broke loose from the men who held him and rushed to help Patene, but was overpowered by numbers and dragged from the office. After a great deal of uproar and confusion, Patene was got rid of also, though he was too great a chief to be violently handled. The printing press was then brought out and loaded upon bullock drays, to be removed to Kihikihi, and thence sent down the river to the Queen's land at Te Ia. Besides the printing press and a mail-box belonging to Government, they carried off some clothes, blankets, and other private property. These were returned as soon as the mistake was discovered. Indeed, throughout the whole riot, private property was scrupulously respected. The young Englishman who was printing had taken off his collar, and left a gold pin sticking in one of the cases of type; though the case was taken, and though natives were going in and out all the afternoon, the pin was found perfectly safe many hours after, stuck in the wall. The rioters even sent to ask leave to have a pot and kettle to cook their food, instead of helping themselves to such utensils as they required. After the press had gone, the eighty warriors, and the women and children by whom they were accompanied, sat down in the road to wait for my return from Waipa, to which place I had gone in the morning. They loaded their guns, and entirely surrounded the buildings by sentries posted at short intervals. Aporo, at the time, gave as his reason for this, that, being responsible for our lives and property, he was determined to keep other natives off the premises while he remained in occupation. There was good reason for his precaution. Aporo's party was accompanied by several Taranaki natives, followers of Wiremu Kingi. That chief and his friends were highly indignant at what was going on at Taranaki, and had the day before, in my hearing, ridiculed the Ngatimaniapoto for not at once attacking and plundering the neighbouring Pakehas. On the way to Te Awamutu, these men had proposed burning down the houses and killing the inmates, which Aporo and his master Rewi refused to permit.

As soon as news of the riot reached Rangiaowhia, Ti Oriori and Taati came down on horseback, at full speed, to Te Awamutu, vehemently protesting against what had been done. They said the words of Potatau and of the present King were—"Be kind to the Pakeha." The Ngatimaniapoto replied, they acknowledged no King but their ancestor Maniapoto, and would trample the words of Matutaera and his father under their feet. Taati called for pen and paper, took down this speech, and sent it off to Ngaruawahia. The discussion lasted till evening, when the Rangiaowhia men returned home, leaving the Ngatimaniapoto in possession, but threatening them with the vengeance of Waikato, if they took any further steps before morning. I arrived at home after dark, and was surprised by the large watch-fires lit round the house. The Ngatimaniapoto took no notice of me as I passed through them; they had done no further damage, having even fetched firewood from a distance, instead of burning the fence; but they sent a message into the house, that in the morning, unless I agreed to go, I was to be shot.

In the early morning, a Rangiaowhia herald arrived to announce that all his tribe was on the way to judge the Ngatimaniapoto. Honi Papita's word was—"We have been treated like slaves by Ngatimaniapoto." It must not be forgotten that Te Awamutu was a debated territory, claimed both by Waikato and Ngatimaniapoto. This was the chief reason why so decided a stand was taken against Rewi. The herald, after making a violent speech, and singing a warlike song in the road, came into the garden, followed by Aporo, who ordered him off the place. He replied—"Is this your place, O Aporo? No, it is ours; it is for us to spoil our own place. You have treated us like slaves." Patene was present and supported the Rangiaowhia men against his own tribe. Aporo said sneeringly, that Patene had been paid by Government for his advocacy. This, which was not true, put Patene into such a passion, that he tried to knock Aporo down. At last, after much uproar, the intruders agreed to leave Aporo's men in possession till the trial had taken place. Crowds now began to arrive from every village within twenty miles. Honi Papita, Taati, and all the Waikato chiefs—Rewi, Wharetini, and all Ngatimaniapoto, Ti Oriori, Wi Kingi, and a vast number of others were present. All sat down in the public road, excluded from Te Awamutu by cords of flax and by Aporo's sentries. The discussion began. The Waikatos expressed lively indignation at Rewi's unwarranted violence, especially in crossing his boundary line, and doing lawless deeds on the soil of other tribes. Rewi replied, that he was carrying out measures for the common good: all had long wished to get rid of the

Governor's officer, sent amongst them to do the work of Satan, to tempt and to deceive: he waited long, while Tamihana and Taati tried slow and effete measures: he was tired of talking and waiting; he was determined to act; and now he should go on with his violence, until the Governor's officer was removed.

It was then suggested that they should ascertain what effect Rewi's conduct had produced on his victim. This was done, in their symbolical fashion, by placing a chair in the middle of the road, on which I was invited to sit down. Aporo then advanced, and said, "Get up, and go." I said, "I shall not." He repeated the order several times, receiving the same reply. He then said, "If you will not go, I shall use force to drive you away." I told him that he had committed a great wrong by invading my land, and taking away my printing-press; and I had a proclamation of Matutaera's Council recently issued against molesting Europeans read aloud, at which they all laughed. I said Aporo was disobeying his King's commands. He said he would disobey his master by driving me away, unless I disobeyed my master by going at once. I replied that nothing but Sir George Grey's orders would induce me to leave the place; and, after saying this, I left the meeting.

The debate was then resumed. Taati pointed with his spear to the house, and said, "If you use violence, I am there." The Waikatos declared that, though agreeing with Ngatimaniapoto in the desire to get rid of the officer of Government, they would not permit violence to be used. Rewi and his men sat on the ground, in dogged silence, merely observing that they should not stir from the spot until their object was accomplished. He also sent off messengers to Hangatiki, to fetch Reihana and reinforcements. Taati and Ti Oriori came into the house, in great alarm; the former wrote to Ngaruawahia for the King, and the latter to Peria for Wi Tamihana, urging them to come with all speed. They said they should remain in the house, because the Ngatimaniapoto would not dare to make an attack while they were seated within. If a house were set on fire with a chief inside, he would, by Maori custom, be considered as burnt, and due vengeance would be taken by his tribe on the incendiaries. At last, Rewi yielded so far to the persuasions of the Rev. A. Reid, as to agree to withdraw his men, and allow time for communication with Sir George Grey. He made a speech to the assembly, saying that, when Governor Grey first came to the country, he (Rewi) had shown no signs of hostility, but had waited to see what the Governor would do. First, at Taupari, the Governor declared himself opposed to the King, and began to make the road to Mangatawhiri. Since that time he had been ceaseless in his machinations against their confederation, and in trying to reduce the Maories under the rule of the Queen. They had never been able to attend to their own internal affairs, but had been constantly harassed by alarms. Lastly, at Taupiri, Sir George Grey said he would dig round the King, till he fell. They looked to see where the spades were at work, and they saw me. They were quite resolved to have no digging in Waikato, but to send me to the Queen's land at Mangatawhiri; there I could dig, if I pleased. He should wait till Sir George Grey's answer came; but he warned me, and begged Mr. Reid and the other natives to note his words, that if the Governor left me there, he left me to certain death.

He then wrote the following letter:—

"Te Awamutu, 25 March, 1863.

"FRIEND GOVERNOR GREY,

"Greeting. This is my word to you. Mr. Gorst has been killed by me. The press has been taken by me. They are my men who took it—eighty, armed with guns. The reason is, to drive away Mr. Gorst, that he may return to the town: it is on account of the great darkness caused by his being sent to live here, and tempt us; and also on account of your saying that you would dig round our King till he fell. Friend, take Mr. Gorst back to town; do not leave him to live with me at Te Awamutu. If you say he is to stay, he will die. Let your letter be speedy to fetch him away within three weeks.

"From your friend,

"REWI MANIAPOTO.

"To Governor Grey at Taranaki."

After writing the letter, Rewi, true to his word, withdrew the men, and said, that for a space of three weeks he would guarantee Te Awamutu from attack. During this period, however, the place would be constantly watched, and, after it, the attack would be renewed. He refused to give up the public property which had been seized, saying that he should send it to Mangatawhiri.

During the interval thus gained, there was an opportunity of determining at leisure the possibility of maintaining the position at Te Awamutu.

The Governor resolved to take no notice whatever of Rewi's letter. General instructions were sent to me, that "in the event of there being any danger whatever to life," I was to "return at once to Auckland, with the other Europeans in the employment of Government on the station." Further than this, no advice, and no help, could be given. One of the Colonial Ministers, aghast at the peril to which the property of the post-office was exposed, promptly stopped the inland-mail between Auckland and Otawhao, thereby cutting off our regular communication with the town, and grievously affronting Taati, whose men were the mail-carriers, although our very lives depended on his firm opposition to Rewi. As Government could give no assistance, the only chance left was to try once more the plan which had so often succeeded before—an appeal to Wi Tamihana, and the more moderate natives, to resist Rewi's violence.

Ti Oriori, to whose tribe most of the young men in the school belonged, sent two couriers—one to fetch Wi Tamihana; the other to summon the Wherokoko, his own section of the Ngatihaua tribe, to attend him armed at Arikirua, for the purpose of defending Te Awamutu. He laughed at the idea of Rewi driving the Maories out of the school, and said he should like to see the attempt made. The boys themselves, who throughout the whole period remained stedfast and obedient, asked Ti Oriori to bring arms, saying, they would then protect Te Awamutu themselves.

The news of Rewi's outrage reached the King at Whatawhata, when Patara, the editor of the *Hokioi*, was the only Councillor with him. By Patara's advice a letter was written, condemning Rewi, and requiring him to send back the printing-press, pay for the damage and the outrage, and leave all questions about the removal of the Governor's officer to be settled by the King himself. Wiremu Tamihana also arrived at Rangiaowhia, in compliance with Ti Oriori's message.

The chiefs of Waikato and Ngatihaua there assembled unanimously condemned Rewi; and Wi Karamoa, the envoy from Ngaruawahia, Wi Tamihana, and their followers, rode to Kihikihi to protest. Rewi consented with reluctance to restore the press, and pay for the damage done. On the question of expelling the Governor's officer, he was immoveable. The party then came to Te Awamutu. Tamihana said no one liked my remaining in the district. Rewi had accused him of having originally brought me there. The accusation was not true. Long ago, before I was an officer of Government, he had invited me to live amongst the Maories; but now that I was working the Governor's works, he himself did not wish to have me. They had no fault to find with the school itself; everything about it was excellent. But the Governor had said at Taupiri, he would dig round the King until he fell, and they could not help thinking that the school at Te Awamutu was one of the Governor's spades. He (Tamihana) had always tried to keep cases out of court, and boys out of the school. But he never had agreed, and never would agree, to my being driven away by force. Te Awamutu was Queen's land, and no one had a right to invade it. He had said this to Rewi, and Wi Karamoa had carried the King's commands to let me alone. But Rewi was mad, and would not listen to them, so they had come in a friendly spirit to tell me this proverb: "Land is a living thing, but man is mortal." Rewi had resolved to use force, and therefore their word was—"You must go."

I replied that, unless they could prevent Rewi from repeating an act which they admitted to be wrong, the Governor's words had already proved true, and the King had fallen. Rewi was now master, and Waikato and Ngatihaua had become his slaves.

When Tamihana found I would not go, he and Ti

Oriori went to Ngaruawahia, and proposed that the King's soldiers should occupy Te Awamutu, to prevent a second attack; but they soon discovered that few would back their proposals. Lower Waikato was charmed at Rewi's daring. Tipene said Rewi's conduct was partly right and partly wrong; but they would accept the wrong with the right, and as he had begun the mischief, it had better go on. The King's Council, frightened and perplexed, set to work to discover the original instigators of the riot: it was proved that Wi Karamoa and two other chiefs of the Council had said or done things which encouraged Rewi in making his attack. Each of them was fined two pounds.

At length, as a last hope, the Rev. A. Purchas, the medical commissioner, and I went to Ngaruawahia, where we were hospitably lodged by Te Paea and Patara, in the printing-office of *Te Hokioi*. The chiefs who had been fined by the Runanga came to excuse themselves. They said that when the first number of the *Pihoihoi* came out, they were very angry at what was written about the King, and asked: "Why isn't the press taken away?" But they were sorry Rewi had construed their hasty words as an approval of his unjustifiable attack.

In the evening there was a Runanga, to discuss the propriety of defending Te Awamutu. Some urged that to do so was their duty; others objected to undertake a task they had not strength to perform. Te Paea sat in our tent, near the house where the discussion was going on. She said it was neither the *Pihoihoi*, nor the words of the Ngaruawahia chiefs, that had caused Rewi's acts; it was Tataraimaka. Rewi had done his best to prevent peace being made in 1861, and had been trying ever since to renew the Taranaki war; he was now doing his best to provoke a war in Waikato. She said that Rewi insulted Tamihana, when he went to Kihikihi to expostulate: she should go too; but it was unlikely Rewi would listen to her, after mocking at so good a man. Finally, having worked herself into a frantic state, she rushed, tears running down her cheeks, into the adjoining house, and addressed the meeting in a very loud voice, abusing their acts and designs for about an hour.

Next morning, I wrote to the Runanga, saying that Rewi had attacked Te Awamutu, and had alleged that he was sanctioned by all Waikato. I asked whether it was true that Waikato abetted him.

Upon this, Patara came out and said, that this was the very question they had debated for three days and three nights without coming to a decision, but they would hold another meeting in the afternoon. A large number of natives were present, strangers from Hawke's Bay and the East Cape, and also several of the Lower Waikato chiefs who had assailed Te Kohekohe. Proceedings commenced by reading out my letter. Herewhini of Te Kohekohe rose to reply:—

"Yes. It is done by all Waikato. Though Rewi did it, it belongs to all Waikato. When we were at Te Kohekohe, we resolved to go up to Otawhao and remove you; but when we arrived at Ngaruawahia, we heard Rewi had done it. The first ground for our wish to drive you away is the Governor's word at Taupiri, that he would dig round the King until he fell; the second is the house at Te Kohekohe, which the Governor and you planned, and which Te Wheoro is to execute; the third is the post set up as our boundary at Te Ia, which you presumed to pull up; the fourth is the house at Te Awamutu; and the fifth is the *Pihoihoi*. We saw that the Governor's words at Taupiri were being fulfilled, so we determined to remove you and all your works and goods to Te Ia, to the Governor's side."

After this speech there was a dead silence, until Patara came to ask privately what we were going to say. We told Patara we were not going to say anything. We did not intend to discuss Herewhini's five "causes," because no cause could justify the act of driving a man from his own land,—all we wished to know was, who had joined in the deed.

This was repeated aloud, and Herewhini again said, It was all Waikato.

We then asked—"Who are all Waikato?"

He pointed down the river and waved his spear round the horizon, saying that it included all, and more than all, that we could see. From Tongariro to the sea, all had agreed.

We said—"Not all."

He challenged us to name one who had not.

We named—"Matutaera Potatau and Wi Tamihana."

He would not believe this unless letters were produced. It was no use to say we had seen a letter of Tamihana; he would not believe it.

A Waipa chief, sitting by, indiscreetly produced Matutaera's letter, written on first hearing of Rewi's outrage. It was handed about among the councillors, but did not seem to be a safe one to read aloud. And so the meeting ended as fruitlessly as the three preceding ones.

Patara at last brought a verbal answer to the question, from Matutaera. I insisted on a written answer. After Patara had returned several times to confer with the King, we obtained the following:—

"Ngaruawahia, April 15, 1863.

"I said to Rewi—O Rewi, leave these days to me. Bring back the property. Let none be lost. I do not say that Mr. Gorst shall stay. He must go.

"*From* MATUTAERA POTATAU."

In explanation of this letter, Patara said, that the King was merely the mouthpiece of his people: he acknowledged that Matutaera had made Rewi's act his own. He said the King could not tell me to remain, because he had no power to protect me against Rewi; and he was afraid of blaming Rewi too strongly, lest he should revolt altogether.

Te Paea and Patara promised, however, to come to Te Awamutu, and make one last effort to induce the Ngatimaniapoto to abstain from violence.

It was just at this conjuncture of affairs that the letter from Taranaki, quoted in the last chapter, arrived in Waikato. The bearer met Rewi at Kihikihi, and gave the letter into his hands. Without waiting to consult with any of his brother chiefs, he turned the messenger back with this answer—"Strike the Pakeha." He then mustered his men, and set off to Hangatiki, leaving Wharetini behind to settle matters at Te Awamutu. The printing press was duly restored very little damaged, and was safely brought down to Auckland. It is an illustration of the fairness of newspaper reports, that though the capture of the press was chronicled, its restoration was passed over in silence, and was, in the *Southern Cross*, absolutely denied.

When the news of the occupation of Tataraimaka by the Governor's troops, and of the message which Rewi had sent back, became known to the Waikato chiefs, Te Paea, Patara, and Ti Oriori, hastened to Te Awamutu. Patara said that, after the message Rewi had sent, there would certainly be war at Taranaki. The coming war would not be like former wars. The young men of the present day would not attend to the words of their chiefs, but would rob and murder as they pleased. No one had any authority over them—not even Rewi; they only obeyed him so long as his commands pleased them. The King had no power at all. I told Patara he was talking like the *Pihoihoi*. He laughed, and said it was very true. They had come out of kindness, to urge us to go to Auckland at once. We had seen how Rewi treated us in time of peace; and we might judge what he would do in time of war; or rather what the people of Hangatiki might do. They said, in very plain language, that as soon as the first shot had been fired at Taranaki, any young fellow who wished to exalt his name would come and murder us, and the chiefs would have no power to prevent it. Te Paea said their warning applied to settlers and missionaries, as well as to the officers of Government. Maories did not care now to send their children to the Mission-schools, and they thought they could read prayers and preach as well as the missionaries themselves. They begged us to go at once, and not to put it off from day to day, waiting till bad news came from Taranaki; it would be too late to go then.

Being without arms, and at the mercy of the first assailant, I had no choice but to abandon Te Awamutu. At the same time, most of the European settlers left the district.

CHAPTER XVIII.

THE OUTBREAK OF WAR.

NOTWITHSTANDING the uproar in Waikato, so long as a shot had not actually been fired there was hope of averting the threatened war. The excitement had originated with the Governor's military movement on Tataraimaka: it was highly probable that the surrender of Waitara would be sufficient to allay the passions thus aroused, and to induce the Waikatos to undo their rash acts.

The Governor and the Colonial Ministry were still debating the Waitara question at Taranaki, when the messenger, sent by the Maories to Waikato, returned. Rewi's reply was reported to Government, and disbelieved. But its effects soon began to be apparent.

The road traversed by the escorts in conveying supplies to the redoubt at Tataraimaka, crossed over Maori land; and, at a place called Oakura, lay for a considerable distance along the sea-beach. On the night of Sunday, April 26th, more than three weeks after Tataraimaka had been occupied, an ambuscade was set by the Ngatiruanui and Taranaki tribes, to watch the beach, and shoot any European who might pass. The plot was discovered by a friendly native, who stationed himself at the Taranaki end of the dangerous passage, to warn European travellers. One officer, at least, owed his life to this man's precaution. It so happened that, during the time the ambuscade was set, no person came from Tataraimaka to the town. At length, at about nine o'clock on Monday morning, a messenger came down from the hills; the ambuscade broke up (no one knows why), and quitted the beach without blood being shed. The friendly native then left his post, went into the town of Taranaki, and told the whole story to the Government, offering to show the trodden ground, and half-extinguished camp-fires, as proofs of the truth of his tale. His account was received with the same incredulity as the report of Rewi's message. The Government had yet a third warning. On the road to Tataraimaka, there was a swampy stream, which drays could hardly cross in summer, and which would be impassable in winter. The military attempted to improve this ford, by throwing stones and gravel into the stream; but the Maories from the hills came down in the night and undid the whole work.

Still the infatuated Government, blind to the need of expedition, continued to debate the Waitara question. At last, the Colonial Ministers, after putting on record their opinions upon the original cause of quarrel at Waitara between Colonel Browne and Wiremu Kingi, and their view of the necessity of a public investigation, concluded, that as the terms on which they held office from the Assembly bound them to second the Governor's policy in native affairs, and as the Governor had the entire control of those British troops, without which no policy whatever could be carried into effect, they would acquiesce in the surrender of Waitara. No great haste was used in drawing the proclamation to announce that Waitara was given up, or to make known to the natives, in any other way, the resolution so tardily arrived at.

Before any proclamation was issued, and one week after the former ambuscade, a second was set on the sea-beach, in the same place, and under the same circumstances. On the morning of Monday, May 4th, exactly one month after the military occupation of Tataraimaka, two officers and seven men, marching along the sea-beach towards the town, were shot down by this ambush, and the Taranaki war was re-commenced.

It must be distinctly understood that this slaughter took place before, not after, the surrender of Waitara. The act was strictly in accordance with what the Maories had said ever since the suspension of hostilities, two years before. Tataraimaka was held as a material guarantee for Waitara; and they had always declared, that an attempt to take the one without surrendering the other, would be resisted by war. The particular act by which they chose to begin the war must excite universal abhorrence; it was a savage act of savages, and was reprobated by all the better men among the Maories themselves. But the deed, though brutal, was not treacherous. Numerous warnings had been given of the intention to strike a blow: these were, unfortunately and culpably, disregarded by the authorities.

In spite of war having already broken out, the Governor still kept to his purpose of restoring Waitara. A proclamation was accordingly issued, stating that the Government would not proceed with the purchase. The troops were withdrawn from the redoubts at Waitara; and, at the same time, the block-houses which held the intervening native territory, claimed under Hapurona's treaty of peace, were silently surrendered, and the troops marched back within our own frontier. These acts, which, if done a week earlier, might have averted war, now only served to increase the contempt with which the Maories regarded us. A Mataitawa chief said: "When Governor Grey heard his men were killed at Oakura, his heart misgave him, and he said, 'Now I must give up Waitara.'" This sentiment was that of all. The conclusion of most persons upon the whole transaction will probably agree with the opinion of two very different men, at opposite ends of the earth.

The Duke of Newcastle says:—

"It would have been better if the re-occupation of the Tataraimaka block, and the abandonment of the

Waitara, had been effected at one and the same time."[1]

Renata, a chief of Hawke's Bay, says:—

"We can see clearly the error of our native tribes in slaying the Pakehas at Tataraimaka; but, at the same time, we cannot lose sight of the error of the Governor in not making known his decision respecting the Waitara at the proper time."[2]

No time was lost in ascertaining the view which Waikato took of the Oakura slaughter. Intense excitement still prevailed among the natives of that district. A party of Ngatimaniapoto had set off to Taranaki, before hearing of the actual outbreak, with the design of attacking the troops occupying Waitara, and other Maori land. Rewi, Reihana, and the principal men, had remained behind, in order to create a diversion by descending in canoes to Te Ia, and making a raid against the settlers. To this scheme Patara, Te Paea, and the chiefs of Ngaruawahia, offered a most determined and successful resistance. Wi Tamihana and Ti Oriori openly expressed their entire disapprobation of the proceedings of Rewi and his people, and declared that the Ngatihaua would take no part in the impending conflict. Waikato was rent, for the first time since the Maori King was established, into two factions at open enmity—Ngatihaua and the chiefs of Waikato, on

[1] N. Z. Parl. Papers, 1863. E. No. 2, A.
[2] N. Z. Parl. Papers, 1863. E. No. 11.

one side, advocating peace; Ngatimaniapoto and a few chiefs of Lower Waikato, on the other, advocating aggressive war.

All the Europeans—missionaries and traders alike—had been compelled to leave the district. The peace party urged and hastened their flight, avowing that, so long as Europeans remained, their Maori friends were in constant dread lest they should be cut off. Their property, as well as their lives, was respected; part was removed, and the rest lay unplundered. The Ngatimaniapoto insisted, however, that all the half-caste children should be seized, as belonging to their race, and carried out their proposal without waiting for the consent of anybody. Several children were thus torn from their European fathers; but I believe all were ultimately recovered, some by stratagem, and others restored by the natives themselves.

The chiefs of the King's Council admitted, that the government which they had attempted to establish had utterly failed. Patara said that it was he who first proposed to send the timber back from Te Kohekohe to Te Ia, but he never expected it would be the prelude to such scenes of violence. The Waikato chiefs, said he, were now ready to propose to the Governor that Waikato should be cut off from all communication with the Europeans until the Maories consented to submit to English law. He thought that the natives throughout the country would be so thoroughly miserable for want of the comforts and help they had hitherto enjoyed, that they would gladly submit to anything in order to recover them.

Matutaera himself was greatly vexed at all that the Ngatimaniapoto had done. He was particularly offended with their conduct to the missionaries, whom he tried to persuade to return, with the proposal to attack Te Ia, and with their talk of taking him away to live at Hangatiki.

The Ngatihaua had assembled in arms under their chiefs to resist the further progress of Rewi's schemes; while the Lower Waikatos, who abetted him, had gathered together at Rangariri, and were busily employed in making a great ditch and rampart from the Waikato river to the Waikari lake, to repel the invasion of the Pakeha, which they supposed to be imminent. This was the work recently captured by General Cameron.

The following letter from Patara to Tamati Ngapora at Mangere, gives a good idea of the state of the Waikato district, and the opinion of the moderate or peace-party thereon:—

"Ngaruawahia, April 27, 1863.

"To Tamati.

"Salutations to our brethren, our fathers, and the tribe. Probably the evil tidings of the doings of Ngatimaniapoto, in violently expelling Mr. Gorst and trampling on the word of the King, have reached you. The present time is a time of darkness; it is impossible to guide matters aright. The Ngatihaua are leading on a straight road; but the tribes that do right are called 'Queenites' by the Ngatimaniapoto; while of those that do wrong, it is said that they belong to the King. At the present time the burden of our affairs is very great. Potatau's words are altogether set at nought, and the word of any common man is by them considered right. They say that by their plans the King will be established: they have not kept one of Potatau's words, nor of his successor's. They say to the Pakehas living among them, whether missionaries or settlers, that if they acknowledge the sovereignty of the King, they will be allowed to remain, but that whoever declares himself a subject of the Queen will be expelled, although the land he lives on may be his own.

"The Ngatimaniapoto are gone to occupy Waitara under Hikaka, Tikaokao, and many other Ngatimaniapoto chiefs: they have gone to drive away the soldiers who garrison Waitara. Perhaps the first mischief may not be at Tataraimaka; those at Waitara may be the most hasty to begin the war.

"Rewi and the Urewara (an East-Coast tribe) have demanded that Te Ia should be given up to them, to do as they may think good. We said, 'He must be a mighty magician who will uncover the incantations which have been laid at that place. Peace has been many times made there. Pukehawani[1] is laid there. Rather let the other side be the first to leap over.' Te Paea and I were at Kihikihi.

"*From* WI PATARA."

In this state of things, Mr. Rogan, officer of the Native Department, was sent, at the risk of his life, with a letter to King Matutaera, detailing the events at Taranaki which had ended in the Oakura massacre, and asking whether, in the opinion of the King, the deed was murder or not. After being several times stopped and searched for concealed weapons, Mr. Rogan reached the capital; but was of course not permitted to see the King. It was well known that the etiquette of Matutaera's Court forbad personal communication between the King and a subordinate officer of Government. But though no expression of opinion from the King himself could be procured, the sentiments of Waikato were delivered with great freedom, and were not different from what might have been expected. Rewi and his allies declared, that the deed was no murder, but the righteous recommencement of a just war. Most of the rest reserved their opinions, until they should have heard the Maori story as well as the Governor's, not placing implicit faith in Government statements. There are several technical words in Maori

[1] A deity of Maori mythology.

to express "killing." It was necessary for the natives to consider, whether or not due warning had been given, whether there was a just ground of quarrel, and many other circumstances, before they could determine whether the word "kohuru," by which we render murder, could be correctly applied to the case. Maories, in estimating guilt, think more of the motives than of the consequences of an act. A man may be "murdered" without being killed at all. I was once "murdered" myself, and was afterwards addressed by my Waikato friends, as—"Oh, corpse!" and by other tribes as—"You food of Waikato." Wiremu Tamihana, and a few others, had made up their minds beforehand, and boldly declared the act was murder. But Tamihana's views of international law were much less civilized than Rewi's. Nothing could, in the opinion of the former, justify the seizure of a "material guarantee." It was wrong, he thought, for the Governor to hold Waitara and other portions of native territory; but the wrong done by the Governor, did not justify the Maories in retaining Tataraimaka. The opposition to Sir George Grey's occupation was unjust, and the slaughter by which it was manifested was a "murder."

A great meeting took place at Rangiaowhia, to determine what part Waikato should take in the new Taranaki war. The first speaker was Wi Tamihana, who, after condemning, in the strongest terms, the whole of those proceedings of Rewi which had led to war, declared his opinion, that the Maories were in the wrong, and announced that the Ngatihaua would take no part in the war. As soon as he sat down, Rewi rose, and, without speaking, thrust out his tongue, and made horrible grimaces at the rival chief. Tamihana asked what this meant. "It means," replied Rewi, "that I shall go." "Where?" "Right on into the mouths of the Governor's cannon." He was asked if he paid no regard to the words of the King. "I care nothing," he said, "about your King. I have anointed my sword and my spear to be kings over me."

The Ngatimaniapoto, however, although bent on war, did not go to Taranaki: they wished for war in Waikato, and they were urgent for an attack upon Te Ia, upon the English villages at Mauku, Drury, and Papakura, and even upon the town of Auckland itself. Nothing but the firm opposition of Wi Tamihana and others to this design prevented its execution in May or the beginning of June, when the bulk of the British troops were engaged at Taranaki, and Auckland lay comparatively defenceless. Rewi, seeing that war was inevitable, wished to strike at an advantage; Tamihana refused to stir until he could fight in a righteous cause. The latter, indeed, carried his opposition to the war-party to such a length, that he went down the river to visit Waata Kukutai, the principal Queen's magistrate, and said that the time was now come when all who desired order and laws must join together to oppose the violence of men like Rewi. The members of the Government, however, in Auckland did not like Tamihana. Few Europeans knew him personally, and it was the fashion to believe him insincere. No encouragement was on this occasion held out to him, nor were any negotiations entered into.

But while leaving Tamihana to struggle unaided against the flood of confusion which the acts of Government had let loose, the authorities were busily employed in preparation for the general war, which was now believed by every one but Tamihana and his friends to be inevitable.

When the station at Te Awamutu was abandoned, a few of the boys, chiefly the younger ones, with two native teachers, remained in the house. Two young men returned to their native homes. The rest went to Auckland, on the promise that, being faithful to Government, they should receive the same benefits as at Te Awamutu. The promise thus made was confirmed by the Governor, who announced his intention of settling the whole establishment at some place in Lower Waikato, where it could be maintained against any further assault, and where the number already under training could be at once reinforced by the young men attached to Waata Kukutai and Wiremu Te Wheoro: these had been awaiting the building of the police-barrack at Te Kohekohe, and the fear of Ngatimaniapoto had deterred them from placing themselves meanwhile at Te Awamutu. The intentions thus expressed had been told to those most nearly affected by them; and the scheme would have been immediately put in execution, had not the tragedy at Oakura prevented Sir George Grey—who wished to superintend the new plan in person—from returning immediately to Auckland.

During this unavoidable delay, a different scheme, which had the effect of making the former no longer possible, was devised and carried into effect by one of the Colonial Ministers, who, while the heads of Government were at Taranaki, was administering affairs in Auckland.

Hona, of Kahumatuku, was directed by Government to leave his village, and settle on a block of Crown land, near Cameron Town, on the Lower Waikato. Te Wheoro, with all his adherents, left Te Kohekohe, and commenced building a Pa, in native fashion, on the slopes of the hills above Te Ia. Waata Kukutai and the Ngatitipa tribe established themselves in Pas at the same place. The two principal chiefs had their salaries raised from 50*l.* to 150*l.* per annum, as a testimony to their loyalty, and the inferiors had presents and pensions distributed amongst them. They all wore yellow leather caps, to distinguish them from their disloyal countrymen. The tools for constructing the Pas, and the food for the working parties, were supplied at the Government expense.

These men were under no orders except those of the distant officials in Auckland, and no attempt whatever was made to reduce them to a state of discipline and obedience. Te Wheoro and Kukutai were, no doubt, perfectly faithful and trustworthy, but neither they nor any one else had the least control over their followers. All were in constant communication with their friends and kinsmen of the King-party, and any person who felt affronted, deserted with the greatest readiness.

Although this measure was wholly ineffective as an attempt to raise a corps of Maories for service as soldiers or police, it had a most important and significant meaning in the eyes of the King-party. Unmistakeable signs now met their eyes, as they went to and fro along the road between Auckland and Waikato, which put an end to all their doubts as to the ultimate purposes of the Government. The soldiers, the military road, the redoubts, the electric telegraph recently constructed from Auckland to the depôt camp at Otahuhu, and being still extended thence to Drury, and lastly, the Pas of Te Wheoro and Ngatitipa—all convinced them that, as they expressed it,—"The evil day was at hand."

CHAPTER XIX.

THE INVASION OF WAIKATO.

THE offensive operations carried on at Taranaki, to avenge the slaughter at Oakura, were brought to a successful issue on June 4th, exactly one month after the murder, when a Maori position beyond Tataraimaka was stormed and carried by our troops: many natives were killed in the assault, and many fugitives fell under the fire of H.M.S. *Eclipse*, which lay off the coast, pitching Armstrong shells amongst the natives on shore.

After the blood shed at Oakura had been thus duly avenged, the troops were withdrawn from Tataraimaka, the bulk of the British force was transported back to Auckland, and Taranaki was once more held by the 57th Regiment alone, while a guerilla warfare was carried on between our men and the Maories over the surrounding country.

In the meanwhile, at Auckland and in Waikato, there was a pause. Both sides felt that war was to come, but each hesitated to strike the first blow. No demand was made, no ultimatum was sent to Ngaruawahia. Although Tamihana and the moderate party had denounced Rewi's policy, and prevented his making that prompt attack upon Auckland which he had planned, and which would, in all probability, have been successful, no effort was made to ally ourselves with these men for the purpose of putting down Ngatimaniapoto violence. Had any just and moderate demand been made by us, it is more than probable that Tamihana and others would have risen in arms to compel Rewi to comply. Had we determined to chastise the latter for his conduct, those who had already declared that he richly deserved punishment, would have sat quietly by and allowed it to be inflicted, if a way of escape had been opened for them by the Government. Such a course, however, would not have suited the colonial policy. Although the Waikatos had been denied the rights of an independent nation, it was now determined to punish them for not having performed the corresponding duties. This was hardly fair. If the Waikatos were really subjects, it was no duty of theirs to punish evil doers like Rewi, and we had no right to confound the innocent with the guilty by a general war. It was rather hard that we should "dig round the King until he fell," and then set him up again to be overthrown by force of arms. But it is the peculiar misfortune of New Zealand natives, that they are alternately treated as British subjects, or as foreigners, according to the interest or caprice of their British rulers.

The Waikatos were soon made to feel the altered circumstances in which they stood. Neri came into town and saw the Governor, to whom he began to talk in his old saucy way about his King, and his objection to the Governor's magistrates. But, instead of his buffoonery being good-naturedly listened to, as it used to be, he was abruptly ordered to leave the Governor's presence, and informed that if found an hour later in Auckland, he would be sent to gaol. Aporo, who had headed the party which seized the Awamutu printing press, came to town with his comrades to sell pigs, as rebels had always been allowed to do without molestation since the Maori King was first established. He was recognised, arrested in the Native Office, brought before a magistrate on a charge of felony, and committed for trial. I may mention here that when, three months later, his trial came on, although throughout the riot at Te Awamutu there was a conspicuous absence of any *animus furandi*, though private property, absolutely in the power of Aporo's men, was scrupulously respected, and though public property was taken with the avowed object of sending it (as they had sent the Kohekohe timber before) to the Queen's side of Mangatawhiri, Aporo was found guilty of theft, and sentenced to two years' penal servitude. At his trial the prisoner was undefended, and had, of course, no witnesses. The jury of Auckland citizens, by whom he was tried, were the enemies of his tribe, and hated the prisoner for his political opinions. It was, in their eyes, "flat burglary" to call a Maori a King, and they brought in a verdict of "Guilty" accordingly, though Aporo was certainly no thief in the common or legal acceptation. It is no doubt better for Aporo to be now at peace in Auckland Gaol, than to be fighting in Waikato; but his condemnation will not increase the respect of Maories for the justice of our courts, in which men are tried for political offences by a jury of their political opponents.

It was expected, and, I am sorry to say, hoped by many, that either the dismissal of Neri, or the seizure of Aporo, would so enrage the Waikatos, that they would attack us; but they remained steady to their original resolution, that the Pakeha should begin the war. They said Neri had gone on his own authority to visit Governor Grey, and if he had behaved impertinently, it was quite right to send him about his business. As for Aporo, a large part of Waikato, and all Ngatihaua, had condemned his conduct from the first; and though Rewi took the opportunity of again proposing war, his designs were once more defeated by Tamihana and the King.

Thus, for a whole month, each side remained in a state of suspense, waiting for the other to begin. The Maories showed what they expected, by removing the bones of their ancestors, buried at Onehunga, and carrying them to a safer resting-place, in the

Waikato country; they felt certain that the day had come when they must fight for their lives and lands, and that the Pakeha would attack, so soon as his preparations were complete. Our side felt sure that the natives were only watching their opportunity, to make an onslaught upon our weaker settlements, or even attempt to sack the town of Auckland itself.

A trivial circumstance precipitated the commencement of war. The news of the Prince of Wales' marriage had reached New Zealand in May; but a later mail brought the additional intelligence, that all the Australian colonies had celebrated the event by public rejoicings. Auckland must not be behindhand in demonstrations of loyalty; and therefore, on the principle of "better late than never," the first of July was fixed as a public holiday, when the citizens were to rejoice in British fashion, by a review, by presenting dreary addresses to the Governor, by climbing greased poles, and other sports, and finally, by lighting bonfires, and illuminating the town at night. The illuminations were no great sight, but the bonfires were numerous and brilliant. They were seen from the Maori villages, in the Hunua forest, beyond Papakura and Mauku, and struck terror into the souls of the spectators. The tidings flew far and near through Waikato, that the Pakeha had made a great war-signal, and was now on the point of marching to the attack. In their alarm, secret Runangas were held, to discuss plans of defence or assault, from which Wi Tamihana and others, who were supposed to have scruples about murder and robbery, were excluded. Letters came pouring in upon the Government during the following week, from chiefs of the highest rank in Waikato, whose names occur continually in the course of this narrative, all warning the Europeans to be on their guard, for secret Runangas were being held, at which the most atrocious plans for misleading the General and sacking Auckland were propounded. All the writers begged the Governor to conceal their names, lest they should be sacrificed to the fury of their countrymen. The knowledge that such letters had been received reached the public ear, with due additions and variations. No one doubted the existence of a terrible plot to murder the Europeans wholesale, in the very streets of Auckland.

The most extreme terror was coupled with savage hatred of the Maori race. A half-caste, who got into some quarrel upon the day of rejoicing, was almost torn to pieces by the mob, and his life was saved only by the prompt interference of a number of gentlemen and non-commissioned officers, who got him into one of the guard-rooms, and kept the door. An attempt was made by the Government to fulfil their promise to the native boys from Te Awamutu, who had been hanging about in idleness and uncertainty, by apprenticing them to tradespeople in the town. But the people to whom application was made, said they would rather drop down dead than let a Maori cross their threshold; they would rather kill a Maori than let him work for them, and so forth. The attempt had to be given up. No one could be found bold enough to defy popular clamour, and take charge of these loyal and faithful young men. Even the very officers of Government refused. Most of the boys and young men went back to Waikato, complaining bitterly of the breach of faith; the remainder were generously taken charge of by the Bishop of New Zealand. The Government were obliged to prohibit natives from going about the town by night; it was thought that, in case of fire or any other alarm, they would certainly be massacred. Every effort was made to get even resident Maories removed as fast as possible from the town. The temper and language of the populace were atrocious. A young half-caste gentleman, in the Government-service, told me that the conduct of the white population made him feel quite ashamed of being partly an Englishman.

In this state of things, the authorities felt constrained to move. They had fresh in their recollection the Oakura disaster, which had occurred because they refused to give heed to warnings from natives. Such a mistake ought not to be made a second time. Letters of the same character as those recently received had often come before, and no disaster had followed. They were, therefore, in themselves no evidence of real danger. It is, without doubt, highly probable that an attack on Auckland was proposed and discussed at war meetings. It would be strange had it been otherwise. We had often proposed and discussed an attack upon Waikato ourselves. But that the Waikatos would have crossed Mangatawhiri to assail us, I utterly disbelieve. Such an act was contrary to their principles, and could not have been carried out without a serious division amongst themselves. As a matter of fact, Tamihana and others kept Rewi from attacking Auckland, for a period of two months and a half, while the town was comparatively defenceless; and there is no reason to suppose they would have failed to restrain him when the town was under the protection of ten thousand soldiers. However, the public believed in a conspiracy, and thought that, somehow or other, the advance of the troops into the Waikato territory would protect their outlying villages from attack. Invasion was thus cried for, and invasion was accordingly decreed.

It was, however, necessary to declare some cause for the intended attack, not so much with the view of producing an effect on the Maories themselves, as of justifying the war in the eyes of the British public. General Cameron was about to advance, and there was not much time left for the manufacture of a proclamation. This proclamation, moreover, proved as difficult to compose as the celebrated one announcing the surrender of Waitara, and, like that, was not finally issued till too late for the purpose for which it was nominally designed. No declaration of war reached the Waikatos until after blood had been shed.

The reason why proclamations to Maories are so difficult to compose, and are couched in such feeble language, is, that they must conform to the prejudices of many different parties. It is, in the first place, necessary to find a formula which expresses the discordant views of the two branches of the double government; it is then necessary carefully to consider what the Home Government will say to this, what the New Zealand Assembly will say to that—whether one phrase will arouse the opposition of the clerical party, or another excite the wrath of the colonial public. What effect the proclamation will have on the natives, is not much thought of; in what light it will be viewed by the Aborigines' Protection Society at home, is a subject of long and careful study.

The proclamation to the Waikatos, after being altered and re-altered, printed and re-printed, finally assumed the following form:—

"G. GREY, *Governor.*

"CHIEFS OF WAIKATO,

"Europeans quietly living on their own lands in Waikato have been driven away; their property has been plundered; their wives and children have been taken from them. By the instigation of some of you, officers and soldiers were murdered at Taranaki; others of you have since expressed approval of these murders. Crimes have been committed in other parts of the island, and the criminals have been rescued or sheltered under the colour of your authority.

"You are now assembling in armed bands; you are constantly threatening to come down the river to ravage the settlement of Auckland, and to murder peaceable settlers. Some of you have offered a safe passage through your territories to armed parties contemplating such outrages. The well-disposed among you are powerless to prevent these evil acts.

"I am therefore compelled, for the protection of all, to establish posts at several points on the Waikato river, and to take necessary measures for the future security of persons inhabiting that district. The lives and property of all well-disposed people living on the river will be protected, and armed and evil-disposed people will be stopped from passing down the river to rob and murder Europeans.

"I now call on all well-disposed natives to aid the Lieutenant-General to establish and maintain these posts, and to preserve peace and order. Those who stay in Waikato to assist the General, or move into such districts as may be pointed out by the Government, will be protected in their persons, property, and land. Those who wage war against Her Majesty, or remain in arms, threatening the lives of her peaceable subjects, must take the consequences of their acts, and must understand that they will forfeit the right to the possession of their lands guaranteed to them by the Treaty of Waitangi; which lands will be occupied by a population capable of protecting, for the future, the quiet and unoffending from the violence with which they are now so constantly threatened.

"Auckland, July 11, 1863."

This date is fallacious. I met the messenger, carrying the first copies printed in the native language, on the evening of July 14th, at dusk. He was then on the road between Auckland and Otahuhu, and did not reach the Waikato until after the battle of Koheroa, which was fought on the 15th.

While the Governor and the Colonial Ministers were thus busily engaged in the manufacture of this proclamation, which was not despatched in time to warn those whom it purported to address, and while General Cameron was hurrying on the military preparations for crossing Mangatawhiri and invading Waikato, an act, which will exercise immense influence on the future relation of the Maori and European races, was performed after the briefest consideration.

There were several Maori villages near Auckland, viz. Mangere, Pukaki, Ihumatao, and others, inhabited by relations of the Waikato tribes. A large proportion of these people were old and infirm. I never heard a complaint of their harbouring dangerous characters, or behaving ill to the European farmers, by whom they were entirely surrounded. Yet our arrangements for governing native settlements, even close to our own doors, were so defective, that the instant war broke out, we found it dangerous, though we had 10,000 men in the field, to allow these poor creatures to remain in their homes. Twenty Maori policemen could have quelled the whole of them even if in actual revolt, but the Government had not a single Maori policeman upon whose obedience they could depend. It was, therefore, resolved to drive these poor men and women from their homes, and confiscate their lands. There was no difficulty in finding a pretext. They were Maories and relatives of Potatau. Underlings of the Native Office were despatched in haste to call upon them to give up their weapons and take the oath of allegiance to the Queen, or, in default, to retire beyond Mangatawhiri under pain of ejection. The first native to whom this cruel decree was made known was Tamati Ngapora, the uncle of the Maori King, who lived at Mangere, in European fashion, receiving a large income from letting his lands as grazing grounds to the neighbouring farmers. After a short silence, Tamati asked—"Is the day of reaping, then, at hand?" Being told that it was, he observed—"Why has not the Governor put Waikato on her trial, before stretching forth the strong hand?" Tamati and the other Mangere natives quite understood the alternatives. They must submit to what they regarded as an ignominious test, or lose the whole of their property. And yet, to their honour be it said, they did not hesitate for a moment.

They all thanked the Pakeha for this last act of kindness in giving them timely warning of the evil that was to come upon Waikato, and an opportunity of themselves escaping; but they could not forget that they were part of Waikato, and they must go and die with their fathers and friends. The officer sent by Government did not deem it his duty to endeavour to turn them, but the Rev. A. G. Purchas, who had been the clergyman of Mangere for many years, did all he could to persuade them to take the oath of allegiance and remain in their homes; he could not shake their determination. All the old people showed the most intense grief at leaving a place where they had so long lived in peace and happiness, but they resolutely tore themselves away. The scene, as described to me by an eye-witness, was most pitiable.

The same answer was returned at Pukaki and Ihumatao. Only one or two at each place accepted the test and stayed behind.

The fugitives were, of course, unable to carry all their goods with them. What remained behind was looted by the colonial forces and the neighbouring settlers. Canoes were broken to pieces and burnt, cattle seized, houses ransacked, and horses brought into Auckland and sold by the spoilers in the public market. Such robbery was of course unsanctioned by the Government, but the authorities were unable to check the greediness of the settlers. Compensation was promised to the sufferers; but it looked strange, in the eyes of the natives, that a Government, which was about to make war on Waikato because the chiefs could not prevent lawlessness, should itself be unable to restrain its subjects from unjust acts.

Meanwhile, the military preparations of General Cameron were completed sooner than the proclamation of Government; and without waiting for the publication of that document, which was yet under discussion, he crossed Mangatawhiri on Sunday, July 12, and, finding no opposition, proceeded to occupy the Koheroa heights, about one mile distant from Mangatawhiri, on the eastern bank of the Waikato.

The road from Otahuhu to the Waikato was thronged with armed men of every description, from the veteran British soldier to the raw colonial shop-boy, shouldering his musket for the first time. Through this martial array the refugees from Pukaki, Mangere, and other places had to thread their way, as they went over to join the enemy. They became alarmed, and with good reason. Two of the chiefs, Ihaka and Mohi, with their women, children, and young men, took refuge at a small native village, called Kirikiri, on the slopes of the

Hunua forest, overlooking Papakura and Drury. There they stopped, and appeared to give up all intention of moving further. Wild reports began to be circulated. It was rumoured that the Maories meant to show fight at Kirikiri, that one hundred young warriors were collected and were building a Pa. Settlers, who had been scouring the bush to bring in cattle, had come upon their encampments; others had seen the Pa; and all were certain that reinforcements had been sent for from Waikato to enable the party to stand their ground. Counter reports were brought in, saying that the Kirikiri party were afraid to stir; that they had a number of old infirm people, women, children, and sick, without means of transport, and were horribly afraid of the soldiers who were scouring the plain below; that they were starving, and if they could but get food and some means of conveyance, would be only too thankful to be gone.

The Government were at this time becoming rather ashamed of having inflicted so much suffering on these innocent old people, and wished to get them away to the Waikato, with all possible speed and humanity. Mr. Dillon Bell, the Colonial Minister for Native Affairs, was therefore specially sent out by Sir George Grey, to visit Kirikiri, and ascertain the real state of affairs, to supply the natives with food, if needed, and to make the best arrangement he could for getting them away from their dangerous vicinity to the outlying European villages. Mr. Dillon Bell, taking me as his companion, left Auckland on this errand, on Monday, the 13th, the day after Mangatawhiri had been crossed. The same evening, at Drury, we met the Bishop of New Zealand, who had been spending the day with the natives in the ranges. The Bishop said that both reports which had been circulated were, to some extent, true; there were a number of sick and infirm people at Kirikiri, who wished to get to Waikato, but could not cross the forest tracks, and dared not go by road; but Mohi and the young men made no secret of their intention to come back and fight in the ranges, so soon as they had taken their old people and children to a place of safety. Next day, we went to Kirikiri. We found Ihaka, very ill, and half-a-dozen aged men, with a few women and children, in one of the houses. They sent for Mohi, who arrived after about an hour's delay, with several young men, and sat down for a talk. The main-body of effective men never appeared at all.

Mr. Dillon Bell told them that the proclamation, calling upon them to take the oath of allegiance, and give up their arms, was not intended as a positive order to leave their homes, as they had supposed. He had been sent out by the Governor himself, who had heard of their destitute state, to give them the choice of taking the test, and returning in peace to Pukaki; or, if they were unwilling to do so, of going unmolested to the Waikato river to join their friends. He urged the former course upon them, declaring that the Government had no wish to deprive them of their property, and promising them protection and good treatment under the Queen's rule.

Mohi replied, by thanking Mr. Bell for the kindness which he had ever shown to the Maories, and specially for his generosity in venturing unarmed amongst them, at such a time, to carry a message of peace and good-will.

If Mr. Bell had arrived, said Mohi, a few days earlier, with such an explanation of the meaning of the test, he and most of his comrades would have returned in peace to their homes. But now, within the last few days, a great change had taken place. The Governor had crossed the boundary, and had invaded Waikato. Mohi said he should not deceive us, but would frankly declare his present purpose. Hitherto, he and his people had strongly opposed the war party in Waikato. Letters had arrived, recounting the violence of Rewi and the Ngatimaniapoto, and they had all joined Tamihana in condemning his conduct. Rewi was utterly in the wrong. Had Sir George Grey declared that he was going to punish Rewi for his crimes, they would have sat by without interfering, and would have said that the Governor was in the right. But, instead of that, Sir George Grey had determined to punish all Waikato. He had crossed Mangatawhiri without notice, and without any investigation into the crimes of Waikato, and was at that very time in occupation of Maori land. Mohi therefore said distinctly, and he begged the Pakehas to mark his words, that they all intended to fight. He was himself a part of Waikato. The Pakehas had attacked Waikato. And he should therefore go to join his people, and live or die with them.

This speech carried an appearance of sincerity with it, as the decision to which he had come, cost the speaker the rental of estates worth several hundreds per annum. Mr. Bell then told Mohi, that the cause of the invasion of Waikato was a secret conspiracy to attack Auckland and murder the Europeans. They all denied any knowledge of the fact, and asked for the names of the informants. Mr. Bell said he could not give the names without the Governor's permission, which he would try to obtain. They said, if the Governor would give them evidence of such a plot, they would take the Oath of Allegiance and remain, as it would be a "kohuru" (murder) on the part of Waikato against them. The old people said they were very hungry and frightened, and accepted gratefully the offer of food, and the assurance of safe conduct. Late in the afternoon, we left Kirikiri, and returned to Auckland.

At ten o'clock that night, a telegraphic despatch was received at Drury from the Governor, ordering the troops to take the whole of the party at Kirikiri prisoners. A detachment was accordingly told off, who marched to the village, captured Ihaka, the sick chief, and all the infirm men, with the women and children; and in some manner, never accounted for, allowed Mohi, the sound chief, with all his able-bodied followers, to slip through their fingers. Mohi, thus relieved of his encumbrances, and of all ground for forbearance, immediately commenced hostilities.

Ihaka, up to December, 1863, had not been brought to trial, but still remained a prisoner. While we were in the ranges, the bodies of a settler and his son, who had been killed by an ambuscade in the forest, near the high-road beyond Drury, were discovered. This was the first blood shed in the Waikato war. But this murder was never laid to the charge of Ihaka, or his followers: suspicion fastened on an entirely different party of Maories, with whom he had no connexion. On whatever ground Ihaka and the innocent women and children were taken, their capture, just after safe conduct had been promised to them by a high officer of Government, had the unfortunate appearance of a gross breach of faith.

Wiremu Tamihana wrote to remonstrate with the Governor, asking how it was that our side had not followed the example of the Maories, who sent away the Europeans from Waikato in safety, with their flocks and their herds, and all their property. "Why," asked Tamihana, "has the property of the Maories been plundered, and why have Ihaka and the women and children been taken prisoners?"

Before this remonstrance had been received, the war in Waikato had become general. While the messenger carrying the Proclamation was still on his way to Waikato, the sudden and unexplained irruption of the British troops had been resisted by force, blood had been shed on each side, and all Waikato banded itself together for resistance to the common foe.

CHAPTER XX.

CONCLUSION.

PEOPLE are suspicious of those who find fault without pointing out a remedy. I must, therefore, in this concluding chapter, try to answer the question, How are the Maories to be managed for the future? I may be allowed to premise that this is the most difficult part of my task. The previous chapters have been mainly a narration of facts, which I can publish without fear of contradiction. The present one is an expression of opinion on a subject respecting which opinions have generally proved wrong.

However many victories may be gained, and however much territory may be conquered, in the present war, we must either go on fighting till the Maories are exterminated, or we must at some point stop the war, and make a new attempt to govern.

It is, therefore, necessary to begin by considering what the invasion of Waikato has done, or can do, to help or hinder this future attempt.

The immediate result of the invasion was the very evil which the movement had been hurried on to avert.

War being declared by the crossing of Mangatawhiri, all those ill-disposed Maories whom Tamihana and his friends had with difficulty restrained in time of peace, swarmed into the Hunua forest, and there carried on a guerilla warfare with the raw colonial levies, in the course of which much property was taken or destroyed, and many of the out-settlers were murdered. The General, in the meantime, after defeating a party of natives, who were rash enough to dispute possession of the Koheroa heights with our troops, had his further advance stopped by a Maori fortification at Meremere, which was too formidable to be attacked in front. All efforts to cut off the marauding parties from the Hunua forest failed; and, in spite of our twenty thousand men in arms, the farms on the skirts of the forest became a mere battle-ground. This state of things continued until the end of the month of October, a period of more than three months.

The arrival of an iron-plated steamer from Sydney then produced a change. By her help, General Cameron was enabled to pass, and so turn, the successive strong positions upon the bank of the river, in which the Waikatos had put their trust. The internal division which existed amongst the Maories before the war, continued during its progress. Rewi and Tamihana still remained rivals. The former led his men into the Hunua forest, to carry on savage warfare at an advantage; the latter sat down opposite General Cameron and the British troops at Meremere, to carry on civilized warfare at a disadvantage. The natives, beaten and almost crushed at Rangiriri, were Tamihana's followers, fighting purely on the defensive, to repel what they deemed an invasion of their country. In December, 1863, the General had reached Ngaruawahia; but Rewi, who is too prudent to meet him in the open field, is still untouched and defiant.

The recent campaign shows plainly what is to be gained by war with the Maories, and at what cost. We have established our military prestige, and, by thus making the hitherto contemptuous natives fear us, have removed one of the lesser obstacles to the establishment of the Queen's sovereignty in New Zealand. In conquering a lesser, however, we have created a greater difficulty. To those who persist in confounding Ngatimaniapoto with Ngatihaua, and dealing with the leaders of both tribes as "Chiefs of Waikato," the result of the war may appear satisfactory; but to those who know that the innocent Ngatihaua have vicariously atoned for the crimes of Ngatimaniapoto and the blunders of the British Government, the war appears unjust, and the victory ignominious. The latter class includes the whole native population of New Zealand. Renata, a chief of Hawke's Bay, who has a reputation for ability among his countrymen equal to that of Tamihana himself, says, in a letter to Dr. Featherston, Superintendent of Wellington: "We have been searching in vain to make out why our Pakeha friends say that murders were the cause of the war in Auckland. Not being able to satisfy ourselves, we sent an express messenger to the seat of war to make inquiries, and he returned last Saturday evening. His report was, that the Governor's war has not been caused by murders, as the Pakehas alleged. Murders could not be heard of. The only grounds that could be alleged were—first, the expulsion of the Maories from Auckland, from their own lands, and the burning of their properties and houses; and, secondly, the crossing of Mangatawhiri. If you know of any other cause, we should be glad if you would point it out to us, that we may speedily know it."[1] In a later letter, the same writer says: "This is what we heard of—Rewi's demand for war, after Aporo had been apprehended and imprisoned. Rewi proposed then to fight; but it was disapproved by Matutaera, by Tamihana, by Te Paea, and the *Chiefs of Waikato.* In consequence of this strong opposition, Rewi desisted, and he came to Taupo, to the 'tangi' for (the death of) Te Heu Heu. On his return, he was met on the road by the news of the driving away of the Maories from their land, of the crossing of Mangatawhiri by the troops, and of the death of Te Huirama."[2]

No one can deny the truth of Renata's facts. Thus, though the Waikato war may have added somewhat to

[1] N. Z. Parl. Papers, 1863. E. No. 11.

[2] Killed in the first battle on the Koheroa.

our reputation for power, it has destroyed what little credit we previously had for benevolence or justice. It has long been a common belief amongst the natives, in spite of assurances to the contrary, that the Pakeha intended, when strong enough, to attack them and rob them of their lands. The invasion of Waikato has proved to them that their apprehension was well founded. The government of an uncivilized people must, as Sir William Martin says, be built upon confidence; there is, among the Maories at the present moment, absolutely no confidence upon which to build.

What, then, is to be done?

One answer to this question has already been given. The colonists, having reluctantly undertaken the management of the Maories, have promptly published their scheme of government and civilization. They propose to take the land of those tribes who have, as they term it, rebelled; divide part among military settlers, who are to protect the colonists in their peaceful money-making avocations; sell part to future immigrants, to repay the cost of the war; and reserve part as farms for the conquered natives, who, it is hoped, will suddenly turn into quiet agriculturalists, and live at peace with the Pakeha intruders.

The effect of this scheme, if carried out, would be to exterminate the natives, upon false pretences, at the cost of the British Government, and for the benefit of the colonists. I do not, however, attribute to its authors a design so wicked. I believe they know the scheme to be impracticable, and have propounded it merely for the purpose of involving the British Government in an undertaking which will require the presence of a large body of troops, thus continuing that military expenditure which is so profitable to the New Zealand colonists. I believe this is the opinion of almost every uninterested person acquainted with the facts. But so long as people in England are ignorant of the facts, the colonists, in reliance on their ignorance, have just expectations of attaining their object. Those facts I shall now endeavour to make known.

The moral ground on which the Act of Confiscation is justified, is expressed in a despatch of Sir George Grey, dated August 20th, 1863 :—

"The chiefs of Waikato having, in so unprovoked a manner, caused Europeans to be murdered, and having planned a wholesale destruction of some of the European settlements, it will be necessary now to take efficient steps for the permanent security of the country, and to inflict upon those chiefs a punishment of such a nature, as will deter other tribes from hereafter forming and attempting to carry out designs of a similar nature."

The reader is aware that most of those chiefs against whom the Governor's accusation can, with any colour of justice, be alleged, belong to the Ngatimaniapoto tribe ; he will, therefore, probably be surprised to learn, that a very small portion only of the lands of that tribe is embraced by the Colonial Confiscation scheme. But the Ngatihaua, who throughout opposed the commission of such acts as the Governor reprobates, and succeeded in preventing them (at least in the Auckland province) until the sudden and unprovoked attack of the Queen's troops, are to forfeit almost the whole of their rich and fertile territories.

So much for the justice of the punishment which the colonists would inflict. Let us next consider how far their scheme would ensure the "permanent security of the country."

When war first began, the design of the Government was to take military possession of the native districts bordering on the English frontier, and draw a line of military posts from the Pukorokoro Creek on the Hauraki Gulf, to Koheroa, on the Waikato river. It was expected that this chain of posts, combined with armed steamers on the Waikato river, would make a safe and defensible frontier for the Auckland Province. Within this frontier, on the southern slopes of the Hunua forest, the military settlers were to be stationed, and there, too, lands might have been reserved for any Maories who wished to share the benefits of civilized government—if, after the evictions at Mangere, such could be found—and live as recipients of colonial bounty. This scheme, though undoubtedly the best for the permanent security of the country, was deliberately abandoned for the present magnificent project, as soon as the fighting began.

In the new plan, the frontier line is drawn from Raglan, through the fertile plains of Upper Waikato, to Tauranga. No one can contend that the new frontier will render the English settlements more secure; but it will give the colonists more land, and increase and prolong the military expenditure of the British Government in New Zealand. Any person who will look at the map of Waikato, and recall the description of the country through which the line of frontier settlements is to pass, can form an idea of the boldness of the design, and of the force that will be required to carry it into execution. The courage with which the colonists have determined that the mother country shall spend vast sums among them, to conquer and protect rich lands for their benefit, is worthy of profound admiration.

The difficulties, however, that beset the accomplishment of their patriotic purpose are very numerous. Passing over the obstacles to the conquest of the territory, let us assume that General Cameron can capture Maori positions at a distance from the river, as easily as those in the assault of which gun-boats can cooperate with the land forces; let us assume, that the Commissariat can furnish the army with supplies in the far interior of a country where neither food nor forage is to be found; and that the natives can be beaten out of the Maunga Kaua, the limestone ranges of Pirongia, and the vast forest which extends from the Thames Valley to Tauranga, as easily as out of the plains below; or, in short, let us assume at once that the Maories agree to withdraw from the intended line of frontier, and leave it open to the Colonial Government. What then? From whence are the 20,000 settlers, who are to occupy the frontier, to come? When colonies in every part of the world are competing for labourers, will a grant of fifty acres of land, overlooked by a rugged forest, the lurking-place of evicted and revengeful proprietors, induce a preference for the North Island of New Zealand? Again, suppose the settlers procured, and placed on their allotments, what security is there that the majority of them will stay? In the probable event of a fresh struggle, a border warfare, like that waged on the edge of the Hunua forest, will break out along the line of new frontier. The change of battle ground would be a great boon to the old colonists, and to the Maories; to the former, because so remote a war would not disturb the equanimity of Auckland, or expose the adjacent farms to the risk of ravage, while the enormously increased expenditure, necessary for carrying on war in the heart of the country, would be a direct source of profit; to the latter, because Maungatautari and Pirongia are more extensive and inaccessible than the Hunua ranges. There is behind them no river navigable by gun-boats, nor any open and fertile country to be conquered. But will new settlers, with the devastation wrought along the old frontier before their eyes,[1] venture to risk their labour and capital in farms along a new frontier? The land is granted to the military settlers for three years, on condition of performing certain military services. If the condition is fulfilled, at the expiration of that time a Crown grant of the fee-simple is to be issued to the settler, who is then free to go or stay as he pleases. It is evident that if any considerable number elect to go, the rest, too weak to protect themselves, would have no choice but to follow. Many of the volunteers already enlisted in Australia intimated, that they should take their grants of land and sell them for what they would fetch. Probably most of the land will be bought up at low prices by speculators; and the Government, by whom confiscation has been devised, will be called upon

[1] "Owing to the disturbed state of the country, a great deal of the growing crop will be lost to the south of Auckland. Hostilities having commenced, the settlers in the out-districts were driven off their farms, and their crops were consequently neglected. The Wairoa district, famous for its thriving settlers and dairy produce, is now a military camp, desolated by the ravages of war, or the destruction which ever follows in its wake. The Pukekohe, Mauku, and Waiuku districts have also been deserted. So also have been the homesteads at and near Pokeno (the Queen's Redoubt). Thousands of acres laid down in grass and potatoes, in the districts named, and around Drury and Papakura, must be looked upon as valueless for this season. We do not speak of the loss of money in cattle, which at this time cannot be adequately calculated."—*Southern Cross*, November 30, 1863.

either to maintain the purchasers in possession, or compensate them for the loss of their property.

That this project will tend to the civilization of the natives themselves, no one soberly believes. The clause in the Act of Confiscation, which requires a hundred acres of land to be reserved for each of the former proprietors, is inserted for the Aborigines Protection Society, and not for the Maories. Even if the natives could so far trust the Government, as to place themselves within its power, and could reconcile themselves to the prospect of living, feeble and despised, in the midst of the white race, no Maori could subsist upon a hundred acres of land, without an entire change of habits, which nothing but long education could produce.

After all, supposing the Government plan in Waikato to be attended with such complete success, as to convert the Waikatos into peaceful and obedient subjects, the question, How the rest of the native race is to be governed? is still unanswered. The Waikato tribes comprise not more than a fifth of the native population; and while the remaining four-fifths are lawless and hostile, permanent peace in New Zealand is an impossibility.

The result of the war, therefore, whatever it may be, will bring us back to the old question—How are the Maories to be managed?

The first step must be to do away at once and for

ever with double Government. Let either the Imperial or Colonial Authorities be made absolute in native affairs. So long as the Colonial Government asks the Imperial sanction to its schemes, and thereby establishes a claim on the Imperial Treasury for assistance in defraying the expensive consequences of error, it will govern the Maories infinitely worse than if left entirely to itself. But, although the natives would be better managed by the colonists alone than by the double Government, it is very questionable, whether government by the colonists would be the best possible for the interests either of the Maories or of the colonists themselves.

Colonial legislatures are ill-adapted for the management of affairs in which much foresight, and provision for a distant future are required. Colonists, who call England "home," and regard the colony as a mere field for speculation, manage their government as a tenant manages a rack-rent farm. The pecuniary interests of the existing colonists are invariably preferred to the future well-being of the community. The New Zealand Assembly contains men of education and ability, who would argue any abstract question with candour and good sense, and come to an honest conclusion thereon; but the moment a question is started affecting any pecuniary interest, the House becomes, as I was once told by a leading member, a mere Assembly of delegates from the various provinces of the colony; each member well knows how he is expected to vote, and knows also, that any eccentricity in voting on his part, would evoke a speedy and unanimous call from his constituents for his resignation. To make matters worse, the New Zealand Assembly is becoming more and more democratic, and experience has proved, that no Government can avoid making so many enemies during a recess, as to ensure dismissal on the Assembly again meeting. A Colonial Ministry has, therefore, no chance of succeeding in the difficult task of governing a subject race. The subject race, moreover, has a strong objection to their government. If conquered into submission, they will submit only to the real conquerors. They are quite aware that they have been defeated by troops of the Queen of England, not by the Pakehas of New Zealand. To the colonists they consider themselves equal both in military power and political ability. They might have remained in allegiance to a distant Sovereign, paramount over settlers and natives alike. But as soon as the former had a Government of their own, the latter began to wish to become a separate nation, and they will never cease to strive for the independence which their rivals enjoy. If, therefore, New Zealand wars are not to be perpetuated, either the Maories must be destroyed, or some scheme must be devised by which they can be civilized and governed, without losing their national independence. Setting aside the question of justice and humanity, I believe it cheaper to stay the work of extermination, and begin the long delayed task of civilization. A whole race will not disappear in a year or two. Even were the Maories wild beasts, a generation or two would have to elapse before they could be hunted down to complete destruction amidst the vast forests of the interior. But they are sufficiently civilized to combine, if driven to desperation, for a bloody and lengthened resistance. It does not require a large force of savages to inflict great loss upon our settlements. The chief mischief in the present war was not done by the 1,000 men who gathered at Meremere to fight the General, but by the small bands of twenty or thirty each, who roamed in the Hunua forest.

If the people of England are willing to make another attempt to govern this race, upon which our colonization has brought such disaster, the first step must be to set all districts inhabited by the natives free from colonial jurisdiction, and to place them under the direct administration of imperial officers.

Under the Act which conferred a constitution on New Zealand, power to effect this is expressly reserved to the British Crown. The native province or provinces thus created would have to be governed on some such principles as the countries of the semi-independent Rajahs in India. A European resident would be appointed, who would make himself the virtual Governor of the province. In the present anarchy and confusion of the native districts, it is not easy to predict what form of Maori authority he could lay hold of under which to gain his influence. During the last year that I was in Waikato, Tamihana and other chiefs were maturing plans for a radical change in the Council of Ngaruawahia. It was no longer to consist of Potatau's kinsmen and chance members, but of representative chiefs, each tribe that had joined the King Confederation sending two. I believe this scheme would have been actually carried out, if the war had not intervened. A Council so constituted would have included men like Tamihana, Rewi, Patara, Renata and others, of whose intellectual power the reader has had evidence, and who, to judge from the example of the actual Council at Ngaruawahia, would have been quite wise enough to govern their fellow-countrymen. A Council of this sort, under the guidance of an English resident, whose power would grow to be greater than that of any chief, would be capable of directing the affairs of a native province.

The next consideration is, how such a Council could be clothed with power. I have no hesitation in saying that this could be done by means of a native police force, consisting of young men instructed and disciplined on a plan similar to that pursued at Te Awamutu, and officered at first by Europeans, but ultimately by natives promoted from the ranks. It would be necessary, to avoid evoking Maori jealousy, to place the force under the nominal command of the Council of

Chiefs; but as pay and promotion would come from the British Resident, he would be the virtual ruler. If this civil arm were once established, the laws made by the Council of Chiefs would be soon respected and obeyed.

It will be seen that the success of this scheme would depend entirely on the personal influence acquired by a British resident. After my own experience in the Waikato district, I am not insensible to the difficulties with which he would have to contend. The first and greatest, which it might probably take years to overcome, would be the deep distrust and suspicion with which he would be regarded. All his promises to guarantee native liberties, all his assurances of non-interference by the colonists, would at first be totally disbelieved; confidence would not begin to revive until after long immunity from molestation. Until, however, some one has surmounted the difficulty of gaining the confidence of the natives, all our efforts to benefit them only increases their distrust. "I would plant institutions," says Sir W. Martin, "by means of personal influence. The first confidence must be a confidence in persons." It is evident that this personal trust cannot be acquired by a Colonial Minister who is not long enough in office for the Maories to become acquainted with his name;[1] nor by a Governor who resides among the Pakehas, and is supposed to be

[1] Since May, 1860, there have been six successive native Ministers.

entirely on the Pakeha side; nor by a mere Government agent, whose judgment is overruled, and whose promises are broken by his official superiors. The Maories could only trust a man who lived amongst them and possessed power to perform his promises.

After gaining the confidence of the natives, the next task would be to teach them to obey. No man could do this unless his own authority were adequately supported. I have already explained to my readers, that the officer of a divided Government in Auckland is regarded by the natives with contempt. It would, therefore, be necessary to give the English officer full power to act independently of the Government of the colony, to carry out his own designs in his own way, and to be free from interference. The Governor alone should have power to dismiss him on the ground of incapacity or misconduct.

The best way of keeping such an officer in check, and of enabling his employers to form a true estimate of his conduct, would be the formation of a Council comprised of men of standing in the colony, versed in native affairs, to which at some time hereafter chiefs like Tamihana might be admitted. The Resident should be bound to keep the Council informed of all that he was doing, or going to do, and the Council should have the corresponding right and duty of expressing a collective or individual opinion thereon. This Council for native affairs should be further required to send one of its members periodically to inspect and report the condition of the native provinces, for the benefit of the Council itself and of the Imperial Government.

The chief objects for which money would be required in a plan of this kind, would be the salaries of a small but effective staff of European officers, and the maintenance of the native police. From the experience of Te Awamutu, I should estimate the cost of the police at about *20l.* per annum for each man. Salaries given to Maori magistrates do more harm than good. The best men will not accept them; and those who do, incur the odium of their countrymen and entirely disqualify themselves thereby from rendering real service to Government. I believe the sum of *50,000l.* per annum, which was voted by the New Zealand Assembly for Sir George Grey's scheme, is amply sufficient to cover the whole cost of governing the Maories. A portion of this might fairly be charged on the colonial revenues, because to those revenues the Maories, as well as the colonists, contribute, by their consumption of imports, their quota.

I must observe, in conclusion, that if this book is considered to have at any rate made out a *primâ facie* case for inquiry into the relationship between the rival races in New Zealand, that inquiry must be made by some commissioner whose well-known ability will command respect both at home and in the colony, and who has no interest to serve by his decision. Such a commissioner would have to collect evidence in the native districts themselves, and not content himself with European or second-hand native testimony in Auckland. I shall have failed in one of my chief objects in writing this book, if I have not convinced the reader that the Maori view of this colonial question is worthy of attention. The Maori story can only be got in full from the Maories themselves. Government officers in native districts know well enough what sort of reports will procure them favour with their superiors, and they are insensibly led into recording that part of the truth which they know will be well received. When these reports get to Auckland, they are subjected to a sifting process by the Colonial Government. I have known disagreeable reports accidentally mislaid; and since, in printing for the Assembly, or forwarding to the Colonial Office, some selection must be made, of course that selection is not unfavourable to the Colonial Government. Original documents are sent home avowedly to illustrate the conclusions advocated in the despatches. The colonial press is very careful about the information sent in its monthly summaries to England, and few facts unfavourable to the colonists are likely to come in that way to British ears. Letters to colonial newspapers are sometimes altered by the Editor, and facts published during the month suppressed in the summary sent home, for fear of the effect which those letters and facts, if copied into English newspapers, would produce. I am informed by men of high standing in New Zealand that, during the last session of the Assembly, every man's tongue was tied, by fear of his constituents, from discussing native affairs, and that even the short debates which did occur were ignored by the dishonesty of the reporters. The press, as well as the House, seemed to have come to the decision that nothing of the past need be inquired into, or even recorded. I am thus justified in saying that the whole truth, if it is ever to be known at all, can only be obtained by inquiries made in the native villages of New Zealand.

THE END.

CPSIA information can be obtained
at www.ICGtesting.com
Printed in the USA
LVHW101928170422
716440LV00004BA/308

9 783752 593105